Praise for Cathy Kelly's irresistible storytelling:

'Honest, funny, clever, it sparkles with witty, wry
observations on modern life. I loved it'
Marian Keyes

'Comforting and feel-good, the perfect treat read'
Good Housekeeping

'This book is full of joy – and I devoured every page
of it gladly'
Milly Johnson

'A heartwarming story about family, love and love'
The Lady

'Packed with Cathy's magical warmth'
Sheila O'Flanagan

.hy Kelly shines an insightful light on female insecurity
.d the healing power of self-belief and family support'
Woman & Home

!led with nuggets of wisdom, compassion and humour,
.thy Kelly proves, yet again, that she knows everything
there is to know about women'
Patricia Scanlan

>ve, laughter, tears and understanding are the perfect
ingredients for a fabulous read'
The Sun

'An involving, heartwarming read about family, friends,
love and disappointment'

Also by Cathy Kelly

Woman to Woman
She's the One
Never Too Late
Someone Like You
What She Wants
Just Between Us
Best of Friends
Always and Forever
Past Secrets
Lessons in Heartbreak
Once in a Lifetime
The Perfect Holiday
Homecoming
The House on Willow Street
The Honey Queen
It Started With Paris
Between Sisters
Secrets of a Happy Marriage
The Year That Changed Everything
The Family Gift

other women

Cathy Kelly

ORION

An Orion Paperback

First published in Great Britain in 2022 by Orion Fiction,
This paperback edition published in 2022 by Orion Fiction,
an imprint of The Orion Publishing Group Ltd
Carmelite House, 50 Victoria Embankment,
London EC4Y 0DZ

An Hachette UK company

1 3 5 7 9 10 8 6 4 2

Copyright © Cathy Kelly 2021

A CIP catalogue record for this book is
available from the British Library.

ISBN (Hardback) 978 1 4091 7926 9
ISBN (Mass Market Paperback) 978 1 4091 7928 3
ISBN (Export Trade Paperback) 978 1 4091 7927 6
ISBN (eBook) 978 1 4091 7929 0

Typeset by Input Data Services Ltd, Somerset

Printed and bound in Great Britain by Clays Ltd, Elcograf S.p.A.

www.orionbooks.co.uk

*To Murray and Dylan, I'm so proud of you both,
all my love, Mum xxC*

Prologue

I park the car on a grass verge at the hospital, ignoring all the signs warning me that it will be clamped.

I don't care about clamping. I have to get into the emergency department. What does a car matter?

I half run because the heaviness in my chest since I got the phone call from the hospital won't allow me to run properly. Or breathe. I need deep, calming breaths.

Screw deep calming breaths.

I need to be with him.

Now. Sooner.

I can keep him alive. No doctor can do it: he needs me, holding his hand, willing him back to life.

I don't have time for the information desk – I know this hospital, see the double doors leading into the actual A & E itself, see a man pushing out of them, and I race, grabbing one swing door just before it shuts.

And I'm in.

Scanning. Peering in past half-drawn cubicle curtains. A man throwing up vile black stuff.

Two cops standing outside another cubicle. A woman on a heart monitor.

And then there he is.

I see his hand lying limply. A hand that's caressed me so many times.

I stand at the edge of the already-full cubicle, about to speak when a doctor hangs her stethoscope round her neck and says: 'I'll talk to the wife.'

She's gone instantly and I follow her, see her approach another woman. The doctor puts a comforting hand on the woman's forearm.

'I'm the wife!' I say, my voice frantic.

And then, as the doctor spins round, I see the other woman, recognise her, see the horror on her face.

'I'm his wife,' I say, 'not her.'

PART ONE

Autumn Leaves Falling

I

Sid

Oscar Wilde was right – work is the curse of the drinking classes. Not that there's any drinking done in Nurture itself. I wend my way through the hordes in The Fiddler's Elbow, neatly avoiding a guy who thinks – mistakenly – that small, dark-haired women in their thirties are only in pubs on a Friday to find handsy hunks like himself, and congratulate myself on not sweeping his feet from beneath him. Krav Maga is a great self-defence tool but there's a time and a place for everything.

I'm heading for the snug at the back of the pub where my Nurture colleagues will be settled in.

Nurture is an advocacy group, semi-funded by the state, set up to improve the health of the people of Ireland and to educate anyone who thinks curry chips, a deep-fried burger and a sugar-laden soft drink is a fully balanced meal.

However, education is a tough job and we need a Friday-night decompress as much as any other worker, so on Fridays, even the most goji-berry-loving among us move blindly en masse across the road to The Fiddler's Elbow to reward ourselves for a week of meetings, phone calls, Zoom meetings and enough unanswered emails to bury us with guilt till kingdom come.

Because of how bad the optics would be if the health gurus were spotted regularly having a drink, eating salt-laden pub snacks and enjoying that ritual of workplace comparing whose week was worse, we converge in the pub's small closed-off snug where nobody can see us.

'The figures came in today from the Department of Health.

Diabetes Two is on the rise, despite the campaign. A year-long campaign,' laments Robbie, who's been in Nurture thirteen years, as long as I have, and is also a campaign director. I'm responsible for school health, which is like trying to hold back a flood with a very small bucket.

I pat a disconsolate Robbie on the back, trying not to spill what looks like a big brandy, and find an empty stool beside Chloe, an intern on a gap year who seems so young, she makes me feel seventy instead of just thirty-four.

Right now, Chloe looks miserable.

'Sid!' she says, eager and anxious in equal measure, and I can sense more misery coming on.

'Adrienne shouted at me today, *shouted*,' she tells me. 'Just because we were out of the coffee pods she likes. It's not my job to replace them, is it? Do you think she has a psychiatric illness?'

Chloe, a wet week out of school and not yet toughened up enough to cope with actual shouting in an office, stares at me over the top of her drink and waits for me to answer. She can't be twelve or else she couldn't be interning, but she looks it, despite the carefully applied modern eyeliner, very grown-up suit and the I-am-clever big-framed glasses.

I think of all the things I could say: 'Adrienne's good at her job but, sometimes, it gets the better of her and she goes into the kitchen for a little meltdown and a caffeine hit.'

Chloe only knows teachers, who are not supposed to shout.

Therefore a workplace meltdown has to be incorrectly cate-gorised into a mental-health box and can't be normal people at the end of their tether. Apart from babysitting, I'd say we are her only work experience.

'This job is not what I thought it would be,' Chloe goes on. 'How do you handle it, Sid?'

Chloe has seen me with my kid sister, Vilma, who is nine-teen, and I'm getting the vibe that she thinks I am Vilma's mother, therefore a nurturing sort.

I am not a nurturing sort. Not by a long shot.

Plus, she can't really think I'm Vilma's mother? I'm thirty-four, not forty-four, although my skincare regime is a little lax, if I'm honest.

The barman finally hands me my large glass of wine and I'm about to test how acidic it is before replying when I think, who am I kidding? I'd drink battery acid at five-thirty on a Friday. Still, the battery acid works and I sigh deeply after my first deep drink.

'Chloe, without meaning to sound unhinged, sometimes I go into the office kitchen and have a little rant at the microwave. It lets off steam.'

I had a mini-canteen breakdown yesterday when a frantic phone call came in about a pancake-and-cream franchise setting up shop right beside a school which famously has no sports area whatsoever. I tell Chloe this.

'But you didn't shout at anyone, did you?' says Chloe, sounding younger every moment.

Patience has never been one of my finer qualities, but I try my best.

'Work can push people, Chloe. Adrienne's brilliant at her job; passionate. It was nothing personal, I'm sure, but I'll talk to her if you like. Did she say sorry?'

Chloe blushes. 'Yes, several times, but that's not the point, is it?'

'The workplace can be a tense environment,' I say, thinking that the pub is doing its job and I am relaxed enough to stop myself throwing the contents of my glass over Chloe to show her how people can really react when they're irritated.

'Want a nacho?' I hand Chloe the packet to change the subject.

'I don't eat processed foods,' she says piously.

'Suit yourself.' I snap my packet back.

Chloe hasn't a clue as to what work is really like as opposed to what young people think it is going to be. The microwave getting shouted at and that accountant who'd faked his CV and nearly lost us our government funding because of the subsequent funds-going-missing fall-out are about the worst things that have ever happened there. The money's not great and I'd be better off if I'd moved jobs years ago, but Nurture is a nice, steady place to work, despite the setbacks like cream-and-pancake franchises. Nurture is truly my second family.

If Chloe knew what horrors some offices held in store for newcomers, she'd take being screamed at in the kitchen any day.

When I finish my wine, I use an app to call a taxi from the only taxi company I ever use. Everyone else has different systems and can't understand why I prefer to wait twenty minutes for someone I know to turn up and bring me home, but I don't care. When the text comes that my driver's here, I say goodbye to everyone and try not to get sucked into any more open-ended discussions about terrible work traumas. Everyone is relaxed by now and it's a good time to go. My own couch, possibly a hot bath and a box set await me. I never drive into the office on Fridays and walk in because my bijou apartment – very bijou – is only two miles away from our city-centre offices. But I never do the walk home.

Tonight, my driver is a lovely man called Gareth, who looks like a bouncer and has a husband and two apricot-coloured chugs (pugs crossed with chihuahuas: 'Their breathing's much better, Sid, love, when they're mixed breed') at home. As he's finishing his shift, he's perfectly happy to sit without much conversation – the chugs are losing weight as per the vet's instructions, thankfully – and listen to Lyric FM playing quietly over the radio.

I phone Vilma from the car: 'Hi, Vilma, tell me – do I look old enough to be your mother?' I ask.

My little sister snorts down the phone, then hits protective mode: 'No! Who said that?'

I sink into the back seat. 'A girl in my office, about eighteen, an intern. She's probably seen you come to get me for lunch because I had the distinct feeling she thought I was your mother.'

'Don't be an idiot.'

'Really.'

'What did she say?'

'It's not what she said – it's that she thinks I'm the motherly type,' I mutter, sorry I started this.

'You're the "take down the patriarchy" and the true sisterhood type,' says Vilma. 'You look out for the women you work with. You dumbass.' She uses the term with affection. 'You like them to be prepared, same way you prepared me for life after school, and *in* school for that matter. That's why my friends love you. You tell us to take no shit and we don't. You're our special ops trainer, Sid: leave no woman behind. Sort of like the Army Rangers – be ready for anything.'

I say nothing for a moment: I always wanted Vilma and her friends to be prepared for life because women are notorious for playing by the rules when the other half of the human race long since ripped up the rule book. I adore Vilma – nobody is going to hurt her on my watch.

'That's probably it,' I say, aiming for cheerful.

'Besides, you've got Mum's skin: olive and anti-ageing, horrible sister. I've got Dad's: pale and liable to burn after five minutes in the sun. You look way too young to be my mum . . . You'd have to have had me when you were fifteen, and in all the pictures I've seen of you at fifteen you look like you're considering entering a convent.'

'I was a nerd,' I protest. 'Nerds wore undistressed jeans and fluffy sweaters with cats on them.'

Vilma laughs.

She and I are technically half-sisters and she takes after my beloved stepfather, Stefan, who required no make-up when he'd adoringly dress up as a vampire to accompany her and other small children on the endless Hallowe'en rounds. He is

9

actually Lithuanian but has the bone structure and height of someone who just drove down from the Carpathians in a black coach. Vilma, whose name means 'truth' in Lithuanian, is the same as Stefan – pale skin, pale eyes, hair like the woods at midnight. I'm like my mother: my hair's chocolate with what Vilma fancifully likes to call bronze highlights, and my eyes are like Mum's, hazel. But Mum's a perfect hippie with her hair long and trailing, which goes with her Stevie Nicks' vibe, while mine's short. And if anyone ever catches me in a hippie outfit, kill me immediately.

'What're you up to tonight?' I ask Vilma, imagining her in the bedroom she shares in a college house, deciding whether it's a jeans night or time to break out the big guns and wear one of the floaty skirts she borrowed from Mum – to be worn ironically, of course.

'Going to Jojo's for a Netflix binge. Drag Race old seasons.'

I can hear the rattle of clothes hangers as she speaks.

'What—'

I know what's coming next.

What are you up to tonight?

'Just here,' I say, as if here is somewhere exciting instead of outside my building. I can't face Vilma's sadness at the fact that my life revolves around almost nothing social. 'Talk tomorrow and be—'

'—safe, yes,' she replies. 'Love you.'

'Love you more.'

It takes another few minutes to get me home.

'Thanks, Gareth,' I say, climbing out right in front of the steps to my apartment-block door. That's the great thing about my taxi guys. There's none of that, 'We'll just drop you on the corner here and sure, you can walk the rest of the way' with them. I tip well and I always ask to be brought as close to the door as possible.

I'm on the tenth floor, which is utterly wonderful from the point of view of getting burgled, because there's a great shortage of ten-storey ladders. Any would-be intruders would have to come from inside the building and, given the concierge system and security cameras all over the place, which I do not regret paying for in my management fees, it's very unlikely that anyone in our apartments would ever get burgled. Plus, I have three locks on the door. And a baseball bat inside it.

Marc, who'd been my significant other for twelve years, hadn't said a word when I insisted on getting three locks. It was one of the many things I loved about him.

Loved: is there a sadder word?

I open my three locks, step inside, relock them quickly and walk through the hall, which, finally, is no longer bare-looking, because Vilma had persuaded me to give her money for frames for some art prints, which we then hung with sticky wall hangers because we are both lethal with hammers.

Marc had taken all his pictures when he'd left.

'Sid, you really don't care about interiors, do you? It looks like you just rent the place and expect to be evicted at any moment,' said Vilma one day when she was visiting. 'Give me a few quid and I'll find pictures to give some vague sense that you're staying longer than a week.'

And she had.

Vilma is a wonderful sister, a conduit to another world. I'm not sure how I would have got by this past year without her because Marc and I were like an old married couple with our own happy routines. Without him, I was rudderless.

There was no one to make me morning coffee, no one to cook up scrambled eggs when we'd run out of groceries, no one to sit with in companionable peace while we surfed the TV stations and our various cable subscriptions.

Sometimes, when I get home, it feels as if somebody has died and left me alone in my little universe.

I conquer this by watching more and more TV and making cocktails – only at weekends – from *The Butler's Friend*, a vintage book from the 1920s which has taught me to make the perfect Boulevardier, where the secret is not just rye whiskey, sweet vermouth and Campari, but to stir and never shake.

Apart from trips home to see Mum and Stefan, my stepfather, and when Vilma comes to see me, I exist in a world of work, home and online supermarket deliveries.

If making the perfect Boulevardier, staying in all weekend and having a loving relationship with my couch cushions were what it took to keep me sane, then that's what I'd do. Marc's leaving had shocked me and made me feel stupid all at the same time. Because, under the circumstances, our relationship was hardly built to last. It was a miracle it had lasted as long as it did, but still, I missed him. We'd grown into adulthood together but that childhood-sweethearts-lasting-forever thing is a hard trick to pull off.

Still, what we'd had was special and I knew I'd never have it again. Besides, I needed another man in my life like I needed a hole in the head. I had everything I wanted. Except for those new biker boots I was longing for.

Who needs men when you've got fabulous boots, right?

2

Marin

I have my hand on the handle of conference room four and I'm steeling myself to open it.

I take a deep breath, hold it for a count of five, and let it out again slowly – a concept brought to me by my daughter, Rachel, who says nobody breathes properly.

'We'd all be dead, then,' pointed out Joey, my other child, nine and three quarters and hilariously determined to annoy his elder sister.

'*Properly*, dopey head,' said Rachel. 'We tense up and don't use the correct muscles.'

She might have a point. To open the door to conference room four, I think I need a brown paper bag to breathe into because I know exactly what I'll find in there and, some days, I just can't cope with the toxicity.

Eighteen years of working as an estate agent has taught me that the early gut impression of a disintegrating marriage can be as good as being their divorce mediator.

In other words: you'd be surprised how much you can tell about people when you are selling their home.

The Ryans, inside the room, are enriched uranium toxic.

Like when I do Pilates and think my stomach might explode with the pain of unused muscles being worked out, I force myself past the feelings and enter the room.

The Ryans are each glaring at the window behind the desk.

They both accompanied me on the initial valuation of their three-bed, semi-detached house in the lovely suburb of Glenageary. Every opened door was a failure of their life together.

For example, the two unused children's bedrooms, one of which was where Charlotte Ryan now stored her clothes.

Leo opened one closet door aggressively: 'See? Half of this stuff still has tags on it. Unworn.'

I like to think I'm always professional but I nearly needed the brown paper bag then, too. Unworn clothes. *Expensive* unworn clothes. I yearned to sort through the piles with Charlotte and offer her anything to try them on. She's probably my height, five six, about the same size – twelve – and is clearly a shopaholic, with money.

There the similarity ends because her hair is expensively highlighted while mine is at the growing-out-the-mistake-fringe stage, and is my natural chestnut colour, constantly tied up at the back of my head and nourished with dry shampoo.

Still, the thought of her wardrobe haul is affecting my brain like the thought of a line of cocaine must affect a coke addict. I stifled the urge but the clothes haunted me all the way around the house.

If only I had the perfect clothes, then everything in my life would be wonderful. I'd feel complete, not less-than.

Random female clients wouldn't look at me as if I was the downtrodden hired help in my black trousers – where are the fashion people hiding the perfect ones? – worn to hide my big hips. My mother wouldn't remark every time she saw me in work clothes that it was a pity my firm didn't have a uniform. My mother has a normal nose but she can look down it as if it was a ski jump in Val d'Isère.

If I had the right jeans, trousers and crisp white shirt, I'd like me more and Nate, my husband, would fancy me the way he used to fancy me back in the days when dinosaurs roamed the earth. But then, maybe marriages are like that, right? Wild lust in the beginning settles down to 'Did you put out the bins?'.

Now that they've accepted my valuation and have chosen Hilliers and McKenzie to sell their property, the Ryans are here in person to discuss the reams of paperwork required to sell a house and sign the company contract. Today.

Charlotte's wearing Isabel Marant. Hideously expensive and, like most high-end clothes, utterly impossible to sell on after being worn. I know because occasionally I shop for expensive clothes, then find out they don't suit me, and try to sell them on.

I know I have a problem, OK? For some people, it's chocolate. For others, wine o'clock.

Anything to fill the gaping hole of emptiness.

For me, it's frantic, addict-level shopping until I'm sitting breathlessly in the car with my haul and I realise, again, that this has all been a mistake. Like all addictive things, my chronic compulsive shopping hits my pocket ruthlessly.

I cannot ask a client about her clothes.

Get a grip, Marin Stanley, I tell myself firmly. You are a professional.

I therefore adopt my professional smile, which is clearly set to 'far too friendly' as its appearance elicits a diatribe from Charlotte about how Leo is keeping the house like a pit and they'll never sell unless he opens some windows and swears off the beer.

'The place smells like a brewery!'

In turn, this makes Leo kick off about how Charlotte had better not start on him now because he can't take any more of her bitching.

I am suddenly annoyed with these people. I steel myself to sound brisk and do what a mentor had told me years ago: carry on as if the argument simply is not happening.

'Your contract with Hilliers and McKenzie,' I say, rapping said document onto the desk. 'I'll go through the details again.'

They shut up.

After an hour of hostility so intense it could run the national grid, I escape the small office to lean against the wall near the giant ficus which brings the dual benefits of oxygen and a discreet hiding space into the office.

From her desk, which is, as ever, perfectly tidy, our office administrator, Bernie, sees me. For once, she appears not to be on the phone, although her ever-present headset is still plugged into her ear. She leaves her chair and is at my side in a moment.

'Do we need someone to go in and clean up the bodies?' she asks.

'No, but I was tempted,' I tell her.

'Ha!'

'I need caffeine,' I mutter, 'then I'll go back in.'

Bernie pats my arm. 'Leave it to me,' she says.

She swoops into the office and closes the door. I imagine her telling Leo and Charlotte that once we get all the paperwork signed and have their booking deposit, we can move on to the other important issues like solicitors, contracts, PSRA forms, money-laundering legislation forms – all the important details of estate agents in a modern age.

I have briefly discussed all of this with them and I should be in there now but, luckily, Bernie can tell when anyone in the office is suffering from Separating Couple Anxiety. Empathy is both very useful and a hindrance in an estate agent.

Five minutes pass and I check the emails on my phone.

She glides gracefully out of the office.

'I have given them all the papers,' she says. 'I considered asking if they wanted more tea or coffee, but thought they might throw hot liquids and we'd get sued.'

We grin at each other.

'Quick, I gave them only one pen. So there is something physical to argue over. Coffee,' she says.

We hurry into the little office kitchen where Bernie, after one crisp conversation with one of the senior partners, had a coffee-shop-standard machine installed. It would be the envy of every other estate agent in the country, I imagine, if they knew about it. But then we are a high-value agency and I doubt if anyone has an office administrator like Bernie. Deftly, she makes us two strong shots of espresso and we drink them, hers straight, mine with a little hint of sugar.

In the interests of full disclosure, I also like sugar, biscuits and chocolates.

'It's sad,' Bernie says thoughtfully, 'how sometimes the separating ones are so full of rage against each other. It's not good for the soul.'

'I don't know how you subdue them,' I say ruefully. 'It felt as if they were about to kill each other and every word was a knife thrown.'

'They are angry with the world and it spills over. We'll let them sit in there on their own for a while and then I will go in and charm them. Don't take on their rage.'

Finally, the Ryans leave the building and I find that Rachel is right. I am breathing better.

I take up my phone to message her something funny about this and find that because my phone was on silent for the meeting, I've missed a call, a text from my mother and that Nate has messaged me.

My mother texts like people once sent telegrams, as if words cost money. Particularly ones like 'please', 'thank you', and 'love': I MUST talk to you about your brother! Phone soonest.

I add so many kisses and hearts to Rachel's messages that they're often a sea of pink and red. I know that when Joey gets a phone, in the very distant future, I shall have to call a halt to this outpouring of love. Boys go off to school holding their mothers' hands, but by the time Joey is twelve and gets a phone, he'll be teased mercilessly at any sign of a heart emoji.

Nate's message is better than my mother's but not much:

Talked to Steve earlier. I asked him and Angie to dinner
tomorrow. Know it's a bit last minute but you're fabulous
at pulling rabbits out of hats. Asked Finn too. He's coming
alone. What about Bea and Luke? Nate

Nate is not a man given to kisses at the end of messages. He finds my outpourings of adoring emojis ludicrous and he teases me mercilessly about them.

In person, however, he's very affectionate, so I can live without smiley faces and hearts. He's also the sort of man who'd have been called a bon viveur in another era. He's tall, strong and muscular from lots of exercise, has a fine singing voice and is always delighted to get his old electric guitar out at parties, so he and his two best friends, Finn and Steve, can sing the folky rock they used to perform when they busked during their college years.

My Nate loves parties, always has, always will. He's never happier than when the house is full of our friends, but these days, I feel too tired to entertain so much. The endless cycle of work, housework, grocery shopping and making dinner is getting to me.

Sometimes, I simply need time to relax with just us. But I can't break his heart like that.

I fire off a couple of messages, telling Nate it's fine – although it's not, really – and texting my mother that I will phone her on the way home.

At my desk, instead of working, I scribble a few frantic menu ideas. I love dinners with my family. Weekend cooking is the best: when there's no rush, I can mess around with recipes and we all have a lazy dinner where there's no studying, homework or anything to hurry us. I don't even mind lazy last-minute dinners where I throw the takeaway menus on the table and we come to a consensus, but there's no hope of that with Steve and Angie.

I like Steve. He and Finn are Nate's oldest friends: they met at college through the running club and now, two and a half decades later, they're still friends. The fourth part of the gang was Jean-Luc, Bea's husband, who died in a car accident nearly ten years ago.

We've kept our friendship going through those awful years

after Jean-Luc was killed, when Bea couldn't cope with get-togethers because it was too painful to remember how it used to be. Somehow, we got her back into the fold because, as Nate insisted, she was part of us. We'd be letting both her and Jean-Luc down if we didn't try.

Bea is amazing: she's raised their son, Luke, on her own, works part-time as a secretary in a dental and medical clinic, so she is always there to collect Luke from school, and she's a lion-ess protecting him, trying to give him everything his dad isn't there to give. Her coming back to our group is partly because of Luke – he and Joey are the same age and, I like to think, because the three men provide role models for a fatherless son.

I like Steve but I admit to loving Finn like a brother. He's kind, warm, clever and, since he broke up with his long-term girlfriend, Mags, has demonstrated unerringly bad taste in girlfriends. I wish I could find someone fabulous for him; I had hopes for him and Bea, to be honest, but they are just friends.

Plus, I don't think you can make other people fall in love with each other – it happens organically or not at all.

Steve used to fly through women as if he thought the world was ending and spreading his seed was paramount. Then he met Angie.

I can't honestly say how I feel about Angie because she makes me feel inadequate on so many levels that I've never managed to reach the bedrock of knowing whether I like her or not. There: I've said it. I feel guilty saying it because she's so nice but I can't help it. Some people push us into being our worse selves.

First time I met her, I saw this vision of sexy, beautifully dressed blondeness getting out of a taxi at the restaurant and my insecurities covered me like a warm, sticky blanket. I felt like I used to when I was a child and my mother was listing my imperfections.

That night, Angie was perfectly pleasant to everyone, talked warmly to me and Mags and discussed work – it would have been easier if she'd been beautiful and brainless but no, she's an award-winning architect in a practice with another woman. She enthralled every guy at and near our table. Her existence pushed every button in me, the ones that said my hair is wrong (goes frizzy so easily), my clothes are wrong and I could lose six pounds without it putting a dent in my overall body mass.

Eleven years later, nothing has changed.

Duh.

A dinner with Angie will mean me pulling out all the stops on my precious Saturday morning off.

Maybe not all the stops, I remind myself, because the grocery bank account is not looking particularly healthy right now. The mortgage is still not paid off and even though people assume that any financial job like Nate's is the equivalent of having a money-printing press in the basement, we are not rich.

I tell myself to go through the bank direct debits and payments this weekend. A financial audit. Although that scares me, because an audit will make me face up to why I bought Lululemon – *Lululemon!* – track pants for running when I never run. But the leggings were so soft and lovely, I just thought, maybe with the right leggings I *would* run? Hopefully?

I work my way through a pile of paperwork, make some phone calls, write some emails and finally finish for the day.

In our business, the working day is anything but a nine-to-five one. Evening and Saturday showings are part of the business and if you're a mother, you need a brilliant child minder.

But I have been in Hilliers and McKenzie for a long time and have moved up the ladder enough to ease that pressure. Happily for me, gone are the days of standing for several two-hour bursts in a series of show houses where you cannot use the facilities, make tea or barely sit on one of the mini-sized couches brought in to make the rooms look bigger, all the while fingering speed dial on your phone in case a weird viewer comes in and you are alone. Now, I am a senior negotiator and handle bigger-value properties and the one-offs, which means I have more power over my own diary. I still have to spend plenty of Saturdays and late nights showing houses but I can arrange it all myself, rather than the more junior staff members who have their showings assigned.

As I head out into the winter rain, I phone my mother and prepare myself for the onslaught.

'Your father's still in the allotment. He should have married that allotment,' my mother shrieks, full volume, down the line.

Dominic, my younger brother who is currently living back home, is in his room 'all hours, never cracks open the window and he doesn't know how to put on a wash!'.

I could mention that if my mother had taught my ditzy thirty-nine-year-old brother how to wash his own clothes when he was a teenager, he might still be married and not be back in the family home clogging the place up like a free-loading guest without the skills to cook, buy groceries, wash towels, clean the bathroom after he's used it, or offer to pitch in with rent money.

But I never point out what my mother *should* have done. My mission, should I choose to accept it, is to listen, agree with her and then nod silently at *how could his wife throw him out of the house?* The irony of this never escapes me.

There are three kids in my family and Dominic, the youngest, could do no wrong in my mother's eyes until recently during the year-long-catastrophe that is Dom's marriage break-up. His wife got tired of being married to a child-man who thinks there's a laundry/cooking/cleaning fairy.

Dominic is not my problem. April, my sister, a woman who believes in romantic fairy tales, is not my problem either. April's the oldest of us three but I definitely parent her. How did this happen? I can't afford the therapy to find out.

As the family fixer, I'm the one who gets the annoyed phone calls from my mother and the begging ones from my father. Last week's instalment in this long-running saga: 'Marin, can you say you need a babysitter next Wednesday? Pretty please? Your mother's got the book-club women in.'

The 'book-club women' are Ma's friends who prefer bitching about their other halves to reading. When they're there, she loudly discusses how bad her life is with my poor father able to hear every word from the tiny den next door, even when he has the sound turned up on the telly.

Being the family fixer also means getting exhausted calls from Dom's wife, Sue-Who-Deserves-Sainthood, who needs Dom to appoint a lawyer so they can get on with the legalities; and then calls from my mother again, who must have got some of the lawyer-type calls from Sue too, because she's got bursitis in one of her knees owing to back-to-back novenas, praying for Dom's marriage. My mother doesn't believe in divorce.

If Ma knew about April's life choices, all of which involve married men, I'd have to call an ambulance.

I know my duty: calm my mother down or she'll have bursitis in the other knee too.

'I'll talk to Dominic, Ma,' I say. 'I think Dad's been planting some Christmas bulbs he wants to force for you. He knows how you love hyacinths,' I add, which is a white lie, because I told him to plant something to keep her happy. 'There's something about the scent of them in the house for the holidays, isn't there?'

Ma is thrilled with this vision of her taste and is mollified. Mollifying my mother is tricky but I am good at it: I've had enough practice, after all. Somehow, after her extracting a promise from me to phone Dom's wife, Sue, I hang up.

Sue's a decent woman who deserves better than Dominic, much and all as I love him. Until he grows up, there is no hope for him having a sensible relationship.

Ideally, he needs to get out of my parents' house, live on his own and reflect that the real world is hard.

Saying you're in love with someone in front of a church full of your friends and relatives is not what marriage is about. It's about respect, compromise, caring, affection, kindness and, sometimes, making dinner for glamorous people who intimidate you because it will make your spouse happy.

It's Saturday evening, I've been out all afternoon showing a lovely late Edwardian house to scores of people who are all interested, but none interested enough to put in an offer. This means that as I stand in the kitchen sweating over a hot stove, I'm feeling irritated and somewhat put upon because of having to cook instead of ordering take out and collapsing in front of the telly. Bea and Luke are late, which is a pity, as Bea is a marvellous cook and always helps, and Luke could play Xbox with poor Joey who is currently sitting silently with Alexandra, Angie and Steve's ten-year-old daughter, while she plays with her mother's phone.

It's my fault: 'Be polite to her,' I always say and he does his best. They're in the same class at school and don't really get on, so I know he feels aggrieved to be stuck with her at the weekend as well as during the week.

Rachel is out at her friend Megan's house, where they're doing something that involves watching TV simultaneously with their friend in college in Galway. It's at moments like this that I question Rachel's – and Megan's – decision to have a gap year before starting college late next September. In March, they'll have earned enough from their various jobs to start a six-month travel fest around the world. The problem is that they're enjoying themselves so much, I don't know if they'll ever go to college.

Her evening out means I'm in the kitchen alone. I have pulled out as many stops as I can and spent far too much buying expensive beef with which to make a teriyaki beef stir fry. No matter how much prep you do beforehand, stir-frying for nine means you end up with two woks and sweat breaking out on your forehead.

'Can I help?'

It's Angie, who always offers to help and I always say no.

Tonight, as ever, she looks immaculate. To a clothes-obsessed woman like myself, I can see that she has the right sneakers (expensive), worn with ankle skimming jeans (also expensive) and a cream silk and cashmere zipped hoodie that clings. You can tell it's got silk in there: the fineness of the cashmere is the key. There's a translucency there to the expert/obsessive eye.

I almost moan. I've seen most of the outfit on Net à Porter: not in the sale part of the site, although that's where I spend hours scrolling. Not buying. Just scrolling.

Angie is perfect.

In her presence, I feel diminished and then ashamed at feeling so. How can I be a fit mother to a nearly grown daughter when I let such stupid things as clothes and body image affect me so badly?

'No, really, Marin. Let me do something. The men are talking work and I am fed up of work.'

She does try but I can't let her.

'You'll ruin your clothes if you fry,' I say. 'How about moving the drinks into the dining area and warming the plates,' I improvise.

'Sure.'

By the time dinner is served, with Angie having carried the plates to the table and having called everyone, I feel like the scullery maid in a period film with Angie as the elegant lady hostess.

'It looks gorgeous,' says Nate, his hand resting on Angie's shoulder as he walks round her to his seat at the table.

He smiles adoringly at Angie – adoringly! There's no other word for it and at that moment, I hate her. She's one of *those* women, I decide furiously, the ones who think nothing of flirting with other women's husbands. Does she want Nate?

Bitch.

'Really, this looks wonderful,' Nate says again and I feel my blood boil.

I cooked it, I want to say. She warmed the plates, nothing more. But then Nate gives me a one-armed hug and says: 'Fabulous little chef, our Marin,' and before I know it, they're all holding glasses up, even the kids with their orange-juice ones, and I'm supposed to smile, even though I'm sweaty, still wearing my apron and reeking of kitchen.

Nate hands me wine and I take a gulp before whisking off the apron.

I fix a smile to my face. *Fabulous little chef?* I'm over-reacting, that's all.

'Enjoy,' I say, and take two more gulps of the wine. Feeling bitchy brings out my inner alcoholic tendencies.

Nate and Steve had argued over which was better: the wine Nate had chosen or the bottles Steve had brought. I hate the stupid male competitiveness between them. But right now, I don't care which wine it is, I finish my glass far too quickly and fill it up again.

It will serve a purpose. And stop me hoping the competitiveness doesn't extend to wives.

When the doorbell rings, I leap to my feet.

'Bea and Luke,' I guess, delighted that a female ally has arrived.

Bea looks so cold, she's actually shivering. Her dark hair is plastered to her face, any mascara she'd applied earlier has slid down her cheeks and I swear there's a blue tinge to her.

'The tyre went flat and we had to fix it!' says Luke, erupting happily into the house and charging off to see Joey.

Bea holds out her hands, which I now see are filthy. 'It's so long since I changed a tyre, I'd almost forgotten. We were stuck because I couldn't get one of the nuts off the tyre and then this man stopped –'

'You let a stranger help?' says Finn, coming into the hall. 'You should have phoned – I'd have come out.'

'I can take care of myself,' says Bea, waggling a penknife she's produced from her coat pocket.

'Hold on, Mr Attacker: just let me get the knife part out – oops, that's the bottle opener, now wait: which end is up?' says Finn.

'Thanks, smartarse,' says Bea, grinning. 'I'm sorry I'm so late, Marin. Go ahead and eat but I'm filthy and wet. Can I borrow something?'

'You'll have to borrow something of Rachel's,' I say, feeling a wobble in my self-esteem. Am I menopausal? That could explain it. 'My stuff will swim on you.'

Bea's tall and naturally slender with legs that genuinely go on forever and, despite all this slenderness, has actual boobs. When I first met her, she was going out with Jean-Luc, I was newly dating Nate, and Bea had been his previous girlfriend. We were early twenty-somethings. Stuff like that happened then. Everyone had said that Bea was so beautiful, I was more nervous of meeting her than of gaining the approval of Nate's pals. But she was so likeable, an intense student studying French and history, which was how she and Jean-Luc had hooked up; he was making a mint giving French tutorials given his Auvergne heritage.

The thing is, Bea is nothing like Angie – she never makes me feel less-than. She never notices her beauty now just as she never noticed it when we were in college and I felt both gauche and encased in puppy fat alongside her slender, fey cleverness.

If Steve had died, would I still be inviting Angie into our lives? Sexy Angie? No.

But Bea's different. Bea has been in my life for twenty years, she's my friend.

I grab her hand. 'Come on upstairs. We can rifle through Rachel's things and find you something dry.'

Upstairs, Bea refuses a shower but towels off and I find her something of Rachel's to wear. Rachel's twenty-seven-inch-waist jeans are perfect, as is a silky black blouse.

'I couldn't get a leg in those jeans,' I say mournfully.

'Nonsense.'

Bea is there, hugging me. She is so very affectionate and I feel for her with only Luke to be affectionate with now and no husband to hug.

'You're gorgeous. You're the sexy, curvy one. I'm the one with bony knees who spent college elbowing people because my limbs had suddenly grown too large.'

We laugh at the memory.

I'd expected to dislike this tall, slim girl with the cloudy auburn hair because Nate had gone out with her before me. But two minutes in Bea's presence had sorted that out. She'd been sitting with them all, chatting mainly to Finn, when Nate introduced me.

'Nate Stanley, in the name of the sisterhood, I am ordering you to be nice to lovely Marin and don't leave her waiting for you in random pubs,' she'd said.

'Yes, or we'll make you suffer,' said Finn lazily. 'He has no manners. Too macho,' he confided to me.

'I am not,' said Nate, stung.

'He's a sweetie,' Bea had whispered to me, 'but don't tell him I said that. He's like the big brother I never had. If he steps out of line, tell me or Finn.'

I wish I could tell her that something feels out-of-line right now but there's nothing I can put my finger on. Besides, Bea has enough to cope with. Life as a widow with an almost ten-year-old boy is not easy. She's been alone since a car crash took her beloved Jean-Luc ten years ago. She doesn't need me moaning on with my wild imaginings about Angie wanting to get her hands on Nate. Because that's all they are.

Bea lost the man she loved in one fatal moment when she was eight and a half months pregnant with their child.

If anyone gets to moan, it's Bea.

3
Bea

'Kite-surfing or hang-gliding?' asks Shazz.

'I'm so much more a kite-surfing sort of gal,' I say sarcastically, hauling the newly changed duvet onto the bed and making everything neat. I love having fresh bedclothes at the weekend. Ironed and everything. The first time Shazz realised I iron my sheets, she said, 'You're fucking kidding me, right?'

'No,' I said. 'I like ironed sheets and a pretty bed, so shoot me. And watch the language – the kids will hear.'

The kids are my Luke and her Raffie, born around the same time, introduced at the health clinic when they were a month old and both of us were single mothers with newborns, reeling with exhaustion. I was thirty-three, Shazz was twenty-three. We had nothing in common except our babies, but we clicked.

Raffie's over here for a play date and there's much giggling from downstairs as they create baby chickens on Minecraft, the current craze. Shazz has stayed to chat and Christie and the girls are coming later.

'They hear bad language everywhere,' says Shazz now, and she's right. Fighting the onslaught of bad language and the fear of social media awaiting them mean mothering is tricky, to say the least.

I neatly arrange the fake mohair blanket in a seafoam colour at the end of the bed, fix my cushions on the pillows and admire my hard work.

Shazz, one of my best friends since that day in the health clinic and a woman whose ultra-pink hair is almost definitely visible from space, is sitting on the floor against the radiator not helping in the slightest.

But then Shazz has seen me at my worst in this bed, like that time when the kids were tiny when Luke and I both had a vomiting bug and she came over to take care of us, which is not something everyone would do. Anyone who's stripped the bed and remade it, while I retched loudly in the bathroom, and then tucked me back into bed with rehydration salts and said; 'Sleep, babes, I'll take care of everything,' never has to bother helping again. They have earned the right to sit on the floor and drink coffee.

'Is kite-surfing that one where they look as if they're being dragged out to sea?' I ask, starting dusting.

'Yeah, I think,' she says, which is her version of ignoring me. She's busy on her tablet writing me up a dating profile despite my protests that hell will freeze over before I go on another date. In the past eight years – since Shazz and our other friend, Christie, started pushing me to try again – I've been on a few dates. Disaster does not come near describing any of them.

At the top of my list of shame stars Ed. He was a set-up by an old school friend and in her fantasy world, her cousin Ed and I – two lonely people – were going to fall madly in love with each other.

This type of behaviour makes a woman wonder exactly what her old friends think of her when they stick cousin Ed on a platter and say, 'Now, there you are! A man! He's just your sort.'

Ed was *nobody's* sort. He had limited small talk unless it was about the rise of right-wing European politics (he was all for it) or model trains. Ed had been searching for love for years. Years. Women were picky, he said with narrowed eyes. Women expect men to buy them dinner into the bargain. Did they think he was made of money?

It was a summer party, so I excused myself to the bathroom, had no coat to find, and headed for home. I'd had the most amazing, wonderful husband and he'd been snatched from me, leaving me a widow at thirty-three. And people were trying to set me up with losers like Ed?

'You're thinking about Ed,' says Shazz, long neon and diamante purple-gel nails working the keypad, looking for hunks who'd fancy single mothers. 'You have an Ed look on your face.'

'Delayed shock,' I say.

'You do French, right?' she asks.

Jean-Luc was French and we met when I was brushing up my French at an evening course he was teaching.

'Yeeees,' I say, dragging the word out. I can see sheer filth coming out of this online profile. Shazz could have so much fun with my ability to do things French-style.

'I *speak* French, Shazz. Mentioning anything else French is asking for trouble.'

'Oh, don't be so picky,' she say blithely, tap tapping away.

I left the dating scene because it was so horrendous and because I'd largely relied on the comfortable route of meeting men via friends. Internet dating scares me. I don't want to swipe my way to love on my phone – Shazz has swiped left many times since she's been a single mum and frankly, I don't know why there aren't more crime shows on how much guys lie about themselves on their profiles, not to mention using other people's photos so that they are entirely unrecognisable.

Shazz found the love of her life, Zephaniah, online, which is why she's keen to get me set up again. She's a born-again romantic. But I'm stalling. I have post-traumatic dating syndrome.

The nail in the coffin, so to speak, was at a party held by Moira, a woman I once worked with. She met me at the front door, utterly excited: 'Bea, I have just the guy for you. Trust me.'

Trust me is what people say when they're about to lie to you.

Startlingly, the guy in question wasn't a weirdo. He was nice, just not my type in the slightest because when it came down to it, I thought ruefully, my type was lying in the cold ground.

The problem turned out to be a guy called Joe who was there with his wife, about whom Joe conveniently forgot as soon as he set eyes on me.

After many glasses of wine, *I* was Joe's type. He happily decided that I was there for him. The nice guy and I agreed that we weren't each other's dream date, so he went off in search of craft beer and a long conversation with some other people about the Champions League. I decided to find my coat with Joe following me around like a dog snuffling for biscuits.

I wanted to escape quietly and I didn't know where the coats were being kept, and Joe followed me into one of the bedrooms on my search. Worse, his wife thought I was encouraging it.

'Leave him alone,' she said, finally pinning me in a corner.

'I do not want Joe,' I said angrily. 'In fact, I have no interest in Joe. I came here for a few drinks with my friend, and it turns out she has a man lined up for me.' I pointed towards the dining-room table area where the food was laid out. 'There he is over there, talking about football and beer. While your husband,' Joe was slinking further and further away all the time, 'has decided he is for me. I have no interest in him. So why don't you bring him home, sober him up and tell him not to run after strange women at parties.'

'It's your fault,' she screeched. 'You skinny bitches with your long hair and no baby fat! You dangle yourselves and your breasts in front of him!'

Clearly this was an ongoing problem and one of the reasons it had not been nipped in the bud was because Mrs Joe always blamed whatever woman Joe had got in his sights, instead of getting Joe and nailing his knee caps to the floor. Also, I am on the bosomy side and Mrs Joe was not. Having big boobs is not all it's cracked up to be but clearly mine had sent Mrs Joe over the edge.

I pushed away from her and said: 'Next time, blame your husband, don't blame the poor woman he is pursuing.'

Still shaking, I found my coat in a chaotic pile in a spare bedroom, walked up to Moira and said hotly, 'I am never coming to your house again. You left me to that mad woman.'

'She gets a bit like that when she's had drink . . .'

'What's Joe's excuse?'

'Over-excitable, loves women.' She looked guilty.

'Why didn't you rescue me?' I demanded. 'In future, we meet for coffee and only coffee. You're buying!'

In the taxi on the way home, I pondered that hitting men like Joe over the head was the only answer. Then, I came to the conclusion that really, the only answer was not going out to parties until people decided that I had actively chosen the celibate life.

But Shazz was convinced in her lovestruck state that I needed pairing up too. Christie – lesbian mother of two exquisite twin girls born via IVF and now living with a female police inspector, Gloria – was on Shazz's side.

The get-Bea-dating-again adventure has been going on for weeks now and I have already seen more dating profiles than I ever cared to. From my glimpse into this world, every man is a hiking, scuba-diving dude who has an Idris Elba/Lionel Messi thing going and plays guitar, or else, they're sex-starved maniacs who imply that what's in their trousers can also be seen from space.

'Can you play a musical instrument?' asks Shazz.

'Does the ukulele count?' I enquire.

'No, smartarse,' she replies. 'Playing the spoons is out too.'

We both laugh.

'I'm going to put saxophone,' she says, concentrating.

'So it's a complete tissue of lies?' I say, the laughing actually beginning to hurt my sides now.

'Absolutely. My cousin Tonya said she kept fit by pole dancing and she went on loads of dates.'

'What are you waiting for, then? Go on! Stick in pole

dancing: I'll practise at bus stops. Far be it from me to get in the way of horny men looking for one-night stands.'

'You're not taking this seriously,' Shazz mutters. 'I'll put in the saxophone. It's very sexy.'

'But I don't play it –' I begin to protest, then try another tack. 'I only said I'd try the Internet once and I want it to be an honest profile.'

'*Nobody* does an honest profile! Relax. This is like leaving bird seed out. You scatter seeds to see what comes along.'

'I know exactly what'll come along if you imply I'm a French-speaking sex kitten who plays the saxophone: sex-starved men. I'm too old, too worn out, Shazz. I want normal. I want romance,' I add wistfully. My bedroom was romantic. From my sea-foam throw to my ruched, frilled cushions, it was a haven for romance. It just never saw any.

'You're never too old for love,' Shazz says, while I hope that there must be one decent, kind, affectionate man out there who will hold me in his arms and make me feel better.

Falling in love with him would be different – in my experience, love hurts too much. Also, people like to believe in an endless supply of true loves. If one dies, you search till you find another one, yes?

No.

But since Shazz fell in love, she wants everyone to be in love. I wish it was that easy.

Late at night, I wonder how being raised without a strong male influence in his life will affect Luke. He has Finn, Nate and Steve, but they have their own lives. We are on the outside, no matter what they think.

I console myself with the psychological tenet that one good parent is all a child needs: I was told that once and I still cling to the idea like a drowning person clinging to a rock in the sea.

When Luke was younger, I used to talk to him about Jean-Luc, show him pictures of his dad, but I do it less now.

We've almost lost contact with Jean-Luc's family in France. His older brother is a lot older, has grown up kids, and has always been too busy to stay in touch, while Jean-Luc's mother, Celine, could barely cope for a long time with seeing the growing little boy who looked so like her own little boy, so our Skype calls have dwindled to almost nothing in the past few years. Honestly, it suits me because I'm terrified Celine would want Luke to come to her for holidays and I can't bear the thought of letting him go.

He's not alone, either: another consolation point. Two kids in his class in school have never set eyes on their fathers, either, although they're still alive. Just vamoosed.

In the case of Shazz, whose boyfriend walked out on her and Raffie when he was a newborn, said boyfriend is looking at certain and very painful death should he ever walk back in.

'That Bastard,' she calls him.

Obviously, That Bastard vanished so comprehensively that he doesn't pay child support. So Shazz does gel nails and beauty treatments from her front room and manages brilliantly.

Since Zephaniah, who is as kind as he is handsome, arrived on the scene, Shazz never talks about That Bastard. She talks about how she never believed in love before but does now.

'Jeez, Bea: you'll be a born-again virgin if you don't get some action soon.'

'Who says I don't get action?' I demand. 'If you could see the way the electricity meter reader and I are together . . .'

'Sparks fly?'

'Exactly.'

Her phone rings and gives me a chance to go downstairs to make coffee for us both. The boys are building a Lego fort with great intent. They play very limited computer games in my house because I won't let them. Since they're both nearly ten later this month, this is still possible but who knows how long my power will last.

Now that she has Zep in her life, Shazz says it's lovely to

have a father figure around for Raffie. She doesn't say it to upset me but to spur me to 'get on with my life'.

'What happens when Luke's grown up? What then?'

'I'll get cats. Or play tennis.'

'Or get the cats to play tennis,' she replies sarcastically. 'He's dead ten years, Babes: nobody said you had to throw yourself on the funeral pyre. Poor Lukey will never be able to leave home: he'll think you've dedicated your life to him and he can't go. I'm joking,' she adds. 'Well, sorta.'

'I don't want to guilt him into never leaving,' I say heatedly, 'but what are the odds of a forty-three-year-old widow with a son falling in love with someone new?'

'You could do with someone to hug who isn't nine and three quarters,' continues Shazz. 'Besides, the dreaded family-tree school project is coming up soon and, apparently, even a hint of "My mum has a boyfriend" makes it easier.'

We've been warned about the Family-Tree project by a friend of Shazz's. In theory: it's a lovely idea. A big chart with as many of the pupil's family members pictured or drawn on it as possible. Lovely if you come from a traditional family but tricky if you're one of the three kids in Luke's and Raffie's class without an actual father.

'Don't remind me,' I groan.

We always talk gently about Jean-Luc the night before Luke's birthday which is coming up. Hearing about the fatal car crash sent me into instantaneous labour. My son was born hours after his father died. I can't see that fitting well onto the Family-Tree project.

As time progresses, I find it harder and harder to remember a time when it was myself and Jean-Luc, when we were a blissfully married couple with a baby on the way. I must have been another person then.

Now, I'm Bea, single parent, widow, adoring mother of Luke, with a tough shell on the outside that I let very few people penetrate.

I was thirty-eight weeks pregnant when my husband died, which means that Jean-Luc never saw his son and Luke, my baby boy who has recently turned gangly and long limbed, never saw his dad.

This is not a sob story – I don't believe in that. I don't want pity. If people dole it out, I smile and mentally give them the bitter version of Taoism: shit happens.

It's true. Appalling things happen amidst the most wonderful of love stories, destroying them.

Love does not stop drunk drivers ploughing into cars.

Love does not mean that your beloved husband will be miraculously revived at the scene of the accident.

Love does mean that when your waters break when you hear the news your husband has died, you fight to bring your son into the world and vow that nothing will ever hurt him.

Actually, that's mother love. The tough kind, the anyone-who-hurts-my-son-will-regret-it love.

Being solely responsible for a child toughens you up. We mothers will do anything for our kids. But for ourselves? Who has the time to do anything for themselves?

Mothers never stop looking after their children. When Jean-Luc's anniversary and Luke's birthday arrives, my mother will bring me flowers and hug me extra hard.

'Love you, darling girl,' she'll say. 'Wherever he is, Jean-Luc is looking down on you and he's so proud of how you're raising Luke.'

My dear mum: I couldn't have got through any of it without her. But I'm not sure Jean-Luc is gazing down at me from anywhere. I truly believed in heaven until he was killed and then – then, I didn't believe in any heaven or deity because no decent God would rip my unborn baby's father away so cruelly.

I've never felt Jean-Luc's presence, although I've dreamed of his arms around me. Once, when that happened, I woke up and cried.

Now, the truth has seeped into my dreams too. I dream of him gone and I'm searching for him, aware that time is ticking and that if I don't find him, it will be too late.

It's hard to know which is worse.

I decided that when Luke was very small and I was weeping – yes, such a biblical word, but it's how it felt – weeping over the only man I think I could ever love, that I would go on because of Luke. I have my friends, mainly women, but I try to hide my vulnerability by holding that rod of steel in my back because it's better that people don't see how broken hearted I am. Fake it till you make it, right?

I feel that dear Finn, one of the people left over from that other life when Jean-Luc and I were together, somehow knows how wounded I still am. Finn will phone and invite me out to dinner for Jean-Luc's anniversary. Loyal, lovely natured and clever, Finn cannot cook, so we have to go out and we have fun choosing restaurants. But I hold my pain close to my heart.

And Marin and Nate, whom I dated years ago when I was a twenty-year-old idiot, will call and say they're having a few people over for supper and would I come?

'Just bring yourself and Luke, no cooking dessert or anything. It's going to be jeans and sweatshirts at the kitchen table, promise.' That's what she always says.

Even though Luke and Joey get on like a house on fire, and I know everyone well, those dinner parties sometimes make me consumed with sadness.

They're a memory of a life I no longer lead.

The doorbell rings snapping me back to the here and now and the two boys yell that it's Christie with the girls.

She's the third part of our triumvirate of square pegs in the round holes of school mums. The girls, Daisy and Lily, who are the girliest girls you will ever see, erupt into the house. Shazz and I go down to meet them. They're non-indentical twins. Daisy is blonde and favours Heidi-style pigtails at the moment with sparkles on everything. Lily is dark and looks like she was ordered from a Parisian catalogue. On her, the cheapest garment looks chic, even at age eight.

'How's the online profile going?' says Christie, herself a stunning blonde with a blunt haircut and a razor-sharp mind.

'I am a French sex kitten with hidden talents,' I murmur, as the four kids get together.

'Shazz!' says Christie.

I cheer up. Lesbian dating websites must be more honest. Or are women inherently more honest? I ponder.

'The picture's the vital ingredient,' Christie goes on. 'Just slap a photo up. That one from summer on the beach where she's in the bikini. No man can resist tits.'

'Tits? Really? Where has the romance gone?' I demand, going into the kitchen and putting the kettle on to boil.

'You got to find the guy first,' says Shazz, 'then work on the romance.'

I give in.

I let them scroll through my phone for photos, saying a clear no to said bikini shots.

One of Shazz's boyfriends once said I had 'a nice rack' and I was mortally embarrassed about this, and have been heading for the minimiser section of the bra department ever since.

We finally settle on a picture of me – fully clothed – on the beach that same evening, a blanket wrapped around me, smiling because the children were all happily tired out and we were heading back to the house we'd rented in Wexford, hungry but full of cheer.

I look just like my mum: hair the colour of the russet apples that used to fall from the tree in our old garden, eyes that are amber in some lights, a honeyed pale gold in others. I know I can look cautious now, as if ready for the next blow.

Tragedy might teach you resilience but it also teaches you to be over-alert about the next pain coming down the tracks.

It's a good photo of me because I'm smiling.

I might be the one faking it on this profile, I think: implying a happy inner world when, in reality, I often feel so lonely and worried about everything.

But still, Shazz and Christie are madly set on this. And I can't let them down.

4

Sid

Vilma's got tickets with all her friends to see some band I've never heard of who are doing a one-off gig in a small venue at the weekend.

'You've got to come!' she says and I can almost see her eyes sparkling with happiness telling me this.

I'm sitting at my desk staring at my inbox, which is full. Again. I've only been out of the office for two hours for a working lunch and despite the new directive from Adrienne that we are too busy to engage in the corporate world's ass-covering cc emails, everyone's still at it.

I start deleting with a vengeance.

'I got a pint of beer spilled on me at the last gig you dragged me to,' I say mutinously, aware that I am sounding childish. 'Plus, it's freezing. Who wants to leave their fire to go out at night in bloody November?'

I do not have a fire, but still. Vilma, who is in college studying political science and seems to have about three lectures a week, laughs.

'You are coming if we have to drag you out of the apartment,' she announces. 'You've had a year of barely ever going out at night, no matter what the weather. It's either one gig every few months or myself and the girls kidnap you and drag you to our flat.'

As their flat is a hotbed of both men and women arriving and departing like a train station, I could not cope with it. I like my peace and not sharing the couch with various happy student types.

'You've got to get over him,' Vilma said as a parting word.

'Fine,' I said in resignation, before hanging up and crossly deleting a few more emails. She didn't understand about Marc and I, but then, I'd never explained it to her. Marc and I were each other's safe harbours in every sense, but I'd messed it up.

Still, his leaving had shocked me because I pride myself on being watchful – hell, I can read a room in seconds – and I hadn't seen the signs.

People always thought we were perfect for each other and in our slender, fine-bonedness, we could almost be brother and sister, although he's taller and his hair is darker than mine.

I'd once had long hair but I kept it in a short cut now: not a pixie but something with a hint of avant-garde to it, half like I went at it with the kitchen scissors, half like some tricky hairdressing genius did it over three hours of aloof thoughtfulness. Nobody ever believes I get it cut in a tiny salon close to the office where most of the customers are lovely elderly ladies having their hair set. I love old ladies – there's not a shred of romantic notions left in them. They've seen Life and know exactly what it brings.

Not that surprising, really, that my world is all safely contained within a couple of miles' radius. Home, the office, the pub. 'You could work anywhere,' Marc would say to me in those early days.

'I like what I do and it's important work,' I said.

And it was. Plus, Adrienne, boss of the organisation, ran the place so wonderfully that it felt like the safest place on earth. Nurture by name and nurture by nature.

During my second year there, when I decided it was the right place for me, Marc and I moved in together. Buying a two-bedroom apartment meant we could afford almost no furniture but as time went on, things improved. We splashed out on a grey velvet couch we could both almost sleep on and a rug in a modern print. And cushions. I adore cushions, the squashier and more velvety the better.

Apart from the cushion fetish, I'm a minimalist. Marc's wallet is testament to his messiness. Receipts hang out of it and if he didn't have me to accompany him around shops, he'd be dressed like a tramp.

Oh but I'm doing it again. Saying 'if he didn't have me'.

It's all past tense now. So past tense that the tumble weeds are rolling through the remains of our relationship.

Nearly a year ago, Marc left me the couch and the rug and I began to think about getting a cat.

'He's gone? Just like that? How dare he dump you. You should have dumped him first,' Vilma said as I told her the news that night on the phone. Vilma, eighteen at the time, was heavily into female empowerment and the belief that girls rule the world. I did not tell her that, in my experience, this was unfortunately not the case.

'I did not know it was over, so he got to do the dumping, which is fine,' I assured her, sounding calm because I was self-medicating with vodka tonics and Haribos instead of dinner. At least nobody could see me, Nurture Department Head, public purveyor of the Sugar is Evil message, doing this.

While Vilma gave out stink about men and how, if she had a staple gun, she'd sort bloody Marc out, with a few well-judged staples and when was I going to tell our mother, Giselle, because she'd be devastated, I ruminated on pets. Cats don't need to be walked. If I had a dog, it would have to come into the office with me and no dog would survive the noisy chatter of our office. A cat wouldn't mind vodka tonic nights. Cats can look after themselves. I didn't want to be alone. Alone scared me.

'Why did you say that about cats?' Vilma asked, confused.

The vodka:tonic ratio was 50:50 at this stage, I should point out. Desperate times and all that.

'I'm just upset,' I improvised. 'He said it was time to end it.'

Vilma hissed, which is what all younger sisters do when their big sister's boyfriends leave. It's a comfortingly feral noise. I adore my sister.

It was just as much my fault as Marc's, but to tell Vilma would be to ultimately hurt her, so I couldn't. But I did miss him, missed having someone to watch telly with or get take-away with.

Which said it all, really: when TV and takeaway are the things you miss most about your relationship, you know it's over.

Vilma's and her friends' delight is infectious as they queue up to get into Whelan's, the venue where an amazing band called Granny's Fruitcake will be on stage from ten.

They've all decided I am to 'have a fun night out!' and are taking this seriously: before long, they have commandeered a high table near the stage, are treating me like bodyguards taking care of a celebrity, and have put a mini bottle of wine, an actual glass and a packet of crisps in front of me. All young men who attempt to infiltrate the group are warned off by them, like lionesses warding off attack.

Despite several nights out with the girls, I am not sure exactly what Vilma told them, but am guessing it involves how poor Sid is lonely, needs to get out more and still isn't over being dumped.

There's no point correcting this version of events and I am happily going along with it because I have no choice, it might be fun and I am out of box sets. Even *I* know it's worrying how I put calendar reminders on my phone diary when new ones are due on Netflix. Life lived through Netflix series is the sort of thing you probably regret when you are dying. But, who knows?

There are five young women: Vilma and her best sister-pack – Rilla (trainee police officer), Sinead (beauty therapist), Svetlana (working in a gym and doing fitness coach qualifications) and Karla (training to be a nurse). They've been friends since school apart from Karla, who's an honorary member of the team because she and Rilla are dating.

I love their protectiveness. I am halfway down my packet of crisps before I get a chance to try my wine.

'The wine's crap here,' says Karla, her spiky haircut coloured an unlikely red. 'Are you sure it's OK for you, Sid?' she asks, as if I am a wine connoisseur.

'Watch her glass, Karla,' says Vilma, looking left and right. 'I don't trust glasses: anybody can slip a drug into one. Bottles are better.' She waved her beer bottle at me.

'Put it down and never pick it up again,' recites Rilla, who has rippling blond hair and the look of a fairy-tale princess, but she's a self-defence genius who learned unarmed combat from her army dad from the age of twelve. I love Rilla.

I pull my wine glass into my embrace and think that if it makes me look like a wino, it's better than being dragged off into the night drugged out of my brain on GBH.

'We take care of each other,' Vilma says, reciting the mantra I taught her. 'Nobody goes to the loo on their own. We travel in pairs. Check in.'

I feel a surge of pride at seeing Vilma and her friends taking care of each other.

'I feel like the older Sarah Connor in *Terminator*,' I say, grinning, 'the one with the amazing combats and boots who has her own rocket launcher. '

We all high-five each other as the band starts up. Their delight is infectious.

Granny's Fruitcake will never be on my playlist but they are earnest, sweet, trying so hard. The lead singer is the youngest, possibly only shaves twice a week and has a lovely huskiness to his voice but the music isn't my thing. Still, that wasn't the point.

After the gig, all of us – happily undrugged by strangers – wander off for something sweet in a cake-and-coffee shop Rilla suggests.

The Cake Shop Café is accessed through a second-hand bookshop that I've been in before. With a mezzanine where books cover every square metre, it would take days to examine all the stock with your head sideways to read the spines before serious neck strain set in. At night, when the bookshop is closed, the café with its outside pergola seating area can be reached by a teeny lane. The pergola area with its trailing plants, fairy lights draping the overhang and tea lights in tiny jars on the tables is buzzing. Heaters keep it warm and there are cheap blankets for anyone who wants added cosiness. The girls slither into a small space and I take the tea and cake orders.

The café's a lovely mix of people, from those retreating after nights in music venues to those having a post-prandial coffee and dessert.

I leave my girls chattering and laughing, exchanging photos and uploading social media things, and collide neatly with a tall man holding an empty tray and staring at the cakes and sugar-laden health balls behind the glass counter.

'Sorry.'

'Fine,' I mutter.

'Did I hurt you?' he asks, staring down at me. I hate being stared down at. Being short is a definite disadvantage in life.

I shake my head. 'Fine,' I say again, about to move past. It was past my bedtime and, jacked up on the 'strangers will put date-rape drugs in your drink' message, I wasn't in the mood for random men talking to me.

'Snap. You've been out with a gang of youngsters in Whelan's,' he says and I stare up, eyes narrowed. Stalker? Random nutter? Nice normal man? It's so hard to tell, as anyone who has ever watched the crime channels will tell you.

'I took my nephews and I saw your gang in there,' he explains, pointing to two lanky youths with broad shoulders who are sitting at a table staring at their phones. 'Actually, they took me,' he adds, semi-bemused. 'I felt like an ancient uncle.'

I can't help myself and I laugh.

'You too, huh?'

'My sister and her friends,' I say, making a snap decision that we were in a public place and my girls would attack him if he tried to slip anything dodgy into my tea.

'Girls' night out?'

'Women,' I say, hackles up. 'We're women.'

He holds up his hands. 'Sorry! Women! No offence. I'm old school in some ways. My nephews seem like boys to me and everyone younger does too. So I say girls . . .' He grimaces. 'I'm making this worse. I suppose I'm saying that they're girls and you, on the other hand, are a woman –'

Poor man is digging a hole so deep, he'll only get out with crampons, some rope and a mountaineer shouting instructions.

I take pity on him. 'It's all right. I'm not going to hit you over the head with my copy of *Feminism Rules*,' I say, 'so cut the cheese.'

He smiles. 'Sounds like an old book title. *Who Moved My Cheese?*'

Against my better judgement, I laugh. 'It's a new title: *Women Who Love Pinterest and Rabbits More Than Men, So Cut The Cheese.*'

'Catchy. I should read it. Shamefully, my own rabbit habit is getting out of hand . . .' he deadpans and it's inexplicably not cheesy. 'I should point out that I am not hitting on you. I was making conversation, that's all. If it helps, I don't date. I'm appalling at it. I have decided to retire from the ring.'

My superpower is a hard-won, near-perfect analysis of people. Near-perfect. I am not counting Marc because just before he left, my superpower obviously left me.

But it's back and I decide that the man beside me is not joking. He is over with dating. He's right: why bother? I chance a look at him.

He's handsome with a lean face, kind flinty grey eyes, a Borzoi-long nose, with short sandy hair going grey in narrow streaks. He could be anywhere from thirty to forty in the dim light of the café. His night out gear is the defiantly undressy: hiking jacket, jeans and an Aran sweater, and his long legs have the hint of someone who trains obsessively for marathons.

'Runner?' I ask.

'Used to be.' He sounds miserable.

'Now you cycle because your knees are banjaxed.'

His turn to laugh. 'Correct. I also swim but am not insane or young enough for triathlons. I like my joints and want to hang on to them. Meanwhile, you work in banking and your idea of a night out is entertaining clients in posh restaurants?' he ventured, taking in my trench coat and trousers, which are from my work wardrobe. Sweatpants were too casual for tonight and my last acceptable pair of jeans have an inconvenient hole in the inner thigh. I am not a shopper.

'Excellent guess,' I lie. 'I have an entire team at my disposal and I scream at them if they annoy me or if my coffee's the wrong temperature. I have two assistants, one I throw my coat at and one who buys my lunch.'

'They'd never have you in the intelligence world, what with being able to lie with ease,' he says, grinning.

I think, *Oh yes, they would.*

'I've seen *The Devil Wears Prada*,' he adds.

'Did sisters or girlfriends make you watch it?'

'My niece – my sister's little girl, Danielle.'

He had, I allowed myself to notice, a nice smile.

'I am putty in her hands. So are her brothers. I was babysitting some years ago, it was a toss up between a Transformer movie or *The Devil Wears Prada*, which is her favourite movie, and she won. Some day, she will be running the country.'

'You are a new man. Congratulations.'

'Thank you.' He inclines his head modestly. 'New man, single man, that's me. Can't get a woman to save my life so have just given up.' He stops dead. 'Sorry – don't know where that's come from. Thinking out loud. All those young people in Whelan's gazing into each other's eyes and making plans for later. I felt both a hundred years old and entirely out of the game. I realised a long time ago that it was time to get out of the game, but a band venue with young people really gets the message across.'

He rubs the bridge of his nose thoughtfully and I think he might be as tired as I am.

We're getting closer to the counter and are standing side by side.

'Do you think,' I say, and I wonder if maybe my mini bottle of wine has pushed me over the edge here, 'that people really weren't meant to date? That somewhere in the whole theory of evolution people are supposed to exist in little extended family groups. And sometimes, if they are very lucky, they make it as couples, but otherwise not?'

He gives me a long searching look.

'You might be on to something there,' he says. 'I thought I had it right with my last girlfriend and – and then I didn't.'

I held up a hand. 'I'm not listening to how she was a horrible bitch, you hate her and she ruined your life,' I say, only half kidding.

'No,' he says. 'It was – forgive the cliché – complicated. But I don't diss and tell.'

He actually sounds forlorn and I think I'll send him over to Vilma so she can counsel him on getting over people. In my experience, straight men don't allow male friends enough emotional access to counsel them past relationship pain.

It was his go with the person behind the counter, and he began politely ordering all sorts of carb-related things to fill the two young guys in the corner. I'd typed in everyone's order on my phone, because I knew I'd never remember it – between chai, lattes and matcha teas and buns with no nuts in them, unless they had anything with Nutella involved, and then the nut-free thing didn't count . . .

'How about your dating history?' the man says as we stand beside each other in what feels like a companionable silence. 'What I mean is, why have you come to the conclusion that dating is over?'

'I lived with a guy for nearly thirteen years and broke up a year ago. Nobody since.' It felt important to say this. The new me was laying the facts out there. I live on my own: so what? 'I'm perfectly happy with my box sets.'

'Me too,' he says. 'Box sets are brilliant.'

'Box sets, a takeaway and a single, perfect glass of wine. Hangovers are just horrendous when you get older,' I add, shuddering. When I make my cocktails at the weekend, I only drink one now. The first post-Marc month involved far too much wine. I do not want to be the single woman statistic who drinks her way through her weekends and gets the shakes on Monday mornings without a shot of vodka.

'It must be age – I can't cope with hangovers either,' he says. 'I swim a lot and I can't go for pints with the lads anymore because I'm not prepared to pay the entertainment tax.'

Suddenly I smile up at him, the irony of it all hitting me as it so often does when I think of the way I live my life now.

'These are supposed to be some of the best years of our lives,' I say, half to myself. 'We are youngish, free, and clearly reasonably solvent if you have a racing bike and we spend our lives eating takeaways and watching Netflix.'

The man looks at me. 'I disagree. The rules of life are societal constructs. Who says these are the best years and to enjoy them properly we have to live in pairs and have children?'

'Teacher?' I ventured.

'University lecturer,' he said, then added, 'I'm Finn. Why can't men and women merely be friends? Honestly, genuinely just friends and let someone else fulfil their biological imperative.'

I raise an eyebrow and decide he's broken up recently too. Only the really recently broken-up talk like this. It's as if being uncoupled pulls out a little stopper in your brain and lets all these random truths out.

We shuffle along as our various teas and foodstuffs are put onto trays.

49

'You and I should be able to see a film or an exhibition and not feel we have to pair up like little robots.'

'Are you asking me out?' I say, grinning, knowing he wasn't.

'I'm sorry,' he says, 'I shouldn't have asked that; you'll think it's a trick. But it's an idea, an experiment. Let's go out – as friends. Then everyone will leave me alone about not having a girlfriend.'

My superpower is still working and he's not tricking me but still . . .

'Tell your friends to leave you alone. I don't do male friends unless I work with them.' He seemed like a decent guy. In another universe, we could have dated – but not in this one. 'Sorry,' I add, 'no dice. Not my thing.' I pick up the tray of coffees and goodies that has handily just materialised in front of me and head back to my crew.

'OK, then. Very nice to meet you.' He smiles at me.

Back at the table, Vilma gives me the laser-eye look. 'So, that dude you were talking to. He was into you, wasn't he?'

'He wasn't,' I say. 'We were discussing how dating is over-rated and humanity should get used to living life alone.'

'Ugh,' says Rilla, without looking up from her phone. 'What about sex?'

I feel Vilma's hand on my thigh and realise she's glaring at me. 'You have no friends, Sid: none, except the people you work with. And us, although I practically had to kidnap you to get you out. You need some life. For fuck's sake, go out with this guy – as a friend. You've got plenty of home-made pepper spray in case he's stalker material, but he looks OK.'

I'm shocked into silence.

Vilma has looked up to me her whole life and now she's staring at me as if I am the weirdest person she's ever met: her crazy sister, the recluse, who never goes out.

I am not going to cry. I never cry. I am going to get angry. Anger works better.

'Fine,' I say furiously, as if I'm raising the stakes on a poker game, 'fine. Let me out, Karla.'

I wriggle out and march up to the table where Finn is now sitting with his two nephews, who are wolfing down cake as if they've been on a keto diet for a month.

They all stare at me.

'Just friends,' I say, ignoring the two younger men. 'No funny business. First sign of it and I'm off.'

'Me too,' he says, looking only a hint startled. 'Film? I have to tell you that I cannot watch – er,' he considers his words, 'sad movies where people cry.'

'Me neither. I like ones where women get to avenge themselves on men. With guns. Flamethrowers, castration, that sort of thing.'

One of the nephews winces.

Finn considers this and nods approval. 'Good plan.'

He extracts himself from the open-mouthed nephews and we move away.

'My name is Sid, short for Sidonie. Never call me Sidonie.' I am aware that I am talking very fast but I think that I may run if I consider how unlike me this is.

'OK, Sid, to keep the ball entirely in your court, I will give you my phone number and if you really want to do this you can ring me, and maybe you should give me your card in case you think I'm being, er, big headed by expecting you to ring me. Because the man rings the woman?'

'That worked in the nineteenth century, but not anymore,' I say gravely. 'Besides, we're in the Friend Zone, which has different rules.'

He grins and it turns out that he really has the most amazing smile. I shuffle around in my purse and take out a card. We manage to swap with only the faintest touch of fingers. But that still feels pleasurable.

'Tomorrow, when we are in our right minds and we have had

some sleep, we will phone each other. And whoever phones first gets to pick the film,' I barter.

'Deal.'

We shake hands and then with one last, bursting grin, he salutes me.

'Comrade friend,' he says.

'Smartass,' I mutter, pretty sure he can hear me.

5

Marin

I can hear my brother and mother arguing before I'm even in the house.

Not all the words are audible but the ones I can hear make me want to run out the door. My mother can start an argument in an empty room. Now she's roped Dom in.

'Lazy . . . taking me for granted . . . disgrace!'

'You said Sue was beneath me!'

My heart actually sinks. Nobody heard me arrive. I could sneak out and –

'Marin!' hisses Dad.

I turn in the hallway and find him peering out from the den where Ma keeps her crafting supplies and where Dad hides himself away during book-club nights and any other night when Ma is in a mood.

'In here.'

I slip in and he shuts the door, delighted to see me.

We hug and I smell that quintessentially Dad smell of Old Spice and fresh ginger. Dad loves ginger and drinks it with lemon, cloves, fresh thyme and hot water every morning. His father gave him the recipe for his arthritis and he's been drinking it for years now, even though Ma rubbishes it as 'an old cure and not worth a patch on modern medicine'.

Ma also has arthritis and now takes a roll call of medicines to cope with the effects of anti-inflammatories on her stomach lining.

'What's the row about this time?' I ask, sitting down on the old worn couch that my father sits on every night to watch his beloved documentaries or gardening shows on TV.

'Divorce,' says Dad. 'Dom told her he was definitely getting divorced and it hasn't gone down well. You'd think he was planning a satanic ritual in the back garden.'

We both giggle. In truth, I think the reason my father has survived so many years with my mother is because he has such a good sense of humour. It's either that or he's growing cannabis in the allotment.

'I've got an old black satin skirt we could repurpose for the altar,' I suggest. 'Doesn't fit me anymore. My hips have spread.'

'I could plant next year's bulbs into a pentagram shape,' Dad says.

We both giggle again.

'I did try to tell her that divorce was a good plan so they could start again with other people but she stormed out,' Dad goes on.

'That was brave of you,' I say, surprised. Dad is very mild mannered and rarely, if ever, goes up against my mother. He gets the full silent treatment for days when he does.

He looks guilty. 'She was going to Mass. Didn't want to be late.'

'Ah.'

My mother goes to daily Mass, is first in line for communion and disapproves of everything the Vatican says she should disapprove of, no matter how cruel.

Her motto in life is 'what will people/Fr Leonard think?'

It's a very hard motto for us flawed human beings to live up to.

'You have to get her to face facts, Marin,' Dad continues. 'With Dom living here, it's like being on the front line. He needs another place to hang around in his old T-shirts and boxers – which he was wearing when he opened the door to Gladys from choir, I might add. I'm too old to be living with this.'

I close my eyes briefly at my father's begging and wonder exactly how I'm going to manage this one.

I'm not sure when I became the family member who was chosen to handle my mother but, somewhere along the way, it happened.

April, despite being the eldest, was always too dizzy and lost in her romantic novels to be of much use. Dominic was a little wild child, everyone's favourite because he's so much fun if utterly unable to do things on his own. Dad is incapable of handling the immoveable force that is my mother. I have wondered many times how they got married in the first place and then remind myself that Ma would have said: 'Denis, church, twelve on Saturday, second one in June, next year. Yes?' And Dad would have nodded.

Which left me, second-born, to keep the peace in our lopsided family. Keeping up appearances has always been the beating heart of our family. We all had to be suitably dressed for morning Mass on Sunday, where my mother would hold her head high and search out those who had not managed this feat of family management.

Dom once naughtily told Ma that sitting in church didn't make her religious any more than sitting in the garage made him a car, but she batted that one right back at him and added a cuff round the ear for good measure. Pure steel, that woman is.

'I'm sleeping badly,' Dad points out, looking mournful.

I give him a stern look: 'That's emotional blackmail.'

'Ah go on, Marin, she listens to you.'

'She listens to you, too.'

'Yes but only for a short while and then she sulks with me. Dom doesn't notice the sulking: he's always been immune. I really can't sleep, you know. I wake up early. That's a sign of stress: I looked it up.'

'Fine. Fill me in, then. Why did Dom tell her he was getting a divorce? He was hell-bent on getting back with Sue last time I talked to him.'

'Sue's moved on. She went out for drinks with an old flame,'

Dad whispers, as if keeping the volume down will make the news easier to impart.

I was getting the picture, finally: my mother has looked down on Sue for years. But now that Sue was moving on, divorce was suddenly in the future and Fr Leonard, very much of the old school of Catholicism, would need CPR if he heard. No wonder there was screaming.

'OK. Let me at them.'

Dad reached under his couch and retrieved an open box of cheap chocolates. 'Have a few. Get your blood sugar up.'

'If she finds these, you're dead,' I say.

Ma prides herself on her figure and does not allow treats in the house.

His mouth full of toffee chocolate, Dad grins. 'I won't tell if you won't.'

The kitchen is uncharacteristically messy when I enter to find Dom, barefoot, wearing ratty sweatpants and a jumper, making coffee in an old Moka machine with the remains of a toasted sandwich on a plate.

The diametric opposite is my mother, who is wearing a neat tweedy-looking skirt to the knee, beige nylons, sedate heels and one of those pale pink twinsets you see in newspaper special offers. Her hair is sprayed into a helmet of frosted curls which dare not move. She is sitting on a kitchen chair, toe tapping, a china cup in front of her and is mid-diatribe.

'. . . You cannot make those vows and then abandon them. New jacket?' she says, catching sight of me and switching her attention from one child to another in a flash.

Ma's intonation is practically weaponised: nobody else can endow two words with such a negative meaning. My mother has been criticising my clothing for so long that this latest statement is like water off a duck's back.

'Work clothes,' I say cheerfully.

'I still think Hilliers should have a uniform,' she says,

reverting to a very old, oft-revisited topic. 'Something classy, a heather tweed, maybe with a plain blazer. Black makes you look old. But a uniform . . .'

She angles her head a little as if to imagine this dream, heather tweed outfit on me. 'Or maybe not. Tweed does add weight around the middle if one isn't careful.'

Fantasy Marin would tell my mother that people in glass houses shouldn't throw stones – my mother is at least two stone overweight – but Real World Marin knows better.

'We can't all have your figure, Ma,' I say, again cheerfully. Because when you deliver a whopper of a lie like this you have to throw in a bit of toadying.

'I know,' says Mum, smoothing down her tweedy skirt.

I often think the problem with my mother is that she has a very limited sense of self awareness. Her focus is always dedicated towards looking at other people's flaws, never her own. I feel sure there is a whole segment of psychoanalysis devoted to this but even when I read *Psychologies* mag, I still can't find the bit to help.

'Hi, Dom,' I say, going over and patting him briefly on the back. 'Is there enough in that Moka for another cup?'

'Yeah, sure,' he says, laid back as ever.

Up close, he has several five o'clock shadows and yet still looks recklessly handsome. All the girls loved Dom at school. But my mother clearly doesn't right now, hence the pained text from Dad begging me to drop in.

Dom has made an almighty mess of the kitchen constructing a toasted cheese sandwich and he stinks. I can see why my mother gets annoyed. But then, she smiled when Dom did this as a young man. Said it was his wife's job to tidy up after him – what does she expect?

Still, I have to make an effort for Dad.

The Moka splutters explosively on the stove top telling us that the coffee is ready. Dom stands watching it, which makes me aware that he's expecting me to take it off the stove and pour the coffees. I am a woman, hence I perform the domestic duties. Poor Dom: he's going to have to cop on.

I have no idea how Sue put up with him for so long. She's a lovely, clever woman – she must have really loved him.

I pour two coffees – I wouldn't dream of asking my mother if she wants one, because she's a tea person through and through – and add sugar into mine.

'Do you want to talk about what's upsetting you, Ma?' I ask gently, hoping to bring the heat in the kitchen down.

'Oh, only that my children have no respect for me or the Church.' She eyes the sugar-laden cup of coffee in my hand like it's an illegal substance. Ma is very anti-sugar. She gave it up one Lent and never went back. Now she views all people who take it in their tea or coffee as people who do not understand the value of sacrifice for one's religion. I much prefer to do things for Lent – help the homeless, that type of thing. Not Ma.

'Respect goes two ways, Ma,' says Dom loyally.

'Oh does it?' she snaps back. 'If you respected me, you wouldn't expect to live under my roof while getting a divorce. How will I ever hold my head up at Mass again? Have you any idea what Father Leonard will say? Imagine the way they'll look at me in the choir.'

'Choir? You all sing like ferrets being strangled.'

I have to hide a grin. He's being childish but, sadly, accurate.

'Dominic!' she shrieks in rage.

Ma is building up a head of steam here and I feel myself assuming the role I always used to as a child: fixer-in-chief. Children do when they're trying to cope with rage and anger.

I feel that familiar tension in my chest and my breathing turns shallow. I can remember the endless arguments at home, arguments out of nowhere that my mother started and Dom somehow ignored, that made April run to her bedroom, pick up another romance novel and escape into it. Dad ran to the allotment and I tried to calm it all.

No wonder we are all the way we are, I think. April in fantasy world hoping that her current married boyfriend will leave his wife; Dom with his head in the sand, ignoring the fact that he has screwed up his own marriage.

I go to the biscuit cupboard and find some very plain biscuits, which are what my mother thinks are suitable offerings in the confectionary department. The only time she bakes nice things are when she is baking for church socials or fetes.

'You're getting a divorce then, Dom?' I say quietly.

'Yep,' he says. 'Sue went out with that bastard Liam the other day. D'you remember him from school? He always said she was the hottest thing. Bastard. I can't believe she'd do that to me.'

'Do what to you?' I say.

'You know, go off with someone else.'

'But you moved out. The two of you have been fighting for about three years, so yeah, I guess she wants to move on.'

'Marin, how can you say such a thing,' growls my mother.

I'm reminded slightly of the satanic voice in *The Exorcist*. I finish my coffee and feel the caffeine and the sugar hit my system.

When home feels like a horror movie, it's time to leave. You never see that embroidered on cushions.

'Ma,' I say gently, 'you can't stop Dom and Sue getting divorced.'

'I can,' she says fiercely. 'I can and I will. I just need somebody to talk some sense into him,' she goes on. 'He got married in a church. Your cousin, Father Michael, came over from Canada to perform the ceremony.'

'Michael was here anyway to visit Auntie Silvie; he didn't fly over on purpose,' huffs Dom.

'That's not the point,' shrieks my mother, and the bell rings for round two.

I roll my eyes and leave them at it, go back into the hall and find Dad in his den.

'Sorry, I didn't help much.'

He reaches under the couch for his chocolates.

'It was lovely to see you, all the same,' he says, offering me another one. 'I'm going to pretend to be asleep if she comes in here.'

I'm almost at the front door when Dom appears.

'Sorry,' he mutters. 'You didn't need to get dragged into all of that.'

I hug him and he leans into me.

'I was thinking,' he begins. 'I need to get out of here and, well, the Sue situation . . . we need time to work it out. I've been investigating flats and I can rent from a pal who's going away but I'll need a deposit.' Dom grins. 'It's just I'm a bit strapped, what with paying my half of the mortgage on our house –'

Dom works in software development and while he could probably write code to make a high-tech fridge do the salsa across the kitchen floor, he's hopeless with money.

'Of course,' I say automatically. 'I'll sell my gold ingots . . .'

We both laugh.

'Seriously, let me check. I'm sure I can manage something. Take care, darling.'

'You're the best, Marin,' says Dom, and I feel so sorry for him. He is a lovely man – just caught in a strange man-child cycle.

I hug him again. 'Love you.'

'Love you, big sis,' he says, and I head off.

When finally I get home, having picked up Joey from the childminder's, Nate's already there and Rachel's left a note on the fridge saying she's got an evening shift in the pizza restaurant, which is her new job. I examine whether tonight's dinner has defrosted.

It has, so I high-speed it into the oven, get vegetables ready for the steamer and am ready to race upstairs to change when Nate wanders into the kitchen.

He's changed out of his suit, is now in jeans and a sweater, and is unruffled because he hasn't gone eight rounds with my mother and brother. He's on the phone, chatting happily: something about a football match and I feel a sudden intense blast of irritation.

I am home late, the oven isn't even turned on, and it would have taken nothing, *nothing*, for him to open the fridge and bung tonight's meatballs topped with mozzarella into the oven. But then, I have made myself indispensable to this family the way I did to my family of origin.

Marin will do it.

From purchasing food to cooking dinner, to laying the table and serving up the meal. Fix, fix, fix. There is nothing Nate has to do except arrive home, change and open wine if he feels like it. I'm the one who's always done the school runs in the morning and picked up the children from childminders: this means Nate has always been free to swim first thing with Steve and Finn.

He's fighting fit and I struggle to do an online Pilates class once a month.

He idly picks up an apple and bites into it. 'What's up?' he asks, seeing my face.

'Bad day,' I mutter, not wanting the fight, but then the irritation refuses to lie buried and squelches out of me, the way my belly does when I wear shaping knickers.

'You could have put dinner in the oven,' I say.

'You should have rung. I would have,' he says equably. 'I can lay the table for you,' he adds.

Lay the table *for me*? It's like, 'I can do the shopping *for you* if you're really stuck.'

It's for all of us. Not just me.

Me wants to lie in a bubble bath, read a novel and not have to look after everyone.

'Really bad day?' he asks, cocking his head to the side.

I have a sudden flashback to the household I have just left where anger ripples through the air.

Taking a deep breath, I say: 'Yes, but I'm OK. Please, do lay the table. Open wine, maybe?'

'That I can do,' says my husband with a charming grin. He kisses me on the cheek, goes to the cupboard in the utility room where he keeps his precious bottles.

Wine will help, I decide. I am lucky. I mustn't forget it.

But to really cheer myself up, I log on to my current favourite account: Vestiare, where delicious and designer things are sold second-hand, so I have a hope in hell of buying them. Vintage clothes porn has got to be the purest art form for the shopaholic, I think, as I begin to scroll. Just something small, perhaps.

Nobody has to know . . .

6

Bea

I'm sitting in morning traffic, edging forward as rain lashes the windscreen and thinking that I'll be at my desk at seven-fifty. According to the car radio traffic updates, there's a blockage up the road due to an oil spill and I wish, as I often do, that my job was on a direct public transport route instead of being inconveniently situated.

In summer, getting to the big medical and dental clinic, where I work as secretary to the medics, means a walk and two buses. In winter, it means either three buses or just two and Scott of the Antarctic outer garments.

I hate the cold, which is why I keep holding off on getting a dog, despite Luke's increasing begging for one.

'Muuum,' he begs. 'I'd look after it. He could sleep in my bed and I'd feed him and walk him and everything.'

His idea of the perfect dog is a Husky, which needs lots of walking, apparently.

Parental Skills Update 2.0 means I know that I will be walking, feeding and cleaning up the poop of said Husky, so we will not be getting one, no matter how beautiful they look. I cannot fit in ten kilometres a day in all weathers. I've been researching, though. Sadly, there doesn't appear to be any breed which doesn't require much walking and is happy to sit at home watching the telly while I'm at work.

Still, making sure Luke never loses out is something of a mission of mine. Maybe it is time for a dog.

In place of a father figure, get a fluffy thing to love?

It does take a village to rear a child and, in our case, that village is almost an all-female one. Alongside myself, Shazz and Christie – or the Single Momma's Club, as Shazz calls us – we have a pretty excellent support system going. My mum, Patricia, is one part of the village. Next up is Shazz's mum, Norma, whom Shazz calls Normal.

I should point out that, sometimes, Shazz calls me Bea-ch for a laugh. You've got to love her sense of humour, and we do spend a lot of time laughing in the Single Momma's Club. 'As long as we're not *Real Housewives of Beverly Hills*,' jokes Christie, which always makes us crack up.

As three women supporting our own kids, anything less like the Beverly Hills ladies would be impossible to imagine.

The final part of our support system is Christie's dad, Vincent. He adores the twins, Daisy and Lily. Christie's mother, on the other hand, has never even met her exquisite twin granddaughters.

'Why?' I couldn't help but ask, the second time we met up, Shazz and I pushing Raffie and Luke in their buggies in the park close to both our homes. Christie, small and with short blonde curls, had her two teeny, gorgeous babies sound asleep in a double buggy and we began, as mothers with small children do, to talk.

Feeding, sleeping, nappies, the great breast-feeding versus bottle-feeding debate: we ran through all the big stuff first, and eventually worked our way round to real life.

'She wanted me to have a happily married, two-point-five-children relationship and I haven't. She thinks there's something wrong with me because I don't fit the mould.'

'You not married, is that it?' asked Shazz, who likes to know all the facts straight up.

For Shazz, it's a point of principle not to let us happily marrieds into our gang.

'No,' said Christie.

'Partner or did he do a runner?' Shazz went on.

Shazz, brought up by a single parent herself, believes that all men leave one way or the other.

Christie gave us an assessing look. 'I'm on my own,' she said.

'Us too,' replied Shazz, happy to have found another member of the tribe. 'My bastard legged it, Bea's fella died. What about you?'

There was a beat.

'I'm lesbian,' Christie said finally. 'It was always going to be just me.'

'Their dad's a turkey baster,' said Shazz in delight. 'Least you don't have to worry about getting child support off it.'

She cackled to herself while I waited anxiously to see if Christie would take offence. People quite often did with Shazz and she'd outdone herself this time.

But no.

Christie grinned. 'I can see I'm going to have to educate you cis girls – that's straight to you. And no, I wouldn't have put it that way myself,' she said, 'no turkey baster involved. The girls were born with donor sperm.'

'I might as well be a bloody lesbian,' continued Shazz, ignoring any hint that she might not be the poster child for political correctness. Shazz doesn't care who someone sleeps with or whether they're gender fluid or celibate as long as they're what she calls 'good people' and enjoy a bit of fun. 'I mean, for all the action I've been getting, I could have turned gay and not even noticed. Not that I haven't tried but the men out there – they run at the sight of a new baby. Since Raffie was born, I'm practically a born-again virgin.'

One of Christie's babies, Daisy, yawned a tiny baby yawn and we all sighed.

Sex means different things to different people. Shattering orgasms, babies or simply the comfort of another human being's arms around you. Sex can but doesn't always mean friendship. Once myself, Shazz and Christie joined forces, we had a friendship force field around us that gave the most earth-shattering sex a run for its money.

We're family, an all-woman village raising four children. I'd do anything for Shazz and Christie, because they'd do anything for me.

Finally, there's a break in the traffic and I manage, with a sneaky five-hundred-metre trip down a bus lane, to get to work on time. I work in a suburban dental and medical clinic, where there are three dentists and five doctors and a multitude of patients coming in and out all the time. I work in the medical section and our desks are in a huge glassed-off area in reception. I spend a lot of time either on the phone or typing up doctors' letters, arranging blood tests, keeping all the doctor-patient communication running smoothly. It's a nice place to work, and I get on really well with the other women who work in the reception area. The other benefit is that I can work part time; I do mornings and share my particular load with another staff member called Antoinette. Up to one o'clock everything is mine; after one o'clock, it's hers. It might not be my true calling but it pays the bills. Ask any single mother and they'll tell you job security is worth its weight in gold, and, most brilliantly, it means I can always be there to pick up Luke from school. Plus, working in such a big practice, you don't necessarily get too close to the people who are coming in, in the same way as you would in a smaller surgery, which suits me just fine. Antoinette used to work for just one doctor and she says it was really difficult.

'You get to know people and you see everything and you see their pain, and I just couldn't do that anymore.'

'Sounds terrible,' I say. And I know I couldn't do it.

I know my mother thinks that Jean-Luc's death has made me hard: on the contrary, it's made me soft, I merely manage to hide it because I can't bear to go through anything like that again. So working here is perfect. I make appointments, type up letters, I'm kind to the people who come in and out, smile at their children. But above all, I do not have to get personally involved with their pain.

The morning's busy and by one o'clock, I'm looking forward to belting out of here and racing home via the supermarket where I'll get some stuff for dinner. The last patient is a red-haired woman who beams as she pays and tells me how lovely Dr Lee is, and how he must be so nice to work for.

'He is,' I assure her as I pass over the credit card machine. In my pocket, I feel my mobile phone vibrate with a text message. When my patient is gone, there's nobody left in reception so I quickly check my phone.

And laugh out loud.

Shazz has sent me a WhatsApp with a selection of photos from her current favourite dating website, which is not quite Tinder but has certainly a hint of its cheeky, straight-to-the-point sexiness.

Yes? texts Shazz beside the picture of one man who obviously owns his own gym or else does not have a job, such is the beauty of his muscles, all on view as he is not wearing a shirt. He has definitely oiled himself up for the photo.

I call her. 'Is he interested in kite-surfing and a girlfriend who's easy-going and loves sexy clothes?' I ask.

'What's wrong with that?'

'I'm a medical secretary. I'm wearing sedate navy trousers, ballet pumps, a navy sweater and you think you can pimp me out to Mr Fun Lovin' Leather Trousers . . .?'

We both laugh.

'How do you know he's wearing leather trousers?' she asks.

'Intuition.' Just so I don't sound like Ms Never Having Fun Ever, I add: 'One day, if we can find me a clever, kind, wise man who happens to be handsome, then sure: I could date him but –'

'Idris Elba's taken,' sighs Shazz. 'There's no hope for you now.'

'Pity, that,' I agree.

I finish tidying up, ready to leave, when Laoise, one of my colleagues, sidles over to my desk looking as if she's about to faint. She's pale at the best of times but now looks so blanched, it's scary.

'Laoise? Are you all right?' I ask, leaping up and steering her to my seat.

'No,' she whispers. 'Bea, I went in to drop some letters to Dr Lee, and he was on the phone. I don't think he even noticed me. He can be very obtuse sometimes.'

I wait patiently for her to get to the point.

'But whoever he was talking to, it was about the practice. They're thinking of downsizing when Dr Ryan retires and breaking up the practice. Dr Lottie wants to work with a woman's menopause clinic, so she'd go too. Dr Lee was talking about some premises they need to look at. A smaller one. I stayed for as long as I could – he was facing the window, you know the way he does when he's on a call, so he honestly didn't notice me. They won't need so many staff, Bea – our jobs –'

I feel an instant clenching of my guts as both my frontal cortex and my intestinal brain do inner shrieks of horror. It's not called the gut-brain axis for nothing.

I also do a rapid mental scan of the staff of the clinic and think that if five doctors suddenly become three, then they have far too many medical secretaries to go around. And the ones who work part-time are certain to go first.

'Of course, we don't know for sure –'

Laoise's trying to talk herself out of the catastrophic thinking but I can't.

She's married, so she has the safety net of another person's salary. I don't.

It's utterly terrifying, one of those moments when the pluses of single motherhood get wiped away by the very precariousness of it all.

'We don't know for sure,' I repeat back to her, and I'm not sure which one of us I'm trying to convince.

7
Sid

Five days have elapsed since I met Finn in the coffee shop, and I still haven't rung, texted or WhatsApped him. His card isn't exactly burning a hole in my handbag, but it's simmering in there.

Vilma has texted me about it several times: Did you ring that guy yet?

Busy. Haven't got around to it. I text back breezily.

On the fifth day she rings. This time, no punches are pulled. 'Have you been talking to that sexy Finn bloke from the coffee shop yet?'

'No, I've been swamped at work,' I protest. 'You have no idea, Vilma: we're juggling so many projects.'

This sounds fabulous and I immediately wonder why I'm not a professional liar. I'd make a fortune. If only I could play poker, I'm sure I could combine the lying with the gambling and earn a fortune.

'I smell bullshit,' says Vilma. 'Ring him.'

OK, scratch that.

'Vilma, honey, the decision to ring him all happened after some wine, it was late at night,' I begin. 'Your generation can do that sort of thing, but mine? Not so much.'

'Millennials get such a tough time,' she says narkily, 'but your generation are the weird ones. What are you? X? Y? Baby boomer?'

'I'm not a baby boomer,' I say, shocked, 'they're ancient.'

'Oh sorry, I forgot, you're the "Nothing good is ever going to happen, so I'm going to just sit here in the dark" generation.'

I have to laugh. 'OK, sis. No, I haven't rung him because I made a decision not to. It was a crazy impulse in the first place. I don't know what came over me.' I'm on a roll with the lying again. 'Plus, I have friends; I don't need any more.'

'No, you don't,' she says, in the way only a sister can. 'I have friends, loads of friends, while you could probably count your actual friends on one hand and still have a couple of fingers left over for typing.'

'I have loads of friends I work with,' I say, stung.

'What about friends *outside* work, friends from school, from college?'

'You're different to me, Vilma,' I grumble. 'You're good at holding on to people.'

I didn't hold on to people – I'd jettisoned them all. Being alone was the only way forward for me all those years ago.

'I thought you were brave and were going to have a new male friend to go for coffee or see a film with.'

I hesitate.

'Just coffee, then?' she says. And I can almost hear her smiling down the phone, like she's boxed me into a corner.

'You're very manipulative, Vilma,' I mutter, 'has anyone ever told you that?'

'Yes,' she says, and now I know she's smiling.

'One of us has to be manipulative. You're a bit clueless, to be honest, Sid, I don't know how you've survived this far.'

For a moment I almost can't breathe because sometimes I'm not entirely sure I *have* survived this far, but Vilma doesn't need to know that.

Existed: that's the word. Some days, I just exist. I don't try to have a good day – I just try to have a day full stop, where I get up, take care of my body, sit at my desk, drink my coffee shakily, and get into bed at night with relief, so glad it's all over.

'What do you suggest?' I say, wrenching myself out of this train of thought.

I've always wanted Vilma to be able to look up to me, to show her that you can have a wonderful, marvellous life and be strong. But I've faked it a lot of the time.

I didn't want to be a horrendous role model for the rest of her life, the cautionary tale. I didn't want to be her sad older sister who never did normal things, never fell in love or settled down.

Vilma thought I'd had a lovely, normal relationship with Marc but I could never explain it to her. Now that he's out of my life, she merely wants me to be happy – and apparently lots of friends is the secret to this.

'Just one coffee,' she wheedles.

'OK, one coffee.' I sigh. 'I'll text him now.'

'Good. Now when you meet people you don't really know, you've got to meet them somewhere really public, never night time, and in a busy area, OK?'

'No shit, Sherlock?' I reply laughing, the big sister letting herself be schooled by the baby of the family. If there's one person I can't say no to, it's Vilma.

I spend so long at my desk composing the text, that I probably could have written an entire report on the negative impact of soft-drink machines in schools in the time it takes me. In the end, I look at my masterpiece and sigh.

Hi, Finn, Sid here. No good films on. Will we meet for a coffee and talk about work?

I send it before I can stop myself. And then I think how lame is that: can we meet for coffee and talk about work? I've basically set us an agenda.

I can feel myself blushing. Me? A woman with biker boots blushing.

I turn my phone to silent and stuff it into my pocket. I don't want to see what he sends back; in fact, he probably won't send anything back because, under the circumstances, why would he? I have made him wait five days and nobody waits five days. Plus, he'll think I'm a nutcase because we discussed the concept of being friends and friends don't say, *Let's talk about work*.

Unless they have no life at all, which makes sense. I have no life at all.

'Are you OK, Sid?' I look up; it's Chloe, innocent intern. She's wearing false eyelashes and I have to admit they look amazing. She's no longer wearing her *I'm intelligent* glasses though: the lashes would probably keep banging into the lenses. I read that somewhere; the two don't go together terribly well.

'Just running through some work problems in my head,' I say with false calm.

In case she asks, I make up a work problem on the spot. I am good at lying, definitely.

Is there an Olympics for that? I was never sporty and it seems that all my skills – being quirky as hell, having weird hair, dressing all in black – are not ones with Olympian categories. But Chloe just nods and floats away, leaving me to ponder my non-existent problems.

The rest of the afternoon passes and I refuse to look at my phone. If the apartment is burgled, the alarm company have my work number as well as my home number. If something happens with Mum, Vilma or Stefan, they all have my work number too. So people can get me.

I stay in the office until six and I'm one of the stragglers, the last to leave.

'Night,' says Eddie, going off with his rucksack. Eddie is a cyclist and makes a round trip of twenty miles every day to get into the office. I have no idea how he hasn't been squashed before now, because I certainly wouldn't cycle along Dublin's roads, but the exercise looks good on Eddie. He is certainly a lean, mean fighting machine.

'See you, Eddie,' I say, 'careful of those trucks.'

'Yes, sir,' he says, saluting me.

Finally, I'm at the door of the office. There's nobody else there except me and the cleaners who are beginning to arrive. I greet them, chat to everyone, particularly Imelda, who's one of my favourites. Imelda has a large and noisy family and it only takes the slightest encouragement for her to start discussing them. Three of her nephews are now in a band.

'I told them they might as well stand at traffic lights washing car windscreens for money because they'll make more cash that way,' she cackles.

I'm comfortable with Imelda, because she's a woman. And I'm comfortable with women. Which is probably why it was days before I texted Finn, and yet I was comfortable with him – so maybe I can be comfortable with some men?

Over the years, I've honed my skills at men-reading. I used to be over-cautious, I have to be honest. But now, I get on well with all the men in the office, have nice chats with the barman in The Fiddler's Elbow on Fridays, say hello to motorbike couriers who arrive, sweating in the office. But I still wouldn't get into a lift with a man, any man. Even if I've known him for years. Politeness has cost many women too much. How often do women feel uneasy at getting into a lift alone with a man, yet do so all the same because not to would be rude?

In my world, be rude. Be as rude as you bloody like. I'm taking the stairs, mate.

'See ya, Imelda,' I say, as I head down in the blissfully empty lift. I pull my phone out of my pocket and look at it and there, top of the list, is a text from Finn.

Hey, Sid, would love to have a coffee. When are you thinking? This evening is good for me or tomorrow lunchtime?

Lunch was pushing it: in fact, lunch was outrageous, ripe with the sense of a date. Coffee was different. I stared at myself in the lift mirror. I looked OK. My hair did look messy, but then it often does as I run my fingers through it a lot and it's not had a cut for ages. I haven't seen my lovely old ladies in the salon for yonks. They're pistols, those women. Seen it all, done it all and can still laugh. I hope I'm like that when I'm older.

I start a text to Finn and by the time I'm in the building's reception, before I have a chance to really think about it, I press send.

> Just finished work, been busy, yeah coffee, I can do a
> quick one, half six, seven, just for half an hour?

As soon as it's gone, I cringe. But it seems the cringe factor is one-sided. His reply is instantaneous.

> I'd love that, how about that little place on Nassau Street.
> Vanilla?

> I know the one, sure.

> See you there in twenty-five minutes?

Great. I stuff my phone back in my pocket and think: *What have I done?*

Everyone outside is windswept. I pull into a shop, find a mirror and decide that at least my eye make-up has stayed on pretty well since half seven this morning. I like a goth eye: habitual ultra-black liner, helped with espresso brown shadow and a hint of silver that brings out the silver in my eyes.

Vilma says she thinks I like this because it makes me look tough, which is actually entirely accurate. I want my eye make-up to say what I could never say: watch out.

Anyone who thinks make-up is all about sexual allure will never understand that for some of us, it's our warpaint. Like

74

tribal markings when the world's first peoples marked their faces for battle. My eye liner is just the same.

Beware: that's what I hope it says.

Vilma thinks I'm just one pair of leather trousers away from going to a heavy metal concert but says I'd look 'cute' in them.

'I am not cute,' I always say in retort. 'It's just I'm short and you're tall, that's all.'

Little is not all it's cracked up to be, I'd like to add. It makes people think you're soft. Hence the all black clothing and the goth eye make-up.

I was soft once, yes. Not anymore.

I scan the rest of me. I'm wearing my normal work uniform of black shirt, black cardigan, of which I have loads in varying shades of greyness, and black jeans. Add to that my equally exciting black runners and black waterproof puffa jacket and I look like I'm hiring for a job as a band roadie.

My hair adds to the look: chaotic and a bit tough, I hope. Rain never bothers it, so I duck back out into the rain and driving wind, nearly at my destination. I have never been in this coffee shop and it's up a laneway off Nassau Street. Presumably the sort of place college lecturers go at lunchtime to mutter about college politics.

When I get there, I see it's a nice mixed crowd of people of all ages and colours. Finn is at the counter having an animated discussion with a tall woman with dreadlocks.

'Sid,' he says, and he smiles, a smile that really lights up his face, and I feel the weirdest quiver inside me, which is scary. I'm not sure where these feelings are coming from or what they are, but they're not bad. There are no internal warning bells over Finn. Instead, I feel . . . warm.

Firmly pushing down any non-friend feelings, I say, 'Hi, Finn,' and give him a manly punch on the arm which comes out stronger than I mean it to.

'Ow, what was that for?'

'Friendly greeting,' I say.

He introduces me to the girl behind the counter. We chat for a moment and she tells me the best coffee of the day is a lovely Colombian roast.

'That's what you always say, Asha,' laughs Finn, and I look at him, eyes narrowed. Is he flirting with her? He's older. She's what – twenty-three, twenty-four? I stare at him, waiting to see something that backs up my suspicion, but he seems genuine. The familiar nervous quiver is somewhere inside me but it's not emerging. Something is holding it back. My hands aren't shaking at all.

'Yeah, professor,' says Asha loudly, 'I say that because it sells well and I get more tips, trying to put myself through college here.'

'Fair enough,' he says, grinning back. 'Just checking you weren't being made to push the Colombian or I'll have to have words with Phil. Phil owns this place,' Finn says to me as an aside. 'I have to keep him on his toes about treating my students with respect.'

He and Asha fist bump.

'Are you really a professor?' I say as we take a seat up against a wall, where all the tables are crammed incredibly close together.

'Yes,' he says. 'I am really a professor. I even have the round-rimmed glasses for work. Joke.'

'Wow,' I say.

He hasn't added any sugar to his coffee. No sweet tooth, then. I'd really like one of the pastries they have on the counter, but I feel a bit shy about getting food. Shy but not tensed up. That's something. Maybe I can do this once and never do it again. Block his number, something like that. *Get a grip, Sid. Just think of him as a work colleague.*

'Are you hungry?' he says. 'You have that hungry look about you.'

'I was working through lunch, though I had a bit of a sandwich,' I say.

'What do you want?' He gets up quickly. 'I'll get us something sweet, savoury? I know you have only half an hour, but let me feed you.'

'I'll have one of those Portuguese tarts,' I say.

'Nice choice, I'll have one too.'

He's back in a moment and we start biting into the tarts.

The glory of the creamy lemony filling lets my lungs expand and warm feelings flood me.

'That's lovely,' I say. 'Sometimes sweet things are the answer.'

'I agree,' he says.

'I thought you cyclists were very careful about what you ate?'

'We are, but that doesn't mean we can't have something nice now and then. Go on, tell me about your day; you wanted to talk work.'

'Well, what else are we going to talk about? We don't know each other.'

'We could discuss our childhoods.'

'New friends don't normally get on to their childhoods until at least the third or fourth meeting. So let's go with work OK? Pretend we are colleagues.'

I blink at him, hoping that didn't sound as mad out loud as it does in my head. I'm not normally like this. I'm a professional, can have professional conversations, but, right now, I feel a little unhinged.

'OK. So, tell me about your work, maybe?' Finn leans in, nodding in encouragement.

I sit a bit more comfortably into my chair now we're on solid ground and I start. He does that lovely thing of listening, of not interrupting every five moments, which was what Marc did, but then, that was different.

'And the people?' he prompts, when I've finished telling him about my new project.

'The people are great. Adrienne is our boss and she's fearless.

I really admire that about her.' I pause, tart gone, halfway down my coffee. 'She's genuinely afraid of nobody.'

I realise suddenly that I've let all my protective barriers down and I can feel the stinging in my eyes signalling that without immediate intervention, my eyes are going to fill with tears.

Startlingly, I get the sense that he has picked up on this too.

'That must be cold,' he says in kind tones, looking into my cup. 'I'll get us more.'

He's back in a minute but it's enough time for me to have recovered, to have dabbed at my eyes and bitten the inside of my mouth, which is a painful but effective 'come back to the here and now' technique they don't teach in cognitive behavioural therapy.

He sits down and says lightly: 'Now, my work. Can't have you hogging the limelight. You need to know what you're getting yourself into. My oldest friends don't ask me about work anymore because they say I get carried away . . .'

I am suddenly annoyed on his behalf. 'Talk,' I command. 'I want to know it all.'

We sit there another half an hour, having gone through his work and then moved on to his family – he's the eldest, has two sisters and five nieces and nephews, both parents living. And then he wants to know about mine.

'My little sister is a lot younger,' I say. 'Vilma, you met her. I was fifteen when she was born.'

'Really? It must have been like being an only child. Was that lonely?'

'No,' I add thoughtfully. If this had been a date I would have stopped there, wary of sharing too much, but since we were doing the friend thing there was no need. It's very freeing, this friend-without-benefits thing. There are no expectations.

'My mum's a bit unusual. When I was younger –' I pause.

'Do not laugh or snigger when I say this,' I warn, 'but our house was a sort of commune for a while.'

Finn's mouth forms a lovely O.

'And you a professor of history and everything,' I said. 'I thought you'd know about communes.'

'I do know about communes, I've just never met anyone who was brought up in one.'

'There is always the odd commune around if there are a couple of hippies. "When two hippies are joined together, there will always be some magical place with weed, a smelly blanket and anecdotes about how life was good when you could drive a VW combi van around Morocco and live the free life." I don't know the rest of the saying,' I said. 'But basically, how it works is that you get a few people who are completely broke and one of them has a house but no money, so they live together and cook horrible things with lentils. My entire childhood was spent farting.'

Finn laughs. 'You do paint with words.'

'Thank you,' I say awkwardly, pleased.

'We also made a lot of jam because we had gooseberry and blackberry bushes in the garden. You have no idea how good I am at making jam.'

He laughs again and we are off, joking, chatting. It's funny and easy. In a way it's like talking to Vilma and her friends: light, interesting, with no side. He's not looking for anything from me except someone to have an enjoyable cup of coffee with.

'Why are you finished with dating?' I ask, and add at speed, 'As a friend. And nothing else. This is not me asking for romantic purposes, OK?'

He nods. 'Message received. I was in a long-term relationship for a few years and we – this is going to sound so clichéd – we began to feel like brother and sister eventually.'

My turn to nod. I understand that one far better than he could know.

'We met just a few years after college and we sort of grew up together, you know the way you're still in your twenties and life's still a big adventure with no plans. Then, somewhere along the way, it stopped working.'

He looks down into his coffee cup now and I'm pretty sure he's not lying. But then, how to be sure?

'Did she feel the same way?'

'She ended it.'

'What's her name?'

'Mags.'

'Are you still friends?' I'm interested because I've only seen Marc once since, and even then it was by accident. When he left, he disappeared.

'No.' He shrugs. 'We tried, honestly tried, but we couldn't go back to that way. We'd messed with the dynamic. I don't think you can date for that long and go back to being friends. Well,' he amends, 'you would if you had children, but not us. Hey, the human race is weird, right? What about you?'

'I was with a guy called Marc for a long time. It ended a year ago.'

Suddenly, I feel anxious. I've talked enough about me. I can't talk about Marc. It's too revealing.

I take a glance at my phone and realise that over an hour has gone by.

'I'm going to be late.'

Which is an absolute lie because I'm only going to be late to my own couch, which never complains either way.

He nods and says, 'Sorry, didn't mean to keep you so long.' He stands as I do and even though he's tall, I don't feel any fear. There is nothing, absolutely nothing predatory about Finn.

'Yeah, this was fun, we can do it again.' I'm surprised by the words as they leave me, and that I mean them.

'We can go on a hike,' he says, 'there isn't anything on in the cinema, it's all useless at the moment.'

'A hike?' I say.

'A hike,' he repeats, grinning. 'I hike with a load of people at the weekend; it's fun, you'd like it.'

'How do you know I'd like it? People are always telling me I'm going to like something. Like skateboarding when I was fourteen. Hated it. Fell off and wrecked my elbow. What's that about, insisting that people are going to like the things you like?'

'Don't know, I'll talk to someone in the psychology department tomorrow. Bound to be a syndrome,' he says, straight-faced. 'But I thought you might like being up the mountains, all the space, feeling the wind in your face.'

'I have had the wind in my face all evening,' I say. 'Do you know what it was like getting here? Twenty-five minutes of rain and wind.'

'No, seriously, Sid, it makes you feel free.'

I look at him for a beat and his face is animated.

'I reckon you'll enjoy it, and two hours up the mountains will show you if you do or not. If you don't, you never have to do it again. And I will then do something that you really want to do like –' his eyes glint – 'rollerblading?'

'Why would I want to go rollerblading? Because I'm a girl?' I sniff. 'I was actually very good at rollerblading when I was younger. I could go backwards and everything. Never knew why I wasn't good on the skateboard.'

'I just fell off the blades,' he says, 'I think I was too tall, the centre-of-gravity issue meant it didn't work. My sisters made me go out with them and they loved watching me fall. But seriously, a hike?'

'How do I know you are not going to bring me up the mountains, attack me with an industrial stapler, kill me and bury the body?'

'There is that,' he agrees. 'But I've got away with it so often before . . .'

His wicked grin is actually lovely. He has a dimple in one cheek.

'Of course, you could tell someone where you are going. Give that younger sister of yours access to your phone's location so she knows where you are at all times.'

Sounds fair. 'When will we do this hiking thing?'

'Saturday? It's supposed to be a beautiful day. I was thinking of going up myself, but everyone who hikes with me is busy. The lure of Christmas happening in the distance is hauling people away from the outdoors and into shopping centres. But I just have to get out: it clears my head, has this meditative quality that I love.'

'OK,' I say, 'if you promise not to attack and kill me, then bury me up the mountains – in which case, I will haunt you forever.'

'Understood. First, you have proper boots, right? Bring a rucksack, water, something to eat and warm clothing.'

'I thought we were going up the mountains for a bit, not to the Antarctic for a week.'

'It's pretty cold up there this time of the year; beautiful, but cold, and it will be sunny, so maybe a bit of sun block.'

'Sun block *and* hiking gear.'

'You're going to love it. I'll send you the details. And if you are going to duck out at the last minute or if it's raining or if there's a gale force blowing, tell me, I'll be going up there anyway.'

'OK, thank you.' I reach into my bag for my wallet and he says, 'Oh, I paid.'

'You are not supposed to pay, we are supposed to be going Dutch on all this stuff, friends do the equal-paying thing.'

'Well, after we have hiked, if we have coffee and buns or whatever, then you can pay, right?'

'Deal.'

'Deal.'

I don't punch him on the shoulder when I go. But I grin at him.

'I'd better enjoy this hiking or our friendship is over. I'm going to have to buy hiking boots; this is a big investment.'

He stares at me thoughtfully for a moment and I have absolutely no idea what he is thinking. His face is so still but his eyes are searching mine.

'A totally worthwhile one,' he says.

As I walk off into the wind and the rain, I'm smiling.

8

Marin

It's a glorious Friday night. No one is coming over at the weekend, there's nothing that needs doing, and I'm feeling the joy of knowing I have got my Christmas shopping in the bag nice and early. Or in the basket, as the case may be. Because I never have time to hit the shops (well, sometimes . . .). I have done most of my Christmas shopping online now before all the good stuff gets snapped up. I have long ago given up the idea of trying to get the perfect present for everyone, because there isn't a perfect present for everyone. Darling April is always happy with beautiful romantic perfumes. And body lotions from Victoria's Secret thrill her to bits. Everything from Victoria's Secret thrills her to bits, even though I feel she's probably older than the target market. But she loves it in there. All those floors of frilly things destined to make the man in her life fall in love with her all over again. Mum is impossible to shop for, always has been, always will be. I get Dad sweets and a jigsaw and a wonderful book about wildlife, same thing every year and he's happy. Over the years I have got him all sorts of things for the allotment. But he now has enough trowels and string and gardeners' hand cream to last him several lifetimes. Dom is getting help with his deposit, which I know he'll appreciate more than any present. Nate is super tricky to buy for, because he's so particular about his clothes. However, I refuse to give him gift vouchers. Instead, every year, I buy him one elegant polo shirt from an expensive brand and he seems pleased. Buying for Rachel and Joey is a total joy, because they both do a list for me about two months before Christmas. It's one of our family traditions. Sort of like a treasure hunt of lovely things, lots of little gifts and one bigger present.

Anyway, the shopping is pretty much done, though it's anyone's guess what I'll be given come Christmas Day.

'Mum, I've done all my homework,' says Joey hopefully, peering into the kitchen. 'Can I have a go on the Xbox now?'

'*All* the homework, honey?' I say, because Joey has been known to fib a smidge when it comes to his weekend homework. Our plan is to get it done on Friday evening and then he's free for the weekend.

'Wait till you're going to secondary school,' Rachel likes to tease him sometimes, 'then you'll be doing homework all weekend.'

'I won't, Mum, will I?' says Joey, horrified.

'Oh it's not that bad,' I always say, giving Rachel the side eye. 'And the older you get, the more homework you're capable of doing,' I add, which is also fibbing.

'Will I check your homework journal and tick everything off, sign it?' I say now.

'Yeah, sure.'

Once the homework notebook has been checked – I see there's a note in there that it's a school photograph day on Monday, and that all the uniforms had better be clean, shiny and the correct colour – I sign the notebook. I give Joey a hug and he belts off to his beloved Xbox.

'You do know that the next generation of children are going to have bizarrely enlarged thumbs from playing games,' says Rachel, who has wandered into the kitchen, holding the takeaway menu.

Sometimes we do takeaways on Fridays and I love it, because it means I don't have to cook. Sheer bliss.

'You are pretty good with the old thumbs yourself,' I say, grinning at her. 'What have you decided? I need to phone the order in now. Dad said he wanted Kung-Po chicken.'

'Oh I don't know, I was thinking more Thai.'

'Ah, honey, it's Chinese this week; we agreed.'

'I don't know if I want Chinese,' she says. 'Megan and I have been discussing how we have to try lots of different foods to acclimatise ourselves for when we go around the world. And we're going to spend a lot of time in Thailand. So I just need to be more into the culture and the food.'

'When you're in Thailand, you can eat Thai food, but tonight we are getting Chinese. Dad's picking it up on his way home, he's not going to two places.'

'Don't see why not,' she grumbles.

Eventually she agrees, chooses a dish and wanders off moodily. I wonder when the difficult teenage years end, because she's eighteen now, nearly nineteen, and there's no end in sight.

Louise, Megan's mother, and I have recently discussed exactly how moody and difficult to live with Rachel and Megan are lately, and we – their mothers – worry about letting two such innocents off on a gap year without us in the background picking up the pieces

'It might help,' Louise's husband, Dave, had said with a hint of bravado, 'show them a bit of the real world. I mean, we do everything for them.'

'That's true,' Nate had agreed.

Louise and I had stared at them both.

'I never did a gap year and I figured out the real world,' I'd said.

This gap year makes me feel sick. Two innocents abroad – it feels like a recipe for disaster.

'It was different when we were teenagers, though,' Dave had said manfully.

'Totally,' Nate had replied. 'It was either get a proper pensionable job or else get a part-time job so you could pay to go to college.'

'Yeah,' Dave had continued, 'no messing in those days.'

'But we don't want to raise our kids like that,' I'd said, 'we want to give them something different.'

'Every generation says that, Marin,' Nate had pointed out. 'You're too soft, that's what you are. They'll cope.'

I remember being really annoyed with him for implying that being soft was somehow a failing, because I'd always tried to be a very different mother to my own mother and nobody could ever call my mother soft. Certainly not my poor father.

I order dinner then go into the sitting room and sit down with a small glass of white wine. I have the room to myself, the TV to myself, and nothing needs to be done in the kitchen. There'd be no washing-up, no cooking, no sweating over the stove: absolute joy. All I have to do is wash up the containers, put the ones that can be recycled into the right bin, easy.

Nate's in a fabulous mood when he gets in.

'Dinner,' he cries, even before he's shut the door behind him. The scent of various meals drifts in with him. I think of Rachel wanting to learn about the culture of the places she'll be visiting, and how much I wish I could go with her. I'd never travelled the way Rachel was going to. I'd gone to college and met Nate and we had married young. I hadn't needed to leave for work like so many other people. And I'd never considered a gap year. But wouldn't it be lovely to take off around the world and see such different places?

Nate and I share the bottle of wine over dinner, me finally letting my shoulders relax, safe in the knowledge no major clear-up job awaits me. Then we find something the whole family can watch, which is almost impossible and, even if it is something a bit action-heroeish for Joey, nobody minds.

'I watch all your soppy girl things,' says Joey, half waiting for Rachel to say, 'Ah do we have to watch this?'

'I know, little bro,' she says, 'you're a really good brother. I'm going to miss you when I'm away.'

'Really?'

'Yeah. You should send me emails, it will help you with your writing. And it will tell you if you spell things wrongly.'

'My spelling is brilliant.' Joey grins.

'Absolutely brilliant, kiddo,' says Nate, ruffling Joey's hair.

'I'll send you all long emails,' Rachel goes on. 'Maybe we can get to China too.'

'I didn't think that was on your itinerary,' I say, but she just rolls her eyes at me.

When both Rachel and Joey have gone to bed, Nate takes me to task about my worries.

'Marin, you need to relax about Rachel's trip,' says Nate to me quietly, firing up my irritation sensors. 'They'll figure it out.'

'I know, but I worry about them figuring it out,' I snap, trying to keep my voice down.

'It will help them grow up a bit,' he says idly and I feel the involuntary shudder that goes through me every time I think about Rachel and Megan on their own going off around the world.

All the things that could go wrong: but Nate seems so calm about it. They'll be fine, end of story.

'But think about the dangers out there, two girls on their own?' I say, annoyed. It's like he doesn't see the gravity of this, like he wants to dismiss it.

I get up and march into the kitchen. He follows me.

'Relax, Marin,' Nate repeats, more angrily this time. 'You've got to let go. You worry over nothing. It drives me mad.'

He reaches for the bottle of wine we opened earlier and pours himself another glass. Not for me, just for him.

Of all the annoying things Nate does, this 'relax, you worry too much' thing is the one that makes my blood boil. And now he's having more wine and hasn't asked if I want some! I want to hit him, hard, and tell him I will worry if I bloody want to, and that if he thinks two teenage girls going off on a gap year is risk-free, then he needs his head examined.

But he's ignoring me now, sitting down at the kitchen table, scrolling through his phone because he's bored with the conversation.

Tiredness hits me in a wave and I snap that I'm going to bed.

I often go to bed before Nate, even though he's up earlier than me, off to do his swimming and his running. He has amazing stamina. But tonight he follows me upstairs, having speedily turned out all the lights and locked the doors. On the stairs I can feel him briefly touch the back of my thighs.

'So?' he whispers. He's tall, so he's already close to my ear, even if he's that far behind me. 'What do you think? End of a long week, a man deserves something . . .'

He has got to be kidding.

And then I stop myself.

Am I turning into my mother? Irritated with my husband at every moment? Look how well that turned out.

So, Nate thinks differently from me about the trip – he doesn't understand the danger out there for girls but I'll make damn sure they both understand it before they get on any plane.

I take a deep breath. I turn around and face him and he grabs me and presses me tight against him and I can feel his erection.

'This is what a man needs,' he says.

It is of course exactly at this moment that Rachel sticks her head out of her bedroom door and goes, 'Ewwee,' at the sight of us and slams the door shut.

'You think we have put her off sex for life?' I say, everything else forgotten.

'Hopefully,' says Nate, unconcerned as he leans in to kiss me.

It's one of the wonderful things about our marriage, how well we fit together sexually, as if just when Nate is ready to explode with wanting, he manages to turn me on so I'm ready too. Equally, when I'm premenstrual and miserable, Nate's always been amazing. Gets a hot water bottle for my belly, tells me to get more rest. It's nice.

He might be useless in the kitchen and thinks I worry too much, but he's amazing at this.

9

Bea

It's Christie's birthday and we decide that a party night out is vital, even if we're all saving for presents for the kids for Christmas. We'll combine it with our annual December party – the Single Mommas' Christmas party. There has been no news on the jobs front – Laoise at work says she has heard nothing else about the practice moving and I am praying that it's just a case of misunderstanding. I cannot let myself worry about it or I will go mad. I need that job: with that, my widow's pension and Jean-Luc's insurance settlement, we can manage – but only just.

'We'll just keep it low key and cheap,' says Shazz, who is brilliant with money.

All our children go to the same school and each class has a mothers' party a month before Christmas, an event lovingly detailed in the class WhatsApp we're all in.

I find the WhatsApp useful but Shazz, who feels that single mothers are treated differently from the smug marrieds, hates it.

We've all been to the ordinary mums' party but, for various reasons, we didn't feel like part of the gang.

'They all sat and bitched about their husbands,' said Shazz, during the post-mortem of the last one we went to. 'It's like they haven't even considered that us three don't have a significant other and that it might make us feel a bit left out.'

So, this year, we're having our own night out.

'I think we need a gang name,' says Shazz, as we sit in the taxi on our way into town for our big night out.

'A gang name,' says Christie, sitting in the middle because she's got the shortest legs. 'Like The Feministas?'

'Not sure,' says Shazz. 'I was thinking something along the lines of the New Normals, something like that.'

'Really?' says Christie.

'Yeah, because we are not like the normals, the women with husbands and partners and fathers for their kids and everything.'

'You've got Zep now,' I point out, wriggling my feet in my high-heeled sandals. I'm already regretting wearing them.

'If we call ourselves the New Normals, then they'll think they are the Abnormals,' says Christie, giggling.

'Yes!' says Shazz delightedly. 'That's it, we're the new normals and they are abnormals. What do you think?' she roars to the taxi driver in front. He's a nice man who appears to be keeping his head down, because all wise taxi drivers know it's more sensible to keep their mouths shut when they've got a cab full of excitable women in it, going out on the town.

'Whatever you say, love,' he says.

'Right answer,' crows Shazz.

First, we're going to get something to eat. Christie was in charge of picking the restaurant, because she has a friend who recently returned to Dublin to open a wildly successful new restaurant off Dawson Street. Usually, it's jam-packed, but thanks to Christie's pal, we're getting a special table in the best location.

'They do cocktails, right?' Shazz asks.

'Lots of cocktails,' says Christie.

'And then we're going clubbing?'

'You know the jury's out on the clubbing,' I say now, 'besides, I'm wearing these stupid shoes.'

'Take them off. I told you they were too high.'

'They're my good high shoes. I don't have loads of pairs of shoes.'

'You could have had my platform ones,' Shazz goes on, 'they

fit you. I know they are a bit dated and everything, but still, you could carry them off, for an old chick,' she adds, naughtily.

'Did you have a cocktail before the taxi?' I ask suspiciously.

'Yeah, Zep mixed me up something Caribbean and it's lighting my fire.'

'Which one of us will be doing the fireman's lift tonight?' I ask Christie, who laughs.

Eventually, we're decanted in front of the restaurant, all dressed up in our birds-of-paradise finery. Shazz's long, artfully curled hair is a lovely combination of blonde with purple tips, mine – rippling brunette – has been blow-dried straight down my back and Christie's got a mop of tousled platinum curls that looks as though she has just come off some Australian beach after doing a bit of surfing.

'We certainly hit all the demographics,' says Shazz looking around. 'I mean, look, we got everything, we've got wild pink, we've got sexy brunette, we've got a platinum modern blonde: there's nobody we can't hook up with.'

'I'm not looking for a man,' I say.

'Me neither,' says Christie. 'I'm woman centric. I'm happy, thank you very much. Plus, you've got Zep.'

'I know,' sighs Shazz happily. 'I'll flirt a bit, that's all. But you should score, Bea.'

Christie and I exchange glances.

'Score? Like round the back of the bike shed? I thought I was going to find hot love on whatever website you've put the tissue of lies on,' I say.

'Bird seed,' she says. 'I didn't tell you but I made it go live before we came out.'

My mouth falls opens. It's live! The stuff about French-speaking, saxophone-playing, who-knows-what-else me . . .

If I was religious, I would say a prayer right now. God, please let someone normal be on the site and like the look of my pic. Then I realise what I've said. Do I want to go on a date?

I feel almost dizzy as we're brought to our tables and I'm not sure if it's the heels or the notion that I'm actually thinking of going on a date. With a man!

Christie's friend has done us proud. Our table is a fabulous spot where we can see all over the restaurant, which is very glamorous and very noisy. Clearly the Christmas spirit is already here even though it's only November, but then, many office parties start early because some companies are far too busy to have December parties. There is mistletoe in tiny silver vases all over the place and Shazz grabs the sprig from our table.

'Now,' she said, 'I'm going to break this up into three bits and when any of us go to the loo, we can bring a bit, and if we see anyone we like, we have to dangle it over their heads.'

'*You* can do that,' I say.

'Spoil sport.'

Despite the noise, we all hear the loud ping of Shazz's phone.

Animal Lover 49 is on the screen.

We lean in as one to examine my first 'I'm interested' single man.

'Photoshopped,' says Christie, staring critically at a very professional photo of a man with greying hair and a big smile.

Shazz shakes her head. ' "Animal Lover". Does this mean he keeps ferrets and bets too much on the dogs?'

Laughing, we decide that he is not for me.

Soon we are deep into starters, finishing a bottle of wine, laughing and joking, discussing our beautiful children and wondering why there's always one Queen Bee who likes to run everything.

'I blame WhatsApp,' says Shazz. 'For some people WhatsApp is like a board room and they can bully everyone on it. No matter what you say back it sounds wrong. So you have to say, "wonderful idea", even if you think it's stupid.'

'Yeah,' I say, 'I hate that thing. When's their Christmas party?'

'Oh, they're having it in January, because they are all too busy with social events.'

I start to laugh. 'We're busy with our wildly exciting social lives too,' I joke.

By the second bottle of wine, I am absolutely convinced that I am not going to any night club under any circumstances. I'm exhausted. My feet hurt and I just want to be at home in my own bed going to sleep.

We have looked at Hot Maaan – 'can't spell,' we all agree; Older But Ready – 'ready for what?' and Hunk of the Year 1968, who gets points for humour but not much else.

'He mentions wine twice,' says Christie. 'Definitely a heavy drinker. Definitely a no.'

'I'm tired, girls,' I say, yawning.

'You can't bail now,' says Shazz, who has had more than her share of the wine. 'This is supposed to be our fun girls' night out.'

'I know, honey,' I say sadly, 'I just don't have the energy, I'm sorry. I'm older, OK, let's have that as the excuse; I'm older, I need to be sitting in front of the box watching reruns of silly films and reading magazines about how to knit sweaters with complicated cable patterns.'

'What's a cable pattern?' asks Shazz.

Christie laughs. 'My mum used to knit too,' she says. And then she pauses, because mentioning her mum always makes her sad.

'Stupid cow,' says Shazz, sounding really drunk now. 'Least you've got your dad.'

We both agree that Christie's mother must have something wrong with her if she's disowned Christie, Daisy and Lily just because Christie's gay.

'Karma's a bitch and it will come and bite her on the ass, because she doesn't realise how precious your girls are,' Shazz goes on. 'None of us had it easy but we are doing this amazing job, we are bringing up four beautiful kids and that means so much. I think maybe that's why the normals or the abnormals get anxious around us, because we can do it. It's not that they think we are going to steal their husbands. It's because we do it all, we're Mum and Dad and every bloody thing. And your mum just hasn't a clue, if she doesn't understand why you love who you love. We have our kids – that's all that matters.'

'Yeah,' says Christie. And suddenly we are taking out our phones and looking at pictures of our children.

All the liquids are making themselves felt, so I head off to the loo and am halfway down the stairs when I hear Shazz squealing with delight. Is this okay. She can't see Shazz only hear her.

Another stud for me, I think, grinning, wondering if any normal man is ever going to appear on the site.

There's no queue for the loo, so I'm speedy and on my way back to our fabulous table when I feel a gentle tap on my arm.

I turn to face a tallish, smiling man with fair hair and an engaging smile who is wearing a beautifully cut suit. Handsome, definitely.

Christie's friend, I think. Not long back from Hong Kong, he's now part-owner of the bistro and is working the room.

'You must be Bea,' he says and I realise he's English, with an exquisite accent that makes me smile far more than the cheesy come-on lines of Hot Man or Older But Ready.

'I'm Sean.'

A little part of me I thought I had lost long ago perks up.

'What do you think of the place?' says Definitely Handsome Sean.

I unperk. He's asking me about his new baby. Just because I have finally decided to get onto the dating scene, doesn't mean the dating scene is keen on me.

'Beautiful,' I say, honestly.

'Really?' His eyes are a pale grey and his face is tanned. Is he looking at me admiringly or wondering why Christie has such a dowdy friend?

At that point, I feel about a hundred.

'Yes, gorgeous. Thank you for the lovely table,' I say politely, excuse myself and leave.

Maybe I'm mad to be thinking of dating. The rules have probably all changed.

Back at the table, while Shazz shows me Good Goods In Small Packages and we giggle at this, Christie gets the bill and divides it up expertly, including the tip.

'I saw Sean talking to you,' Christie says as we leave. 'He'd come over to say hello. Isn't he a darling? So handsome.'

'Yes,' I say, a shade too brightly.

I debate asking if he's involved with someone but then decide he showed me not a hint of interest. It's not him, it's me, I think with a private little laugh.

Outside, Christie, who has mastered the taxi-driver alert whistle, summons one to us in a moment.

'Wish I could do that,' says Shazz. 'You know I used to be able to drink three times this much and now I can't.'

'It's called having a child and a job,' I said. 'You're not twenty-one or in Kansas anymore, Dorothy.'

'Yeah,' says Shazz, as she's helped into the back of the cab.

She falls asleep as we drive home. Christie and I talk quietly over her.

'This was fun.'

'We are lucky to have found each other.'

'Do you think our kids will grow up different because they didn't have what everyone else has?' asks Christie.

'I'm always wondering the same thing myself,' I say. 'But you know they just need one good parent who loves them unconditionally and they've got that. Lots of people have two parents and it doesn't work out. And who knows what goes on in other people's lives? We don't. Look at your mother, pretending everything in the garden is rosy, not telling her neighbours that she has two beautiful granddaughters, all because she doesn't want a lesbian daughter. She doesn't want a daughter who got pregnant with a sperm donor. She wants a son-in-law with a big car, whom she can boast about. What's fabulous about that?'

'Yeah, you're right,' says Christie, sitting back. 'I forget that stuff sometimes.'

As the cab drives into the night, I wonder just who I'm trying to convince.

10

Sid

I'm really sorry I decided that a movie would be too intimate and that a hike was a good idea, because it's November, it's cold up on the mountains and it turns out that people with long legs move faster than those of us with short ones. Funny that.

Finn strides on ahead of me, as if he's got some sort of motor in his butt. I look at the way those long legs move in a fairly smooth motion from his hips. From a panting four feet behind him. I try and concentrate on the way I am striding along the path and realise that I'm not walking the same way; I am walking the way I walk when I am trying to get a bus in a hurry and there is a certain frantic pacing in keeping up. Shit. I'm not doing this right and my hiking boots hurt, which is unsurprising as they are new and cheap. Thoreau was right when he said to beware of any enterprise which required new clothes.

'Why did you buy cheap boots?' says Finn, spotting them the moment I arrived.

'Because you might turn out to be a friend I want to dump because you are really boring, what with all your hiking,' I say, half sarcastically, half humorously to him as we stand in the car park and he looks at my footwear. 'And I can't afford a quarter of a month's mortgage on proper Mount Everest boots.'

'I should have come with you to the shop. I could have got you a discount.'

I don't say that I nearly didn't buy any boots, nearly cancelled full stop. Why did I think I could have men friends now? What madness was this?

'Men should be kept out of shops,' I mutter. 'In fact, I should be kept out of shops, I don't do shops.'

'Really,' he deadpans.

We both laugh and I feel some of the tension leave my body. I was over-reacting: this might be OK after all. If it's not, I'll never see him again.

Finn turns round to check on me and catches me wincing. 'You've really never done anything like this before?' he asks, looking at my hodgepodge outfit. I am not a woman well equipped in the wardrobe department for unusual trekking up the mountains. I go to work, do the occasional weight class and collapse onto the couch. End of.

'I don't hike.'

'What did you and your previous – er, friends, do?' says Finn, gesturing for me to sit down on a rock so he can re-lace my boots.

'We didn't hike,' I say. 'And that's a very datey thing you're doing, trying to fix my boots,' I say, but his presence is calming, not threatening. I like the way he's gentle, as if he senses I can get nervous.

'This is what people who are on a group trek do for each other. They generally don't have to fix boots but if there's a newcomer, they will. They make sure that their backpacks are comfortable and they adjust them on their shoulders, because if they're not right, you're in trouble.'

'What do you mean you're in trouble?' I say, eyes narrowing. 'Is this one of those ultimate-challenge army rangers/SAS survival adventure things, where we hike over the mountains for eight hours and then somebody – with luck – picks us up in a Land Rover? Or, worse, if we miss the pick-up point, we have to throw ourselves in a sleeping bag on the side of a hill for a night of hypothermia?'

'Yes.' Finn grins. 'Second option.'

We laugh again. Must be the briskly cold air, I decide, that's making me laugh so much. And relax. Because the mountain air is relaxing. He's right. Just not about any army ranger shenanigans.

'Hypothermia. For real? Forget it. I'm not doing that, I am good for maybe an hour of hiking and then I was thinking about a pub and nice food: chips, ideally. A cup of coffee, a good stretch and then someone to magically transport me back to the car. Then I'm going to go home, have a bath, put on fluffy PJs and lie down in front of the television. That's what I was thinking.'

He rolls his eyes. 'Boots are finished.' He stands up. 'You're sorted. Now,' he moves behind me to adjust my rucksack, 'that's a useless rucksack. Plus, you've only brought one bottle of water.'

'Should I have brought one of those enormous pig bladder things from the camping shop?' I say.

'Yeah,' he says and then laughs again. 'No, only kidding. That's for really long hikes. Would it lower your stress levels to tell you I've chocolate, too?'

'I didn't know chocolate was allowed in health activities,' I say, delightedly.

'You have so much to learn. When you have done this much walking you are allowed to have chocolate. Now check my rucksack.'

'I don't know how to check your rucksack,' I say. 'What am I checking it for, squirrels?'

'Beginners,' he sighs and starts to demonstrate that everything is in the correct place. There follows a short lecture on how having the straps in the correct place mean his ruck-sack – which feels like it holds rocks – will be comfortable.

'OK, lead on, McDuff,' I say, once he and his bag of rocks are sorted.

After about fifteen minutes of his leading on, I realise that he is actually getting further and further ahead because of this hip movement thing that I do not have. I call time.

'We've only just started.'

'I'm just asking for a little break; you did say you'd go gently with me.'

He laughs.

'If you were in my hiking team, we'd all be talking about you behind your back,' he said.

'You sound like complete pigs,' I remark.

'How are you not fit?' he said. 'I mean you work in Nurture.'

'There was no room for a gym in the office,' I say with a hint of sarcasm. 'I work in development, which means I am very involved in schools and community projects making sure that people in communities are fit and have correct nutritional advice, plus helping raise funds for facilities within less advantaged regions. I do not go out on hikes at weekends. Although we do have people within the organisation who fundraise and do that sort of thing.'

'And you never have to help?'

'Of course I help, I just don't do any marathoning,' I say.

'And your man Marc, did he help when you were together?'

'If you are trying to find out what Marc was like I will tell you everything,' I say, astonishing myself.

I am telling him nothing, surely?

'But I'm only going to tell you because we are friends, nothing else – so if you are enquiring because, well –' I stop. Suddenly I didn't know where I was going with this. If I was about to say, *because you were trying to fill his position*, that would sound very big headed of me.

So far, Finn hadn't shown the slightest romantic interest in me. Bizarrely, I trusted him. What was not to like?

I make one of what Vilma calls my 'executive decisions'.

Why *not* talk about the past. That's normal behaviour, isn't it?

'Marc and I were very lazy,' I admit. We did canal-bank walks and he once – briefly – was in a gym with a climbing wall, but he fell and fractured his wrist, so it put him off.'

'Poor guy,' says Finn.

'I did karate for a while but I had to leave because I whacked the instructor over the head with a pole when he was showing us how to block blows.'

Finn stops and bends over, he laughs so much. 'Really?'

I nod. 'He wanted me to hit him so he could demonstrate blocking – I'd only started. So I bashed as hard as I could and – well, he wasn't ready.'

I can still remember the man swearing at me as he clutched his head and howled.

'I did point out that the whole point of martial arts is that people don't announce they're going to hit you with a pole.'

Finn is still laughing. 'You are priceless. A tiny ninja.'

'Still a ninja,' I say proudly. 'I never learned karate but I have my own moves.'

And then we're both giggling and it's lovely: up in the clear, fresh mountain air giggling with a nice man who is funny, kind and doesn't make me in the least scared.

'Ivanna, my most recent ex, who came after Mags, was very into the gym, never hiking,' says Finn, when we're back walking. 'I like a bit of gym work but I love swimming, especially wild swimming when I can manage it, but I swim in a pool several mornings a week. This, though, is like meditation. You can see for miles.' He gestures at the broad expanse of the Wicklow mountains around us, strewn with gorse and heather, the odd mountainy sheep still grazing and giving us beady eyes.

We stop and admire the view.

'You liked different things,' I say.

'Yes.'

'Marc and I liked a lot of the same things,' I say. 'We liked cheap restaurants and box sets.'

'Partial to both of them myself. So, what went wrong?'

Given how comfortable I feel with Finn, I answer.

'The things we liked turned out to be different after all,' I say, 'so he moved out. What about you?'

'I'm not sure,' he says. 'She turned out to be tricky. I'm not dissing her. I genuinely thought she was fabulous. But my friends called her Ivanna the Terrible.'

'Were they your male friends?' I say, in an accusatory voice.

'Yes, but also one of my best friend's wives: Marin, who is a real woman's woman, or so people tell me.'

'Another woman dissed her?'

'Yes. I had to push her to say anything. But she said –' his eyes glaze over as if he's remembering –'that she didn't really trust Ivanna. It turned out she had another man at the same time as she was seeing me, which was not part of my master plan.'

'Sounds like Marin has good instincts. And in my experience, master plans don't work out,' I commiserate. 'Still, we've given up all that now – we are happy celibates who have friends.'

'That would make a snappy business card,' says Finn.

'Definitely going to have some printed up,' I deadpan back. Having a friend is nice, I think.

'OK, we have stopped for two minutes.' He's looking at his watch, a manly sort of piece of machinery that was half-divers' watch, half-'I am going to haul a submarine up with one hand, while I'm at it' thing. 'You can't stop too often or you seize up.'

'This is a military exercise, then, is it?' I say, heavy on the irony.

'Nearly.'

We set off again slightly more slowly. He keeps his pace slower so that we're walking together and he talks, explaining about the peaks in the distance, showing areas where his hiker pals go on different days, how it all looks beautiful on a day like today but once the mist comes down and it gets dark, people get lost. Fog can be dreadful, hypothermia can set in. You have to be fully prepared to go out and hike, otherwise you could get the poor rescue helicopter circling the area trying to find you.

'You wouldn't believe the number of people who get lost up here at weekends,' he says.

'Yeah,' I panted, 'I would, I really would. I would never be one of them, though, because I would not be up here in the first place.'

Three hours later, after managing a sit-down on a rock where we ate some sandwiches that Finn supplied, because he figured my jar of peanut butter, two spoons and a flask of coffee was not sufficient, we arrived back at our cars.

Every bit of me aches and I feel exhausted but pleased with myself. I did it. I have hiked, high up on top of the mountains in winter. Colour me achieved.

'Now wasn't that wonderful?' he says, stretching.

'Sure.' I've been dreaming of a hot bath for the past thirty minutes, boiling hot with possibly some Epsom salts in it and lavender and I will lie there for an hour until my limbs melt . . .

'Come again next weekend?'

'Are you mad?' I say. 'It will take me three weeks to get over this.'

'No, it won't,' he says fondly. 'Epsom salts in your bath, you'll be grand.'

I laugh. 'Already there,' I say.

We fist bump and head to our separate cars. He waits until I get in my car and start to drive away, waving me off. He really is very gentlemanly, I think, with a nice warm glow inside me.

II

Marin

It's true: when your children are teenagers, you never sleep at night when they're out until they're home in their beds again. Sleeping implies an inability to leap out of bed and rescue them from the emergency that will surely find them.

Rachel and her best friend, Megan, are out. It's a Friday night and my mama-radar is on high alert.

I've dozed but, suddenly, I am wide awake. Two a.m. The girls insisted they'd be home by one. An hour ago. I grab my phone and dial Rachel's number. Straight to voicemail. I try Megan. No answer.

She's never been out this late without it being an overnight. They are *eighteen*. Kids.

Something's gone wrong; I feel it.

The bed beside me is empty because Nate is at a schmoozing-client event in the city and though he said he'd be late, did he mean this late? Did the client fall asleep in his soup?

My brain sloughs this off as unimportant – what matters is that I feel, *I know*, something's wrong and I need to rescue my daughter.

But who will mind Joey, nine, blissfully asleep in his bedroom, the walls of which are innocently covered with robot posters? I text Rachel, saying that if taxis were a problem, Louise, Megan's mother, would have to pick them up as I couldn't leave Joey.

We don't have a blood pressure machine, but I'm sure I can feel mine increasing silently.

I give up trying to sleep, switch on the light and grab my phone again.

There is still no reply to my text – it just says 'delivered'.

You hear anything? I text Louise. We've been pals since our daughters bonded when they were four. Not best pals or anything, but we're on the same page when it comes to parenting.

Not a dickie bird, texts Louise back at speed.

I stare at the words, feeling utterly powerless.

I never felt like that when they were younger on sleepovers. The Network of Mothers would have got in touch by phone, text in those pre-WhatsApp days, Morse code, if necessary. Discussions about how much children's paracetamol to give, any allergy information, nightmare procedures, etc. would have been had in advance.

'If Megan loses her bear, she will sob and then scream,' Louise told me when Megan and Rachel were eight, on their first sleepover. 'She can lose him in a heartbeat. He must stay in her bed until bedtime. Check. She will try to smuggle him into the cinema. We lost him there once – worst twelve hours of my life.'

That sort of thing. It's our life's work – taking care of our children.

Now Megan is also eighteen, somehow looks twenty-five, and has buttery blonde highlights that go perfectly with her buttery skin (amazing fake-tan application by herself). She and Rachel, also with buttery blonde highlights and a couple of silvery purple hints around the tips, were going to a club tonight.

The club – Les Cloob and no, I am not making this up – admits over twenty-ones only but the girls in their silky vintage dresses look older. Les Cloob likes attractive young women and will not card them. Where gorgeous girls with no money go, less gorgeous men with money will follow. The eternal cycle continues.

Rachel read *The Handmaid's Tale* when she was fourteen. And still, four years later, she wants to go to Les Cloob. A hotbed of men who think a questing hand on a girl's rear end is a compliment. Both girls did Tai Kwan Doh for two years – they can handle a questing hand. But afterwards, tipsy on expensive cocktails, leaving said premises – what then?

A vision of both girls leaving the club, tripping along on ludicrous shoes, pulled into an alley, assails me.

The phone rings.

It's Louise, with the words no mother wants to hear.

'There's a problem.'

'Jesus.' My hand is at my mouth. 'What?'

'They got into the club, were dancing and got separated. Megan has spent the last hour looking for Rachel. She can't find her.'

'An hour . . .'

'I know. I said why didn't she call –'

I'm not even listening.

My flight response doesn't stand a chance – the fight one kicks in instantly. I press the phone's speaker buttons, and am out of the bed, dragging on clothes, trainers, grabbing my bag, while speaking: 'Did Megan tell the doorman, any of the staff, that Rachel had vanished?'

Louise doesn't hesitate. 'Yes and they've looked too.'

'CCTV,' I say. 'Someone's dragged her out of there. We need the police. I'll ring Nate, get him home. Can you get over here and take care of Joey until Nate comes home?'

Louse lives one street away. She doesn't question the plan. My daughter is missing, therefore I have to go into the city.

'I'll be right there,' she says.

Nate's phone goes to voicemail. Sweet Jesus.

'NATE!' I yell into the phone. 'I need you!!! Rachel is missing. Come home to take care of Joey. Please!'

I keep ringing until I've rung three times and still nothing. Voicemail each time. What has he done with the bloody phone?

Damn it, I need him.

Louise meets me at my door and hugs me, her eyes red.

'She's going to be fine,' she says walking in, trying for cheerful. 'You know how dizzy they get when they're excited.'

'They're joined at the hip, Louise,' I say grimly. 'Nothing would make Rachel go off and not come back.'

I watch too many news reports on TV. Far too much. But I know something isn't right.

'Megan's in the back room with the manager,' explains Louise. 'He doesn't want to call the police.'

I bet he doesn't.

I phone the police as I reverse the car out of the drive. It's been five minutes since Louise rang. Five more minutes of Rachel not being attached to her friend.

The police are amazingly helpful. They have a squad car a minute away from the club.

I wish I was a minute away. The drive into the city centre usually takes twenty minutes, but I make it in fourteen. Screw the red lights and God help anyone who tries to stop me. I can find Rachel: nobody but me. I know her, understand her: she came from my body, covered in blood and vernix, she's mine to protect.

I throw the car vaguely at a parking space, leap out and run up the street, noting the ridiculous number of alleys lining it. A couple emerging from the basement entrance of Les Cloob are shoved rudely aside as I two-step-it-at-a-time down metal steps. I push pass the bouncer and something in my face tells him not to bar my way.

Inside, people are dancing, music's playing, but it's all white noise to me. I scan the room for the bar, find it, then shove viciously past a crowd, mostly half-drunk who complain and I shout 'back off' at them with such ferocity that they move back.

'The manager's room, the police? Where are they?' I snarl at a young barman when I get to the counter.

He gestures to a door in a wall and I take the shortest route, pushing roughly through dancers. I don't care who gets flattened. I have to find Rachel. Nothing else matters.

A man in dark blue serge is at the door and I shove past him too, spotting Megan in an armchair and, beside her, sobbing and dishevelled, with vomit on her silky vintage slip dress, is Rachel.

I sink to the floor beside my daughter, looking for signs of assault, hurt.

'What happened?' I ask.

'Oh Mum, I went outside for –' She stops in her shaky confession and starts crying again.

'It was only a cigarette,' says Megan quickly.

'Nobody hurt you?' I demand. I don't care about cigarettes, even though she swore blind she'd never smoke.

'The door got stuck,' my daughter goes on.

'She went out the wrong door into the stores and she couldn't get back in,' adds the manager.

'And nobody hurt you?' I ask again.

Rachel shakes her head. 'I felt sick and I kept banging the door but nobody heard me –'

Uncaring of the vomit, the way I never cared about it when she was little, I pull her close to me and croon her name as I stroke her hair. My girl, safe, unhurt.

Scared but unhurt.

We phone Louise, who's back in her own house, which means Nate must have reared his head at last. I can almost feel the tension flow out of her at the news that Rachel's safe.

Once Megan's in her own home, and both Rachel and I have been hugged by Louise, we drive home, Rachel drunkenly apologising, for the cigarette, for everything.

My hand finds hers in the dark of the car.

'We'll talk in the morning. I love you so much, Rachel,' I say, determined not to cry in front of her. 'You're safe, that's all that matters.'

That's all we care about, us mothers.

At our house, I help her out of the car in those daft shoes but Nate is out the front door in seconds and sweeps her up in his arms, his face white.

'Oh my baby,' he says, half to her, half to me.

I cling on to him, letting myself breathe deeply for the first time in hours. Nate's here – it will be fine.

'I'm so sorry . . .' Rachel is saying brokenly.

He carries her quietly upstairs and lays her on her bed, kneeling beside it, clutching her hand.

'Where were you?' I mouth at Nate.

'Later,' he mouths back, face filled with guilt.

I clean Rachel up, get her into pyjamas, leave water beside her bed and plan to return to sit with her in case she's unwell – six varying cocktails, Megan admitted tearfully in the car, all different, all very strong – in the night.

But first.

Nate's half undressed in our bedroom, sitting on our bed, as if he can't get any further. His shirt is off displaying the admirable physique of someone who swims every second day and does the weight room when not swimming. Nate's hair, like his chest hair, is still dark. I keep finding grey ones in my shoulder-length chestnut curls. Forty-eight to my forty-three and I am not ageing as well.

'Is she going to be all right?' he asks.

I nod, sitting beside him. 'Where were you?'

'We were late but it was only half one and then Anton, he's the main client, says let's go to his hotel and have a cognac in the hotel bar and –'

Nate looks up, his face wracked with remorse. 'I'm so sorry. There was a noisy crew in one end of the hotel bar and I just didn't hear the phone. I had trouble getting a cab – you know what it's like – and when I got a cab and saw your message . . .'

He shudders and looks as if he might cry. Nate never cries, except for when the children were born.

My blood's fired up. I want to rage at someone and he's

sitting there, being nothing like the alpha male I know and love.

Then I think of the bullet we dodged. How Rachel is not sitting mutely in the sexual assault unit, her life changed forever.

We have everything.

'There's nothing I can say, Marin,' Nate says, looking broken as he sits there. 'Rachel needed me, you needed me –'

I stop him by reaching out and taking his hand.

He's the warmest human being I know – never cold, despite his low pulse rate, needing only the lightest duvet, even in winter. His big hand feels warm to my cool one and he grips mine tightly.

Rachel is safe: both my children are safe. I say a gratitude prayer to whoever is listening.

'I'm sorry, so sorry,' he says again.

'I was here, Rachel's OK,' I say and I let myself go, finally crying, as my husband holds me tightly.

12

Bea

I used to take Jean-Luc's anniversary off work but now I don't. I need to be busy. Frantic, actually, as the day after Jean-Luc died is the day Luke was born and each year since he was three, we have a party in the house. Our funds never reach to adventures out but I am getting McDonald's for his five chosen pals this year and Mum has made an amazing cake in the shape of a Formula One car.

'Magic,' says Shazz, when I tell her about McDonald's. 'No cooking!'

'Double figures, Mum!' says Luke at breakfast the day before his birthday, oblivious to the three special anniversary cards on the kitchen window.

There's one I buy every year, an unusual type I have to order off the Internet. It says: *We miss you, Dad!!*

I don't want Luke to forget. I need to keep his father's memory alive but it's getting harder and harder. I never know whether showing Luke pictures of his dead father will help or not. How can one tell? Yes – you have a dad, but he's dead, so this is what he looked like, endlessly. Or simply let Luke know he has me and a wonderful support system. I feel freshly guilty of not pushing contact with Jean-Luc's mother more often – she's a nervy woman – because I'm terrified she'll want Luke to go and stay with her and I couldn't bear that, being alone here. One day, but not yet.

Then, every year on his birthday, I wonder if I've failed Luke somehow in not reminding him enough about his dad.

'It's OK about the dog, Mum,' says Luke, looking at me

with Jean-Luc's eyes, which are blue with startling shards of copper close to the irises.

'Heterochromia,' Jean-Luc told me when I fell in love with his eyes. 'When you have completely different-coloured eyes or a very obvious combination of colours in both.'

'Rare?' I asked him. It was so early in our dating career but even then, everything about him seemed rare.

'Very,' he said, moving in to kiss me so I had to close my eyes and stop staring at his.

Luke is a beautiful mix of his father and I, but I no longer see any of that: I just see Luke. A gangling boy with a warm heart, large hands like his dad, a glorious sense of humour and thick dark hair that defies any comb.

'I know it's not a dog,' Luke goes on. He is so stoic and strong, my little warrior, kindest boy ever. 'I know we can't have one. When I'm a grown up, we'll have a dog.'

'The dog might eat tomorrow's birthday hamster,' I say, deadpan.

'Hamster?'

Luke looks joyous and leaps up to hug me. 'Mum, I'll look after it and –'

'– walk it,' I say, still grave.

He giggles. 'You don't walk hamsters,' he says.

He's so happy at the thought of any living animal to care for. I think of the small bundle of fur I've been waiting several weeks for, ready to be picked up by my mother today. The rescue people Shazz knows are desperate for homes for two lots of puppies rescued from inept puppy farmers trying to make a living from beautiful animals for the Christmas market. It's due to Shazz and the abandoned dog overload that we're getting any puppy this close to the holidays. I can't wait to see Luke's face.

Later in the day, I get two texts from Marin.

The first is: We are thinking of you today.

The second is an invitation to Joey's tenth birthday party to me, to my phone, but written to Luke as if Joey had written it with his mother watching. It's sweet:

> Dear Joey, will you come to my party because it will be boring without you? It's the cinema, Joey. p.s. I'm ten and I'm not supposed to ask for presents.

And then I can see absolutely where his mother takes over. 'No presents! Your presence is enough!'

Marin knows that money is tight in our house and that while Joey goes to a private school where kids get things like iPhone ear-buds for Christmas, Luke goes to a school where lots of the kids don't get anything if the Vincent de Paul do not step in.

Honestly, just bring yourselves, is written firmly in Marin's utterly detectable text.

Friendships are strange. They start off one way and twenty years down the line they become something totally different. When I met Nate, Finn and Steve, and later met Marin she was dating Nate, we were all young and full of beans, going to change the world, have fabulous adventures, travel, never be tied down and be friends for ever, obviously. It sort of worked out like that. Marin and Nate fell in love and they were right for each other, absolutely. I was the crazy one for a while, travelling a lot, a variety of jobs, interesting six-month relationships around the world with interesting men. And then I met Jean-Luc and that was it: he was the only man for me.

In those early years, the four of us saw each other all the time. The men clicked and Jean-Luc became part of the Steve/Finn/Nate gang, going to the pub and playing snooker, watching sports together, supporting opposing teams just so they could rib each other.

There was a rivalry between Nate, Steve and Jean-Luc that somehow Finn never took part in – which would wind the others up even more. The secret, I always felt, was that Finn was so fiercely intelligent, a polymath, and utterly confident in his own skin that he never had that need to compete with his friends. We'd meet Finn's girlfriends, and for such a clever man, he had an unerring knack for picking totally the wrong people for him.

Jean-Luc and I wanted a family, but it didn't happen for years. We turned to infertility treatment and, finally, I became pregnant. It was amazing, joyous. Marin was one of the few people who knew about the infertility treatment, and I begged her not to tell Nate. I knew he'd have felt superior to Jean-Luc if he knew: Nate could be childishly macho. If he became aware that we'd needed help to have our baby, then he'd feel superior to my darling husband in the ultimate way.

Marin was delighted. She was pregnant with her second child – due almost the same time as me.

'We can go through it together,' she said, happily.

Afterwards, did it really matter that we had spent three years and so much money trying to have a baby by IVF? Was that important? No.

Nothing was important but looking after my beautiful little baby boy all the time I was grieving. Without Luke, I don't think I could have kept on living because my beloved Jean-Luc wasn't in the world: suddenly he didn't exist, he was gone.

At the time, so many people said the wrong thing. *Everything happens for a reason.* I blocked those helpful souls from my phone. Or worse, 'God has a plan'. What plan was that, precisely? Needless to say, the 'God has a plan' people were immediately blocked.

The people who said, 'I don't know what to say, because I have no idea what you are going through, but I am so sorry, and if I can help,' they could stay.

I culled a lot of friends in those months. But Marin, Nate, Finn and even Steve made the cut.

Finn, dear man, would come round with supermarket groceries when Luke was a tiny baby. He'd bring it all in, put it all carefully in cupboards, tell me just to sit up at the counter and direct him. I got used to it, got used to his calm, gentle presence. He wasn't asking anything of me, he wasn't expecting to be entertained, he just was kind and practical.

In times of tragedy, practical helps.

It meant I didn't have to drag food and boxes of nappies home from the supermarket when my heart hurt so much, I thought I'd cry with the physical pain.

My mother was my birthing partner. My mum had never had it easy, but she was strong. My father used to say there was a rod of steel in my mother's spine and he was right, there was. There was a rod of steel in mine too. And together the two of us got Luke into the world squirming, roaring, a long baby with lungs like a sailor. He was going to be tall like his father, we decided, wiping away tears and sweat. The change-over midwife – because the original had gone off because the labour had lasted twenty-eight hours – said, 'Will we call the dad?'

Mum and I looked at each other and neither of us had cried. We just held on to Luke.

Marin was almost the first person into the hospital with lots of useful things, soft baby onesies and cream for my nipples just in case I decided I was going to breastfeed, because the jury was still out on that one. I cried when I saw her because she was ripe with pregnancy then, nearly nine months gone and her baby was going to have a father.

I felt so bereft and I sobbed when Marin was gone.

'It's the baby blues,' the nurse said kindly, putting an arm around me and a note on my chart simultaneously, probably recommending the psych team come in to assess me.

It wasn't the baby blues – it was the widow's blues, which is a different song altogether, like a long jazz note blown on a sax, wavering into the night. 'My man left me . . .'

It still surprises me now, the word 'widow'. Widows are supposed to be older, having had a lifetime of love, but I'd had so little. I'd imagined us growing old together and once Jean-Luc was gone, that dream died with him. Everyone gets one love story and I'd had mine.

Yet now . . . it must be Shazz and Christie with their pushing me to go on dates because I keep thinking about it now. It could never be what I had with Jean-Luc but could I have happiness again? Just a hint? Someone to hold me, to kiss me, to remind me that I'm a woman in her forties, that there's plenty of life ahead.

There's no time limit on grief – so what if I am ready for someone new?

The day before Luke's birthday, Mum phones about the surprise present and she sounds a bit flustered on the phone.

'Did you get it?' I asked, glad that the puppy code emergency would soon be over and that the little bundle of fur which was allegedly a terrier girl puppy, would be ours.

Mum had gone to pick up the dog and this evening, when we went to Mum's for dinner, his present would be there. I don't know which of us is more excited – me or Mum.

'I did –' says Mum, hesitantly.

'Is she OK? Did she get sick all over the car?' I asked.

We'd had a small poodle when I was little, an adorable bundle of grey who loved eating grass and doing tiny, discreet vomits on the rugs.

'No. Well, the thing is . . . they gave me two,' says Mum rapidly. 'Someone didn't come for the other one and – well, I took her.' She says this last bit in a rush and I laugh. Of course she took two!

'So we have two puppies?' I say, half laughing. In for a penny, in for a pound.

'Yes. I had to, Bea. I couldn't separate them. They snuggled together and cried. I'll send you a picture.'

She didn't really need to send anything. It wasn't just Luke who wanted something fluffy and warm to love: I did too.

'Beautiful,' I sigh. 'We'll be over to you in ten minutes.'

Luke never suspected a thing.

He and I chat about the party the next day, whether he'd get homework from school that night because 'it is my birthday . . .' and he looks at me sideways and says: 'Where will the hamster sleep? They can't sleep outside because they're tiny. I'd like him – or her – to sleep with me but it's fine if he can't, because he might get lost in the bed the way small things get lost in couches, the way Rhianna from my class lost her pet rat. She called it Snowy because it was white and rats are clever but I'd never ask for one, Mum, because I know you're scared . . .'

Inside, I glow with happiness.

The thinking part of my brain is already going over the logistics of having two small dogs in the house. The crate to keep them in for puppy training was certainly big enough: it had fitted a Rottweiler puppy once from someone on the road where Shazz lived. I had soft blankets, puppy food, food and water bowls and even training mats to put on the floor so that the dog would know where to pee. I doubted this would work at first but you've got to try.

My mother is at the door as we drive up. Her cardigan is definitely sporting puppy slobber but her face is alight.

'I've got cake!' she says, fizzing with excitement. 'Special cake.'

'More cake? Not the one for tomorrow?' Luke likes getting things sorted out.

'No, special cake. It's . . . it's in a box.'

The cake box was on the floor of Mum's kitchen and it's making very un-patisserie-like noises. Squealing noises, unhappy squealing noises.

Luke is on his knees in front of it in a flash.

'Mum?' He looks up to me.

'Happy Birthday, darling. It's from me and Granny. Or rather, they're from us. Because we love you so much.'

He opens the box flaps as if opening an organ donor box,

carefully, breath held and then we all saw the two inhabitants: short-haired, fluffy and with their little puppy faces in full moan as if the world was a cruel place and if they had someone to lick, it would all be rosy again.

'Mum! Granny!'

Instinctively, Luke reaches in and gently lifts out the first puppy, who has a patch of dark brown over one naughty eye and an entirely white body. Left alone, the other puppy's wails rise.

Luke scoops the second one out with one hand, this one dappled dark brown, pale brown and white. She looks scared and whimpers to be out of her box, but Luke gently holds the two of them close to his face, and croons at them.

'You're safe, we're going to take care of you. And love you and kiss you and maybe you can sleep on my bed, but you can't fall out in case you get hurt and I am going to love you and love you so much.'

The puppies start licking him ecstatically, as if Luke is what they have been waiting for all their tiny lives.

My mother and I look at each other and the tears in her eyes are reflected by the tears in mine.

Everything doesn't happen for a reason, I know – except, perhaps, two puppies instead of one for a fatherless ten-year-old's birthday.

13

Sid

Another Friday night, and it's sleeting mildly as I hurry across the road from the office into The Fiddler's Elbow to join the rest of the Nurture crowd for our Friday-evening drink. I had some last-minute emails to catch up on, so I'm all on my lonesome as I dodge traffic and arrive in the pub in a panting mess with sleety snow clinging to my hat, which is a very attractive item, being another of my black fluffy much-washed items.

I wriggle through the crowds thronging the pub, all festively celebrating as I make my way to the snug. And suddenly I'm tapped on the arm.

'Thought I'd find you here,' says a familiar voice.

I turn around and there's Finn, standing with two other guys. I can't help it, I beam at him, and say, 'What are you doing here?'

'All his old friends are bored by him so he says he was going off to see his new friend,' says one of the other guys, a slender man with very professorial round glasses and a beard, who is wearing what looks like three jumpers all at the same time. 'We had to come along. Old Finn here needs help from time to time.'

'What sort of help?' I say, grinning.

They're grinning back and the other guy is poking Finn in the ribs.

'Basic conversation,' says Mr Round Glasses.

'Poor thing,' I say, 'so, doesn't have many friends, does he?'

'Well, we're not his friends either, we're colleagues,' says the other man. 'Friends with this fella? Are you mad? I'm Philip

McDonald.' He holds out his hand. 'Modern Irish History.'

'Lovely to meet you.'

Finn is openly amused and watches.

'Michael O'Shaughnessy, Medieval,' says Round Glasses.

'In truth 'tis beautiful to meet with you too,' I say and then laugh. 'That wasn't really medieval, was it?'

'No,' he laughs.

'I didn't know you came in here,' I say to Finn.

'Ah, myself and the lads were getting bored with our usual watering holes, so we thought we'd drop in here for a quick pint before heading home.'

Cue more naughty beaming.

'He told us that he had a new friend who worked in Nurture who came in here.'

'Ah,' I say, and I had to work very hard not to grin. 'And that's cause for excitement, is it?'

'Well, he's got scads of male friends and there are plenty of female colleagues. But apparently he's enjoying your company and he says he's never had a female friend like you before. Probably because you don't know him well enough yet and you haven't got annoyed with him. I mean, we get annoyed with him all the time. He gets very carried away with politics in the 1800s. Drives us nuts.'

'Shut up,' says Finn mildly. 'Don't give away all my secrets.'

He turns to me and his smile is wide, warm, welcoming: 'Can I offer you a drink? We've been here a few minutes and I've been looking around for a group of healthy-looking people all drinking sparkling water.'

I laugh so loud, I'm afraid I might have peed a little bit.

'That,' I say loudly, 'is exactly what myself and my colleagues do.' Then I beckon the men close and begin to whisper. I was going to give away one of Nurture's great secrets. 'We drink in the snug,' I look at Philip and Michael, 'and we try not to be seen necking bottles of wine and eating crisps and snacks and chicken wings in baskets in the pub after work. Because that would look bad, given that we spend a large portion of our work telling people that they should all be following the Mediterranean diet and avoiding trans-fats.'

'All things in moderation,' says Philip.

'Absolutely, but some enterprising young photographer might get a picture of us all sitting there with glasses lined up in front of us and packets of crisps littering the place and . . .' my voice trailed off. 'It's about reputational damage. We have to consider the optics.'

'You're far too clever to be Finn's friend,' says Philip happily. 'Finn's last girlfriend was –'

'I'm not his girlfriend,' I interrupt. Although I couldn't deny a faint frisson at the thought that these men assumed this might be a possibility.

'We're friends, didn't he explain? That's the whole point; friends. Non-dating friends. It can happen in the twenty-first century.'

'Oh we know that,' says Michael quickly.

'Will you stop,' says Finn. 'I just said I was going to come down and say hi to Sid, and you pair tagged along, and now you're making me look like some lunatic.'

'I think the three of you are looking like lunatics with no outside interference,' I say gravely. 'But you're harmless lunatics, so I will go and say hello to my pals in the snug and tell them I'm going to drink with some non-Nurture people outside.'

'Can we not come in?' says Philip, looking excited. 'Only we normally just get to talk with other people from the university and it's nice to meet civilians.'

I laugh loudly at this. 'Civilians?'

'You really know how to insult people,' Michael mutters to Philip. And Finn puts his hand up to his head and closes his eyes.

'Sorry, Sid,' he says, 'I just thought it would be nice to drop in and say hello, that's all; I didn't mean to bring these two eejits with me.'

'No, it's fine,' I say. 'Come on. Let's go in and meet the civilians.'

The three of them pick up their drinks and follow me into the snug, which is already quite jammed with people.

'Friends of mine,' I say, holding up a hand to the assembled company. It wasn't unknown for friends of ours to drop in. The snug couldn't be entirely cut off for Nurture's use. And plenty of people had friends, girlfriends, husbands, wives, drop in.

'What are you having?' says Finn.

'I thought this was my go?' I say.

'No, mine – to make up for ambushing your evening,' he replies.

I accept a glass of red wine, the red being more drinkable than the white in The Fiddler's, and we find ourselves a bit of window to lean against. There is no hope of getting stools, of course, not at this point in the evening. Occasionally, someone goes out into the main bar, steals a stool and drags it back in triumphantly like a Neanderthal belting out of the cave to steal a bit of someone else's woolly mammoth.

Philip is regaling us with stories of the Drama Society Christmas party when he'd been a student, and is on his third hot whiskey – he drinks hot whiskey because, he says, he is always cold – when Adrienne arrives and inserts herself into the group, demanding introductions. The trio of newcomers are delighted to see her and chat away. Not a hint of shyness among them.

Finn turns to me and says quietly, close to my ear, 'I hope this was OK. Should I have rung beforehand, or texted? I just thought it would be nice to drop in and see you. Otherwise we'd be going to the same old dull pub. And I thought it would be nice to say hello. How's your week been?'

'It's fine to do this,' I say, trying to sound blasé, 'absolutely fine. I just come in for a couple of glasses of wine and then I head off.'

'You're not heading off yet,' he says, looking upset in a way

I find deeply flattering and then, instantly, bewildering. What is wrong with me?

Even though it's too early to phone a taxi at this point, ready to hear about Gareth's chugs, Pickle and Kiki, I shake my head.

'No, not heading off yet,' I say and his eyes glitter as he looks at me.

Just then Adrienne appears at my side. 'I like your man,' she whispers into my ear.

'He's not my man,' I hiss back. 'He's a friend.'

'Oh, well, I like your *friend*,' says Adrienne naughtily. 'Can I be his friend too?'

'He has enough friends,' I say primly. 'Besides, I thought you were seeing someone?'

'I'm always seeing someone,' says Adrienne. 'I don't know why. You'd think I'd know better after being married twice.'

'Third time's the charm,' I say.

'And you know this, how?' she asks. We both laugh.

'Isn't romance a triumph of hope over hideous experiences or something like that?' I say.

She gives me a searching look. 'Yeah, right.'

'Nice to meet you,' she says to Finn and wanders off again.

'It's noisy here,' he says. 'Is there a quieter bit of the pub where we can talk?'

The Fiddler's Elbow has no quiet bits. It's like a giant cocktail party on acid on a Friday night, full of revellers, loud stories and, soon, live music, which just means people have to roar their stories at full volume.

'There's a teeny wine bar down the road. I've had lunch there with my boss Adrienne, whom you just met, a few times. I've never been at night but it might be quieter.'

We quietly make our escape from the crowd at The Fiddler's and, ten minutes later, we're installed at a small table in the wine bar and have two glasses of decent wine in front of us, along with menus.

'Oh, mushroom risotto,' says Finn, almost moaning. 'I can never resist it.'

I look up at him. 'That's one of my favourite things to eat.'

'Really?'

'Really. But the portions are huge here. We could –' I pause. 'We could get a big one and share.'

'Excellent plan.'

I used to share meals with Marc but with another man – never. Yet this feels utterly normal. As if I've known him for years. Weird.

We order and chat idly, getting to know each other.

'First pet?' asks Finn.

'A kitten called Miaow when I was three. She was what they call calico – many colours – and she adored me. We had lots of animals, including, once, a cockatoo, but we were only taking care of it. But Miaow was my first baby. You?'

'A wheaten terrier called Lucky. He was a rescue, had only half of one ear, was nearly totally deaf and had a limp. The vet used to laugh every time we went because he said if this was Lucky, he'd hate to see Unlucky. Gorgeous dog, though. Very sweet. Right . . . death row meal?' continues Finn, as if we're about to do a quiz on each other and need to know everything.

I shudder. 'No, not death row. Too sad. Final meal, if I was well enough to eat it.'

He smiles at me. 'You're a softie, despite the biker boots. I knew it.'

'I am sort of soft but I can be tough when required,' I say, attempting hauteur, and failing. 'Don't forget my karate skills.'

We both laugh as the risotto arrives. It's huge, in one bowl and with two forks. The intimacy of the situation hits me but I dismiss it. Finn is good people. He will not read anything into this – unless I want him to. Maybe I do . . . Or maybe not. To cover my confusion, I launch into telling him my final meal.

'A veggie burger with lots of mayonnaise, sweet potato chips and steamed broccoli. Then, for afters, a giant coffee cake, which would make me sick, but I'd be dead, so it wouldn't matter.'

Finn's just looking at me, elbows on the table, staring. At me. Like he's drinking me in and liking it.

'Eat up,' I say, both unnerved and excited. 'We have a trough of food to get through.'

The risotto is delicious and I can't help but moan at my first forkful.

Finn's head shoots up at the sound.

I feel the oddest quiver inside me. What is happening? Stop this, I tell myself sternly.

'Or maybe I'd make this my last meal,' I say, to cover up my blush.

'Are you vegetarian?' he asks.

'Pescatarian,' I say. 'I eat fish. Meat is murder but fish is justifiable homicide,' I quip. 'So, your last meal of choice?'

'You'll hate this but it'd be steak. The French way, almost bleu, which is when they show the steak the pan and for a brief moment, the two are joined.'

I am definitely blushing now. 'Gosh,' I say, 'you are a carnivore. Am I safe?'

As soon as the words are out, I regret them. What is happening to me? It's like careful Sid has been body-snatched by flirty Sid who can't open her mouth without a double entendre emerging. Flirty Sid is a new person, and I have no idea what planet she has come from but she needs to go back there.

'People probably taste like chicken,' I continue weakly, and wonder if I am making it worse. 'Everything unusual is said to taste like chicken.'

'Moving on from the cannibalism, I'd have chips, ordinary ones. Very boring,' Finn adds.

I can't help it. I look up at him, taking in the breadth of his shoulders, the warm, open face, the kind eyes searching mine, and I say: 'You're not boring at all, Finn.'

We both eat some more risotto and he tells me how he read *The Lord of the Rings* at fourteen and scared the hell out of himself, and adores any movie made by Wes Anderson.

'I like any movie with a woman on a revenge kick,' I say before I can help myself and he watches me carefully, saying nothing. 'And *Little Women*. Oh, I loved that book.'

'My sisters do too,' he says.

The risotto is finally finished and it's getting late. Despite the fact that I feel so utterly safe with Finn, I feel I should be getting home. It's hours past my normal Friday evening leaving time.

'I'm tired,' I say apologetically. 'Long day.'

'Of course,' he says. 'I dragged you out, I'm sorry.'

'Don't be,' I say, and feel the dreaded blush again. Quickly, I make my normal phone-call arrangement with my taxi guys. Finn's watching me as I come off the phone.

'You don't use an app?' he says.

'No,' I say, looking at him straight on, 'I don't. There's this lovely company I use and I trust them.'

He seems to be thinking, but he doesn't say anything.

'Good plan,' he says. 'Good plan.'

We split the bill after a verbal struggle of 'me', 'no, me'.

Then my phone pings. My taxi's outside. I grab my coat, shrug myself into it and turn to say goodbye.

'I'm walking you out,' he says.

It's a nice feeling having him at my back. The street is busy, people belting up and down, heads bent against the rain which has replaced the sleet. Plenty of people have started the Twelve Pubs of Christmas early now December is officially here and there is lots of laughter and high jinks in the air.

'I think I'll head off, too,' he says. 'You hiking tomorrow?'

'No,' I say, 'I can't. But maybe next week.'

'Great,' he says, looking pleased.

He opens the cab door for me, waits till I'm inside, then leans in and says, 'Night, hope you get there safely.'

'Don't worry, she will,' says a voice from the front, 'she always does; we take care of her.'

Finn's eyes smile as they meet mine. 'Good to know,' he says, and he shuts the door.

And my heart does a little weird skip.

14

Marin

It's nearly the weekend of Joey's birthday party and today, Thursday, two days before the party, I realise I will have to order a cake. Because work has been so manic, I haven't managed to bake one. I've been trying to sell a lovely cottage in a prime location in Dalkey for a sweet elderly lady who wants to move into an apartment and the sale fell through at the last minute. She's devastated because it means she might miss out on the apartment she wants to buy and I'm devastated because the would-be buyers have been stringing me along for weeks now.

And then Nate ruins everything by mentioning that Steve and Angie might hang around for a drink when they come to pick up Alexandra on Saturday evening after the party.

I don't know why but this sends me into orbit.

'I'll be tired,' I snap.

'It's only a few friends, for God's sake,' he says, irritated.

I'm cleaning up after dinner and even though the kids usually take their turns, this is mine and Nate's evening and yet, somehow, I am scrubbing the frying pan that can't go into the dishwasher or the special coating will come off, and he's sitting at the kitchen table with his phone and the work diary that Rachel says is 'soo old fashioned, Dad!'.

'Once, we didn't have mobile phones, kiddo,' he likes to say back. 'I prefer to make notes and this is how I do it.'

He's using the Mont Blanc pen he's had for years which was the source of one of our rare early rows as money was excruciatingly tight at the time – Rachel was two and I was only working part-time. I like to think I don't hold grudges but clearly I do as, lately, I cannot even see that pen without thinking of that time when we were living on the budget from hell.

Mind you, I think guiltily, I was better at budgets then. Now I am afraid to look at my credit-card bill. I did some online shopping during the week – new winter boots from Acne and some perfume, the exotic Atelier Cologne's Grand Néroli, which I read about in a magazine and then fell in love with. It's so expensive I feel a frisson of guilt every time I spray it on.

I can hardly feel annoyed at Nate's expensive pen when I can't be let near a website without flexing my credit card.

'If you really don't want Steve and Angie coming, I can put them off. It's just drinks and a little something to eat. But if it's too much trouble . . .' he says now, a hint of acid in his voice.

Irritation at having to magic up nibbles as well as drinks ratchets up to rage. How dare he dump Steve and Angie into the mix on the same weekend as Joey's party? It's costing us a fortune – in money, time and energy. Most of which is mine.

'I like our friends coming to have drinks,' I snap, 'but in order to have Alexa at the party, as she is hardly Joey's close pal, I had to invite the whole class, Nate. Twenty-five kids.'

'You didn't have to invite them all,' he says.

'You don't understand school politics,' I reply. 'It's all or nobody.'

I wish it wasn't this way but I can't risk upsetting any of the mothers – and then I think: why not? Why do I always have to please everyone?

This party is genuinely costing a king's ransom in both food and entertainment. As all twenty-five children are coming, it means myself and a few other parents will be ferrying the lot to ours back from the cinema where already I will have forked out shedloads of cash on tickets and nachos and heck knows what bad food groups to keep them happy.

Nate and Rachel will be there, but hopefully some other

kind parental soul will stay to help? Some parents belt off at high speed, delirious to have got shot of their little darlings. Others stay because cinema trips with lots of kids are recipes for disaster. Back at our house, they will have cake and party bags, and be picked up. An entirely plausible plan when it was six boys: one verging on insanity when it's twenty-five.

I'm annoyed with Nate but I say nothing because it occurs to me that this is precisely what my mother would do. I always swore I'd never be like my mother but lately, I have a horrible feeling I'm turning into her.

My mother is the most dreadful martyr – every action has to be accompanied by a diatribe about how she's the only one who can cook dinner/shop/organise the washing. When we were younger and I was there to help with all of this, Ma found other things to be a martyr about. I didn't have a birthday party after my seventh because Ma said it gave her a headache baking a cake. From then on, I made cakes for April and Dom because I liked baking. Am I turning into her? A martyr, the way Dom described it.

A martyr with an added extra: an addiction to shopping.

Friday morning, I'm early to the school for drop off and find myself beside Angie, who gets out of her sleek sports car and runs over to me.

'Anything I can bring to dinner tomorrow night?' she asks.

Dinner? I have that falling-through-a-hole moment when I feel the ground vanish beneath me.

What happened to *drinks*?

After Joey's party, I will be able to manage a drink and a bowl of crisps afterwards but will be found lying on the couch immediately once all guests have gone. Dinner was going to be cereal.

'Er . . .'

'He told you it was just drinks, didn't he?' she says, perfectly volumised blow-dried head at an angle. 'Men!'

'Yeah, men!' I join in, wondering if I am grimacing instead of smiling. Hard to tell. 'Dinner is fine,' I lie.

I don't know why I am doing this but I will not let this woman think I can't handle twenty-five kids all afternoon and a few people round to dinner afterwards. She could probably do it. Mind you, she'd probably have it catered.

'We can have takeaway,' she adds, cheerfully.

'No,' I say immediately, my mustn't-let-the-side-down genes coming to the rescue. Damn, I am my mother. This is a deeply depressing thought. 'I love cooking.'

Angie looks at me oddly but I am not going to break my false smile. If she's coming, if Nate has dropped me in it again, I shall be the perfect wife. If it kills me.

Half an hour and one fabricated dental emergency excuse for the office later, I'm in the nearest shopping centre in the most expensive shop, determinedly ignoring sales assistants watching me rifling through casual T-shirts that run into treble figures and fingering buttery leather biker jackets that cost more than my yearly car insurance.

Sometimes I can ignore the urge, can abstain. The trick is not to go near the posh shops or onto Net à Porter, which raises a lust that sends the neurons in my brain berserk.

The site is effortlessly clever and once you pretend you can afford something on it, it delightedly shows you other beautiful things you might also like.

I like them all. Want them all. With this jacket, that silk blouse, those heels, that mouse-sized handbag – with a handy shopper for holding actual stuff – I will have achieved perfection.

My breathing is definitely faster now as I gather a great armful of clothes and march into a changing room, storming past the assistants who are wondering if a woman with a seven-year-old Coach tote bag and rather tired office flats can afford this or should they call security?

I slide the lock across, in my happy place now.

This stuff is brand new, picked by clever, fashionable people. It's expensive and that means it's good. Every item an investment.

My favourite words.

An investment piece. The words to justify it all.

Today, I will find the one missing piece. I always knew it was out there in the wild. A work/home jacket I can wear forever and people will say 'Marin's so cool, effortlessly so.' A coat for the school gates that screams 'her life is sorted!' The jeans. The ones that make my legs look thinner, longer, that flatten my belly with its overhang of two-baby flesh.

I will look like Angie. I will be able to tell Nate I am not a dogsbody and to stop with the one-armed hugs. I will reclaim my life –

'Do you need any help?' says an assistant outside.

'Uh . . .' I mutter, looking round at my haul.

Boots, I ponder? Or cool-mum-around-town trainers. Like the ones Angie has. With the right footwear and a fabulous jacket/coat/pair of jeans, it doesn't matter where you bought the rest of it.

'Boots,' I say, deep in the throes of it now. Those Acne ones I bought online haven't come yet. I need boots now. 'Like those ones by Balenciaga but not them, obviously. Trainers too. Size 37. White. Not the Veja, as they're too tight. Had to give my last pair away.'

Sometimes my choices are questionable. I nearly once bought a Hermès handbag but when I realised the girl was looking at both my unmanicured nails and the rather battered leather tote that's perfect for all my files and brochures, I was shocked back to reality. Like most ordinary humans, I could not afford the bag. Not under any circumstances, short of selling the car and my body. I'd shuffled away and then almost ran out of the shop.

Not so today. Boxes of boots and trainers appear, and I rip clothes on and off, admiring myself in the special changing-room lighting.

Each piece is perfect but I'm not greedy.

One thing, I tell myself. Just one.

I'm in the car driving back into work when the fever breaks. A rash of hot shame and then the sudden plunge of guilt.

What have I done? Beside me on the seat is a bag holding two items. The black jeans and one of those elusive 'perfect' white T-shirts.

'Those jeans look incredible,' the assistant said.

Clad in my borrowed finery, I step out to look at myself in the big mirror. Transformed.

'The T-shirt is flying out of the shop,' she pointed out gravely. Sensible Me knows this is fabulous upselling. Shopper Me nearly buys two.

Now that the shopping adrenalin rush has left me, the fear and guilt are overwhelming.

I cry as I drive and the precious shopping bag beside me on the passenger seat doesn't help in the least. Shopping is an urge to fill that great gaping wound inside me. The one from my childhood that tells me I'm not anything special and really, once you get to seven, you don't need a birthday party, do you? Some people use alcohol or drugs to numb pain. I buy things.

But still, clothes don't hurt anyone, do they? And all women love to shop. It's what we do, right?

But I know I've gone too far this time. I've spent too much. I don't need to look at the bank statement to know that I won't be able to afford to pay even a quarter of my credit card bill this month. I shudder to think of the interest ratcheting up. Why do I do this? Why?

When I get in to the office the rest of the day stretches ahead, made longer by knowing that the contraband is in my car. Guilt-inducing contraband. Our bank balance has not been good lately but this will push it over the edge. I bought the stuff out of the housekeeping money and I haven't dared look at the balance on my phone. Only if I shop in the low-cost shops for the next month will we be able to manage – which is hardly realistic given Christmas is coming. The guilt ripples through me.

The day is not made any better by a text from April, the oldest of my family and the one whose entire life I have to keep a secret from my mother.

That's me: secret keeper extraordinaire. All weird families have them and my family of origin certainly is weird.

Jared's leaving her! Today!!!!! Phone soonest!!!!

April, I mutter to myself as I tidy up my desk.

My sister is one of life's innocents, so trusting of the world that she sees only what it shows her on the surface. This trait makes her both a genuinely lovely person and a magnet for men attracted to naïve women with shimmering sex appeal.

Essentially, we're alike: short, chestnut-haired and blue eyed. But that's it. I have kindness writ large on my face and April's has a look that says '*You!* I've been waiting for you for a lifetime . . .'

Plus, she's very slim, more hourglass than I am, which means a tiny waist and boobs men speak to. She has full lips and always wears lip gloss, a combination that has an almost mesmeric effect on men. Between the lips and the boobs, she's a walking *Playboy* girl, despite being close to fifty. The trick is that April does not behave as someone who is or who believes she is, in her forties. She is excellent at escaping reality.

If I am the fixer in our family, April is the runner. She left home as soon as she could to escape our mother, and she's still searching for someone to save her, like a fairy-tale princess, and even though I have bought her many self-help books, she does not get that she has to save herself. But then, who am I to talk, shopping myself to happiness?

'Thank goodness you rang,' says April, picking up after the first ring. 'It's happening, it's really happening. Today, finally –'

'April,' I interrupt her as a blast of icy wind hits me on my walk to the car, 'we've talked about this: don't get your hopes up.'

'Please don't say anything negative,' she begs. 'Can't you believe in me for a moment?'

I don't answer. I believe in her. I just don't believe in Jared. Not that I have met him. Jared is either a practised adulterer of enormous skill or can disappear over rooftops like Spider-man. I went through a brief phase of trying to catch him at my sister's apartment, just to size him up for myself. But he must have superhuman powers of evasion. I never managed to meet him.

This, given that their relationship has been going on for two years, makes me think it's highly unlikely it's going to end well for April.

'Darling,' I say, trying a different tack, 'I just don't want you to get hurt. He's said this before. Nothing has changed.' I stop, not wanting to hurt her, but she's my sister, I owe her honesty. 'He lives in a very big beautiful house with his wife and adult daughters, and if he leaves her, he's going to be giving up all of that. So it's going to be ugly.'

Being at the property coalface of divorcing couples is too in-structive. Generally, the more money and prestige people have, the more enraged they get when one spouse ups and leaves. People frequently rely on their homes as barometers of their success in the world. *Look at us: big house. Architect-designed extension with floor-to-ceiling windows and a terrace overlooking the sea/mountains/Italianate gardens. We are fabulous!* Until one of them falls in love with another person and packs a suitcase. Or an antique Vuitton steam trunk, whatever.

Jared Quinn and his wife live with their two college-going daughters in an exquisite Georgian house on a whole acre in Killiney. It's a stunning property and hasn't been on the market since they purchased it twenty-five years previously. Jared would be leaving the cachet of his address to move in with my sister in her six-hundred-square-metre apartment with south-facing balcony along the river. About three million euros less cachet. I have no idea of what Mrs Quinn looks like or how lovely his two daughters are, but that house is something special.

'I know all those things,' she says, as I wriggle into the car, 'but this time it's going to be different. He rang first thing this morning. He hadn't slept, poor darling: he'd had a nightmare.'

Other people's nightmares are generally boring, but the nightmares of your sister's married boyfriend are in a class all of their own, particularly during your commute.

Poor April. I know I shouldn't be on the phone in the car but I can't face this at home: better to get it done now, so I half listen as I sit in lines of traffic to my turn off.

'So he's going to tell her tonight and then come over here.'

I tune back in. 'Is he telling her before or after dinner?'

'I, I don't know. Should it matter?'

'Before dinner makes more sense because then he can collect his stuff and leave. But after dinner implies everyone sitting down together and –'

There's a silence and I fervently hope April is seeing the Quinn family sitting around whatever sort of table rich people who live in Georgian mansions eat their dinner on.

Nobody split up during dinner. 'Pass the salt. By the way, I'm leaving you.'

Cue crashing of precious, lead-bottomed wine glasses. There are far too many items to fling at a departing spouse at meal times. No. I just didn't see it.

'Marin, you're so lucky, you have everything but, this time, I'm going to have it too.' She hangs up abruptly.

Given the newly organised dinner tomorrow, I should stop off and get some shopping for it, but I'm too worn out. I'll get up early to shop. I want to go home and hug Joey, Rachel and even Nate, which is a plus, since I was so cross with him this morning.

I can't help April. Not tonight, anyway. Tonight I have to pick up Joey's birthday cake, finally ordered at lunchtime, and get the house balloon-ready for the after-cinema party tomorrow.

I want it all to be *perfect*.

15

Bea

There are so many SUVs crowded in the car park of the small cinema where Joey's birthday will begin, that I think they must be breeding there.

Women with glossy hair, expensive clothes and perfect make-up are dropping off children, while Marin and Rachel stand at the door counting kids off and putting stickers on their tops. There are some fathers too, which always hurts – imagine having a man to bring Luke places, to be a dad to him, to say: 'You rest, honey – Luke and I are going off to discuss manly things while walking the dogs.'

I could have that, I think – have been thinking about it a lot lately. Nobody says I have to be alone forever. Shazz and Christie aren't anymore. But it's such a leap.

'Mum, Mum, park there,' says Luke excitedly, showing me a sliver of a parking space near the door that will fit my small Nissan perfectly and which would never have been big enough for one of the posh cars with their new registrations.

The puppies, Sausage and Doughnut, are in the back of the car, squeaking with the excitement with which they treat every trip out. They're too little to actually go on a walk, not having had their three-month booster shots, but Luke begged me to bring them today, 'so I can show Joey'.

Sure enough, amid the sea of faces and big cars, Marin sees us. I've told her about the dogs and she knows nothing will please Luke more than to show off his birthday present to his friend. Joey races over and is soon in our small car, with Sausage and Doughnut clambering all over him, their little puppy tongues licking as though their life depended upon it. The scent of them fills the car. There's something about the smell of puppies. A smell of joy and happiness.

'You're so lucky,' says Joey, hugging Sausage close and I see Luke's face surge with pride. For once, he has something Joey does not, and I let myself breathe out. Who cares if I am cleaning up puppy poop for time immemorial? My son is happy.

Finally, Joey and Luke get out of the car.

'Can we bring them in, Bea?' begs Joey and he looks just like Nate – he's going to be a heartbreaker for sure. Before Nate went out with me, he'd cut quite a swathe through the college. It was one of the reasons I'd broken up with him all those years ago. I never entirely trusted him, but then Marin came along and the rest is history: Nate finally hung up his bad-boy spurs.

'You can't bring the puppies into the cinema, Luke, lovie,' I say, 'they're too little. It's not safe for them because they haven't had all their vaccinations – the way you had to have measles shots when you were young. And they'd be bored in the cinema –'

'– and do poos. They do them everywhere!' interrupts Luke joyfully. 'Squelch, poop, squelch.'

Both boys erupt into fits of giggles and I laugh. *He* has not been trying to wash the cream fluffy rug from in front of the fireplace. I swear, that puppy poop was green. It's like having two small babies running around *without* nappies. I am not sure how I'm going to manage to take care of them and walk them when they're bigger, but we'll cross that bridge when we come to it. Besides, and the fear hits my heart afresh, what if Laoise is right and there are job losses on the horizon in work? This is not a good hiring economy right now, particularly for lovely part-time jobs where you share your job with a woman who has grown-up children and can help you out if your small son is sick and you can't come in. Where would I get a job like that again?

Trying not to shudder at the thought, I manage to put the puppies back into their little car crate and get out with the boys to go to see my friend at the cinema door.

'Marin,' I say, hugging her.

She's dressed beautifully – in something wonderfully expensive, I think, and she looks happy. I'm glad. Marin does love her clothes but her mother, who can do passive aggressive and plain old aggressive like a veteran boxer, knocks her confidence all the time. It's wonderful to see Marin here today among the glam posh mums, looking confident, although she is a little tired around the eyes, I notice.

'I'll be back at five,' I say, 'to get Luke and anyone else who needs a lift to your place.'

'Yes, thank you,' she says gratefully. She comes closer to whisper. 'Some people literally want to dump the kids and run till six-thirty pick-up at my house. How do they think I'm getting them back to ours? In a bus? On my magic carpet? I do not understand some parents.'

I laugh out loud. 'See you later,' I say. 'I can't arrange the magic carpet but I have room for two more in my car.' I hug her again and look around for Luke, but he's already inside, talking to Rachel, delighted with himself.

My afternoon passes in a blur of life admin and puppy fur. At five-twenty, myself, Luke and two other boys arrive at Marin's house, which is remarkably SUV-free. I park carefully then let everyone out on the side of the footpath.

I always feel anxious when I'm taking care of other people's children; Shazz says it's post-traumatic stress disorder. This is her latest kick – that I have PTSD after Jean-Luc's death and that's why I can't date.

'Don't be ridiculous. I just don't want to lock lips with some of the idiots that put their names into the online dating hat. You saw those guys . . . Would *you* date any of them? No!'

'We'll find the right website,' insists Shazz. 'Give me time.'

Marin and Nate's house is a testament to Marin's perfectionism.

It's large, beautifully decorated in elegant creams and whites, but it's cosy too. That's Marin's touch: dried flowers and wicker hearts hanging from the bannisters, Rachel's tiny old ballet shoes in a framed box beside a miniature pair of Joey's shoes from when he was born and somebody gave him adorable but deeply silly Converse shoes. He couldn't wear them but they look so sweet in their box frame.

The party is in the living room where three other parents, all mums, are trying to calm things. I stay there for fifteen minutes and help out, then, knowing the food is due because there's a bit of moaning going on about people being hungry, I head into the kitchen.

Rachel and Marin are shoving McDonald's, purchased by Nate who has just arrived, onto plates.

Nate is ticking off a list of orders and when he sees me, he puts it to one side for a hug.

'Hi, sweetheart,' he says, planting a kiss on my cheek. 'Now, I think we might have too many packets of fries, but then you can never have too many fries, can you?'

'No,' says Rachel, grabbing a pack and stuffing a few into her mouth.

I laugh and for a moment, myself, Rachel and Nate grab fries, moaning at the taste.

'I love this stuff,' says Nate.

'I don't know why it took you so long to get it,' hisses Marin at him. 'You said you'd have it all laid out when we got home. I thought we'd have to give them the cake next and they'd all be hyped up on sugar.'

'Even more hyped up,' says Rachel. 'You want to see how many sweets they ate at the cinema.'

'I had a work call,' Nate bites back. 'Life doesn't stop for parties. Jesus, it's not exactly hard – amusing twenty-five kids in a house with a giant TV, every cable channel you could ask for and a giant cake.'

I'm caught in the middle of a deeply uncomfortable family scene, so I grab the first three plates and head back into the living room.

'I have chicken nuggets, barbecue sauce and fries,' I announce, slightly shaken by what I've just witnessed.

There's a wild scramble and, luckily, Rachel comes in with more food before the riot starts. For once, I am glad that Luke only has small parties. The very notion of entertaining twenty-five kids is overwhelming. But even more overwhelming is the thought that things are tricky between Nate and Marin, whom I have never once seen bicker like that.

I am very anxious about change. Even if Shazz is right about me having some syndrome as a result of Jean-Luc's death, change is never good.

Not in my experience, anyway.

16

Sid

I always feel the thrill of going home when I reach the crest of the hill into Greystones. Until that point, I've been driving along with only mountains in the distance, but at that crest, suddenly sea is spread in front of me like an iridescent cape of blue, shimmering into the curve of the harbour, reaching out into the distance along the horizon.

Whatever the season, it's beautiful and today, sharply cool with the low winter sunlight dusting the world, it's magical.

The Christmas spirit is probably responsible as every house seems to have a gleam of fairy lights from their windows, even though it's only half two in the afternoon. I know our house will have been given the fairy-light treatment to within an inch of its life. My mother, Giselle, loves Christmas and has never been able to pass a charity shop without searching out any baubles someone else has discarded.

Stefan spends a lot of his December weekends stapling icicle lights to the whole outside of the house and wrapping white fairy lights round the maple trees in the front garden. Even the hen house gets fairy lights, although the hens don't seem in the least put out by the added shininess.

Giselle, wrapped up in her olive-green home-felted coat with her silvery hair hanging in a long plait down her back and looking like a faery person herself, directs it all like the art director on a fantasy movie. Adding in some of the ivy she spray paints silver when it dies and then working out which of the metal artwork she makes will look best in the right spot, is her next job, with Stefan holding the ladder and saying he should do it and then watching her anxiously as she bounces up each rung without fear. With a house called Rivendell, what else can you do? Giselle is a huge *Lord of the Rings* fan and had renamed the house instantly when she moved in. This and the fact that I call her Giselle rather than Mum almost tells you all you need to know about my mother, except that she is utterly special, one of life's truly good people who never sees the bad in anyone.

My Great-Granny McNamara left her the house and apparently, my grandmother, who was not a person to be trifled with, was outraged. But Giselle, already a fully fledged free spirit, pointed out that Great-Granny McNamara had always had second sight and that the house needed her. She was also pregnant at the time and when my father said he was too young to be a dad and maybe after he finished college he'd consider it, she needed a place of sanctuary. Rivendell became that place. My father never returned.

Before long, Giselle installed herself and a few equally free-spirited friends in the house to keep her company. They dallied with New Romanticism, attempted to grow their own vegetables and failed miserably until it became clear that some of them would have to get jobs.

'Jobs.' Giselle smiles dreamily whenever it's brought up today. 'We were so innocent. We thought we could live in the wild and be our own people but it turned out that we still needed money and you can only eat so many turnips.'

Despite the gardening disasters, the turnips grew. They bought lentils. I still hate both.

The garden's fruit trees, hidden behind a tangle of briars, became the Rivendell family's saviour. They learned to make jams. Apple jellies, French apple and almond marmalade à la Madeleine, rhubarb and ginger jam, gooseberry jam. If it stood still long enough, it was made into jam.

The house was an ancient Edwardian wreck which gradually improved as the various shifting inhabitants got better at fixing plumbing and shoring up against the damp for a few more months. I grew up with lots of people and children: artists doing things with tiny canvasses and nearly dried-out paints to sell in the city squares at the weekends; sculptors busily making insane wire sculptures in the huge back shed; one enterprising girl who thought she could start a business by growing cannabis in her bedroom.

The gardeners might have been useless with anything that wasn't a turnip but they could recognise hash plants when they saw one. She'd had to leave. A little recreational smoking was fine – growing with intent to supply was not.

Other kids in school thought I was a bit weird as a child, but they envied me too because it was quite obvious I didn't have to do my homework. If Mum was called into the school for some infraction of rules, she'd trail in happily and tell them that Sidonie was a free-spirited child and that children should be allowed to make their own decisions. Not the big ones, but the ones that called to them. 'One day Sidonie might under-stand the value of education. And then,' my mother would say happily, 'perhaps she might settle a bit more at maths.'

I never settled a bit more at maths.

Nowadays the house looks a bit better, which is 100 per cent due to Stefan's inhabitation. Stefan and my mother fell in love twenty years ago when he came along with some rather more industrial jam-making equipment he was selling. With him came stability and most of the commune moving out, because for the first time, my mother envisaged a life with just the three of us – and eventually darling baby Vilma in the house. With, of course, the dogs, the cats, the collection of hedgehogs and the two African grey parrots that nobody had known what to do with when their owner, old Mrs Ryan up the road, had died. It was a very happy menagerie.

Giselle was at the kitchen table stirring a giant bowl with Christmas cake mixture in it, watched hungrily by two dogs and one cat, when I arrived. The scent of cinnamon, which I adore, was heady in the air and the sixty-year-old cream range, which had defied all of us until Stefan moved in, was quietly heating the room to a blissful warmth. Blue, the other cat, was curled up on a couch beside the fire, warming his arthritic bones and ignoring the culinary efforts.

'Sidonie!' exclaims my mother, throwing down her wooden spoon to throw her arms around me. 'You're early.'

'We only did a small hike today. Everyone's exhausted: work parties, Christmas madness, etc.,' I said, holding on to her tightly. This had been my third hike with Finn, the second where we'd had company and while it was fun hiking over the mountains, chatting and breathing in fresh mountain air, it was weirdly not as much fun as when we were alone. 'I thought you'd made cakes already.'

'Oh I have,' says my mother, helping me out of my coat, 'but myself and the Romantics are doing a cake run next weekend for ten of our darling older inhabitants who we feel could do with some cheering up. We've got very gentle chilli jam, plum relish, a few tiny bottles of sloe gin because we don't want them all to get sozzled and Rowena's sloe gin is like rocket fuel, and the cakes.'

The Rivendell gang from the early days had nearly all settled nearby. They drove sensible cars, had normal jobs and astonished their children with stories of how they'd lived for several years in the Rivendell house and survived on their pooled resources. Their nickname for themselves was the Romantics as it made them laugh, thinking of the days when they'd thought they could survive outside normal life without rents, mortgages, car loans, pensions and school shoes. Carrie, who was a couple of years younger than I was and had moved out of Rivendell with her mother when she was seven, was an accountant, having watched her mother qualify as an accountant and marry another accountant. Every once in a while Carrie and I met up, normally during the holidays, and Carrie would tell me that she couldn't really remember much about Rivendell, apart from the fun and the menagerie of animals and the first hedgehog. We children called him Hedgy and we went to great lengths to ensure that he was happy and that the dogs, cats and the goose we owned for a brief period left him alone.

Hedgy had eventually shuffled off into someone else's garden one day and we were heartbroken, because he never came back. We used to love his adorable little snout, and how he'd look at us with great intensity when we got down on our knees to gaze into his eyes. Contrary to popular opinion, hedgehogs don't immediately curl up at the first sign of people looking at them. While Hedgy didn't precisely let us stroke him, he was perfectly happy to snuffle around near us when we weren't with the dogs. And whenever we had to lift him out of harm's way, his spikes weren't spiky at all, but were like delicate bristles. I loved that about them.

But our garden's suitability for hedgehogs must have spread among the community because we were always being gifted with ones wandering into tiny gardens or found perilously crossing and re-crossing dangerous roads despite all attempts to put them into fields.

'I wish I could have a hedgehog now,' Carrie once said mistily, 'but we have two Labradors and they'd probably think he was a football.'

I had met her two Labradors, and they were so adorable I couldn't imagine them treating a Hedgy with anything but respect. But perhaps she knew best.

I think about my first beloved cat, the little calico called Miaow, and telling Finn about her. I feel so strange when I think about Finn – feelings I thought I'd never feel again. Different from the way I was with Marc. We had been running away together, from our situations at first and then later from real life. Not the basis for a relationship, as I've found out.

Maybe I was a bit like Hedgy the hedgehog, not quite as spiky as I tried to imply, but gently bristled. To keep people out.

'Tea?' says Giselle now, after I have hugged her. She abandons the cake for a moment to sit down on the couch beside the fire, and I join her and stroke Blue gently. You have to be gentle with Blue, because his poor joints ache so much. But I have discovered a tiny little nodule at the base of his spine, whereupon you can massage gently and he arches his back ever so slightly because it's pleasurable. Hours on the couch on Pinterest can come in handy, it seems. I am not wasting my life.

'No, I'll make the tea,' I say, kissing Blue on the top of his grey furry head, 'then I'll do some stirring.'

Passing, I stick a finger into the bowl and scoop out a squelch of the delicious mixture. 'Oh,' I say as a moan emerges from me. 'I think it's better uncooked.'

'Everyone says that until they've licked three bowls,' Giselle says matter of factly. 'Then they say they are going to be sick. I have made a lot of cakes and a lot of children have passed through this house.'

'I know,' I say, 'I was just thinking about Carrie. I'll have to give her a ring over Christmas and perhaps we can meet up.'

'She has news,' says Giselle, suddenly busying herself with the cat.

'What?'

'She's pregnant.' There's a pause. 'It's twins.'

'Wow,' I say, catching myself and trying not to sound shocked or envious or any of those other emotions that might betray how I feel. I'm not sure how I truly feel, but I do know I'm not ready to feel it now.

'Tony's thrilled but Rowena is delirious,' my mother says to my back as I fill the teapot with boiling water from the stove.

'Course she is,' I say, putting a smile in my voice. 'What mother wouldn't want grandchildren?'

As soon as the words are out, I wish I could put them back in the bottle.

My mother: kind, loving, one of nature's born magnets for children and small animals.

'Yes,' she says, and I can hear the pain in her voice.

It's primeval, that pain: it comes from wanting love and happiness and family for your own children.

She tries to hide it but she can't. I'm very good at hiding my emotions now but my mother never learned.

I can't tell her I never want to bring children into this world because how could I protect them? I won't do it. It's all I can do to protect myself.

I could never tell her what happened, kept away from home for weeks afterwards – the shame stopped me telling, shame that I had done something wrong, coupled with the fear of what it would do to her. Shame reminds me of those pictures of beautiful sea birds covered in oil after an oil spill: it sticks to them, blackly, dangerously, stopping everything. Their wings cannot move, they cannot breathe and only if they are helped is there some hope for their survival. But if the shame goes unnoticed or if people do not recognise the wounded, utterly broken look in the birds' eyes, then they lie down in the shame of the oil and let it encompass them.

My mother tried so hard to take care of me all my childhood and it was all ruined in an instant. I can never tell her the truth now. It would devastate her, truly. She'd tried to protect me and it had gone wrong. I would never break her heart with the truth, that it was all my fault.

A stamping of boots announces Stefan's arrival in the kitchen.

Even in his socked feet he's incredibly tall but has the gentle empathy that a woman like my mother needs. He can sense the tension between us and, in a moment, he goes over to my mother and kisses her against her temple, his long arms encircling her. I see her lean against him, just briefly, their love almost tangible.

Then he comes to me, bends, kisses me on the forehead, before gently putting his arms around me, as if I am something very precious and fragile. It requires no effort to see why Stefan has changed all our lives for the better. He is the most gloriously kind man. My mother, fey, wild at heart, has blossomed with him in her life.

Today, with thoughts of shame in my head and Finn creeping daily into my heart, I wonder if I could ever have what my mother and Stefan have? Love, happiness, the simplicity of a life well lived?

Tea inside us, I stir the cake with my mother assisting, and when it's neatly in the oven in its sheath of baking tin, brown paper and string, I help Stefan with dinner while Giselle drives down to the train station to pick up Vilma who's also home for the weekend.

She comes every few weekends, the way I used to in the early days, apart from that first six weeks when I was twenty-two, when I didn't come home once.

Giselle rang me, Stefan rang me, Vilma rang me and I did a pretty good job of saying I was really busy and the new job was fabulous and the little apartment I was sharing with three girls was just so full of fun, that I couldn't leave but I'd be down soon.

Because I couldn't see them, or I'd have broken down.

Staying away was the only option. I was so wounded and covered in the vicious oil of shame. I could not have pretended to them, the people I loved. I felt complicit, as if I had done something wrong, because I must have, mustn't I? The shame went that deep.

So I stayed in my tiny apartment and drank neat vodka, which I had never done before, because I had to numb the pain and it seemed like the only way. I didn't cry. I merely made myself numb. I could not think of what had happened without wanting to make the cut in my wrists that would end it all.

As if some deity is helping me emerge from my dark thoughts, Stefan puts on music, Nina Simone at her happiest, singing 'I Want a Little Sugar in My Bowl' and I grin.

Finn, I think: he could be the sugar in my bowl . . .

I'm smiling as I slowly heat up the smoky goulash Giselle made earlier, a recipe she had picked up from some of their travels around Europe, while Stefan's in charge of the kibinai, tiny little curded cheese pastries we're going to have as a starter. Stefan has brought so many glorious Lithuanian foods into the house. Although we had to stop getting him to make fried bread because, Vilma said, exactly around the time when she started doing nutrition in Home Economics, it was bad for us.

'It's not bad for you,' Stefan had said, laughing, 'but it's probably not good for you either. Still, we enjoy the simple things in life while we can.'

Which sums up Stefan's motto.

We assemble dinner companionably, with him asking me questions about work and my friends. He's much better than my mother at getting information out of me, but I'm wise to his ways. No matter how much Stefan loves me and wants me to be happy, I don't want anyone looking at my life and seeing what they perceive to be wrong.

I always loved going home to Rivendell and just enjoying myself without any reminders that I wasn't ticking off the boxes for husband, children, super job: all these markers people are supposed to have achieved by the time they get to my age. Is that what life's supposed to be about? Ticking off the boxes?

I wasn't ticking off any boxes, but I'd never hurt my beloved Stefan or Giselle by saying such a thing. But now . . . maybe things were changing. I wouldn't say anything, though. I held the thoughts of Finn close to my heart. I liked him – I could admit that – but it didn't mean he'd love me. I came with so much baggage I could fill a 747's baggage hold. Who'd take that on?

Vilma arrives in a flurry of hugs for everyone and a bottle of wine she's picked up somewhere that was cheap, but 'it's supposed to be really, really good'.

Stefan hugs her. 'Cheap and really, really good, my favourite words,' he says, 'apart from Giselle, Sidonie and Vilma.'

'You forgot the cats and the dogs and the goose,' says Vilma.

'The goose met with an untimely death,' my mother says gravely.

'Not another one.'

We could never keep geese very long; they were always escaping and getting out onto the road and terrorising passers-by. Geese were the untrained attack dogs of the animal world, ferocious fowl with teeth.

Dinner is lovely. We talk and laugh, though the wine is sadly tragic. And Vilma insists we don't drink it, and says she'll bring it back to the shop and make the man in the shop drink a bit of it until he sees that cheap and nice are not the same things.

'No, no, darling,' says Giselle, 'there is no point. But you shouldn't be spending your money on wine for us anyway, you should be spending it on you.'

'I know but I brought home most of my washing,' says Vilma.

'And you can do it yourself,' Giselle laughs.

My phone pings with a text and I see, with a dart of excitement, that it's from Finn. He's asking me to dinner at his friend Marin's. She's the one married to his pal, Nate.

'I'd love you to come,' the text finishes and I feel myself fill with excitement. You didn't invite people you didn't like to dinner with your friends, I think. Then my crazy mind gets involved and reminds me that we said we'd be friends. Just friends.

'Must go to the loo,' I say idly, and rush off to sit alone and examine each word of the text. It's all straightforward except for the last line.

I'd love you to come.

You don't say that to someone who's a friend, do you?

I beam at myself in the foxed old mirror that's been in Rivendell forever.

'Finn,' I whisper into it. 'Finn and Sid. Sid and Finn. Imagine if that came true . . .?'

I'd love that too, I text back and feel a quiver of excitement run through my whole body. I've met Finn for coffee twice since our meal in the wine bar and we've gone for another two walks, which weren't quite as much fun because we weren't alone. His fellow hikers are nice but they're not his real pals.

I feel schoolgirlish at how anxious it makes me that his friends will like me.

Me: biker-boot chick, wanting a guy's friends to like me. I must be going a little nuts.

As I come down from my girlish fantasies about Finn, I tell myself that it's simply nice having a male friend. It doesn't have to go anywhere. We talk about work and sometimes he talks about sport, and I tell him sport is really boring, which makes him laugh. We talk about all sorts of things. Sometimes Finn tries to subtly meander the conversation around to Marc. And I just as subtly shove him off.

I can't go there with him.

He thinks I had a normal relationship with Marc. I can't tell him the truth.

I flush the loo for the sake of noise and return to the kitchen, my phone hidden in my pocket, like something precious.

After dinner we sit in the big old sitting room with the funny purple velvet couch we have had for years, and the old brightly coloured carpets that feel like they have been in Rivendell as long as I have. We love cards and we play all sorts of games and when there are the four of us together, it's so much fun. Vilma's the most competitive, with Stefan being the gentleman banker of all the pennies we keep in a jar so we can place bets. Blue curls up behind me on the couch and it's lovely to feel his gentle feline heat in the small of my back. Soot, who has mixed parentage but is certainly over half dachshund, sits on my mother's lap, eyes closed in blissful contentment because he's with his dearest person in the whole world. There is the faintest hint of fox poo off him and Giselle says she's going to have to wash him properly tomorrow.

With the fire roaring in the grate and the house cosy and happy, outside lit up with its twinkling of fairy lights, I think that Rivendell must be one of the happiest, most magical places in the world, and I'm so lucky to have it, to dip in and out of. If I am really lucky, I think dreamily, slipping into fantasy land, I might even have someone to bring here one day.

17

Marin

It's another Saturday morning when I should be lying in bed with a novel, but instead I'm drinking a strong coffee, figuring out what I'm going to cook for dessert. Tonight, Finn is bringing his new friend who is not, repeat not, his girlfriend.

'Don't treat her like that,' says Finn to me. 'She's –' he pauses, thinking – 'just don't treat her like that. I haven't asked her out or anything. I need to go slow here.'

'Why?' I ask.

'Just because,' he says enigmatically.

So, no pressure. Finn – a gorgeous human being – has, since he split up with Mags some years ago, had the taste in girlfriends of someone who's suffered a lot of concussions. But this sounds different. I hope.

Once, I harboured plans that he'd fall for Bea or even my sister, April, but Bea isn't interested in anything but friendship from Finn and April only likes those men who are permanently unavailable. It's a mystery why Finn – decent, a gentleman, funny, kind to children and animals and good-looking – is still single.

His break-up with Mags seems to have affected his ability to recognise women who are all wrong for him. His last girlfriend Ivanna – whom Steve and Nate cruelly called Ivanna the terrible – was far too cold and humourless for him. And this woman, this Sid? Who knows – time will tell.

'Mum,' says Rachel, moving into the kitchen with speed and snagging a banana from the fruit bowl, 'since you have got people over tonight, could I possibly borrow your car?'

'Where are you going, darling?' I say idly, as if I wasn't checking up on her, but I so am. Since the Les Cloob incident, I am terrified of something happening to Rachel. My motherly fear sensors have edged up a notch because of it. Now, I see, she's truly at the age where she can go off into the world on her own and I cannot be beside her every moment. Another lesson in the painful and lifelong parenting journey, for which there is no damn guidebook.

Louise, Megan's mother, is more sanguine: 'They learned their lesson,' she says.

'No they didn't,' I say. 'They're kids and at that age, the brain tells them to take more risks.'

I feel generally more anxious lately and I don't know it if it's because of what happened with Rachel and Megan or because of how Nate's becoming more and more distant. The one-armed-hug king. Not a single sexy moment on the stairs for weeks. I might as well be invisible. And now, another bloody gang over for drinks and food, which means another family Saturday evening gone. When do we ever get to have time to ourselves?

Despite the Rachel incident, I have to be careful not to imply that this one-off means she is untrustworthy. You can't keep harping on about don't drink and drive, or never get into a car with anyone who is drunk. You have got to let go or they won't tell you anything at all.

'Megan and I were thinking of seeing a band, just a small indie thing with some of the guys,' says Rachel.

'Guys?' I can't help myself using an inflection to imply that I need the names, addresses and photo IDs of these men. As soon as I have said it, I'm sorry because you are not supposed to enquire as to the identity of your eighteen-year-old daughter's friends.

The modern parent is, apparently, supposed to cheerfully say: 'Yeah, fine.'

And the next morning, when the police come round and

say, 'do you know who your daughter was with last night?' you are going to look like you really don't care. How to strike that balance?

Rachel takes pity on me.

'Matt, Lorcan and possibly Cameron.'

'Sounds lovely,' I say, much more enthusiastically. They're nice young men. Responsible. I have had them in my house many times and I have given them fierce looks, analysed them, looked at the way they filled the dishwasher and said, 'thank you, this is lovely, Marin' politely as they ate meals I prepared for them. And basically did my best to frighten them so they will not even dream of hurting my daughter. Nate always laughs at this.

'You are so soft in every other way, Marin,' he'll say. 'But you're like someone with a copy of *Guns 'n' Ammo* under the bed when it comes to those guys, and that's supposed to be my job.'

I agree that he's the one who should be doing the tough dad thing – but Nate is very laid back lately. Honestly, he's being useless.

I want to make sure that Rachel is hanging around with decent young men who get the concept of consent, full stop, and that when they are out they stay together, and they understand that drunk and unable to say no does not mean yes. I want to be sure that she'll be safe. Because I will find those boys and rip them into pieces if she is not.

'Sounds fine,' I say to Rachel now. 'Can you give me a hand for a few minutes and get some eggs in the corner shop? Finn's bringing a new woman who is a friend, and not a date,' I add, 'so all stops are being pulled out.'

'Hope she's better than the last stupid cow,' says Rachel.

'Rachel, we do not diss other women,' I say sternly, even though I had been dissing Ivanna in my own head. 'If you're still around when this Sid comes, drop in and give this nice new girl/woman the once over,' I said. 'Just don't push her up against the wall and ask her too many intense questions.'

Rachel laughs. 'That's your job, Mum,' she says.

Then Joey is at the door, an empty cereal bowl in his hand and a look of hunger on his face. Joey, almost taller than me already at ten, is always hungry. There's something of the monster about him in that he can keep eating the way Godzilla keeps eating things, even when there really can't be any more room for stuff in there. But Godzilla's not lanky, with ruffled hair and that lovely half-little-boy, half-tweenager look of my darling Joey.

Rachel grabs the keys.

'We need Cheerios,' says Joey, as she disappears out the door.

'Sure,' she calls out.

'I'll text you a list,' I add and can hear her groan. 'Pay off for taking the car tonight,' I say.

'Stop having dinner parties, then,' she yells.

Tell your father that, I think grimly. He's the one who keeps organising things for every weekend.

I turn to my darling son.

'There's a box in the corner cupboard up high, Joey. Don't forget to put the bowl in the dishwasher after, honey,' I say, which is half for me and half for him. I have to stop doing everything for him. When he clatters his bowl into the dishwasher, I give him a big hug. He's such a pet. Ten years old, still happy to hug me.

The same age as Bea's Luke. I hope he's still hugging her, I think.

Poor Bea – proof that being beautiful means absolutely nothing in the lottery of life. Bea's stunning, and has the best work ethic of anyone I know – she's had to single parent her son, after all. But we were on the phone this week when I asked her here tonight and she admitted – rather reluctantly – that she was going on a blind date the following week.

'Two of my girlfriends set it up and you probably think I'm crazy –' she begins, but I stop her.

'No! I think it's wonderful!' And I do. The thought of beautiful Bea with someone makes me so happy. If anyone deserves happiness, it's her.

Nate walks into our bedroom and looks at me as if I am stark raving mad as I pull garment after garment out of the wardrobe, put it on and find it wanting.

Clothes litter the bed like the end of an everything-must-go sale day in a posh shop.

He's wearing chinos, a T-shirt and a light sweater, all of which took precisely two moments of effort, but now that he's dressed, he's staring at me.

'Dejunking?' he says mildly.

'Yes, that's exactly it,' I say with heavy irony from under a coral-coloured top that was cheap but somehow draped well. I drag it down. Once clingy, its cheapness means too many washes have shrunk it, so I pull it off.

'Okey doke, I'll go down and open the wine.'

He plants a kiss on my head and leaves, at which point I sit on the bed on my coral top, in just my bra and slimming black jeans and tell myself that crying won't help. I know this is stupid but I can't look bad in front of Finn's new girlfriend/friend. I have to look like my best me.

I don't want her to judge me. It's bad enough to feel so beneath Angie, even though yes, it's not her it's me, but still. I can't have another person in my house making me feel inadequate. Why am I like this anyway? I never used to feel so unsettled.

'Mum?' Joey is at our bedroom door.

I am frozen. Shame floods me. I've been trying to bring up my son and daughter to feel good about themselves and how are they going to do that if they see me rejecting every item I own in case I look fat in it?

'Hi, honey,' I say, trying for breezy. I grab a T-shirt and pull it on. 'Come in.'

'The bed's all junky,' he says.

'I was tidying up,' I lie. 'The wardrobe was untidy.'

'The bed's untidy now,' says Joey. 'You really messed up, Mum.'

He turns and heads off.

I stare at the pile of clothes and my eye catches a black T-shirt thing that was supposed to be either a dress or go over trousers but looked wrong as both.

There's the one I lost the receipt for so I couldn't take it back. A shameful purchase: full price, had us eating very, very carefully for a week because I blew so much of the housekeeping on it. Turns out that silver sequinned blouses are only flattering in the shop's lengthening, low-light dressing-room mirror. The bed is littered with my sartorial disappointments, my dreams as wrinkled and crushed as the cottons and silks.

It's nearly time for everyone to arrive and there's a ring at the doorbell.

My heart sinks but I take a deep breath and put my game face on.

Nate whisks the guests into the kitchen and it turns out to be Angie, who is wearing an entirely wet blouse and holding out the remains of a bouquet of flowers at arm's length.

'We collided because we'd parked round the side and I came round the corner at speed,' says the woman following her. This must be Sid. 'You know how fast I walk, Finn. We were like two wildebeests at the watering hole. Some of my flowers are in a heap in the ground at your front door.'

Steve and Finn follow them, laughing.

Sid puts down the remains of the flowers. 'I wasn't sure about the lilies,' she says, wiping her hands on her black trousers and extending one forward.

'It's fine,' I say. And I'm beaming at her because Sid is as straightforward as they come and her smile is utterly genuine. She is dressed in possibly the least pretentious way I have ever seen and, believe me, I have seen them all. She's wearing a black T-shirt, a black cardigan, black trousers and black train-ers. Nothing looks expensive label-y. She has short, messy dark hair, quite a heavy splurge of dark eyeliner and eyeshadow and possibly a swipe of lip balm. That is it, the extent of it. There's no, *I am here and I am fabulous, look at me in my cashmere.*

I have to stop thinking like that, it's not normal.

I immediately let my stomach out. It's fine, so what if the ludicrously expensive jeans I bought recently do not suck the two babies' worth of belly in.

'Will we leave the flowers out there?' I say.

Angie has dumped her flowers in the sink and gone off in search of the loo.

'I'll get scissors and go out,' says Sid thoughtfully. 'Snip off anything that's still salvageable. But all in all, I think we did a really good job of destruction there.'

'Knew you'd get on,' says Finn.

I look at him and I think he's glowing with happiness. They might be friends but I sense it could easily segue into something more. Or has it already . . .? Once, I would have whispered this to Nate as soon as we had a moment alone, but not tonight.

'So, this is Sid,' he says, ready to welcome them now they're in his castle, and I watch my husband go to Sid to kiss her on both cheeks, Continental-style, which is his normal greeting of women in a social setting, even those he doesn't know. But a weird thing happens. Sid moves a step back and extends a hand.

'You must be Nate,' she says, in a low, firm voice, hand fur-ther extended than normal.

She doesn't like being touched: it comes to me in a moment. No, she doesn't like being touched by men, because she didn't mind colliding with Angie, seemed to think it was funny, and was relaxed about shaking my hand.

Nate seems taken aback, cross even, and for some reason I can't explain in my rational mind, I decide that she is fabulous. FABULOUS.

Steve and Finn burst out laughing, as if at some private joke.

'The old charm doesn't always work,' says Steve and he digs my husband in the ribs.

Yes, Nate, I think – the old charm doesn't work.

Sid says, 'If you could give me scissors and a compost bag for the flowers?'

I laugh. 'You are kind but, honestly, it's fine.'

'No, really,' she says. 'I hate when there's mess, I like to tidy things up.'

'Right,' I say, knowing determination when I see it. I see it in Joey every day, when he tries to get out of doing his homework. And even though Sid is a lot older than Joey, I can see absolute firm determination written all over her. I hand her scissors and a compost bag.

'Won't be long,' she says. And she's off out.

'She's great, isn't she?' says Finn, leaning against the cooker, which is where he normally stations himself when he comes to our house for dinner parties. 'Knew you'd like her.'

'I love her,' says Angie, coming back into the room having removed her blouse and now clad merely in an elegant camisole with a silky wrap around her shoulders.

'That's because she's normal,' says Steve. 'You were expecting Ivanna the terrible.'

'She wasn't terrible,' says Finn. 'She was just high maintenance.'

'You don't need high maintenance,' says Nate firmly, as if he needs to be top dog again. 'You need someone like Marin, only you can't have her because she's mine.'

'I don't need anyone. I'm off dating, I've told you. Sid and I are pals.'

Yeah, right, I think.

Finn begins lifting lids off saucepans and doing the sort of thing that you only allow a person who is very familiar and adored to do in your kitchen.

'I love that seafood chowder,' he moans. 'Could you make

me up a bucket of it, I'll pay, bring it home and freeze it into little pots, and then I won't have to shop for a week.'

'I promised to show you how to make it,' I tell him sternly, the way I tell him every time. 'Rachel has learned. Teach a man how to fish and all that.'

'I'm unteachable where cooking's concerned,' says Finn.

'Nobody's unteachable,' says Rachel, coming into the room and smiling at everyone.

Finn and Steve hug her.

'Off to break a few hearts, eh,' says Steve.

'No,' says my daughter loftily. 'Off with friends. No hearts involved.'

'Our daughter is going to be running her own accountancy firm before she's forty,' says Nate proudly. 'So none of this breaking-heart stuff, she doesn't have time for men.'

Everyone laughs.

'Enough, proud papa,' I say. I've been a cow, I decide. Nate can be self-absorbed but he adores the kids, loves us all so much. He's just not always brilliant at showing it.

Sid comes back and is introduced to Rachel, who seems to approve.

'Your hair,' Rachel says, awestruck. 'I love it.'

Sid puts a hand up and ruffles it. 'A no-effort hairdo,' she says, grinning.

'It's so *now*,' Rachel goes on.

Now is the best thing of all for Rachel and Megan – encompassing the right clothes, shoes, hair, make-up and views.

'Who does it?' Rachel asks and Sid looks bemused.

'Small place in the city near the office. Nothing fancy,' she says. 'I just wash it, towel dry it and I'm done. Had it for years. Fifteen, actually,' she adds and she sounds different for a moment, a less cheerful tone to her voice.

Who, I think, knows how long they've had their hair cut a certain way? I forget my anniversary, never mind the length I've had certain clothes or hairdos.

'Muum,' interrupts Rachel. 'Earth to Mum. I'm going.'

I abandon the cooking. 'Excuse me,' I say to everyone in the kitchen. 'Nate, fix the drinks, I'm going out to say goodbye to Rachel.'

Rachel is hugged and admired as she makes her way through the kitchen. They have all seen her grow up from a little child to the beautiful girl she is now. She definitely looks more like Nate than me with that incredible streaky blonde hair that's rippling down her back and the brown eyes, although hers are wide apart whilst Nate's are narrower, shrewder.

I wonder is it some strange evolutionary fact that makes mothers think their own children are the most beautiful creatures in the world? And does that in its place make us more protective? It must do. Evolution at work.

'Now you will be careful, won't you, honey?' I say as we get to the front door.

'Mum, I will,' she says with a hint of irritation. 'I'm driving, I'm not drinking, we are going to see a band. End of. I'll park the car somewhere safe, the lads will be with us, you have my phone number, you have their phone numbers, their addresses, probably their social security numbers too.'

I laugh. 'You got me, darling. Have fun,' and I watch her head off to pick up Megan.

All's right in the world.

18

Sid

Rachel seems like a very put-together young woman, a lot more together than lovely dizzy Chloe from my office, I think as I watch her and her mother head out. I really like Marin, even though I wasn't sure if I would from the way Finn was describing her. She just sounded perfect and I've never liked perfect people. Perfect is boring. But she's warm, if a little frazzled, but that's probably just due to an influx of guests.

She likes looking after people, I think, which is lovely. Makes me think of my mother and her collection of artistic strays always littering up our table, and I grin because looking at Marin in her lovely silky shirt and black jeans, I know she's a million miles away from my mother and yet similar. Both part of that decent crew of women who take it upon themselves to take care of people. It's clearly not genetic.

Rachel and Marin head out to pass over the essential wisdom that goes between a mother and her daughter going out for the night.

I accept a glass of juice, grab a handful of nuts from a bowl, and wander over to Finn. Seeing a person with their friends is very instructive, but tonight, I find that I merely want to be close to him. There is nobody I want to impress, not Nate, Steve or Angie. The person I like most apart from Finn is Marin. So I'll whisper to Finn that if we could sit close to her, that would be lovely. It would be too much to say I want to sit close to him . . .

'I'm not used to going out much lately,' I say, knowing this is a huge admission, but I don't care. If he doesn't understand, then he isn't the man I think he is.

One large hand pats my arm.

'Message received. And thank you for coming. I didn't want it to be a baptism of fire.'

'This is nice, they're good people.'

Rachel has just gone when there is a ring on the door, and Nate goes out to answer it. He comes in with a woman I assume is Bea, who's tall, slightly too thin and is dressed in a pretty but old floral dress with a heavy knitted cardigan on over it. She'd be utterly beautiful if it wasn't for that hauntingly sad look in her eyes. In fact, I can imagine her as a model when she was younger. Nate is all over her.

'Let me take your cardigan, are you too hot, too cold, will I throw another log on the fire? Now, did you get a taxi, I told you to get a taxi because you can have a drink. You didn't, I don't know what's wrong with you.'

I steal a look at Marin as this is going on. And even though nobody else appears to see this as a little over the top, Marin is watching Nate with a slightly resigned look. I sense that she is anxious about Angie because Nate seems delighted to talk to Angie and tell her how marvellous she is. But, this is different. This is like he's taking care of Bea, some special command from his royal master and he's doing it to the tee, because Bea is precious and must be looked after. And yet there has been none of that in his conversations with Marin, no thanks for cooking this amazing dinner.

I don't know what it is about Nate, but he rubs me up the wrong way.

It's not Bea's fault. She's not looking for this. She comes in and embraces people, comes to me, holds out her hand formally, says, 'Hello, so nice to meet you.' And sits down quietly. She's compact, neat for a tall, elegant person. And I wonder about this group of friends and how they all fit together, because something just feels a little odd.

The food is fabulous. Every time I try to get up and help Marin, she says, 'no, no sit, I can do everything.' Angie offers too, but Marin absolutely insists *she* sits down. The person who does most of the helping is Finn. Nate just sits at the head of the table, holding court, laughing, chatting, making jokes, pulling people into the conversation if he feels they are at a loss. It's like he's taken a course in how to be the centre of attention at every party. It's strange, he's one of Finn's best friends and Finn is such a decent man. But this guy, I don't like him. Don't like the way he tried to touch me when we met. Nor do I like the way he's letting Marin run around like a little creature on batteries while he just sits there. If he's the one who loves giving dinner parties, why isn't *he* killing himself? Eventually, I get up.

'No,' I said calmly, as I walk behind Marin carrying some plates. 'I am going to help, I just cannot sit down, I'm not good at sitting down. I grew up in a house where there were loads of people hanging around looking for food. And the rule of thumb was, bring your own plate back to the kitchen and wash up.'

'You're really kind but –' she says.

'No buts,' I say.

She looks tired. She's an attractive woman, dark hair, beautiful eyes. But she's worn out. And I feel she didn't really want to do this.

'I'm sorry,' I said, suddenly knowing I'm right. 'You had to pull all of this out of a hat because someone decided a dinner party would be a good idea, right?'

'No, no, honestly.' She almost looks panicked. 'I really love having people over.'

'Sure, but sometimes it's nice to sit and hug your couch cushions and watch the box. I mean, I know it's different when you have kids and a husband,' I add, because she might think it's different, but I feel that somehow even if I did have a husband

and kids, I would be very slow to deal out dinner-party invitations the way this nice woman appears to. 'I quite like to couch surf a bit on a Saturday night after a busy week.'

'But I always love it when we have people over,' protests Marin. 'Specially this lot.'

I think of Angie in her beautiful clothes, a very poised and elegant woman, who seems perfectly nice but doesn't have the womanly talk gene thing going for her. Watching Nate fussing over her or Bea wouldn't be my idea of a nice evening at home.

'You haven't known Angie as long, no?'

Marin blinks at me. 'Not as long as the others, no. I love her clothes, don't you?'

I shrug. 'I don't do the clothes thing,' I say. 'I've a nice simple uniform going for me, and I could probably wear the same thing every single day and nobody would know. Although I do have loads of this particular outfit so I can have a new one every day for two weeks.'

Marin laughs and sits down at the table.

'I'm terrible with clothes,' she says. 'I always look at Angie's and I feel like a slob.'

'Well, she's five foot ten, everything hangs well when you're five foot ten and she works out, I can tell.'

'Sometimes I work out too,' says Marin thoughtfully. 'But I don't have a lot of time.'

'Course you don't have a lot of time, you've a big job.'

'Oh, it's not a big job –'

'Who says it's not a big job?' I say and suddenly I feel as if I'm hearing Nate's voice. 'You're an estate agent, which is a big job, and you're a mum, and you run the house and you clearly do all the cooking.'

I don't know why, but I want to shake her and tell her she's incredible. And that good-looking dude in there doesn't deserve her, because all he wants to do is show off his lovely house and his great choice in wine. And she's running around exhausted. I stare at her and I realise I've upset her.

'Oh don't mind me,' I say, 'I shouldn't really be let out to see the general public. I'm a bit eccentric, I think.' I'm exaggerating, but I want to make her feel better.

'Are you seeing Finn?' says Marin hopefully. 'He's gorgeous. I know he says you're not, but I would love to see him happy. I used to long for him to get together with Bea because he's such a darling and so's she, but they're just old pals.'

At that exact moment, I want to say no, that she can't have him because I want him. And then I think, don't be ridiculous, where did that come from?

'No, we're friends,' I say quickly, 'just friends. It's good to have friends, right, you know, like dinner parties: fun.'

'Yeah,' says Marin, 'fun.'

19

Bea

I feel like someone from Hollywood being primped for the Oscars.

I'm standing up in my bedroom with Christie and my mother sitting on the bed, watching, while Shazz fusses over me. I'm wearing a tight black skirt, black nylons and a low-cut top from Shazz's wardrobe that says 'come and get me, baby'. Or so I'm told.

'It's too low,' I say for what feels like the tenth time.

I bend forward. 'Look, if I do this, you can see my bra.'

'But it's a nice bra,' says Shazz, utterly delighted with herself.

We have very different ideas about clothes and while Shazz thinks there is no such thing as 'too tight', I do. The top is satin and I feel I should be standing on a street corner telling people how much I cost.

'I'd fancy you in it,' says Christie.

'You are not my target market,' I reply. 'My target market might think I am asking for it. Imagine what Tom will think.'

Tom is my date for this evening, picked after enormous examination of all the prospective dates and while his looks do not fill me with excitement, although it could just be a bad profile picture, he sounds mild. Mild is what I want for this first date.

'Tom will think all his Christmases have come at once,' says Shazz, trying to decide whether her vermeil heart necklace – which nestles just above my breasts – is better than my own tiny gold and lapis lazuli beads, which circle my neck.

'I wish I could become a lesbian,' I say to Christie, with a sigh as I have often said before. She laughs, as she always does. 'Women are kinder and have much less testosterone,' I add. 'Testosterone is the problem.'

'It doesn't work that way, sweetie,' pipes up Mum, who has never heard this conversation between me and Christie before. 'I don't think you get to choose. You just are what you are.'

Christie leans down and hugs my mother tightly. Her own mother is devoutly religious, thinks any variation of homosexuality or gender issues is bad and has never even seen Christie's two beautiful daughters because they weren't born in a straight family. Her predjudice is her loss, Shazz and I always say when Christie gets sad.

'I know that, Mum,' I say. 'It's a joke between us but it would be easier.'

Shazz has been ignoring us. 'Tom is going to love this,' she says thoughtfully, deciding – to my relief – on my own beads. Her necklace would be like a sign pointing down to my bosoms.

'I still feel like I'm hooking in this outfit,' I say.

'You're too classy, Bea,' says Shazz and both Christie and my mother agree.

'You look elegant,' Mum says. 'Now have fun.'

Tom and I are meeting for drinks in a pub not too far from my home.

'Dinner's too risky,' says Shazz. 'If he turns out to be a total weirdo, you're stuck.'

I park the car, because I plan to drink mineral water, and enter the pub, keeping a wary eye out for a 'tall man wearing a navy cashmere sweater and with blond hair.'

That's Tom's personal description and it fits with the profile picture. If he is everything he says he is, he sounds lovely. A lawyer, divorced, with two daughters and heavily involved in his local sports club. What's not to like.

But there is no sign of a tall man in navy cashmere. I stand, like a flamingo, on one leg because when I'm nervous, I tend to do this. The lounge part of the pub is small. Unless there is another bit, Tom is hiding. Everyone is in groups or couples, apart from one guy . . .

'Bea! I knew it was you. You're beautiful!'

A distinctly short man stands on tippytoes to kiss my cheek and I think that someone with a legal background must know that it's illegal to pass oneself off as something else. But then, probably not on dating websites.

I'm five eight, tall for a woman, and there is no way Tom is over five foot six. Which is fine. But he's lied.

He grabs my hand and leads me over to a table, where he's clearly already downed one pint and a packet of peanuts, and is half-way into another one.

'I'm nervous, so I got here early,' he says and smiles. Truthfully, he has a sweet smile but there's a bit of peanut stuck in his teeth and the hair – the blond hair that looked outwardly tousled in his profile picture – is almost definitely a wig.

He's also older than he said he was. Tom fifty-four is more like Tom sixty-three or older.

'You're even more beautiful than your picture,' he gabbles on.

'Thank you,' I say because I don't know what else to say.

Am I so shallow that I can't allow myself to like a shorter, older man with a wig? Who knows what sort of wonderful person Tom is?

Except, I think, as he energetically waves at the barman for drinks, he lied. My profile told the truth, even though Shazz says this is the kiss of death.

I order my mineral water and sit back against the banquette. I soon realise that sitting beside Tom is a mistake. He's very close to me, saying he's been looking forward to this ever since I messaged him back and that he doesn't mind that I'm a widow.

'No competition, eh?' he says jovially.

'That's one way of putting it,' I say, bristling.

'My girls are thrilled I'm seeing someone else,' he goes on. 'The ex has found herself some bit on the side. "Dad," they said to me, "you need someone to love, someone to enjoy the rest of your life with".'

'How old are your girls?' I ask politely.

Next second, his phone is out and he's scrolling through pictures, showing me two women who are either very late twenties or early thirties.

'You must have married young,' I say, thinking that maybe I'm wrong and he's younger than he looks, that divorce must have shattered him so much he's aged.

'No, had Lara when we were just thirty. Right little chip off the old block. Got into law first try. Doesn't work in my firm, though.'

And he's off, showing me old pictures on his phone that he must have transferred from actual hard copies. Tom is a doting dad, for sure. But the sight of him and a woman with a very 1970s haircut and their two small children clarify the fact that he's lied about his age.

He manages to drink his second pint too and is soon ordering another one. He's chatting garrulously about his life, not asking me anything about mine, and I can see that for Tom, this date is going swimmingly. I feel as if I am floating above myself - witnessing it all with the mild disinterest of a television camera person.

'Have a real drink, love,' he says. 'It'll loosen you up. You're stiff as a board,' he adds, running one finger down my back against the silky top and pinging my bra strap as he does so.

I jerk away.

'Tom, we have only just met and that was entirely inappropriate,' I say, trying not to sound harsh. But real anger has sprung up in me.

'Oh honey, look at you – you came here all dressed up and

you can't just drink bottled water and expect a man to just look. This is one helluva sexy outfit.'

His other hand touches my tight skirt and begins to slide it up my thigh.

The last bit of calm snaps inside me. Tom is lucky I keep the snapping internal or else he'd have broken fingers. I am stronger than I look.

I grab my handbag and push myself out of the banquette.

'Thank you, Tom, for the water. I don't think we're suited,' I say icily.

'Don't tease, honey,' he says and, unbelievably, he's still smiling, still convinced this is salvageable. 'With no man at home, you must be lonely . . .'

'I have my husband's old double-barrelled shotgun,' I lie. 'It keeps people away and I'm never lonely.' I stare full-on at Tom: 'I'm an excellent shot,' I say. The whole thing is a lie: there is no gun but I am suddenly furious that this complete stranger has invaded my personal space, touched me inappropriately and lied solidly to get me here.

Holding my head high, I march out to the car, daring him to come after me. I swear, I will kick him in the nuts if he attempts it.

I'm halfway home before I stop shaking and I realise that this was a horrible encounter. Liars cannot be trusted, no matter how smiley-faced they are.

Mum reaches the hall as soon as she hears me unlock the front door. She takes in my face, which I know has two bright red patches on my cheeks – I always get red in the face when I'm shocked or angry.

'Not so good?' she asks tentatively.

I lean down to hug her.

'Oh Mum, it was awful. He lied about his age, looked nothing like his photo, had a wig . . . And he ran his hand down my back and up my leg, *and* pinged my bloody bra strap. One minute we were talking, the next: ping!'

'Bastard!' she says, shocking me. Mum never swears.

'Why did I let Shazz and Christie convince me to do this?' I say into the warmth of her shoulder.

'Because you're ready,' Mum says softly. 'You've grieved for long enough. There's no time limit on grief and you had so much to grieve, but you are ready for someone else in your life, someone to hug, someone to hold you and make you feel like a woman again. Though this Internet thing might not be the way . . .'

'No, it isn't,' I say, shuddering.

She leads me into the kitchen where the puppies are in their bed but come awake and waddle out of the cage to see me.

I sink onto the floor and Sausage tries to climb my leg, ripping the hated slinky tights as she does so.

'You little darlings,' I croon and they lick every bit of my face they can reach, making their happy little puppy noises. 'I don't think I am ready, Mum,' I say. 'This is enough – Luke, me, you, my friends and these little angels.'

'No, you are ready,' Mum repeats. 'Let's try the old-fashioned way of finding someone.'

'Blind dates? Remember crazy Ed and the man who was married who thought I was his?'

'They were disasters,' Mum says, boiling the kettle. 'No, there must be nice men out there somewhere and I have plenty of women friends with sons and nephews and contacts who will know someone.'

'What are you going to say?' I ask. 'My daughter is desperate –'

'No,' Mum interrupts firmly. 'I'm going to say that my beautiful daughter, whom many have admired, has finally finished grieving her husband and that she might welcome a lovely man to take her to dinner.'

'I draw the line at wigs,' I say. 'I'd far prefer someone who was bald and honest than someone with a bad wig. I'm too old to be in a relationship with someone who can't be honest with himself, never mind with me.'

'Good thought to start with,' says Mum, making tea and smiling her Cheshire Cat smile, which only comes out when she's got a plan. 'Leave it to me, darling. Just leave it to me.'

PART TWO

Christmas Lights Sparkling

20

Marin

Ma has a task for me. She wants me to phone Dom's beleaguered wife, Sue.

'Talk to Sue and tell her we want her here for Christmas,' commands my mother early one morning, as I'm shaking off my coat after arriving into work. It's freezing, the week before Christmas and I don't want to be here and I don't want to be in the middle of my mother's nefarious plan.

I nearly hadn't answered the call, but some Pavlovian response made me.

'Ma, she's probably going to her own family for dinner, you know how it is.' I'm thinking of Nate's vast plans for Christmas. The party he wants to give just before Christmas. The flying visit we'll make to my home, the equally flying visit we'll make to his. And then the supposedly grand dinner in our own house where he'll want to somehow round up a few of his random friends to come in and enjoy his largesse. I'm going off parties. Seriously. I did try looking up if irritability was one of the signs of the perimenopause, but there are so many signs that any normal woman could have them all. Sadly, there is no special mention of disliking parties.

'I don't see why she's not coming here, she's still married to Dominic,' Ma bleats, 'and he'd love her here, I know he would. I have no idea what April is up to, she doesn't tell me anything.'

There's a very good reason April doesn't tell my mother anything. Most of April's Christmases are spent waiting for phone calls from her married lovers, or occasionally the odd torrid session out when one escapes the marital fold for half an hour, to get over to April's to hug her, kiss her, bring her some ludicrous present and then disappear, leaving her that strange combination of happy and sad. Only *then* can she actually go anywhere for Christmas. This Christmas, there'll be no waiting-for-Jared time as he, predictably, didn't leave his wife or his house.

I realise Ma is still talking about Dom and how Sue is being so tricky.

'Why isn't Dominic ringing Sue?' I ask suddenly.

Big mistake. There's something about being in the office that brings out the professional woman in me, and I come over all direct, which is not something I normally do with my mother. In our house, you kept your mouth shut and let Ma run things her way. If you did anything she didn't like, she would deploy the silent treatment. Which I feel sure has already been banned under the Geneva Convention.

'Of course he's not going to ring her, because she's not answering his calls,' snaps my mother as if it's all perfectly plain and I must be an absolute cretin not to have thought of this.

Why does she talk to me like this? I think.

'She'll listen to you. You need to do this, Marin.' I know this move, it's like one of those marvellous chess games that have names. The Immortal Game. I am the pawn and my mother is the Grand Master. 'It's not as if I'm asking for much!' Ma says in a more heated voice.

Ah yes, the 'I'm only asking this one little thing of you' gambit.

Like the good little girl I am, I slip back into my role.

'Of course, I'll ring her later. Ma, I'm just at the office, I'd better go.'

'Fine, fine, busy busy, I know, bye,' she huffs, as if my having a job is something I do purely to annoy her.

I sit at my desk and tap out a text to Sue. I don't really feel up to ringing her just yet. But I know I can be honest with her.

Hi, Sue, Ma has been on because Dominic apparently
wants you to see him on Christmas. I know – he should
be texting or phoning. I apologise for my family in general.
Can we talk, so I can say I've done my best? xx Marin

Sue and I have always got on. She's normal, far more normal
than anyone else in my family, so I have absolutely no idea how
she managed to get married to Dom. But I can only assume
that his good looks, and he *is* very good looking, somehow
blinded her to his ability to seem like a grown-up but act like
a teenager.

What's your day like? she texts back quickly.

I scan down my calendar. Sue works about a mile away in an
office in the city.

I could manage a coffee at about twelve, I say, I can come
close to you. But I've literally got half an hour.

Great, she says, let's do it.

The city is no fun this time of the year. There's a wild Christmas frenzy in the air as if people will actually implode if they
do not wave their credit cards enough. Nobody looks happy,
just harassed, belting along the streets, going to meetings and
fitting in a bit of Christmas shopping along the way. Or just
in town to buy the perfect gift, which, of course, doesn't exist.

Sue and I arrive exactly at the same time in front of the
coffee shop.

'Good timing,' she says. She's taller than me, younger, fair,
athletic. Could have had her pick of any number of men. I
remember their wedding day, and she looked like a goddess
in a long cream sheath. Dominic had the faint air of a young
Hugh Jackman: the shoulders, the face, everything. He's even
nice. But being married to him must be like being married to
a large child who wants amusing all the time.

We hug, grab two coffees and find a corner.

'I knew you'd draw the short straw,' says Sue, drinking her

coffee black. This is obviously the secret to the athletic thing. I have milk and sugar.

'I'm sorry,' I say, 'I really am. I wish it had worked out, honey, but you know, you've got to do what's right for you. I adore Dom but he hasn't quite grown up yet.'

Her eyes are sad as she looks at me.

'I love him,' she says, resignedly. 'But I can't live with him, I can't stay married to him. He's useless around the house, even though I work longer hours than he does. He honestly can't even work the washing machine.'

I feel a faint stab of recognition. Nate claims that only women understand laundry equipment. He always says it as a joke but it's not, I realise. He never does the laundry. He can put things in the basket all right, but he never carries the damned thing downstairs or puts on a wash.

Sue's still talking: 'And the lads, those idiots he's in "the band" with. They're all adults but they still harbour this belief that they could make it big. Every damn weekend, he wants them round so they can pluck their bloody guitars and I'm supposed to provide food.'

Another stab. Nate may not be in a band but he's obsessed with having people in our house. It's very similar.

'Plus, your mother's always on the phone to me these days, blaming me. Drives me nuts. I just wanted a quiet life, and kids. I want kids.'

I stare at Sue and grab her hand across the table.

I suddenly realise that I have been a hopeless sister-in-law: there was lovely Sue, married for years, and not a sign of a child and I had never noticed, never wondered if it was choice or circumstance. I bet my mother noticed. Bet she mentioned it to poor Sue too.

'My darling: infertility?'

'No.' She sounds weary now, as if she has thought about this so often, it's imprinted in her brain and she can speak without engaging anything but the most limited mental circuits:

'Dom's "not ready for kids". He wants us to do fun stuff first before we settle down. I'm thirty-three. My body's about to hit the downhill slope and he doesn't care, never thinks about that. Just wants to have fun . . .'

There it is: the bitterness of pain long kept inside.

Something in me reacts to it. Dom doesn't really care what Sue wants. Not because he's a horrible person but because what he wants comes first: it always has. Ma adored him and he could do no wrong.

Nate is the same. We do what he wants all the time. Case in point: endless entertaining when I am so tired working and rushing around after Joey and even Rachel, who always wonders where her new sweater/skirt/jeans are.

There's no comparison, of course. Sue is in deep pain and I'm merely irritated. Isn't that all it is?

'He does want children but not yet and he never thought to mention that to me. Because you don't talk about that stuff in advance. Why the hell not? Why do you need to have the wedding dress booked months in advance, spend hours discussing invitations, all that superfluous stuff and never sit down and have a serious conversation? Let's discuss these important things – like how do we feel about money, where will we live, do we both want children and when? What do we want out of our lives? Would we like to retire and live in the country when we hit fifty? Are we going to argue about how to bring the kids up? Are we going to try and live like vegans and have no TVs?' Sue sighs. 'Stupidly, I thought we were on the same page plan-wise but Dominic doesn't have any plan. He thinks planning is boring. And he sulks if I bring anything serious up now. He could sulk for Ireland, but I guess you know that?'

'Yeah,' I say, 'I thought you knew that and got it?'

'No, I didn't know it. He hid it. He hid it until we were married. It's like he's hardwired to sulk. Then I realised it's just the family hardwiring – no offence, my family has its own hardwiring but with yours, April is hardwired to try to have what she can't, Dom is hardwired to be a child and sulk, and you're hardwired to try to keep everyone happy and take care of them all.'

I look at her, and my eyes fill with tears.

'Yeah,' I say, suddenly sad. 'I am. I'm hardwired to keep everyone happy, because you know Ma, you know what it's like.' I'm half-processing this statement but Sue has rushed on with the conversation.

'When I married Dom, I didn't know it was going to be like that. I want a family and a life and I can't have that with your brother because he's totally messed up. Dom hates plans but I've got a plan, Marin, a plan to have a good life. And I'm never going to have that with Dom. That's why I want to get divorced so I can start again. Your holier-than-God mother is going to have to deal with it, because it's her bloody fault.'

'I know,' I say sadly.

This time Sue grabs my hand.

'It's not your fault, Marin,' she says. 'You've always been so amazing to me. I love you, you take care of Dom, you've done everything for everyone, even April, and her problems are pretty unsolvable.'

I smile sadly. April has that effect on me.

'I don't think I'm doing very well there.'

'You can't fix April because the fact is, nobody can fix anyone else. The fixing up is an inside job.'

'Did you mean it when you said you had a plan?' I say suddenly.

'Yeah sure,' says Sue. And I'm struck again by the fact that she is thirty-three and that thirty-three-year-olds might have plans. Whereas people like me never had a plan. Nate came into my life and there was no need for a plan. He was the prince on the charger. I always thought April wanted the prince on the charger who was going to rescue her, but now it hits me. April wants the unavailable, because that's what she knows, has read about since she was young. It's me who wanted rescuing. And instead I'm still trying to fix everything for everyone and it turns out that nobody is rescuing me at all.

'I've upset you, I'm really sorry,' says Sue shrewdly. 'I just can't deal with your mother at Christmas or Dom. I'm not going to be around for Christmas, I'm going away with my sister; we're going to go skiing. I thought it would be fun. I have only done it once and it's horrendously expensive, but whatever.'

'New beginnings,' I say, pulling myself together. 'If you don't go, we'll be having a big party at my house and I will control Ma.'

She laughs so loudly that the other people in the coffee shop look around.

'Marin, honey: nobody can control your mother. Have a good party.'

I feel suddenly sick at the thought of Nate's big party. He's obsessed with a big Christmas bash, has already bought the wine, discussed canapes with me. I haven't had a chance to get my roots dyed and yet I already know I'm making asparagus wrapped in filo pastry because Nate loves it.

'I will,' I say, forcing a smile. 'Enjoy skiing.'

'I can't wait,' she says, beaming, and I'm struck by her fresh youth and the fact that she's prepared to let my poor brother and all his baggage go and move on. At that moment I want to slap Dominic and my mother. Although I think my mother might get the biggest slap.

'I'd better get back to the office,' I say.

She stands up and hugs me. 'I'll pay for this, go on. We'll talk after Christmas, OK?'

'Yes, right. If you need me to intervene in the whole legal thing talk to me.'

'No, I don't,' says Sue firmly. 'You're not fixing this, you are not helping me, you are taking care of yourself. Hey, maybe that can be your Christmas present to yourself, Marin, you taking care of you. Your mother shouldn't have sent you here. It's none of her business.'

She gives me an extra tight hug and releases me.

I walk down the street and I feel shaky, as if someone has just ripped a veil from in front of me and shown me something I didn't know. People have plans and they can choose what they want, they don't have to get tied up in the past, they don't have to follow the old message. And I thought, I really thought, that April was the one searching for the prince, but it was me, and Nate's the prince and I'm always trying to do the right thing for my prince in case he goes off me. I don't want a Christmas party. I don't want to go to my parents' house for Christmas – well, I do to see Dad. But Ma, I could give her a miss and it wouldn't bother me.

And I don't want to go to Nate's mother's house on Christmas Day, because Nate's mother always looks at me as though I'm some consolation prize he was made to marry. I want to be at home in my own house with maybe April coming over whenever she's freed from waiting for the current married lover. I want to have simple food I haven't spent four hours preparing and play Monopoly or cards with the kids, watch a Disney movie, and just have fun.

That's my plan. It may not be a five-year one, but it's a plan all right.

21

Bea

Antoinette is sick so I have to do her shift and stay for the full day in work, which means Mum picks Luke up from school. I'm tired and anxious by the time I drive in her gate to pick him up, and I hope she's fed him because I am literally too shattered to even think of heating up the mac and cheese I made at the weekend in one of my ultra-organised cook-and-freeze days.

At work, Laoise was muttering about the practice being halved although she has no more evidence than she had last month.

'Why don't we just ask Dr Franklin?' I say to her.

Laoise goggles at me. 'Ask?' she says, as if I have suggested a day trip to Mars.

'Yes, ask. This is our job security we're talking about.'

Laoise deflates. 'I don't know anything else. I was just worrying out loud.'

'I wish you wouldn't,' I say, 'because when you worry, I worry and the week before Christmas is not the time to think about possible job losses.'

I'm thinking of this as I let myself into Mum's and feel the huge relief I always feel when I'm there. I'd never have managed without her all these years. She's had my back in every way: I am so lucky to have her.

This whole week, I feel as though somebody has got a giant Christmas tree and bashed me over the head with it. The practice is madly busy with people determined to have doctor's visits for random complaints because they know we'll be closed over the holidays.

I've also been working hard the way I do every year to make everything Christmassy for Luke. We're going to have Christmas in Mum's house this year. And she's very excited because a new neighbour moved in next door, a very charming sixty-something gentleman with rippling silver hair, who was apparently something big in the boat-building industry.

'I think they're boats but they might be yachts,' says Mum. 'Maybe you could ask, because I have sort of forgotten and I don't want to let on. His name is Cliff and he's coming in for a pre-lunch drink. I did think of asking him for lunch but . . .' Her voice trails off. And I realise she's anxious about what I will think.

'He's a widower. I told him all about you and Luke and he says this is a very precious time with your daughter and your grandson. Is there anything I can bring? Imagine, he thought of bringing something. You do think it's all right, darling, don't you?'

I beam at her. I'm genuinely so thrilled for Mum, it's completely wonderful. But it makes me feel everything is changing. Mum is looking at a man in a romantic way and it's startling. I never thought there'd be anyone for her but Dad. And, Lord, I hate those kids who expect their parents to remain surgically attached to a corpse for the rest of their lives. But it's just so unusual. For so long it's been her and me and Luke. And then Shazz and Raffie and Norma and Christie and Vincent; it's our little gang, and Mum's changing it.

'You don't mind, darling, do you?' she says, still anxious. 'Do you feel I'm being unfaithful to Dad?'

'Mum, you loved Dad so much and he loved you, but I want you to be happy. For goodness' sake, you do realise that people who have happy marriages often get married again really quickly if something happens to their spouse? It's proof of how wonderful marriage was for them.'

'Well, yes,' she says, flustered. 'I'm not going to marry Cliff; he's only coming in for a drink.'

'Why doesn't he join us for dinner?' I hear myself say.

Imagine – darling Mum thinking of falling in love again.

She chatters happily as she makes us both tea and I think idly of Nate and Marin's annual Christmas party and how I'm dreading it. I'm tired of these parties. I'm tired of being the single woman like a splinter in a thumb. The person who used to be part of their gang and is now the pity element. Not that Marin thinks like that, or Finn. But sometimes I think I'm stuck and I'll never get out of being stuck. Yet, if I move away from everything that Jean-Luc and I had together, then maybe I'll be nothing. I'm stuck in limbo – unable to get a decent date, destined to be alone until I'm Mum's age and meet a sweet widower from next door.

Myself, Luke and the puppies drive home, Luke chattering excitedly about the Christmas play where he is playing a Christmas pirate, which makes no sense but then, Christmas plays aren't supposed to, I think, being a veteran of so many of them. He was a rainbow fairy angel once and I made his costume out of an old sheet, glitter and lots of stick-on rainbows. We still have it.

Our house is almost the most Christmassy house imaginable – with the possible exception of Number Twenty-six on our road, where they have practically wiped out the national grid system with twinkling lights, a giant Santa and a complete herd of reindeers perilously perched on the roof. My Christmas extravaganza is confined to inside and our indoor lights are so pretty. I've always wanted the holidays to be incredible for Luke. When I was a child, I loved Christmas. And just because his dad isn't here, it doesn't mean he's going to miss out.

'They definitely know,' Shazz says to me the day before the Christmas play.

'You think?' I say miserably.

'Oh come on, kids know about Santa younger and younger; we're kidding ourselves.'

'But Luke hasn't said anything, I so want him to believe, it's part of the magic. And if the magic is gone, I feel he's growing up and moving away from me, and everything is changing and I can't cope with change. I don't know, when did I get so weak and frail and frightened?'

'I don't care,' says Shazz, 'if Raffie doesn't believe – well, that's fair enough. I mean, we don't want them getting on for eleven and having kids in class slag them because they don't know. And there is always some little gutter snipe whose mother or father or big brother told them. Don't know why that isn't on the mothers' WhatsApp,' she says, grimly. 'But I'm going to say to Raffie, if you don't believe, you don't receive. So he knows but we still have the fun. It's a win-win situation.'

'Yes, you're right,' I say. 'If you don't believe, you don't receive.' I think of the presents, even presents for the dogs. They've got special dog-food stockings and a fluffy teddy for each of them. Even though I know said fluffy teddies will be disembowelled really quickly. Sausage knows how to de-squeak a teddy faster than you would think possible.

Luke and I have just got inside when Luke, instead of racing into the kitchen with the puppies, who head for their bowls expectantly every time they get home, stops and gives me his serious look.

'Mum,' he says, slowly. 'The thing is –' He pauses. He's such a fast thinker, and normally, he talks quickly and excitedly but now he's slow, thoughtful. 'After Christmas we're doing this thing and it's, um –' Another pause.

I smile but I feel my heart sink.

'Yes, lovie,' I say cheerfully, implying in my best motherly way that whatever happens, we will manage it gloriously.

'We've got to do a Family Tree project. We've got to put pictures of people in it, like our families and –'

'That'll be great fun,' I lie, managing to look as if I mean it. I put an arm around him. 'We're so lucky to have such lovely family and friends. Can we put the puppies in too, do you think?'

He smiles and I know he's relieved, that he was hating having to tell me this. 'Yes! Christie has ink in her printer and we can print them there. I want colour ones so everyone can see how adorable they are.'

'I bet nobody has puppies like them,' I say, continuing to squeeze him as we walk into the kitchen.

The girls are looking up at me expectantly, then back down at their bowls. They think food should be a 24/7 sort of experience.

'I love you,' says Luke, launching himself onto the ground and grabbing them both.

They squeal delightedly and I think that Luke's birthday dogs were simply the best present he's ever had. What a pity dads can't be put on Christmas lists.

22

Sid

'Going to a pre-Christmas dinner with his best friends sounds more than "just friends" to me,' says Vilma slyly as we meander through the food market in the city and try free samples of juicy olives and just-baked bread with a new type of goat's cheese smeared on top.

'We are just friends,' I mutter with my mouth full.

Vilma pokes me gleefully in the ribs.

'Don't believe you!' she says. 'You like him! It's about time. Are you going to buy him a present? Or is he getting you one? Because if you get him one and he hasn't got you one, then that's awkward. Maybe he's in the Brown Thomas lingerie department as we speak, standing in front of a sales lady, cupping his hands and saying "she's about this size"!'

Vilma goes off into peals of laughter at this notion and I feel myself turn pink.

'Course he's not,' I say, although I wish he was.

Finn is haunting my dreams now and my favourite fantasy is of us together in bed, curled up, looking into each other's eyes as he gently touches my body, running his fingers over my skin as if I'm a precious gift.

'You bought bloody Marc that cashmere sweater for Christmas and then he dumped you. OK, it was TK Maxx and only cost forty-five quid, but still. Cashmere!' Vilma has moved on at speed. Marc still rankles with her. I wish I could tell her that poor Marc had to leave me, really. I was too broken. We'd tried intimacy and, eventually, it had petered out. He deserved a woman who'd make love to him.

And as for Finn . . . *he* makes me think of making love. I stop by the Christmas gift area and see a body butter in a jolly jar, something chocolatey designed to be spread on a lover's body and licked slowly off. I have never licked *anything* off *anyone's* body but I have the fiercest desire to buy this for Finn and to tell him what I want to do with it.

'Can I phone Marc up and say Happy Christmas?' asks Vilma, suddenly at my side. She looks younger than her nineteen years.

I forget how young she is. Marc was like a big brother. I vow to phone him and make sure he talks to her.

'I'd love if you did,' I say. 'It hurt me so much when he left, honey, but we had moved apart.'

It's the only way I can explain it to her.

My sense of betrayal at his leaving had far less to do with him than with my past – Marc's leaving meant I was on my own and he had been my security blanket. But perhaps he had to leave to free us both to move on? Of course, I can never tell Vilma any of this. I want her to believe in romance.

'I still think Finn must fancy you,' Vilma says now. 'Go on, get him a pressie.'

My eyes swivel to the chocolate body sauce and I gulp at the thought of his beautiful head bent over my body, licking it off *me*.

I'd love to be able to tell Vilma how groundbreaking this feels but again, I can't.

'Something funny,' she suggests, mistaking my silence. 'Or foodie things. Something from here. Like cherries dipped in dark chocolate? I love cherries.'

I imagine Finn dangling one over my mouth, feeding me.

'Biscuits,' I say quickly. Nobody can feel erotic over biscuits. This madness has to stop. Body butter, indeed. 'Really special shortbread.'

Which he might ask me to his place to eat . . .

*

One of the many things working at Nurture has given me is the ability to put together a wonderful healthy food package. After all, we do tell people how to eat healthily and if I can't get it together to put a Christmas package of glorious and sugar-free goodies together, then nobody can. So after my shopping trip with Vilma, my basket of gifts for Marin and Nate's big Christmas party is a combination of semi-naughty, but nice. There are the delicious home-made beetroot chocolate brownies – I know that sounds like an oxymoron, using the words beetroot and delicious in the one sentence, but it's true. Also, I didn't home-make them myself, obviously. Somebody else home-made them for the beautiful deli and I just bought them and made them look a bit home-made, because I tied them up in the tissue paper and added the ribbon. That has to mean something, doesn't it? I have also put in Fairtrade chocolates – dark, naturally, because it's healthier for you – and some really beautiful olive oil. I controlled myself from adding the special booklet on the correct sort of oils because I suspect that everyone in their house already knows that. There is loads of other stuff, including the decidedly unhealthy two bottles of wine I drop in at the last minute. I also stick in some of the grapefruit juice I love, because I have absolutely no plans to be standing on the side of the road trying to hail a taxi on Christmas Eve evening, because I have had a couple of glasses of wine.

'I can drive you there and back,' Finn says when he phones later to chat and check if I'm still coming, sounding slightly put out that I didn't already expect this.

'Don't be daft,' I reply. 'I'm just dropping in for a couple of hours. You'll definitely be there longer than me. So don't drink and drive is my motto. And besides, I might head down to Giselle's and Stefan's earlier than I had planned.'

'Fine, your choice, Sid,' he says and I feel crushed.

After all my fantasising earlier, Finn hasn't said a word to me about us doing anything special over Christmas in our conversation.

I feel very stupid for having indulged in chocolate-based fantasies about him now. I am clearly just a friend. I bet he's found a girlfriend now; he's too handsome and lovely not to. Biker-boot Sid will just be one of his old pals he occasionally hikes with and if I was said girlfriend, I'd make him ditch all extraneous female friends instantly.

This thought makes me laugh to myself: he isn't interested in me and yet I still know that if he was, I'd be possessive about him because – well, just because. I think that if Finn was really in my life, I'd never let him go.

But that's not happening, is it? I mentally let go of the chocolate sauce.

'There are so many crazy drivers on the road at Christmas,' I add, putting on my cheerful act. 'I'd prefer to drive off earlier and avoid the madness.'

The official story – I love having an official story, which means I can hide the real story – is that I'm spending Christmas week with my mother, Vilma and my dear stepfather Stefan and whoever else they decide to invite. The reality is I think I might just do one overnight there, because it seems that Giselle has a load of nearly homeless sculptors and potters who are a bit stuck for somewhere to stay over Christmas. Because Mum has a sprawling back garden with the big shed that's housed both humans and every sort of art medium going over the years, I'm quite sure she can fit in a couple of potters, but sculptors . . . I'm not so sure. They need spaaace. Either way, I'm not entirely sure that Mum will not have loaned out my bed to one of these people and I'm not bunking in with Vilma because she wriggles.

Our work party was two nights ago and some of the office are still nursing hangovers because Adrienne put money behind the till in the little Argentinian steakhouse we went to and copious bottles of red wine appeared on the tables.

'I am never drinking again,' was the most repeated phrase the next day, apart from 'Does anyone have any paracetamol left?'

Adrienne sent most of them home at lunch.

'It's my fault,' she said ruefully. 'I didn't expect everyone to go quite so wild.'

'The owner did play all that tango music after twelve,' I reminded her. I had no idea there were so many different types of tango music and after a while, everyone – well, obviously not me – was up swinging their legs as if they were on *Strictly* and kicking their partners in the shins.

'Painful sort of dance when performed by amateurs,' said Adrienne. 'I always wanted to be good at the tango. I'm very disappointed in myself.'

'Freddie could hardly walk in a straight line by the time you and he got up,' I reminded her. 'You can't gauge your fleckles, or whatever they're called, when your partner has to be held up.'

'True.'

Nobody brought partners to the Nurture party – it had always been just for staff – but as I watched people giggling as they tried to dance, I'd found myself wishing I could try a little dance in someone's arms. Finn's.

In honour of tonight's party at Marin and Nate's I apply my party make-up, which is a good, heavy brown eyeshadow with hints of bronze to liven it up and a nice nude lip. Vilma and her friends love this look. They think I look like a goth French lady. For total excitement, I wear my newest black jeans and a black shirt with a hint of silver in it. Wild, huh? That's me.

I can't help but close my eyes and wish, just a teeny bit, that Finn would see me as more than just a friend tonight, but I can hardly make the first move. I'd pushed us into the friend zone – and now I was stuck there.

23

Marin

On the afternoon of the Christmas party, Nate walks into the kitchen looking both casual yet dressed up in a shirt I am convinced I have never seen before, in a wonderful cornflower-blue colour, which looks marvellous on him.

'Have you been shopping?' I say, astonished.

'Yes,' he says, like a delighted small boy. 'Couldn't resist it, everyone slags me off for wearing boring old business shirts, so here, look at me.' He holds out his arms and does a full rotation. 'Treated myself to a new shirt for Christmas.'

'Oh darling, you should have said and I'd have bought you one.'

'No, sweetheart, it's fine.' He comes over and kisses me lightly on the forehead. 'You have quite enough to do, what with catering for the hordes. How are we getting on?'

'Food for the hordes, all made, present and correct,' I say opening the fridge and then the oven, to stuff in some filo pastry things. 'You said you saw Louise yesterday – did she say she was coming to the party?' I ask. 'She hasn't replied.'

'No.' He hesitated there for a moment and I don't miss it.

'What do you mean, "no"? She's not coming or you didn't ask?'

'Er . . . didn't ask,' he says.

'But you hesitated. Has she said something, is there something wrong with the girls, do you think I – I don't like to ask Rachel, because who knows what madcap plan they've come up with now . . .'

Lately, I feel as if Louise and I are no longer on the same

page. She's so much more relaxed about the girls' gap-year trip and it's stressing me out.

'You worry too much, Marin,' says my husband.

And I think this is possibly one of the most dangerous statements in the entire world.

'You worry too much, dear.'

Probably every police report where a woman killed her husband, starts with, 'Well, then he said to me, you worry/talk/drive me nuts too much and then I picked up the shotgun.'

I have never been a sulker, but I decide that Nate could do without my attention for a while. I dump the wiping-down cloth into the special washing basket I keep for dishcloths, extract a new folded one from the cupboard, slam it down on the counter and leave the room.

Nate is not even aware of this, does not even say, *Did I say something?* Nothing, I think with irritation, absolutely nothing.

He's accused me of being a worry wart and we have a teenage daughter who is going away soon with her friend, across the world, for months, and of course I'm worried. I'm worried sick!

Right now, I'm filled with an intense rage against Nate. Is it the menopause or the perimenopause or one of the bloody pauses? Please don't tell me it's happening now. There has got to be a reason I'm this irritable, it's not normal. Normal people don't feel irritable like this, do they?

Then I try to rationalise: it's the day before Christmas and we are doing what we do every year, which is to have a massive party with friends and family. It is stressful enough to drive a lesser woman to drink.

Of course I'm stressed and irritable. My husband has just marched downstairs, having done practically nothing except buying in wine and arranging it lovingly, and then has accused me of being someone who worries all the time.

Plus he's wearing a new shirt and he hates shopping. I'm stung that he's gone without me. We always head into the sales together and he finds some good work clothes, while I look longingly at nice things at 50 per cent off and dream about how they'll change my life.

I hope he felt in just enough of a shopping mood to buy me something nice for Christmas, I think mutinously. Nate is a terrible shopper. He goes into the pharmacy and asks them what the most fabulous perfume is at the moment and buys that for me. It is one of his grander flaws as a husband, I must admit. He is brilliant in so many other ways, and I do love him, but that man can't shop – unless it's for beautiful party shirts, it seems. I feel like I'm being a bitch but at the same time all my anger feels entirely, totally justifiable.

I go upstairs into our room, shut the door, thankful that my two offspring are both doing other things in their rooms and I practise some deep breathing. This party will be lovely, I will be calm. I breathe and count to ten. Is it breathe in for six, hold for seven, out for eight or the other way round? Oh hell, I just breathe a bit. In, out, in out. Breathing is supposed to come naturally but it doesn't feel natural right now. I'll be OK, I tell myself, when the party has started and everyone is here: then I can relax.

I open my wardrobe and take out tonight's outfit. I know I shouldn't have bought it but it's a very sexy velvet dress in midnight-blue with some magical properties that make me look both taller and thinner. If Nate's been buying things for himself, then I'm allowed a treat, I reason? His shirt *probably* cost as much as my dress . . .

With this happy thought in mind, I race to his drawer where he neatly stores all receipts. He's so anal about things like that, whereas I just dump everything into a big box and try not to look at it again because of how guilty my shopping receipts make me feel.

Finally, I find the receipt for his shirt – except it's not a proper receipt. It's a gift receipt. From an expensive store – the kind Nate would never visit without me dragging him in there.

This time, I'm not the one who has something to feel guilty about. Why would he lie to me?

24

Bea

Luke is staying with Mum tonight, along with the puppies. When she heard that Nate and Marin's party was today, she insisted on a sleepover. 'Just in case you meet someone, darling, and end up staying later, having a drink and getting a taxi. Christmas parties are very good for that, you know.' Unlikely, since I'll know everyone there, but I'll welcome a sleep in.

When I arrive with Luke and the puppies, who go everywhere with Luke now, an elegant older gentleman with white hair and a sailing tan is busily doing something to the hinges on Mum's cloakroom door, which has been hanging badly lately.

'I'm sure you could do it yourself, Mabel,' he's saying. 'You're so very competent but you need the right tools.'

I think he might be a tad deaf as he doesn't hear us at first but then Luke and the puppies make themselves known.

'Hello, there,' he says and I instantly like him. He could be a model for an attractive older gentleman in a knitting catalogue with twinkling eyes and an engaging smile.

'I'm Cliff and you must be Bea. And this young man must be Luke – how lovely to meet you all.'

The dogs, whom I believe are great judges of humanity, fling themselves on him and he instantly crouches down, which pleases Luke no end.

'This is Sausage and this is Doughnut,' he says. 'Sausage is not allowed to eat sausages. The vet said so.'

Within moments, Cliff has shaken my hand and he and

Luke are on the floor with the puppies, engaged in conversations about what dogs cannot eat – grapes particularly bad, they both agree, and Cliff is talking about his first dog, a small Labrador. Mum comes through from the kitchen, a big smile already on her face.

'That dog was so very lovely to cuddle, just like Sausage and Doughnut are,' he says and I have a vision of him being wonderful with grandchildren.

Mum must have read my mind.

'Cliff has three grandchildren but they live in Japan, which means he doesn't get to see them all the time.'

'We Zoom,' says Cliff proudly.

Nothing wrong with his hearing, then.

By the time I leave, I can see that Mum is nearly as besotted as Luke and the dogs, who are now sprawled on Cliff on the floor and Cliff is telling Luke how his youngest granddaughter wants a kitten for her birthday.

'He won't stay long and don't worry, I won't leave them alone for a moment. I know Cliff is still a stranger to us all,' she says to me quietly.

I smile gratefully. I'm fearfully protective of Luke.

As I drive away, I'm still smiling because I can see how Mum's face lights up at the sight of Cliff. But if she moves on, everyone in my little circle of love will have found someone. Everyone but me.

As I near Marin and Nate's house, I have reached that surge of emotion I haven't felt in years: a swell of pure loneliness. It's not fair, I want to wail out loud as I drive along the Christmassy streets. Everyone has someone, except me.

I park on the street, make a vague attempt at wiping my eyes, but decide that I'll fix myself up when I get in. I can race upstairs to Marin's bathroom and do a make-up repair job before entering the fray. Hopefully, Marin or Rachel will open the door. But they don't – Nate does and he takes one look at my tear-stained face and puts his arms around me.

'Bea, honey,' he croons, and I'm held against him, feeling the strength of his body as he hugs me tightly.

It feels so long since anyone did this – so very long – and I let out a sob.

He leads me into the cloakroom in the hall, shuts the door and goes back to hugging me.

'I'm really sorry,' I mutter. 'It's just . . .' I can't continue the sentence, can't explain how lonely I feel.

So we stand there, hugging, and it begins to feel better.

'Everyone thinks ten years is forever but it's not, it's the blink of an eye and I still remember him.'

'Shush, I know,' he says gently.

The door rattles and suddenly it's opened and there, looking astonished at the sight of the two of us hugging, is Angie.

'Hi, Angie,' says Nate urbanely, as if he's always being caught in tiny cloakrooms with women other than his wife, 'poor Bea was upset.'

'Really?' says Angie, staring at both of us in a blast of ice-cold disapproval.

Mortified, I push out past her. 'Sorry, Nate. Sorry, Angie,' I say, and rush out the front door. I can't stay. What will this look like?

25

Sid

I rock up at Nate's and Marin's to find it's a winter wonderland. There are people all over the house. Marin and Rachel have obviously been working incredibly hard decorating, because everywhere is festive in a pretty and warm way. There are no expensive decorations, just nicely thought-out ones. A tree in a pot so you can plant it again, which I approve of, all sorts of elderly decorations, including lots of rather battered children's ones, presents under the tree. In one corner there is a table set up and several people are playing cards with much squawking and giggling. Holding my juice, I wriggle into the room and begin to circulate with Rachel introducing me. There are lots of little groups of people here and children running around. I don't know many people but that's one of the benefits of growing up in any communal sort of living: you get used to fitting in. I look at the party of card players, one of whom turns out to be Marin's mother, who looks fearsome and is crammed into a fire-engine-red dress.

'Granny's very into her cards,' whispers Rachel, who has shown me in. 'Likes to win.'

There's Marin's father, who is sitting quietly talking to a glamorous-looking blonde who might be Marin's sister, and he's eating chocolates out of a box as if someone is about to come over and wrench them out of his hand. Steve's mother and Angie's father are there, Rachel points out, along with another lady who lives next door, who is clearly thrashing them all at poker.

'Aha,' says this lady, who looks by far the oldest person in the room and is already wearing a gold hat from a cracker. 'I win.' And she hauls the coins across the table, starts gleefully piling them up. They are only copper coins and I suspect none of the people playing would care if they were playing for matchsticks or buttons, because it's the joy of winning with this lot.

'Beryl, I am sure you have several cards stuffed up your jumper,' says one of the women.

Beryl, the older lady, laughs uproariously. 'You are a terrible tease, Millie. You say that every year. Just because I beat you every year.'

Great roars of laughter come from the table and it's clear that this is not some serious accusation of cheating, but more an enjoyable tradition that goes on every Christmas.

Granny in Fire-Engine-Red looks up. 'Hello,' she says, with very unfriendly eyes, 'you're new.'

'Sid,' I say. I hold out my hand, amused.

No surprise as to how Marin is always racing around doing things for other people if this gorgon is her mother.

'Sid – that's a strange name. I'm Eithne, Marin's mother. You're with Finn now?' The woman looks at me shrewdly. With interrogation techniques like that, she could work for any of the Interpol-related agencies.

'He's just my friend,' I say, which is an understatement, 'and he's not here yet, is he?'

I looked very hard when I came in but there was no sign of him.

Rachel, who is obviously trained at rescuing people from her grandmother, appears beside me. 'Now, ladies and gentlemen, can I get you anything else? I know you already have some punch but I am also serving teas and coffees, because we don't want anyone staggering.'

'Are you talking to me, young lady?' says Beryl in a pretend annoyed voice. 'I can hold my liquor.'

The others start laughing again. Clearly this is some joke and Rachel and I look at each other.

'They are like this every year,' she says. 'Respect your elders, I'm told.' The giggling goes on, except that, clearly, Eithne is not a giggler.

I help Rachel distribute tea, coffee and what are undoubtedly home-made mince pies to the card players, who nibble and drink and then shove it all to one side, so they can get back to the game.

'Who,' I whisper to Rachel, 'is the lady beside your father?'

Rachel whispers back: 'My aunt, April.'

At this precise moment, April bursts into tears and Nate hugs her.

'I thought she might be,' I say. 'Should we do something?'

Rachel stares at her aunt, who's still crying.

'I know you think you can help,' she says, 'but you can't really. April has always got a drama going on and you just have to let her get on with it. That's what Mum says. I love her, but, you know, some men are unobtainable. And April loves them.'

'Ah,' I say, understanding. 'Is this one of those, he's with his family at Christmas and she's here alone without him feeling neglected?'

'Got it in one,' says Rachel. 'Poor April, she doesn't know how to be happy on her own, she has to have some complication connected to her. I don't understand it. Feminism passed her by.'

I look at Rachel thoughtfully. 'You really do remind me of my sister, Vilma,' I say. 'Girls don't rule the world. Not yet, anyway. We're trying, but it's not an even fight. Don't think we've won because then you underestimate them. Feminism 2.0.'

'Oh I know,' she says grimly. 'I had an – er . . . little incident one evening my friend Megan and I were out. Some guy did his best to put his hand up my skirt and I literally had to run. Got stuck outside the back of the club and Mum ended up racing in because Megan couldn't find me. I never told her about the guy, by the way,' Rachel adds, looking panicked. 'I mean, it was nothing.'

'It's rarely nothing,' I say carefully. 'It leaves a mark.'

'Yeah, taught me not to wear short skirts,' says Rachel cynically. 'But that's wrong, isn't it? Why can't I wear what I want without some dude thinking he has the right to stick his hand up it?'

'There's what *should* happen and what does,' I say. 'The two are often different. In an ideal world, you should wear what you want and be alone with anyone you feel like, but in the real world, the rules of the jungle apply.'

She nods and looks at me thoughtfully.

Just then, I see Finn arriving. Our eyes meet and he strides straight over to me, which makes me light up inside.

'Hi,' I say breathlessly.

'See ya,' whispers Rachel, and she's gone.

'Sorry I'm late,' he says. 'Traffic.'

I have this overpowering urge to reach up and pull his head down to mine, to kiss him, but at that moment, Marin whizzes past, says 'Hello all!' and the moment is gone.

I let out a shaky breath and watch as Finn hugs Marin hello and thanks her for inviting him.

He didn't hug me, I think, suddenly hit with the realisation. He has never really touched me.

All this fantasy is on one side because if he liked me, really liked me, he'd have put his arms around me and given me a friendly hug, one that could gently segue into something else, but he hasn't.

My silly head, my crazy heart, has invented this great romance.

Stung, I lower my head and remember his present. I'll give it to him but then he needs to be out of my life because I like him too much. And it's not reciprocated.

'I got you some nice chocolate today when I was out with Vilma,' I say, offhandedly.

His eyes stare into mine.

I can't read the look in them: guilt that he hasn't bought me anything? Horror that I'm overstepping the friend thing with a Christmas present?

Bloody women, that's probably what he's thinking.

I shove the gift into his hands and stalk off towards the kitchen. I'll help Marin out and then I'm gone. Rachel is still on service duty and seems to welcome the help. I'm doing one last run of goodies with Rachel and we end up in the kitchen again where, miraculously, Marin is not racing around.

Rachel's intelligent young gaze turns to me. 'Are you dating Finn?'

I am used to this utter honesty from young women, seeing as I have Vilma doing it to me all the time.

'Don't forget I have a sister around your age,' I say, 'so I am immune to being interrogated,' and I manage a brave grin at her.

She grins back.

'It was worth a try. We are just friends,' I say, over-brightly. 'It's a great thing to have male friends. You probably have some?'

'Yes,' she says thoughtfully, 'but I look at them as guys I have decided I won't go out with, so then they can be my friends. It doesn't work otherwise. Is that what happened to you and Finn, you met him and decided he was nice but you wouldn't be interested in going out with him, so then he can be your friend? Or do you actually want to go out with him?'

This takes me aback.

'Eh, no, well,' I stutter, trying to buy time. I can only do this for so long. I just might cry soon. Finn hasn't come searching for me. I embarrassed him with the present. I need to get out of here, soon. 'My sister keeps trying to bring me out with her friends because she thinks I'm going to moulder away in my apartment with no cat and turn into an elderly spinster lady who never has any fun. But it's all right, I don't see it that way, I'm happy.'

'I didn't mean to offend you,' says Rachel. 'Honestly, did I offend you? If so, I'm sorry.'

'Course you didn't offend me,' I add quickly.

'Because Mum thinks you're brilliant and she'd kill me if she knew I said that to you. It's just – well, you are younger than all the other grown-up people, and I felt I could say that to you.'

'It's fine,' I say. 'Lots of women are alone, and might stay alone, a changing world and all that. You get to choose how to live your life. '

'Yeah,' Rachel nods, 'as long as you are happy.'

'Exactly,' I say, 'as long as you are happy.'

26

Marin

Both ovens are going full pelt and for some reason the air extractor is not working terribly well. The place is hot, steamy and I can feel my hair that I carefully set with my heated rollers early this morning drooping. The playing of carols has been taken over by something totally else and I suspect that Megan and Rachel are now in charge of the music. There was no more George Michael's 'Last Christmas' or even Mariah Carey belting out, 'All I Want for Christmas Is You' – no. We had moved on to all sorts of songs that had no Christmas relevance at all, and I wasn't sure that the varying ages of guests would appreciate it, but oh, whatever.

I'm alone in the kitchen because everyone else has decided that they do not want to be hot and bothered and it is much more fun being in the open-plan living area, sitting down, standing up, laughing, talking, drinking, eating nibbles or mince pies. The children are probably close to requiring their second batch of food of the day so I shove a load of home-made sausage rolls into the oven.

Then Sid comes into the kitchen.

'Can I help?' she says. 'I'm pretty useless at cooking, to be absolutely frank, but it's getting crazy and noisy in there and I just thought you might need a bit of a hand.'

'Oh Sid,' I said, thinking I could have hugged her. 'That is so nice of you, but you don't have to.'

She cuts me off. 'I know I don't have to, but I'm here. So, what can I do, why don't you sit down and instruct me. I have an office job, I take instruction extremely well, I can open the oven and close the oven and put things on plates and open bottles and make tea.'

Somehow her voice has a calm commanding air to it.

'Are you in charge of many people in the office?' I say, sitting down on one of the kitchen chairs, realising that I haven't sat down for ages and my lower back is starting to ache.

'I am in charge of a department, but I run it with a very light hand,' Sid says, 'I'm not cut out for bossing people around. But when I see another woman who needs a helping hand, I like to be there.'

'Thank you,' I say, knowing I sound tearful and not even slightly like myself. This is not me, nobody in my own office would recognise this version of Marin, but it's Christmas and I'm tired and maybe having these parties is just too much . . .

'Are you teetotalling or do you want tea or a drink or what?' says Sid, standing midway between the fridge and the kettle.

'Coffee,' I say. 'I know I shouldn't or I won't sleep well, but I don't care. I'm just tired, that will perk me up.'

'Coffee coming up,' says Sid, and she goes and stares at our complicated machine, finds a cup and works it expertly.

'I love practical people,' I say to her back. 'You're very practical. That's nice, it helps.'

'Well,' says Sid without turning around, 'my mother is a glorious woman but she has never been practical and one of us had to be. So I pretty soon learned how to do everything. This coffee machine is easy – we have one quite similar in the office. I look at things and I figure it out. Now, the stuff in the oven – does that need to come out soon? I do not have the cooking gene so have no clue. Give me timings.'

'No, it's got at least seven more minutes,' I say, 'but we could probably heat up some more mince pies and get the shortbreads out.'

I direct her to where the spare mince pies are sealed away and she takes them out and looks at them.

'Did you make these?' she asks, astonished.

I nod.

'So you have a full-time job, a family and you still made all these mince pies?'

'Yeah,' I sigh. 'Am I nuts?'

'No, each to her own,' says Sid. 'You will find no judgement here. I'm just in awe of you. I was thinking of getting a cat but what if I have to make special dinners for the cat if it was sick?'

'I think they have special sicky-cat, cat food,' I say.

'My mother always looked after the cats at home, we had loads. My mother takes in strays, you see, stray animals and stray people. And I like to look after her.'

She sits down beside me.

'She sounds wonderful,' I say, 'tell me more.'

'We lived in a big but absolutely shattered run-down house when I was a child. There was no heating, so if there was a room that didn't have a fireplace in it you were in terrible trouble. We went through a lot of hot water bottles and blankets: you needed blankets. I still don't like being cold,' she admits. 'People would turn up at the house with kittens and puppies because they knew that Mum would take them in. Maybe because lots of women stayed with us over the years, the locals thought she was gay, so random strangers would turn up at the door and say, "we were told that the lesbian lady would look after the cats/puppies/whatever".'

I laugh.

'That's so funny,' I say and then realise I might have just insulted her mother if she is gay.

'She's not a lesbian, but two of the women living there for a few years were, so people assumed any woman in our house was a lesbian until my stepfather came to stay. Where we lived, if you didn't have a family and two point five children, you were weird. Mum's different, lovely and kind. She likes having a lot of people around, likes rescuing people. So she rescues cats, dogs, a hedgehog, several hamsters, a very aggressive rabbit and lots of people. Somewhere along the way she rescued Stefan, my stepfather, although really Stefan rescued my mother and turned things around. There were less people coming in and it was all less chaotic after he arrived.'

'Sounds wonderful,' I say wistfully, thinking it does. This marvellous bohemian lifestyle seems gloriously different and at odds from our very ordinary world where we have a party every year and invite the same people.

I am fed up with doing this, I realise. And Nate knows I'm fed up. But he's just not listening to me.

'Yeah,' she says wistfully. 'It is. They're very in love, my mother and Stefan. Makes you almost believe in love.'

I look at her because I swear I can see the glint of tears in her eyes.

'You OK?' I ask. 'Things all right with Finn?'

'Oh we're not going out,' she says almost harshly. 'We're friends. I'm not exactly girlfriend material.'

Strange, but she sounds almost childlike for such a practical, grown-up person. I get the sense she's been badly hurt somehow in the past. And I don't believe for a second that Finn isn't interested in her. He's never brought a female friend to our house before if he wasn't interested in them romantically. Never.

I decide that some matchmaking is in order.

'Just nipping out to the hall to er . . . check something,' I say.

The mistletoe is in the hall. I'm going to hand it to Finn and tell him he's going to lose this lovely woman if he doesn't do something. Delighted with my plan, I rush out only to see Nate and Angie coming back into the house, clearly after being outside, both looking as if something has just gone on.

They don't see me in the dimly lit hall and I step back into the doorway, shaken.

Nate and Angie? What were they doing outside? Kissing? What other explanation could there be? I knew there was something wrong. Knew it.

She's the difference. He's having an affair with her. Is he?

She bought him that damned shirt. Or am I imagining it? I've always felt so anxious around her – now my insecurities are rushing through me and I can't think straight.

I wait for them to join the others in the living room and then slip upstairs, locking myself in our bathroom. I can't cry when we've a houseful of guests but I feel as if my world has just ended. If I'm right, it just has.

After a moment, I sit up, dab away the tears under my eyes and determine that I can't be right. I just can't. I must have misunderstood.

I've left my phone up here on the dressing table out of the way and I have a quick check now, several notifications flashing up on the screen. One is a message from Bea:

Sorry, Marin, I got held up and won't make it after all.
Happy Christmas xx

I deflate a little – it would have been lovely to have Bea's warm, calm influence here right now. I hope she's OK.

Heading back downstairs to the party, I make my way into the room where all the guests are. Nate and Angie are at the opposite ends of the room and I'd swear there's a tension between them, almost as if they were arguing.

I look around for Finn and Sid, determined to do one thing right tonight but Finn is Sid-less.

'Where's Sid?' I ask.

'She gave me a lovely present and then disappeared into the kitchen,' he says, running his long fingers through his hair distractedly.

'There! She's feeding the masses with Rachel.'

I call Sid over and she gives both of us a forced smile.

Finn's body language is so obvious, I don't know how she can't see it or feel it. But she puts down her plate of mince pies, pats him on the sweatered arm, hugs me quickly and says: 'Sorry, have to head off now. Have a lovely Christmas.'

And like a little runner, she turns and dashes through the party and is gone.

Finn's face is stunned. 'I wanted to say thank you . . .' he begins.

I look at him sadly. Earlier, I might have said something wise to him but now . . . I have nothing wise left to say. Nothing.

27
Sid

I continue to stare at Finn's WhatsApp as if it's an unexploded bomb.

> *My cinema mates are all busy, but there is an old showing of Casablanca on in the Stella next week, do you fancy it? Totally non-date, fellow hiker. Say no if you don't want to, but there's something relaxing about old movies. Finn.*

I have never been to the Stella in Rathmines, an old cinema that, legend had it, had been a bit of a flea pit in its time. In recent years, however, it's been updated into a 1920s centre of glamour, where the modern world stops at the door outside. Apparently, cinemagoers sit in beautiful and glorious comfy seats in a perfectly recreated twenties setting and have drinks and nibbles brought to them. There were possibly even girls going around in mad little 1920s outfits selling cigarettes like in the old movies.

But it was very datey, wasn't it?

Vilma has been asking about Finn since our shopping trip when I bought his Christmas present but I've been deliberately vague. I don't want her thinking I've had my heart broken. Because it's not. No. Course not.

Vilma wants me to fall in love again – she still believes in the fairy tale and that, after Marc, I will find another prince and can be a princess again. I didn't want to go into that.

I can't ruin fairy tales for her. Maybe she'll have one, after all. One sister learning that life is more Grimm's fairy tale than Disney is enough for any family.

Adrienne, who runs Nurture and is not much older than me, is my go-to person for lots of things. We can talk but we don't have girlie drinks or dinners. We work together, we share problems occasionally: end of. It works for both of us. As I've said before, I do not have a vast circle of friends, but if I'd met Adrienne outside of Nurture she might have become one of them.

First up, Adrienne is not a girlie woman. She owns no lipstick and her haircut is also done in the same tiny local salon as mine, where shampoos and sets make up 90 per cent of the business. A shade under forty, she runs an average of sixty kilometres a week and unless she has an actual meeting in government buildings, lives in jeans. Even on those government-buildings days, she often wears her newest jeans with a smart jacket.

'I do the work, I don't model,' she told one reporter dumb enough to ask her about her 'casual style'. 'Would you ask a man about his choice of clothing?'

Said reporter disappeared, tail between legs, but there followed a raft of predictable articles on 'why women were judged on what they wore rather than on what they achieved'.

Adrienne had refused to comment. We had a book on it in the office. Long-time Nurture workers, like myself, put our money on her not commenting. Newbies were sure Adrienne would make a stand. They didn't get that by saying nothing, the stand was made. 'I don't comment on my clothes.' QED.

Today, I run the boss to ground in her office where she's staring out of the window and drumming short fingernails upon a window ledge which has already been drummed to bits, if the peeling paint is anything to go by. The Nurture offices are not establishments of glamour like the Stella Cinema.

Yeah, subconscious, I hear you. Now shut up.

'Oh, sorry, you're on the phone,' I say, as she turns and I see she's got the phone clamped to one ear.

'No, on hold,' she mutters, eyeballs rolling. 'What is it?'

'Nah, this isn't the time.'

'Please. Come in and sit down. I've been on hold for twenty minutes. I'm giving them five more minutes before I'm going to send them a strongly worded email with the words "off" and "fuck" in it.'

I grin. When Adrienne says stuff like that, you know she means it.

'Just a real quickie, OK. Non-work.'

She looks at her phone. 'OK, that's twenty-two minutes I'm on hold, that's just too long.' She pokes at the phone screen as if she's poking someone's eye out in person, throws it onto the desk with a clatter, sits back in her chair and puts her cowboy-booted feet up on the desk. 'Oh wow, what a day. So, problem?'

'The circular argument of hell.'

'My speciality,' she says with a grin. 'Spill.'

'There's this guy, Finn – the one you met at the pub,' I say, 'and he's nice, but we were supposed to be friends, platonic. And now he's asked me on a date but . . .'

'Is he hassling you?' says Adrienne, giving me a fierce look. She's ready with the 'do we need to kill him?' face. She's tough for the boss of a charity.

'No, he's not hassling me, he's –' I search for the word – 'lovely. But I don't know if I'm ready. We're in the friend zone.'

She snorts. 'Friend zone. So he's friend-zoned you?'

'No, no,' I say, 'I friend-zoned *him*. I wanted him to stay there because, you know – what with Marc . . .'

For a second Adrienne's eyes, shrewd enough to see through every possible lie on the planet, laser me with intensity.

'Tell me if I'm getting any of this wrong. You put him in the friend zone because you're not ready but now you're in here discussing him with me? I'm calling bullshit. You want to go on this date and you're looking for permission to do it.'

'Look, it's just –' I stalled – 'I'm not over Marc. I'm not ready to date.'

'Sid, stop with the you-and-Marc thing. It's so old. Marc was nice, but you and him, really!'

'OK, I'm sorry I came in without senior counsel,' I say crossly. Adrienne knew me so well. I'd never told her the truth of my relationship with Marc but she'd obviously figured it out.

'Don't shoot the messenger,' she says.

'I thought you'd understand.'

'Because I'm divorced?'

'Yeah, you get men.'

'If I got men I wouldn't be divorced,' she reminds me.

'OK, you get men better than I get men,' I say.

'True. I would not ever say that you *get men*. But maybe you are getting men now. Progress, right?'

'Adrienne, you're really annoying, you know that?'

She beams back at me.

'People tell me that all the time. My ex certainly did. So where does he want to take you?'

'The Stella.'

'The Stella! If you said he was booking the Presidential Suite in a swanky hotel and had the pink furry handcuffs lined up and a bucket of oysters so you two could keep going all night, I might say yeah, he's moving a bit fast, but the Stella? It's not exactly Ferrari speed yet, is it? It's a definite sign of intent but he could be a metropolitan man who likes classy spots and old movies.'

Finn is not a metropolitan man, I think. He's kind. Gentle. Sexy . . . Oh hell, this is killing me. I'd made up my mind not to see him again after Christmas. I'd felt so hurt because it was obvious he wasn't into me the way I was into him, but now he's asking me out on what is clearly a date. My brain feels like it's going to explode.

'Sid?' Adrienne is looking at me.

'Should I go?'

'You like him, don't you?'

'Yeah, I like him.' It stung that I was finally admitting it out loud and not just to myself. And I do like him. I like him a lot. Maybe I do want to date him. Dammit – this was *impossible*.

'Go. State your parameters. Bring your highly illegal pepper spray. But you're a good judge of character, Sid. The best. If *you* like him with all your antennae up like you're looking for life in outer space, then he's good stuff.'

I let the crack about my antennae go.

'What if it hurts, emotionally?'

'Life is a risk,' said Adrienne, picking up her pen and her phone at the same time. 'Everything we do is a risk, so take some of your own. Marc's gone. He flew the nest. You can fly too. Now I'm going to ring those people again. No, I'm not, I'm going to ring the press office. That normally scares the shit out of them. Should have done that in the first place.'

Delighted with herself, she scrolls through her contacts and I leave.

I think about what she'd said – life is a risk. I knew that. I'd once blindly stumbled into a risk and it had ripped me in half so badly that I'd been hiding from any risk at all for fifteen years. Dare I risk anything again?

28

Marin

I'm not a fan of January – January means cold weather, rain, grey skies and if a bit of low winter sun manages to pierce through the clouds, it only stays for a moment and then it's gone. The plus about January is that it's sale time. Normally, I go shopping to fill the hole in my wardrobe and my psyche – now, I'm going shopping because I feel so empty and alone.

Nate seems the same as ever but I'm not. I can't unsee what I saw at Christmas: him and Angie coming back into the house. I should ask him about it all but I'm afraid he'll have some glib explanation for it, which would be worse because I'd know if he was lying.

This year, I'd had so many plans for New Year resolutions involving things like doing more exercise, cooking more nutritious food (too much cheese is creeping into everything!) and, most importantly, staying out of the shops. Pre-Christmas, I'd been doing very well at this. I felt like a junkie looking for a fix every time I passed one of the little boutiques I love and saw the word 'Christmas party sale' winking at me from the window, like it was covered in glorious diamonds and it was calling just to me. *'Marin, we have the perfect outfit for you, this will change your life, this will let you be the person you were always meant to be . . .'*

The new me is supposed to be walking firmly past, nose in the air, ignoring the siren call of the sale rail. I've been caught that way so often before. I could show you the pink satin opera coat thing I bought once, that looked spectacular in the shop and was down to fifty euros and was a bargain, if, for example, you were a bit taller and went to the opera, whereupon you might *need* an opera coat.

However, not being an opera-going person and not being tall enough to wear it, I just looked like a meringue in a tightly belted coat, who'd never be knocked down because she was almost luminous. I never did manage to sell that one, the charity shops got it. Now, however, I'm buying like the end of the world is nigh and the only way to save us all is for me to shop.

But, and this is the really scary thing, something that would worry me senseless if I wasn't so anxious anyway, we seem to be running low on money. And I can't figure out why.

Nate and I rarely talk about money. Why is money such a tricky subject with couples? We can go to bed and kiss and exchange bodily fluids and lie there bathed in each other's sweat. But we can't say, you know we are about four hundred quid down, what's happening there, was there some bill I didn't know about? Did you buy something for some woman? And I can't tell anyone, certainly not April, whom I'm rushing to meet through the horrible rain. I've got an hour for lunch today and then I have to drive out to a beautiful house in Shankill that I'm showing.

January is not a prime time for selling houses, but needs must. April has been in a very sad, depressed mood since Christmas, when Jared inevitably did not leave his wife. I have not said, "I told you so", because it would be cruel and I love her to bits. She needs support from the only member of her family who knows about her life. Ma would stab her with a sharpened crucifix if she knew about April's fondness for married men.

We have arranged to meet in a small café around the corner from my work, so I can belt back to the office, grab my car and change into my nice showing-house jacket.

She's sitting in the corner of the restaurant and I go over to her and give her a hug. Even miserable, her eyes swollen with tears and her lips quivering, she manages to look desirable. Poor, poor April.

'Do you want anything else?' I say, looking down at her cup of coffee and sandwich barely nibbled, which is how she has always kept so thin. She doesn't do that 'leave half of what's on your plate' thing. No, April does the 'leave three quarters of what's on your plate' thing. When she was younger, April was a more rounded girl and Ma never let the opportunity to tell her so pass by. It's meant a lifelong aversion to eating for any reason other than pure sustenance.

'No, this is enough,' she waves an airy hand, 'maybe a water. Still, bottled.'

'Of course,' I say, determined not to transform into my mother and say, *It's far from bottled water you were reared, what's wrong with tap water?* Instead, I go up to the counter, order a sandwich, a cup of tea, bottled water and wilfully add a chocolate muffin to my order.

Then, I sit down beside April, reach over and grasp one long elegant hand with its beautifully manicured nails. April so often works in terrible jobs because she's never found any great ambition for her own career, so she never has the funds to get her nails done professionally. She's brilliant at doing them herself though. Today, they're a delicious rich espresso brown.

'So, how are you?' I ask. I haven't seen her since our Christmas party.

'How am I? How do you think I am?' she says, and tears well up in those huge beautiful eyes and it's easy to see how so many men have fallen into their depths. However, the men always seem to scramble out at some point and go back to their wives.

'Is there any word from Jared?' I say. Jared went long before Christmas but she's still been holding out hope that he'd come back to her.

'Don't speak his name,' she says brokenly. 'He was full of lies, why did he tell me he wanted to be with me, why did he say that I was his immortal beloved?'

The part of me that knows how to placate and the part of

me that really, really wants to tell the absolute truth, battle for supremacy in my head. Absolute truth wins. I poke my teabag around in the little teapot until it's nice and strong, pour it, add milk and begin.

'April, you know I love you.'

'I don't want a lecture,' she interrupts.

'This isn't a lecture, it's your life, you can do exactly what you want to do with it.'

'I didn't ask you for lunch just to be told where I'm going wrong.'

'We all go wrong,' I say in exasperation, 'every single one of us. Do you think I'm perfect?'

'Yes,' she says, pain evident in every angle of her face, 'you have everything, you have Nate and he's so handsome and attractive and you know other women love him and look at him. And then you have Rachel and Joey and you have your job and friends and everything. And what do I have?'

Inside, I feel a little nauseous. I have Nate, have I? I wish I knew if I did.

'You have what any of us have,' I say, ignoring the inner me. 'We have ourselves and you keep giving yourself and your power away to men who are not worthy of you.'

The anger fades from her face. She still looks beautiful and I wonder idly what it must be like to have that power and still for it not to bring happiness.

I'd always wanted to look like April when I was younger. Once she'd conquered the puppy-fat stage, she was so sexy and glamorous, capable of making men watch her as she walked past. People didn't watch me as I walked past and yet my life had worked out better. I had my children, my work, I had Nate . . . it kept coming back to Nate. Was he my sum total?

'I don't feel like I have any power,' she says, 'I just wanted someone to take care of me. Do you know, I never pursued any of the married men I've been with?'

I stop drinking my tea and shake my head. There's nothing

predatory about April – she is no femme fatale. I always knew this and yet I never fully put it into thoughts.

'They asked me out and I –' she pauses – 'I never asked them to leave any woman for me. I never said: "leave her and live with me". Not once, never. I didn't think I was worth it. I've never thought I was worth it. I thought I was lucky to get just a piece of pure love. If life was different, then maybe these men would have met me first and I'd be married to them. But it didn't work that way because I am unlovable. I need to see myself reflected in their eyes because they love me – for a while, anyway.'

'April, that's not true,' I say kindly. 'I love you, my children do, Dom does, Dad adores you.' I leave Ma out, another irredeemably sad omission.

'Thanks, sis.'

'You really never asked Jared to leave?' I am truly astonished.

She shakes her head. 'He kept saying he couldn't live without me and I believed him. He hurt me more than anyone else because I thought he loved me but he said –' she's crying now – 'he said I'd be fine on my own and he didn't want to regret leaving and he would: regret it.'

Regret leaving that lovely big house, more like.

'Oh April,' I say.

At this point, big tears began to slide down my sister's perfect face.

'Oh darling, I'm sorry, I'm sorry.' I shove the chocolate muffin over to her side and she begins to eat it mechanically.

I can almost see her thought processes because I understand them: *I'm going to eat this because it's bad for me and it will stop me being beautiful, and then men will have more reasons not to want to be with me.*

I thought of all the ways April had learned to dislike herself. Our home had never been an easy one in which to grow up. Dominic had stayed an eternal teenager because it was the only way he could cope with our family's dysfunction. As for me,

I'd read the mood of the family and tried to keep the peace, and Dad had hidden in his allotment. Finally, April had re-treated into the fantasy world of the princess being rescued by the prince. And the princess must be thin, of course, because that was what fashion dictated. Princesses did not wear a size-fourteen dress, therefore neither would April. It was all cruel, wrong and ultimately destructive.

'I just want what you have,' April says, between mouthfuls of chocolate muffin, 'just happiness, someone to come home to, someone who can cook dinner.'

'Nate can't cook dinner,' I say, 'he's useless at it – in fact, I think he's getting worse. Once upon a time he'd heat up some soup or something, but now he comes home and he's exhausted, between the gym and work.'

The gym – that's a sign, isn't it? Men who have affairs are always going to the gym. But then, Finn, Steve and he have always swum and gone to the gym.

'But men are different,' says April, as if this is self-explanatory. 'We're supposed to look after them.'

'No, we're not, we're equal.'

'Ha! If we were equal, men would be buying lipsticks and suck-it-all-in knickers and having their legs shaved. So it's not equal at all. We're supposed to make ourselves desirable for them. And not earn too much or be too successful. I just want someone to take care of me the way Nate takes care of you.'

'He doesn't take care of me,' I say a little dully, because as I say it, I realise he doesn't. If anything, I take care of him. And look where it's got us now – me wondering if he's being faithful, too scared to ask in case I find out.

'Marriage is never what it looks like, April,' I say, 'it's hard, you get annoyed with the other person. But you stick it out.'

'I made a New Year's resolution.' She laughs and there's no humour in her voice. 'I'm going to give up men for six months, totally. I'm not even going to speak to a man unless he's some-one I work with. Don't tell me that I need friends and that if you have lots of friends, then you will find someone to date, because it doesn't work that way. I'm nearly forty-six, no matter how good I look, I'm still nearly forty-six. Men want a younger model.'

'Oh April,' I say, taking both her hands in mine. 'So what exactly are you going to do?'

'I'm going to concentrate on work,' she says, 'I'm going to stop going part-time, if I can, and I'm going to get some hobbies. I'm going to stop waiting. I'm going to get some rescue puppies. This year is going to be different.' She looks defiant.

Ma never allowed us to have dogs in the house. 'Dirty smelly things,' she called dogs.

'Good for you,' I say.

'And if a man invites me out in that six months, I'll tell him no. And if at the end of it he's still there, well, we might give it a try. But I will be looking for upfront disclosure. If he's married or *about to be divorced*, and that happens more often than you think, then no. Or is *living separate lives* with his wife, that's another big no-no. If only you knew all the stories they tell . . .'

I don't want a story from Nate. I'm going to find out myself what's really going on: no excuses from him, the actual truth. And if he has been cheating, then he'll be sorry.

29

Bea

Mum's been very busy finding me dates. New Year, new love life, apparently.

'It's my new mission,' she says cheerfully, as she lists her friends' relatives, who generally sound as if they should be attending some sort of group therapy after tricky divorces/relationship break-ups.

I have had coffee with some of them and I think that if work goes belly up, I could always retrain as a counsellor with a view to working with the recently divorced.

There's Jim, who married a Brazilian lady, who ended our two-hour coffee session in a local Starbucks by saying he was very dull, which was why the love of his life had left.

He told me all about her during our 'date'. Two hours is a long time for a blind date but I felt so sorry for poor Jim and it ended up with me almost counselling him about how he might get help so he could recover some of his lost confidence.

There's Leon, who has three daughters, has been though an epic divorce battle and cheerfully told me he'd never have a bean again.

'Cleaned me out,' he said. 'Still, I want the girls to have a good life. The flat's fine, although they have to share the second bedroom when they come to stay. Mea culpa,' he added. 'I had the fling, it was my fault.'

I said I didn't know this and Leon looked a tad annoyed. 'I was sure Aunt Josie would have said that, just to warn you. She says you went through a hard time, what with your husband being killed and all that.'

'Yeah, hard time,' I agreed. Leon is too much of a player for me to want to say any more.

Mum is sorry that Leon and Jim weren't keepers but she's still hoping and it keeps her amused. Plus, it's keeping my mind off the absence of news at work about our impending doom. Dr Ryan discussed it but now isn't going anywhere after all, says Laoise, who has taken it upon herself to be the bringer of news on the office front. 'I think the move is off.'

Myself and Antoinette, with whom I job share, discuss that we now get anxious whenever Laoise approaches either of us on our shifts in case she has newly gleaned bad news about the doctors' plans to downsize.

'I need this job,' says Antoinette.

'Join the club,' I agree.

So I'm kept busy until, suddenly, the day the Family Tree project hits Luke and I, and it blows our lives out of the water.

To families with two parents living with their child, it must be easy, I think.

But not for us.

Worse, I didn't think it would hurt us and I had advance warning.

'That family tree bullshit – it's coming up,' Shazz says to me one week. We both knew it was coming, had been waiting since before Christmas.

'Lori reminded me,' Shazz went on. 'It's part of the New Year curriculum, always is in fourth class.'

Shazz has a friend with an older girl in the boys' school and she's like us, a single mother. She's very helpful for filling us in on issues in senior classes, so we're ready for them when they occur.

'Kids want both parents,' Shazz said to me one night while we're discussing the issue of being single parents. 'Why? Why aren't we enough? We give them everything.'

I swirl the wine around in my glass.

'They want to be like everyone else,' I say. 'We talk about

Jean-Luc, maybe not a lot, it's a long time ago now, so I try and keep his memory alive and say things like, *your dad would be so proud of you, Luke.* I mean he never asks anymore, which is odd. He used to wonder if he was like his dad but he literally never does these days.'

'No, Raffie doesn't do that either,' says Shazz, 'although he's nothing like that bastard.'

'One day he'll hear you, you know,' I say to her. 'You just can't call him that.'

'Yeah, you're right,' she said. 'I just get so angry, the fact that he just left, couldn't cope with it. Why can men father children if they are not going to go through with it properly? It's about more than just producing sperm, it's about being there, being a parent. Evolution got it all wrong.'

'Well,' I say, shrugging, 'Jean-Luc wanted to be a parent and he never got his chance, so I guess life doesn't work out the way we want it to, evolution or not.'

The school has always been pretty good when it came to looking after the kids who were in single-parent households. But there were still parents' evenings and teachers would forget and say things like, *Oh, maybe ask your dad about that.* The first time that had happened, the first time it had actually penetrated Luke's brain that he didn't have a dad, he'd been six years old, and when I picked him up from school he was crying.

'Mr McManus said I have to ask Dad something, but I can't and Raffie can't and we don't understand, and you have to make Mr McManus understand.'

Mr McManus was the boys' teacher at the time and he wasn't long out of teacher training college.

We'd got through that and when Lori had told us about the Family Tree project, we hoped we'd be ready and now it was here.

I tried discussing it with him in advance.

'Honey, I think the Family Tree project is coming up soon. We must get photos of the puppies for it,' I said brightly.

'Sausage and Doughnut will look beautiful. And maybe one of your dad? We can look through the box of photos together.'

I had photos of Jean-Luc in the house but somehow, they'd become part of the place rather than objects that stood out anymore. I'm not sure how that happened – maybe I was trying to protect Luke by not highlighting what he didn't have.

Luke didn't tell me the day they were given the project to start at home, but I knew. Shazz texts me that afternoon, when Luke had stomped upstairs to his room.

They got it, she says. Raffie is miserable and is sulking in his room. I didn't know what was wrong and he said, he's not going to school tomorrow, he's not doing his homework. I thought what the heck? Then I remembered, family-bloody-tree.

I think of Luke's pale little face as he sat in the back of the car coming home from school earlier, because he still isn't quite tall enough to sit in the front yet.

I go upstairs and he's sitting on his bed, not doing anything, not looking at a book or messing around, just sitting there.

'Mum,' he says, his little face serious, 'is my dad dead or did he just go? I know Raffie's dad is gone. But you have just been saying that, haven't you? Dad's not dead. All that stuff about how he'd have been proud of me doing stuff, you're making that up. He just ran away like Raffie's dad, didn't he?' I think my heart is going to shatter into a million shards. All these years I thought I was being a good mother, and I was holding it together and instead, I've ruined everything. I didn't want Luke to feel he was missing out by not having a father, so I tried to be Mum and Dad. And I'd mistakenly let his father figure drift into the background, because I didn't want Luke to know he'd lost so much. My son is ten and he thinks his father is a waster who ran away and left us, left *him*.

'Darling,' I stammer, 'I . . .' It's like the words are stuck in my throat; I don't know what to say. 'He's dead, your dad is dead, he died. I never showed you the piece from the newspaper but it was an accident. You have to believe me. Ask Granny.'

I sit down on the bed beside him, and then I slide onto the floor because I'm not sure what to say. I don't feel like the calm mother anymore. I feel like someone who has failed utterly. I turn around so that I'm facing him and I say, 'Luke, your dad and I were so in love and I was pregnant and none of this is a lie. A driver who had been drinking smashed into his car and he was gone.'

His little face stares at me, those eyes so like Jean-Luc's, and I think of all the things I have done wrong. Like nails shattering down out of the sky, piercing every part of me.

'I'm sorry, I'm sorry, Luke.'

Luke stares at me and I start to cry. I always swore I wouldn't cry in front of Luke, not letting him have to be my protector. He was a child and blast it all to hell, he would be allowed to be a child, not have to comfort his grieving mother.

He wouldn't have to be the man of the house, I could be both the mother and the father.

Or I thought I could.

He's staring at me, his face white.

'You still don't believe me, do you?' I say, shocked.

He shrugs, doesn't say anything. I can see the shimmer of a film of tears on his eyes. I get back up on the bed to try and get close to him, but he moves further away. 'Please let me hold you, let me hug you, please darling,' I say, begging.

'I just want a dad, like everyone else. Raffie wants a dad and he's got Zep now. I don't have anyone. Even the ones who live with their mums, they still see their dads at weekends, but I don't. What did we do wrong?'

'Nothing! We did nothing wrong. He died. Oh Luke, please believe me! I'm sorry, I'm so sorry,' I say. 'Will we look at his photographs?'

'I don't want photographs,' he says angrily.

'I'll ring Granny, get her over here and she can tell you.'

'She'll lie too!' he yells.

And it's like my beautiful, gentle son has turned against me.

233

He's angry because I have hurt him. In trying to protect him, I did it all wrong.

Then all my plans not to fall apart disintegrate.

'I love your dad, still love him, actually,' I say, and now I'm really crying. 'I love him for himself and I love him because he gave me you, but he died.'

'You just say that,' Luke shrieks at me.

'Oh Luke,' and I pull him to me. He's in my arms crying like he used to when he was smaller. I suddenly feel so angry with Jean-Luc because if only he was here, we wouldn't be going through this. I'd be happy and Luke would be happy and he wouldn't think he'd been abandoned.

'We need help with this, Lukie. Some clever person who can talk to us and will talk about how it's different when your dad dies instead of when he leaves.'

'I don't want to talk to anyone,' he says mulishly.

'We need to, darling. I've messed this up and we're going to do it right. Plus, we're going to talk more about your dad and you are going to tell me about how you feel, because you don't talk about this anymore.'

'Didn't want to hurt you,' he mutters, 'because I knew Dad made you sad. I hated him for that.'

So I do the thing I haven't done for a couple of years. I get down the big box of photos of pictures of myself and Jean-Luc when we were younger and I go through it slowly, pointing out places we went, things we did.

'See the way you are just like your dad there?'

'Yeah,' he says and he's smiling again. It's like he was afraid to ask, afraid of hurting me by bringing up his dad.

The pain nearly kills me. 'Do you feel different in school?' I say delicately, thinking of the Family Tree project. Why had I not been more ready for it?

'Yeah, there are kids like me and Raffie, but most of them have two parents, even if they are divorced, they've got two. Some of them have stepmums and dads and that's good and that's bad. Henry hates his stepmum. Says she's grumpy in the morning. But we just have you guys and the grannies and you know that's different. The other kids have dads that take them places and play football with them and . . . I don't have that.'

'You lost something precious, Luke, and so did I. And I thought it would be better if we just kept going, just you, me, Granny, Shazz, Norma and Raffie, and I thought we were family enough.'

'You are, you are,' my strong little boy says, 'but just some-times it's – you know –' he can't find the words and I understand because I can't find the words either.

'OK, let's talk about Dad more. We'll go to France on holi-days, see your granny and granddad there. Let's write them an email now, OK?'

'Why don't they come over here?' He's still suspicious.

'They did a little bit when you were younger, but it's been sad for them too. They weren't like Granny –' I pause – 'they didn't want to travel too much.'

'Why didn't we travel to see them?'

The truth was I'd always feared that Geneviève, Jean-Luc's mum, blamed me in some way. If Jean-Luc hadn't been living in another country with me, he'd never have been killed. 'I made a mistake and we are going to change that,' I say firmly.

I turn a few more pages of the album. There's the funny ones Jean-Luc took of my belly as I was getting bigger. The ones he took of both of us with him on the timer and him kneeling down and kissing my growing bump.

'See,' I say, 'he wanted you so much, darling. But your dad was very strong. He'd want us to miss him, because he was a super person and he'd want us to talk about him. But he would hate you to think that he didn't want you or that he left you.'

'No, I didn't think that,' Luke says suddenly, taking a deep breath, 'it was just this family-tree thing made me sad, and we have to bring in pictures.'

He's being brave, my strong darling son.

'How about we make it the best family tree in the class,' I say fiercely, 'the very best. We're going to email *Grandmère* right now and see what wonderful pictures she can come up with, ones I don't have.'

'Maybe we could Skype her?'

'Sure,' I say. We'd tried Skyping when he was little and Geneviève, found it very painful to look at the little boy who looked so like her lost son. I should have pushed it. I shouldn't have let the contact slip away. She's his grandmother. I have to make this right.

Finally, Luke's in bed asleep and I sit in the kitchen and cry. I have failed him so badly. I kept all men away thinking it was the right thing to do, but now it feels like I was wrong.

I find a bottle of white wine in a cupboard and open it, not caring that it's not the right temperature – the sort of thing Jean-Luc used to worry about. I've been holding on to the pain from the past too much. It's time to think about the future.

30
Sid

Friday evening and the January rain is coming down as if every cloud in the sky got an urgent memo to dump all supplies, now. I'm getting soaked as I run through the puddles, wondering why I'd got a bus rather than a taxi and was wearing a skirt and not my combat trousers.

Yet, I know why. Because I don't want to talk to one of my nice taxi drivers who know me well and will wonder about my outfit – very un-me – or why I'm quivering with weirdly excited nerves. I feel incredibly first datish, which is ludicrous because I genuinely can't think of the last time I went on a first date.

Head down, I make it to the Stella and Finn is there, waiting for me with a big umbrella, and I hurry and stand under it because, naturally, I have not brought mine.

'It wasn't raining when I left,' I say, and he smiles down at me. I've forgotten how tall he is, six something, Stefan's height. I'm useless at height. Most short people are. For the first time since I've met him, Finn is not in casual, where's-the-mountain clothes. He's wearing dark trousers, a very non-casual grey woollen jacket, white shirt and a fine grey sweater. He's dressed up. For this non-date involving two just-friends meeting to see a movie.

'Should we go in?' he says, his eyes never leaving my face and yet I feel he's taken in the skirt of my dress, my sheeny-hosiery legs in the neat little pumps I break out for important meetings.

And against some of my better judgement I nod, and with

one long arm he pushes the doors open and I brush past him into the heat.

I had gone online to look up the Stella. An old 1923 cinema, it's been refurbished to look like it might have done in more glamorous 1920s style, complete with a ritzy cocktail bar. It's an elegant cinema with lots of little table lamps and fabulous seating. He takes off my coat and gives it a little shake, because it's now just a soggy mess, and reaches out to touch my shoulders to see if I'm dry. Normally, I don't let people touch me, but this is OK, this is Finn checking whether I'm dry or not, the same way he needed to check if my rucksack was on correctly.

The cocktail bar is glorious with a chandelier and an air of utter excitement and glamour to it.

'This is beautiful,' I say.

'Yes, isn't it. The photos don't do it justice,' he says, looking around.

'You mean you haven't been here before?'

'No,' he says, 'not the sort of place I normally go.' He smiles at me, a smile that crinkles up his eyes and sucks all the oxygen from the room.

'But, you know, on other dates,' I ask, shocked to find that I'm actually angling for information about other women he might have taken out. Like Mags, or Ivanna the Terrible – was she tall and beautiful? I want to know. And what was so high-maintenance about her?

'You're the first person I thought of to bring here,' he says, 'because it's different, special, like something out of another age. And that seemed to sum up you.'

I keep my head down until we find a banquette, not wanting him to see that I'm blushing. We sit down and a waitress comes by and definitely shoots Finn an admiring glance. Hey, sister, hands off, he's mine, I want to say.

I recklessly order a Martini, while Finn sticks to sparkling water.

'I brought the car,' he says, 'so I could drive you home.'

We sit there for a minute in silence while I look around and I shiver because my cardigan is damp. Despite the heating, I'm cold, but I'll wait to take off my black cardigan when it's dark and he can't see.

'Take my jacket,' says Finn.

I look at him and his face is a little set, different to the way it normally is.

'Please,' he says, 'take off your cardigan and I won't look.'

I'm touched he's picked up on my shyness. Underneath I'm wearing a sleeveless dress, which is probably not the right thing to wear in Ireland in icy, wet January, but it was the most date-like thing in my wardrobe. I put his jacket on over me. It's huge and the soft silkiness of the lining is like a living thing draped around me, like his arms, and it feels wonderful. I fold it around me.

'Thank you,' I say.

'No problem,' he says.

'Gentlemen used to always provide ladies with their jackets when they were cold, didn't you ever see it in movies? And I used to wonder why the guys would sit there and not shiver?'

'Because it was the correct thing to do and gentlemen in those movies were not allowed to shiver; it was written into the contract: no shivering. Ruins the effect,' he quips, deadpan.

The film is starting, according to an announcement, and we get up. Me, bringing my wet cardigan with me.

'We can spread it out somewhere and it will dry,' he says. 'Here, give it to me.'

And he takes my cardigan and offers me his arm as we go towards the cinema.

'Is it this place?' I ask. 'Or have we slipped back in time to the nineteen twenties?'

Finn looks down at me.

'I think it's you,' he says and I feel that quiver inside.

He has got us an amazing seat to the back. Not the single luxurious seats further up, but curved, soft bench seats. The sort of ones all cinemas once came with, where courting couples could sit together, wrap their arms around each other and basically do things that did not involve looking at the screen. But I don't mind, I don't mind at all.

'It's a great place for a date, isn't it?' I say.

For a second his face is conflicted and he says, 'Sid, I didn't want to trick you but I thought you'd like this place and these seats were all they had. There was a cancellation.' He looks forlorn. 'We don't have to do this, we can go, we can find some pub where there's mad, loud music and people are getting happy and where we'll have to shout all evening to be heard above the noise. I'm sorry, I didn't mean to do this, it just fell into place and –'

I thought of Adrienne, 'life is full of risk'.

I haven't risked anything for fifteen bloody years.

'It's perfect,' I say. And I reach out and I take his hand. 'Let's go.'

And then we're sitting in this beautiful cosy seat. The space means we naturally sit quite close to each other and Finn turns and says to me gravely, gesturing with those large hands.

'I honestly didn't mean to do this to you, this wasn't my plan.'

'So you don't want a date?' I say. Whatever happens, I can take it. Just because I've built myself up into a state of excitement doesn't mean I'm going to crumble if he just wants to be friends.

'I'd love this to be a date,' he says slowly. 'I just didn't mean to bulldoze you.'

For the first time in forever, I reach up and touch his face and say 'No, this is lovely, perfectly lovely.'

He smiles and I allow myself to breathe out.

'Where is Sid and what have you done with her?'

'Still here,' I say lightly. 'Settle up there. Don't get any ideas but I want to lean back against you so I can stop shivering. Let's watch the film.'

I hear him sigh with contentment as I lean back against his big body and feel his warmth. I am not afraid. If this feeling of happiness is a risk, then it has to be risked. Just for this.

The film is wonderful, I'd forgotten how wonderful. I can remember watching it when I was a kid on our old, tiny, hopeless black-and-white television as Mum had never gone in for proper colour TVs or anything along those lines. But on some Saturday afternoons when Vilma was little and Mum would go back to bed for a rest, Stefan would take Vilma off to the park to wear her out, and I'd lie down on the squashy old couch in the big room and watch old movies, let myself fall into that romantic world where love conquered all. I thought that was the way life was supposed to be. I don't know how my father had left my mother when I was only little. But there had always been so much love to go around and I don't think I ever missed him. Stefan loved us all, we were his family, he would protect us, and I saw the way he and Mum were. I could believe in true love back then.

'They don't make them like that anymore,' says Finn, when it's over, as he unfolds his length and stands up in the cinema and stretches.

'No,' I say, 'they don't. That was wonderful, thank you. Can I go Dutch with you on the tickets?'

He looks at me assessingly.

'Well, it wasn't supposed to be a date, and it cost more than it should have cost for a non-date friend-zone thing, so just let me deal with this one.'

'I'll do the next one,' I say.

He beams. 'Perfect.'

Outside, the rain has stopped but Finn insists I wear his jacket as mine is still wet through.

'You'll freeze,' he says.

'And you won't?'

'I'm a big strong man,' he says jokily, walking along beside me, hovering protectively.

I feel strangely safe and I *never* feel safe. Not really. And then I check myself, because safe isn't always safe. My brain runs its circuit of checks and it still comes back to the same answer, this is OK. Finn is good, he isn't going to hurt me, I can tell.

'*This* is your car, really?'

We stand in front of a rather old, battered Mini. It's small and he's tall. A vision of getting a certain number of clowns into a Mini comes to mind.

'How do you even get into it?'

'With the seat pushed all the way back,' he says. 'I think I have made a sort of bump in the ceiling where my head is,' he adds gravely. 'It is not the ideal car for someone of six foot three, but I have the motorbike, and I couldn't exactly drive you home on that.'

'You didn't know you were going to be driving me home?' I counter.

'I sort of hoped I would be. Have I messed up with the friend thing?' he says, looking me straight in the eye when we are both in the car, and I have stopped laughing at how amusing it is, watching a man of his size folded up into a Mini.

I look down at my lap.

'No, you haven't messed things up,' I say, 'not one bit.'

I direct him to my apartment, and I know absolutely that I could invite him in, but I'm not going to. I'm not ready, not yet.

Gallantly, after unfolding himself from the car, he helps me out. He then walks me up the steps to the apartment-building door.

'You're still in nineteen-twenties mode,' I say.

'It's you,' he says, 'you do that to me.'

'Really? A nineteen-twenties gentleman would not have made a lady go on a twenty-kilometre hike,' I point out, and he laughs.

'It wasn't twenty kilometres.'

'It felt like it.'

I slip the jacket off my shoulders and reach up to him, put it around his, but I can't quite make it. Instead, he balances his jacket over one arm and then two hands with their long fingers catch my face.

'Thank you,' he says. 'Thank you, Sid. Tonight was lovely.'

His lips come down on mine, warm and soft. I'm not afraid. It just feels right. I feel a pooling of warmth deep in me, and I think, oh right, yes. Then the heat of his lips is gone and he's standing up.

'Go in,' he says, 'you'll get cold. Is it safe in there?'

'Security cameras all over the place,' I say.

'Text me when you're in your apartment.'

I nod.

'I'm not saying that in a crazy, possessive stalkery way,' he adds, as he shrugs back into his jacket. 'But just text me.'

I nod and I slip in. As the lift doors close on me, he's still standing outside watching, like a knight.

After I bolt the third lock on my apartment, I send him a text. Thanks for a beautiful night, I'm home, Sid. I don't add a kiss or a funny emoji, I'm not a funny-emoji sort of person, except for Vilma and Mum.

The lovely glow inside me continues, something I don't know if I've ever felt before, something soft. But I do know I don't want it to go away.

31

Marin

Louise phones me up so we can talk about our beloved daughters going off on their six-month trip around the world.

'Hello, stranger,' I say, and I know there's an edge to my voice. I feel as if there's a permanent edge to my voice these days. Even Bernie in work has mentioned it.

'You doing all right, Marin love?' she's asked more than once when I've been sitting at my desk, knowing I look glum and not being able to change my face. Not even having bulging shopping bags in my car boot can cheer me up. I'm spending worse than ever and Nate seems to think I'm in perimenopausal hell as he's giving me a wide berth.

I still haven't asked him if he's having an affair: instead, I'm buying the world.

'I can't believe they'll be gone in a few weeks,' sighs Louise on the phone, ignoring my edgy tone.

At the thought of Rachel being gone away with Megan, I burst into tears.

Bernie looks up from her notepad where she's been writing something about a showing in Shankill that's been cancelled.

'Marin,' says Louise in surprise, 'what's wrong?'

'Nothing,' I lie.

'Are you in work?'

'Yes.'

'Can you escape for an hour?'

I look at my desk with all the things I have yet to do, think of the house I have to show this evening at seven-thirty, and tell her I can't.

'Tomorrow, after school drop off. Come for a ten-minute coffee in mine,' she says. 'I'm working from home and you won't be late – you'll speed into work because you'll miss the worst of the traffic.'

'Yes,' I mutter. 'See you then.'

The next morning, I arrive at Louise's house and think that it is simply months since I've been here. With Megan and Rachel so close, I used to spend hours here. Louise and I became firm friends and it's only in the past few months that she's more or less vanished.

Louise is dressed in her at-home gear of jeans and blouse, in case she has to do a Zoom call. She's a banking executive and has one day a week working from home, which she says she loves. 'I get far more done on those days than when I'm in the office.'

She hugs me. Louise is such an affectionate person and as she holds me, I feel as if we're connecting suddenly in the way I've missed for so long.

'Now, in case you're worried about the girls' trip, I've been making lists for them – calendar reminders of when they're to email and WhatsApp us, notes on the consulates in every place they're going. Even a book on customs for single-female travellers!' She waves the book at me. 'But Marin, is that what's wrong? Is it the girls' trip, or is it something else?'

I want to bleat that she's been avoiding me, that we haven't had a heart-to-heart talk for ages, but I don't.

Instead I say: 'It's Nate and me . . .'

In a quieter voice, she says: 'Come on in, I've got coffee on.'

We sit in her kitchen and she finally tells me.

'I'm sorry, Marin – I didn't know what to do. If I told you and I was wrong, you'd never forgive me. The messenger is always the one in trouble . . .'

'If you told me what?'

She hesitates, then says: 'I saw Nate coming out of a hotel

in town one afternoon, with a tall blonde woman. I didn't see her face because she was facing the other way, but he kissed her goodbye.'

My heart doesn't sink: it plummets. I've been kidding myself that I was imagining things. But here are two riddles solved: the one about why Louise hasn't been able to talk to me and the one about Nate.

'Do you think it could be Angie, Steve's wife?'

She considers this and shrugs. 'I can't say. Honestly. But I'm really sorry for telling you, Marin. And for not telling you. It could be totally innocent –'

'Hardly,' I say, and I fill her in on what I saw at Christmas.

With a willing listener, it all comes tumbling out. The gift receipt, his cornflower-blue shirt, all my fears.

'I didn't want to believe, but I knew something was wrong,' I say, 'and I kept hoping I was imagining it, that he was going through a mid-life crisis or something. But it's not just me who's seen something, you have too –'

'Nate loves you, though,' Louise says. 'Men – men are different. We love with all our hearts but they're not the same. They can honestly have sex and it can mean nothing to them. For us, it does.'

'So it meant something to the blonde woman and nothing to him? I don't care!' I cry. 'It matters to me. I love him and he's slept with another woman.'

'I didn't see that –' she begins, but I stop her.

'What else would he be coming out of a hotel with another woman for?' I say. 'It's got to be that. He's got someone else.'

I feel like I'm crumbling from the inside: my security blanket was that I was loved. Without that belief, I am nothing.

I sit at Louise's kitchen table and sob. My breathing is laboured and I think, brokenly, of how Rachel and Joey argued about people breathing properly, and how I was happy then. Or maybe I wasn't really happy – I simply didn't know all the facts. I was unhappiness in waiting. Now it's arrived in all its painful glory. I try to work out was I better when I'd just wondered if Nate was unhappy – or if the proof is the rock falling onto me, crushing me. I don't know the answer. But I feel crushed, all right. Crushed into pieces.

32

Bea

I walk through the front door and begin texting Mum to let her know how it went.

'Piers was lovely, Mum, but no romance. Sorry!'

Mum has almost given up the blind-date thing because it's been so bad, but finally she's met one of her friends' nephews and says, 'He's good-looking and funny. I think dinner wouldn't be a hardship.'

It's not a hardship at all, even though Piers and myself know within five minutes that there's not a spark between us, but he's truly entertaining. Luke and the puppies are staying over at Mum's, so we linger over coffee and tell stories about our blind dates from hell.

'If you ever need a fun night out,' he says to me as we leave the restaurant, 'give me a buzz.'

'Right back at you,' I say, cheerfully, thinking that if only all the dates were like this funny, non-date one, then who needed a man in their life?

I'll fill Mum in on the details in the morning but now, I angle my head as I hear something odd.

Water, water dripping from somewhere. It's coming from the kitchen.

I race in to find the floor near the sink awash with water. Something is leaking and, after ten minutes, I still can't stop the leaking or figure out what to do. The pool of water is growing slowly, so I've thrown towels on it. I'm worrying about the cost of getting a plumber out at half nine on a Saturday evening when the phone rings: Marin.

Briefly, I consider not answering because I have this crisis to figure out, but autopilot kicks in and I pick up.

We haven't talked since Christmas and she's ringing for a chat.

'Nate has had some work thing on,' she says brightly, and I'm not sure why, but she sounds a little off.

'Myself, Rachel and Joey are here and we've had a takeaway – bliss not to cook. They're arguing over what Disney movie to watch.

'*Frozen Two*,' I manage to joke, because Joey's true adoration for this movie shows no sign of abating. Nate hates this, he doesn't understand why Joey doesn't want to watch some macho little boy movie. But, no, he's a *Frozen* boy. And Marin, normally so yielding with Nate, takes no crap when it comes to Joey's obsession with the Disney princesses.

'Possibly,' says Marin, and I'm distracted from her odd tone by the continual leaking of whatever it is under the sink.

'Ah, that sounds lovely,' I say, 'but you know what, I'm going to have to hang up. I'm going to try Finn and see if he's around because I've got a leak in the kitchen and if he's not there, it's time to call the emergency plumber.'

I'd had to ring the emergency plumber before. And when he left, I was quite surprised he wasn't driving off in an S-Class Mercedes because of the amount he charged me just for the pleasure of coming out to my house on a Friday evening.

'Finn's out with Sid,' says Marin. 'I'll phone Nate,' she offers.

'That's so kind of you, Marin,' I say, mentally shelving the option of phoning Finn, 'but if Nate is at a business thing, you can hardly get him out on the grounds that his wife's friend is having a problem with a leak.'

'Just let me ring him, OK? He said he wouldn't be late, would just be out for a couple of hours. So you never know.'

She rings back to say he's coming, so I make tea and wait. Twenty minutes later, a taxi deposits Nate at my door. He's been drinking and he looks even more piratical than normal, dark hair ruffled, smelling of strong woody eau de cologne and brandy. He's wearing a suit too, although he's loosened the tie. These are clearly important clients, which is why he's dressed up so much.

'You're home early,' I say. I haven't any energy for conversation. The buzz of the evening out with Piers has worn off. I wish I'd made it just drinks so I could pick up Luke instead of letting him sleep at my mother's. The house feels so lonely without him.

'Oh, I managed to pawn them off,' he says. 'Some of these people would wreck your head, Bea, do you know that?'

'No,' I say. 'Listen, Nate, far be it for me to refuse an offer of you coming to help me with my plumbing but you're plastered. What good are you going to be? Really kind of you and everything, but let me call you a taxi and send you home, OK? We'll manage tonight and I'll send Finn a text in the morning, he's normally up early on Sundays.'

'I can handle a boiler just as well as Finn, drunk or not.'

Nate is always the most competitive person in the room. He has macho running through his body like whorls of writing through a seaside stick of rock.

'Come in,' I mutter, 'and let's get you a cup of coffee while I call the cab.'

I need this like I need a hole in the head. It's time for the emergency plumber.

'No,' he says, taking off his suit jacket and hanging it on the newel post. He loosens his tie and undoes the top three buttons. 'You just need to shut the water off, silly, and yes, coffee would be good. They were throwing wine into us earlier.'

He follows me into the kitchen. My cottage kitchen is big enough for possibly three people at a stretch, but only if they're small people. I'm tall and Nate is altogether too big for my kitchen. I try to think of the last time he's actually been here alone without Marin, and I can't. It was the way it was. My friendship was with Marin now, and when I saw them, it was as a couple. Finn drops over from time to time, but that's different. Finn's a friend, but Nate, leaning against the door jamb watching me intensely, feels weird tonight.

'Show me your tool bag,' he says.

'How'd you know I have a tool bag?' I ask.

'Because Marin told me. She says you are brilliant, you can do everything. Except think to turn off the water.'

I open the cupboard under the stairs, where I keep the tools along with the vacuum cleaner, the ironing board, ancient bits of discarded sports equipment of Luke's. And all sorts of other odds and ends that I'm always meaning to tidy out but never get round to.

Nate pulls the bag out.

'All right,' he says, examining it all like a surgeon looking at new theatre equipment. 'I can fix whatever's wrong. I'm pretty handy around the house, you know.'

'Have your coffee,' I say, handing it to him, 'and forget about the leak. I'll cope till tomorrow.'

But Nate's already pulled off his suit jacket and is under the sink, strong shoulders and arms reaching in and doing whatever it is that men do when faced with plumbing problems.

'Look, just leave it, will you, you're plastered.'

'I think it's nothing more serious than a burst pipe,' he says.

'Really?'

'Yeah, it's obvious.'

I stifle the urge to slap the back of his head.

'Bet you I figured it out quicker than Finn.'

'God, you're so competitive,' I say, laughing at him, because it reminds me of him all those years ago.

'What's wrong with that?' he demands. 'Men are competitive, Bea: it's testosterone. Evolution, etc., etc.'

He takes a slurp of coffee and grins suddenly.

'Can you stick a bit of whiskey in it?' he asks. 'And a dollop of cream?'

I raise my eyes to heaven but give in. As he fills a couple of big saucepans with water and then searches for the stopcock to turn it off until the morning, I make two Irish coffees. It's probably last Christmas since the bottle of whiskey came out in this house, I think, as I take a sip of mine.

'I won't send a bill,' he says, standing up to take his.

We sit at the kitchen table drinking slowly, not talking, and I enjoy the subtle sweetness of the Irish coffee. I used to have a drinks measure, I think. This is definitely a double but I know I'll sleep after it.

'Another one would be lovely but a mistake,' says Nate, finishing his and getting to his feet. I finish mine too and stand up. He'll need a taxi now, I think, and wonder where I put my phone so I can check the taxi app.

But suddenly, Nate smiles that lazy smile, pulls me towards him as if we were still going out like crazy twenty-year-olds, and I'm held in Nate's arms, my whole body pressed up against his body. He's lowering his mouth to mine. The first flare of wrongness disappears.

It's the first time I've been held like this since Jean-Luc died.

And, oh forgive me, I don't push him away.

It's like some ancient body memory, this being held.

You've missed this, my body is saying and I lean into him and as if I have no control, I kiss him back. My hands go round to hold him and he fixes his on my waist, large hands, then splaying down to cup my buttocks and pull them closer.

I know this is wrong, wrong on every level, wrong because he's Marin's husband. Marin, my friend! Wrong because me and Nate were in the past when we were kids.

But then his hands are in my hair and he's whispering to me, and even though I know it's utterly wrong, I don't stop him.

I'm held against his chest and he's murmuring into my ear about how beautiful I am.

'Fragile and elegant,' he murmurs.

When his fingers reach up under my silky sweater, I moan. It's like having somebody point something out to you that you had never known you'd missed and I am lost. I kiss him back, just one kiss, I think, letting my body press even more closely against his and it feels so lovely just for once to have this closeness, this tenderness, in my life.

It's dark. I wake up and sit bolt upright in the bed. There's something wrong. And I can't think what it is and then I realise; there's a strange smell of alcohol and beside me in the bed is Nate. Nate is in bed beside me and he's naked and snoring. I'm in bed with him. Naked. Oh Jesus. We had sex. Actual sex. I can't believe this, I cannot believe I did this. I know I was at a low ebb with the sense of a sweet date that would never mean anything behind me, and no sign of true love ahead of me, and he was there. I just wanted to feel held and not the person who was always in charge . . . but how could I let this happen?

What have I done?

I have to get Nate out of the house and nobody must know. But I know.

I know, oh God, I know.

I close my eyes and I cry, great heaving sobs. I wriggle out of the bed, because I don't want to be beside him.

I'll have to burn the bed. I can't have him in it. I can't have his memory in it. This was the bed I shared with Jean-Luc and it's old and needs a new mattress and now it's tainted for good.

I reach for my phone. Half two in the morning. I've got to get him out of here. Now.

I go into the bathroom and stare at myself in the mirror and I look the way I always look: pale, my hair dark, grey bits, my eyes shadowed.

Why now, why now? Look at all those stupid men people have been pushing towards me at parties for years, people's nephews and friends and 'oh he'll be perfect for you'. Men like the Teds of this world who are never going to be perfect for anyone. And I said no, because I didn't need them. I didn't want them.

Me and Luke are perfect together and now in this moment of weakness, not long after the pain from that bloody Family Tree project, just because I was lonely, I have fallen into this hole of disaster.

Just then, a thought occurs to me. Maybe he's done this before. Marin had told me about Rachel and that horrible night when she was missing in town for an hour. Nate was supposedly off with colleagues and his phone wasn't working, or he didn't hear it or some ludicrous excuse. Is this what he's been doing with other women? And now I'm just as bad, worse even, because I'm her friend.

I can't ever be her friend again. The thought makes my heart ache.

I run back into the bedroom, grab a pair of jeans, boots and pull on a sweater. Downstairs I make some very strong coffee and order him a taxi.

I bring up the coffee and I shake him hard.

'Drink this,' I say loudly. He wakes up blearily and looks at me.

'Hi, baby, that was sexy, you were always sexy.'

'Nate!' I say, horrified the way I wasn't horrified a while ago. 'Don't. We've done a dreadful thing.' I hand him the coffee and try not to cry.

Two-shot espresso, no sugar, no milk, straight-into-the-vein caffeine. If I had a syringe I would stick it straight into him.

'Drink that, throw on your clothes, you're getting out of here. You've got to go home.'

'No rush,' he says reasonably, 'maybe we can do it again . . .'

'No we cannot! I was weak, weak! We cannot ever let Marin know or it will destroy her. I haven't had a man since Jean-Luc. I now realise you might do this routinely, but I do not.'

'Shit, Really?' He looks horrified at the idea of no sex for over ten years.

'Yes, really. And I would not have chosen you if I had been in my right mind. I do not mess with married men.'

Saying the words makes me feel how much I've betrayed Marin. This is her husband, not mine. Why didn't I send him away, why didn't I push him away earlier?

'Nate,' I say in desperation, 'get up, get out and be quiet. I don't want my neighbours seeing you leaving.'

Dublin is a village and word spreads. I can't bear the thought of how this will hurt Marin.

I send him outside as the lights of the taxi appear in the dark and lean against the door, locking the big lock. I can feel the fear in me, making my body vibrate with fear and anxiety. Then I go back upstairs, strip the bed. Stuff everything in the washing machine. Have the hottest shower I can bear, put on different clothes. Make my bed again after turning the mattress over.

I lie in an uneasy sleep until dawn comes. I wake up every half an hour, shaking, anxious, aware that some fabric of my life has shifted and there is nothing I can do about it.

33
Sid

The poster for the Rape Crisis Centre parachute jump practically leaps out at me. It's synchronicity at work, I think, as I stare at it. The traffic has stalled on my route into the office and because the car simply isn't moving, I have time to look carefully and note the website.

At work, I check the site and see that if I can raise two thousand euros, I can do a tandem jump in ten days and all but two hundred euros of the money goes to the charity.

There's a fundraising page and I join it, looking at all the eager faces who've already posed excitedly online about how much money they've raised. I'm coming late to the party when it comes to fundraising. But without even considering how much I don't like heights, I know that this is something I've got to do.

Fear keeps you in your little cage so that you can see the outside world but not get out.

Not anymore, I think. Time to fly.

You're doing what? Finn replies to my text.

You read it right, I answer back happily. Can you forward this to anyone who might donate a fiver or a tenner?

Of course. But can I come?

I don't have a lot of time to raise the money but Mum, Stefan and Vilma come to my rescue, along with what must be everyone in Finn's college.

With four days to spare, I've raised more than two thousand euros.

On the Friday evening before the jump, Adrienne and I are last in the office.

'I'm skipping the drinks this evening,' I say, as we walk out the door, with us both saying bye to Imelda, who has nearly finished the evening clean.

'No Dutch courage,' she says.

I glance at her.

'Tea,' I say. 'Lots of herbal tea to help me sleep. The last thing I want to do is drink too much to blot out the impending fear, then wake up with a dreadful hangover and not be able to do it,' I reply.

Adrienne nods. 'It does sound scary but anyone who's jumped always says it's amazing. One friend's mother is still sky diving at seventy.'

'I'd say this will be my only jump,' I say with total confidence. 'I'm terrified of heights.'

'What?'

I realise that I have actually shocked Adrienne. Which I'd thought was impossible up until this point.

'*Now* you're shocked?' I demand. 'I thought you belonged to the "do what scares you" school of thought?'

'What scares you in a metaphorical sense,' she says. 'Not what bloody terrifies you. Why put yourself through that?'

I don't answer straight off. Instead I explain about Vilma's roof climbing: 'When she was about ten, Vilma used to climb onto the kitchen roof from her bedroom, and I was terrified the first time I saw her do it.'

I can still see it in my mind.

'It's safe,' Vilma had said airily.

'Get in!' I'd shrieked.

'You get out,' she said.

I hadn't. I'd run downstairs to find Stefan.

'Fear is what terrifies me,' I tell Adrienne. 'I can guarantee you that I won't jump again but I'm jumping tomorrow.'

*

Finn is driving me down to the Kildare parachutists' club where the gang of Rape Crisis Centre charity jumpers are to gather. It's a cool morning and I'm nervous but Finn drives most of the way with his left hand holding on to my right one, only taking it off to change gear.

We don't talk and it's strangely peaceful in the early morning light. Because the weather is changeable, we have to be there at half eight, so we can complete our training and be jumping by lunch.

I'm jumping out of a plane in a few hours, I think, watching the landscape pass by in a blur. But it's going to be all right, I know. I hold on to Finn's hand and I know this is the right thing to do.

He hasn't asked me why I'm doing it: he's simply there with me, supporting me. I haven't explained a thing. I don't need to.

Only jumpers are allowed into the training area and once we're in our flight suits, all twenty-four of us, twenty women and four men, are brought through the training technique over and over again: how to exit the plane, how to use our emergency chute if we need to and how to land, which is a tricky manoeuvre unless you fancy breaking your legs.

'Just because it's a tandem jump, don't think you can coast,' says the instructor, 'no puns intended.'

We have coffee before it's jump-off time and I'm happy to be in the second group of four going up. The clouds are moving in and if they do, the jumping will stop till tomorrow. I'm ready now – I might have become properly frightened by tomorrow.

Finn's sitting in a cosy room with some other drivers and one half-asleep father who has brought twin daughters for a twenty-first birthday jump.

I go straight to Finn and hug him.

'I'm scared,' I whisper, now that it's almost time. I can hear the whine of the plane taking off with the first team. I have ten minutes to be out there for my turn.

'You'll be safe,' he whispers into my hair. 'I'll be waiting for you.'

On the plane, it's so loud that I can't hear my teeth chattering with fear. The other jumpers are grinning, and the tandem instructors are so relaxed, I almost can't bear it.

'You OK, Sid?' says Carla, the female instructor jumping with me. 'It's a blast but you don't have to. There's no shame in admitting that it's not for you.'

It's that word again. I can feel my spine strengthen as the steel comes back into it.

'Oh, I'm jumping.'

I must have spoken out loud.

Carla grins at me.

She expertly hooks us together and when the small plane's engine is shut off and we're flying on the wind, coasting like a bird of prey riding a thermal, Carla and I make our way over to the fuselage door which has been pulled open.

Beneath us, two thousand feet below, everything looks like a child's toy farm, with fields spread out around us and the parachute centre nothing but a tiny little collection of buildings.

I know the statistics: two minutes for me and Carla to land, if all goes to plan. Thirty-seven seconds to drop to earth if not.

I'm frightened but I've been far more frightened and that fear has held me in its grip for too long. Not anymore, I think.

'Ready? Three, two, one –'

And we're gone, into the air speeding down until Carla pulls – I mean, she must – the rip cord and we jerk up.

'Look up,' she yells and I look to see the beautiful sight of an opened chute above me. I breathe in, letting the glorious air fill my lungs.

'See?' she says joyously. 'Isn't it amazing!'

I exhale slowly and yell back. 'Yes. Amazing.'

Some fears are meant to be faced after all.

PART THREE

Witch Hazel Blossoming

34
Marin

I wake up in the morning and I'm in bed alone. There's no sign of Nate and I'm feeling ripples of fear run through me. It's a combination of everything I've been feeling and thinking for so long. I get out of bed, race into the shower and let water stream over me. I don't just want to wash him out of my hair, I want to wash him out of my life. I get dressed quickly. It's half six; normally I'm not awake or dressed this early on a Sunday morning. But I get myself ready, because I feel I have something to face.

It's an instinct. Ancient.

I refuse to sit in bed waiting for him to come home on a Sunday morning, smiling and saying: 'Oh babe, how are you, you were out all night?' I've just had it up to here. I go downstairs and make the strongest coffee I can cope with and some toast. But I can't eat the toast. Who can I ring? I need to talk to someone.

April, who warned me, of all the people to warn me. That it should be April, still astonishes me. I dial her number.

'What's wrong, Marin?' she says, answering instantly. 'Has something happened? Is it Ma, Dad? Tell me.'

'It's Nate,' I say. 'He didn't come home last night. And you know what, he's been late home so often and I couldn't tell you. I think he's having an affair with Angie.'

'Angie?'

'Yeah, Louise saw him with a blonde woman, although she couldn't see who it was, and then I saw them having a weird moment at the Christmas party. It has to be Angie. I haven't

had the courage to confront him. I thought he'd leave me . . .'
There: I've admitted it.

'I'm so sorry, lovie,' she says. It doesn't escape me that April, who is always the other woman, is feeling sorry for me because my husband is cheating on me. 'But how do you *know*?'

'I just know,' I say.

'Well, you can't put up with that, I mean, he's got –' she stops. 'No I'm not going to tell you what he's got to do. What do *you* think he's got to do?'

'I don't know,' I say and suddenly I want to cry. 'We've got two children, we've got a life. What do I do? Just say get out of here now and let's sell the house and I'm going to try and make it on my own. I don't know what to do.'

And then I hear a noise downstairs.

He can't have been here all along? His side of the bed wasn't slept in. But –

'I think he's home,' I say suddenly. 'I'll ring you later.'

I stalk downstairs and he's in the kitchen, in underpants, socks and a T-shirt he must have found in the laundry basket.

He's clearly just woken up, so he must have been here.

'When did you get home?' I demand.

'Too late. I didn't want to wake you,' he mutters. 'I slept on the couch, which is bloody uncomfortable and oh hell, have we got any of the strong ibuprofen because my head is splitting?'

In his half-dressed state, smelling of alcohol and looking unshaven, he looks precisely like he slept on the couch.

'I'm really sorry, Marin,' he said. 'I just got pissed and when I got home, I made it into the kitchen and some bit of brain came alive. I couldn't crawl into bed with you like that . . .'

And he falls into my arms and somehow my arms go around him.

'You weren't with anyone,' I say, my voice shrill.

'Jesus, don't shout so close to my head,' he says. 'You know, Marin, stop imagining shit. I went out, I got pissed, and I am a moron. At least I didn't wake you at whenever time it was when I got here.'

'I didn't think you'd come home,' I said and I don't know how, but normality is restored. And I'm not thinking he's cheating or that he's cheated. He couldn't come in and be like this, be normal. Nobody can lie like this, surely? No, I'm imagining it.

'Get upstairs and have a shower and get into bed,' I say, 'and just try to do dry spring. There's far too much drinking in your job.'

'I'm not an alcoholic.'

'I don't think you're an alcoholic, I think you're a moron,' I say.

'Why are you up so early anyway?' he says, his eyes bleary.

'I woke up and you weren't here and I was worried.'

'Oh baby, you thought I was in hospital or somewhere, I'm so sorry.'

He hugs me. I don't smell anything on him, I don't smell any perfume or any woman or anything, it's just unshaven man. His teeth aren't brushed, surely if he was sleeping with someone else he'd have made a bit of a better effort?

'Go to bed,' I say.

It's like a weight has been lifted. How could I think the worse of him. Sure, he's a selfish bastard sometimes but I don't get him doing enough around the house and with the kids. That's my fault for needing to do everything. Things are going to change around here. First, I'm going to cut up all my credit cards. That would be a wonderful start. Yes, that's it. That's a big part of the problem.

35
Bea

How do you measure the worst week of your life?

On Monday I can't go into work.

'Mum, what's wrong?' says Luke.

'Just feel sick,' I say, 'I don't know what it is, it's a bug.'

It's not a bug, but I am sick, I literally haven't been able to keep any food in my stomach since I got Nate out of the house and I feel so weak. I'm drinking those replacement salts because I'm afraid I will actually get sick. But all I can think of is, what have I done, what have I done? Just for a moment of not thinking. And I've hurt Luke, because he's so precious and to think that I'm his mother and I've done something like this. And Marin, and I love Marin . . .

How I've betrayed her. I think of the time she came to me when Luke was a newborn and she was so heavily pregnant with Joey and she waddled in the door with another gift, with some food, with something, *anything* to help me.

'What's up with you?' says Shazz when she comes to pick up Luke to bring him to school.

'Just feel like shit,' I say.

'You look like shit,' she says.

'I must have some sort of bug or something, I can't eat.'

'But Luke's OK?'

'Luke's fine.'

'You sure you don't need to go to the doctor, get a – I don't know, injection or something?'

There's no injection for this, I think, absolutely no medication whatsoever.

I take the week off work. I'm so reliable, nobody suspects a thing. I literally cannot face people. In the day time, I sit with the puppies and I hold them and pet them. And Mum and Cliff, who's been partnering her in bridge recently, come and walk them for me.

'You poor darling,' says Mum. 'Now, I've brought you some chicken soup. You know it's the best thing.'

'Penicillin,' says Cliff, smiling in that lovely paternal way he has. He'd be a lovely granddaddy for Luke, I think. What sort of person would he think I am if he knew what I'd done? Mum won't judge me because she loves me and she loves Luke. But how can any other normal person think I'm anything but dirt? One of those other women. Before, I just thought of other women as Shazz and Christie, women who held me together, who were my family. Now I realise there can be many types of other women.

Somehow the week passes and it's Thursday. Shazz calls me first thing, before Luke has left for school.

'Why doesn't Luke come and spend the night with us and we'll bring him to school in the morning? It will be sort of a bit of fun, you've had a low week. And it's been hard on him too. Send him in with an overnight bag, your mum can mind the dogs and you can just sleep and do absolutely nothing.'

I'm beginning to feel marginally better. I can eat a little. The chicken soup does work. And the thought of being on my own in the house, even without the beautiful dogs, helps; it would be peaceful. I can exorcise the memory of Nate in here. I could pray in each room, pray for forgiveness, even though I'm not religious.

'That would be lovely.'

Shazz is off organising it in a flash.

That evening I fall asleep in front of the TV. I started watching a thriller and then the tiredness pulled me under, and suddenly I'm awake. I hear a tapping noise on the window and I get an awful fright. I look at my phone quickly, it's ten-forty.

Only Shazz would do this – but she has keys . . .? Something must have happened to Luke. I run to the door and unlock it and wrench it open. And there is Nate.

'Hey, babe,' he says, and he's smiling at me like it's over twenty years ago and we're dating.

'Nate?' I say in disbelief. 'You can't come in. Not now, not ever again.'

'Oh, honey, don't be like that. I've thought about nothing but you all week,' he says, and before I know it, he's in the house.

'Get out,' I say.

'Babe, don't be like that,' he says. 'Look, last week was such a wake-up call for me. I've always been crazy about you, Bea. You must know that.'

I can't think of a thing to say for a full minute.

'No, I don't know that,' I hiss. 'You're married to Marin, we're friends, remember?'

He's back in the kitchen and he looks, in some automatic male way, under the sink. 'You got this fixed, right?'

'Yes and don't change the subject.'

'I can do things for you like that now,' he says, going for the kettle.

'Nate, what are you talking about?'

'Now we're together. Where do you keep the glasses? I'll have a straight one of those whiskeys from last week.'

'We're not together.'

'Bea, last weekend in bed, it was amazing. I know you felt it too. Then, your mum was talking to Marin and said you weren't well, needed a little time on your own. I can pick up the hints, you know. Of course it would have been easier if you had rung me yourself.'

I feel something akin to panic. This cannot be happening. Nate is a good man – dumb, for sure, because how can he not be reading my reactions, but a good man. Has he lost the run of himself entirely? He's had a few drinks, I can tell. He likes good wine. How am I going to get him out of here?

'We are not a thing,' I say. 'Last week was a mistake.'

'You don't mean that,' he says, eyes glittering.

Yes, definitely a bit drunk.

'Darling Bea, I can't stop thinking about you, how lonely you've been. I'm not leaving Marin, I love her, but I hate to think of you being so lonely.'

'I'm not,' I say. 'And marriages don't work like that – you don't come round to your old girlfriend's every weekend and then play house with your wife the rest of the time, Nate!'

I am so angry, I think I am going to hit him.

He honestly thinks this is a helpful plan.

'There's always been something between us. And who's to know? It's not going to do anyone any harm. You don't want anything serious, you still love Jean-Luc, we all know that. But everyone needs love in their lives, Bea, and you're so lovely. Jean-Luc would hate to see you so lonely.'

I stop backing away at this ludicrous statement.

'You want to have sex with me because Jean-Luc would want it? Seriously?'

'Well . . .'

I have to get him out of the house. I left my own phone on the couch in the living room, which makes me furious because it's far easier to ring the emergency services from a mobile than it is from a house phone. Mobiles are easier to tap out numbers on.

'Why don't you take your coat off,' I say, stalling for time. If he's preoccupied, I can run to the living room and phone someone – but who? Finn? How would I explain this? My mother and Cliff? Worse. The police. Say he's drunk, an old friend, can they get him home . . .?

'Aha!' He's found the whiskey and he's got two glasses. 'I believe we have the house to ourselves.' While he's taking his coat off, I run into the other room, grab the phone and I dial 999. I'm just about to press the green button and he appears at the kitchen door and says, 'What are you doing?'

'I'm ringing the police,' I say. 'You've got to get out of here.'

'You can't do that, you can't ring the police. I mean Jesus, stop it.' And he lurches towards me.

I run away into the kitchen and slam the door and shove the kitchen table in front of it, which is absolutely no good because Nate is strong, he's like a bull, he'll get through anything.

'I am going to ring the police,' I shout. 'Or would you like it if I rang Marin first? Your call.'

Please let him just go home and leave me alone. I am not able for this.

'Don't ring Marin,' he says. It's the first time he doesn't sound like Mr In Control.

'I'll ring Marin,' I warn. 'She is my friend.'

'You weren't thinking of that last week.'

'Last week you caught me at a weak moment and I did something so stupid and shameful. But you – you put your arms around a woman who was vulnerable and we hurt Marin . . .'

Suddenly there's this weird, lightly strangled noise outside the door. I hear the door creak, like something has just banged into it and an odd noise like someone being kicked.

'Nate, Nate?'

I run around the other door of the kitchen, the one that leads from the dining room to the living room back into the hall. Nate is lying on the ground crumpled up, holding his left arm. His jaw constricted, his face white.

I click the green button on the phone. 'I need an ambulance,' I say. 'I think he's having a heart attack.' And I give them my address.

36
Sid

Stefan has just cooked us the most incredible dinner and myself and Mum are sitting in front of a roaring fire, with the kittens playing on the rag rug in front of us. Mum has been telling us all about one of the old gang who's getting married in Hawaii and we're all invited.

'Hawaii,' I say dreamily. 'I love the sound of that. Is it true that the word for hello and goodbye is the same?'

'No idea,' says Mum, smiling at me. 'Probably a crazy rumour the way people think Ireland is full of weird little men with pots of gold.'

'Yeuch, the whole leprechaun thing,' I say, shuddering. 'We have so many lovely legends, so many ancient stories. How have horrible little green men with pots of gold come to be an actual symbol people associate with this country? Where are the tourist statues of powerful Morrigan or the Tuatha de Danann?'

'All countries have their burdens,' says Stefan gravely. 'You know nobody can talk about Lithuania without discussing the kaukas, same as the leprechauns. Evil spirits. Nobody is talking about the higher beings, the gods and goddesses. My mother was called Laima, named after the goddess of Fate and women bearing children.'

'I prefer Vilma to Laima,' Mum says to him grinning. 'Stefan wanted your sister to be Laima but Vilma, truth, has such purity to it.'

They share another glance with such love in it that I'm smiling at them both, and then Mum turns her eyes to me. This time, she's beaming at me.

'So, truth, my darling. Tell us about this man.'

'What man?' I ask, blushing so much that Stefan laughs.

'The man who makes you so happy, of course. Why have you not brought him to see us?'

I laugh then. How do mothers know these things?

I tell them how wonderful Finn is, how we've gone walking together, how he came to my charity parachute jump, how I had to meet his friends, how gentle he is with me, how gentlemanly, and how I'm going to his house soon for dinner.

'He's been learning to cook,' I tell them, grinning like a loon, because it is adorable. ' "I want to cook things for you, feed you up, look after you," he says.' Just thinking about this and telling them makes me feel full of joy. I never dreamed there could be such happiness. All those years with Marc, thinking that I was safe because I had a man living with me, a man who was more of a brother than anything, a friend who shared my bed but never touched me because I couldn't face the intimacy.

And then I tell them how it was all down to Vilma and her friends insisting that I go out with them one night.

'I'd met him in the queue and she could just tell he was special,' I recount. 'You want to have heard her when I came back to the table with the food and drinks and hadn't agreed to be friends with him.'

'I knew Vilma had something to do with it,' Mum crows. 'She's been keeping the secret very badly, you know. No talent for keeping things to herself, your sister.'

'It is why she is called truth,' says Stefan.

'She told you?' I ask.

Mum laughs. 'She may have said something. But I can see it in you, Sid. You look –' she pauses – 'you look like you haven't looked for years. You look like you did all those years ago before you went to the city.'

I stare into the fire. I never wanted to tell them because it would hurt them, but now that I am happy, now that I am healing, I can. So I do.

37
Marin

The phone rings, jerking me awake and I sit bolt upright in the bed. What was the noise? Then it clicks into my brain.

The house phone, Nate's side of the bed. He's not there, working late. Again.

I'd gone to bed early because I have an early meeting in the morning and was in a deep, heavy sleep – I feel like I'm underwater. I lunge across Nate's side of the bed and drag the phone out of its cradle.

'Yes,' I hiss.

'I'm looking for Mrs Marin Stanley,' says the voice.

'This is me, Marin, she, whatever.'

'My name is Dr Luther, and I'm calling from the Emergency Department in St Vincent's Hospital. Your husband Nate is here. He's had a cardiac event.'

'Is he all right, is he dead? Tell me.' The words just keep tumbling out of my mouth.

'No, he's OK, stable for now. Do you have someone to drive you, to be with you?'

'Yes,' I say, 'but, but what happened?'

'That's really all I can tell you over the phone.'

'And what do I do when I get there?' It's like all my synapses are fried and I can't think straight.

'Just come to reception, ask for me, Dr Luther, or say who you are and you'll be led in. You'll be able to see your husband.'

'But is he going to be all right?'

'He's in good hands.' It's the voice of a woman used to saying things like that to people, I think blankly and then she's gone.

I'm left holding the phone, sitting on the edge of the bed, feeling the blood pumping through my skull and my chest as if I'm the one having a heart attack.

I stuff the phone back down and race into Rachel's room. She's there, in bed asleep, looking younger than ever, her long dark hair spread over the pillow. I can't wake her, but somebody needs to be here for Joey. I run to Joey's room and look at him, slipping in to stroke his face because he won't wake up. Nothing short of an earthquake wakes Joey when he goes to sleep.

I race back into our bedroom and grab a bit of paper and scrabble among the detritus of the dressing table for a pen.

Your dad not well, in Vincent's Hospital, gone to see him, stay here with Joey. I'll call you if I need you, it's . . .

I realise I don't even know what time it is, so I look at my watch and it's 1.05 a.m.

I grab my handbag, throw my phone and charger into it trying to think sensibly but it's impossible. Then I strip off my clothes and pull on leggings, a bra and a sweatshirt, all of which I was wearing around the house yesterday evening. I don't care. Socks, runners, I don't even pull a brush through my hair – it's not important. And then I'm out and in the car, shaking as I grab the steering wheel.

I turn the radio off, I don't want to listen to any music. I drive quickly, thinking of the last time I sped out of our suburban village towards the city, the night I thought Rachel was in trouble and I knew that if I had met any police car that night I'd just tell them and they'd help me, bring me, and now they'd do the same, wouldn't they? But I can't crash, so I slow down and try to breathe. He was OK, he was in good hands, he was stable, those were the words she said. They are good words, good news.

I park the car on a grass verge at the hospital, ignoring all the signs warning me that it will be clamped.

I don't care about clamping. I have to get to the emergency department. What does a car matter?

I half run, because the heaviness in my chest since I got the phone call from the hospital won't allow me to run properly. Or breathe. I need deep calming breaths.

Screw deep, calming breaths.

I need to be with him.

Now. Sooner.

I can keep him alive. No doctor can do it: he needs me, holding his hand, willing him back to life.

I don't have time for the information desk – I know this hospital, see the double doors leading into the actual A & E itself, see a man pushing out of them and I race, grabbing one swing door just before it shuts.

I'm in.

Scanning. Peering in past half-drawn cubicle curtains. A man throwing up vile black stuff.

Two cops standing outside another cubicle. A woman on a heart monitor.

And then there he is.

I see his hand lying limply. A hand that's caressed me so many times.

I stand at the edge of the already-full cubicle, about to speak when a doctor hangs her stethoscope round her neck and says: 'I'll talk to the wife.'

She's gone instantly and I follow her, see her approach another woman. The doctor puts a comforting hand on the woman's forearm.

'I'm the wife!' I say, my voice frantic.

And then, as the doctor spins around, I see the other woman, recognise her, see the horror on her face.

'I'm his wife,' I say, 'not her.'

She looks white and, at first, she runs to me, then stops dead, her hands flying to her mouth.

Bea.

Nate has been with her? In all my horrible imaginings about other women, I never thought it could be Bea.

'I'm his wife,' I repeat to the doctor, who looks startled and then immediately a blankness falls over her features.

'Right,' she says. 'Do we need to sort out some identification?' she asks.

'I was just with Nate when he collapsed,' Bea says. 'Marin is his wife. I'll leave now that she's here.'

I don't give her a second look, I only want to see Nate.

'He is under sedation,' the doctor tells me, matter of factly, as we walk back to the cubicle. I take Nate's hand and hold it. None of this seems real. He's hooked up to machines with the reassuring beep of the pulse, his chest a tangle of wires ready to connect him to the ECG machine. But there is nothing reassuring about this scene.

I can't speak. My fingers keep stroking the cold part of Nate's hand encumbered by oxygen monitors and wires.

'I'll get the cardiac consultant to talk to you in a little while, but we are slammed tonight, big traffic accident.'

I nod.

'Is there anything more you can tell me?' I find my voice.

'No. Your husband is stable for now. It's important we get him upstairs to the cath lab.'

'OK.' I take the news and nod, as if I'm used to hearing this every day. And then she's gone, whisking out, pulling the curtain back into place. Bea has followed me in, and now the three of us are in the tiny narrow cubicle, Nate's breathing even, the beep of the machines the only sound I'm taking in, although it's chaotic outside.

She doesn't leap in with excuses or lies. Instead she says, 'Marin, there's a chair, please sit.'

I don't sit. 'Get out.'

I can see her eyes fill with tears but I feel no pity.

I cannot work out which of them I hate most at this moment.

She slips quietly away and I'm alone in the cubicle with my husband, who isn't really my husband, who's only been pretending to be my husband. I look at his face, touch his brow, his nose, his lips and I lean over to kiss him on the forehead because I love him, he's the father of my children. And then I allow myself to cry.

After a little while, an older doctor arrives along with the porters.

'Mrs Stanley?' I can tell that he knows Nate has come in with another woman: the look he gives me is pitying. 'I'm Dr O'Donnell. We are moving your husband up to cardiac care where we'll perform more tests. He may need an angiogram to see what the problem was; we need to keep him stable and you probably won't be in with him for a little while. Do you want to go home?'

'No, I'm going to stay.'

'OK, go back out and someone will show you how to get up to coronary care and wait near the nurses' station, and we can talk to you up there.'

'Is he going to survive?' I only have one question I need answered. 'Is he going to be all right?'

'I can't say right now, we are doing our best. You have got to trust us.'

And, with that, the nurses and the porters organise my husband so his trolley can be wheeled away from me and I am led to the doors out of the emergency department.

I find coronary care on the fourth floor, although I am feeling weaker with every step closer to it.

Nate has had a heart attack. The words sound too serious, too dangerous, to apply to Nate.

And he'd been with Bea.

How could he do that? He loved me, he loved our children; none of it made any sense. I'd suspected Angie, had on-and-off conversations in my head about confronting him, kept putting it off because I wanted to believe that Nate would never risk

277

what we had. Would never have an affair, certainly not with his friend's wife.

And all along, he had been doing just that. Except that the friend was Jean-Luc and the wife was Bea.

I have to sit in a little ante-room beside coronary care. I hold my phone in my hand, wondering who I can text to say, you won't believe what's happened. In hospitals, people ring family and friends so that these loved ones tell them it will all be OK. How can that happen here? Who could I ring?

April, who probably knew women who'd accompanied men who weren't their husbands to all sorts of places, if not hospitals. No, I'd talk to her in the morning. I thought of Rachel, happily asleep in her own bed with the alarms on and Joey tucked up in his room. How could I ever tell them? Did I have to? I couldn't.

There was nobody I could phone and tell, nobody to cry to.

38
Bea

Outside the hospital, there is one lonely taxi. I get into it and give the driver my address. I don't look at him. I don't want to look at anyone. I'm still shaking from the combination of shock and grief. I slept with another woman's husband, not just another woman, but Marin's husband, and that single act of selfishness has brought us here to the hospital. I could have just left, but that would be the coward's way out. No, I had to stay and make sure he was all right and greet her.

'You all right, love?' says the taxi driver. He can see my undoubtedly white face in his rear-view mirror.

'Not really,' I whisper.

'Sorry, love,' is all he says.

Even he can see that I am not to be spoken to.

The driver takes me to Shazz's house because Luke was staying over with her and Raffie last night so I could rest, all of which seems like a million years ago.

I wish I'd told Shazz before what had happened last week; I can't have her thinking I planned for Nate to come, that I made them all complicit in a lie. What happened tonight was all because of one weak moment, for the momentary sense of comfort of having another human body wrapped around me. Because that's all it was. It's like my brain had deserted me and all I needed was the comfort of someone to hold me and love me. All these years of saying I didn't want anyone and then these stupid dates, all culminating in me having sex with the very last person I should ever be intimate with.

I've got Shazz's keys in the same way she's got my keys. So I let myself in, turn off the alarm, turn it on again and realise it's four in the morning now. There's no way I could sleep, although Shazz has a very comfortable couch in her kitchen. I take off my coat, throw my handbag on the floor and make myself a cup of herbal tea. Chamomile, although it will take more than that to make me sleep. It's closer to morning than night – how can I sleep now? I sit on the couch, pull a throw around myself and wonder what the hell I can possibly say to my friend about this. How am I going to live with this knowledge forever? That one act of stupidity brought Nate back to my door and now look where we are.

'Jesus, you frightened the shit out of me,' says a voice. It's Shazz, standing at the door to the kitchen with a baseball bat in her hand, dressed in her woolly pyjamas. 'What are you doing here?'

I look at her and no words come, only tears.

'Are you OK?' She's by my side in an instant kneeling on the floor. Putting down the chamomile tea and taking my hands in hers. 'Did something happen?'

I shake my head.

'No, Shazz, no; I've done the stupidest thing, I can't explain. It all started with that horrible family-tree thing and you know how that threw me, how Luke thought I was lying to him about his dad. And I felt I'd failed, I felt so lonely. And then, I went out with Piers last week, which was fun but would never amount to anything and then Nate turned up when I had a leak in my kitchen.' I let the tears fall onto the blanket.

'Last weekend?'

I nod.

'I knew you were freaked by something.'

'He put his arms around me. You know how that feels when you've been lonely for so long. But I could have said no, I could have hit him over the head, I could have rung Marin up and told her.'

I start to cry properly. Shazz goes to a cupboard high up and takes out a bottle of brandy. She pours two glasses.

'This is my medicinal brandy,' she says, 'it's actually not bad, not that I like brandy, but it has a bit of a kick in it and reminds your body that it's still alive. I think possibly because it makes your heartbeat go up, but you look like you are going to pass out, so maybe having your heartbeat go up is a plus.'

'I can't drink brandy,' I say, shuddering at the look of the glass.

'You can and you will; get it down you. The kids sleep well but you never know, any minute now they'll suddenly erupt downstairs and want to know what's going on. So let's get our plan organised and sort things out.'

'There's no sorting out,' I say. 'He turned up out of the blue tonight and I told him to go or I'd phone Marin or the police. I began to and he had a heart attack with fear, so I called an ambulance and I brought him to hospital.' Shazz's mouth falls open. 'And I gave them Marin's number and they rang her and I stayed until she got there.'

'Jesus wept,' says Shazz.

'And they were carrying on as if I was his wife, although I kept telling them I wasn't and that his wife would be there. But I mean they all must have known. And then she came in, and her face, oh Shazz, her face. She looked so heartbroken.'

'Yeah, well, I'd look heartbroken if I was married to that bollix, I never liked Nate.'

'You know Finn's new girlfriend? She doesn't like Nate either.'

'Smart woman.'

'The first time she met him he went to do the kiss on both cheeks.'

'Yeah, pretentious wanker,' interrupts Shazz.

'No, but she pulled back instantly, it's like she knew.'

'Clever chick must have met his type before. It's nice that Finn has got someone with a bit of sense. If Marin had any sense, she'd dump Nate. I know you're feeling like shit right now, Bea, because you have never done anything like this before in your life. But you have some sort of excuse. Nate hit on you when you were really, really low and he did the hugging and the minding and the *I'm always here for you*. And then suddenly he's kissing you and it feels nice to be held. Guys like him, it doesn't just happen once. I bet there's a trail of women. I bet he has his own football team of them.'

'You could be right,' I say. 'But that doesn't take away from the fact that the football team are not friends of his wife, part of his circle. I've just destroyed that.'

'If you've destroyed it, he's destroyed it too. Now you're going to get over this and you're going to stop beating yourself up. People are complicated, and life's mental. That's my mantra, babes. Drink your brandy, one gulp, go.'

We drained our glasses together. The brandy burns the back of my throat and I start to cough.

'I thought you said this was good stuff?'

'It's all relative,' says Shazz, pouring us each a smaller shot. 'It's good stuff to me, Lady Muck. OK, one, two, three, shot!'

With two brandies inside me, I'm slightly stabilised, although I doubt if the hospital advise brandy for helping people with shock. We sit together quietly and I myself relax as much as I possibly can. Finally, Shazz looks at her watch.

'Now, you've got to get back to your house, lie down for an hour, get up early, wash your hair, do your make-up, have a lot of strong coffee and face the day as normal. I'll bring Luke to school. You go into work and don't answer any phone calls, except if they are from me or your mum. Marin might ring you from a different phone, you don't want that, you're not ready for it now, OK?'

'OK,' I say. 'OK.'

As I start the short walk home along the totally deserted streets that separate our houses, I think about how grateful I am for Shazz's friendship.

But mine and Marin's will never be the same ever again. I've broken it.

39

Marin

They won't let me into cardiac care but a nurse suggests I have a tea or coffee from the machine down the hall.

'It's working at the moment,' she says, as if this is an unusual occurrence, 'do you have change?'

'I think so,' I say, looking around in my purse, 'yes.'

'Come back and hopefully in the next fifteen minutes you'll be able to come in, OK?'

'Thank you,' I say.

It's now half four, and I feel as if I'm starring in a nightmare, somebody else's nightmare. The machine coffee is horrible, but it's strong and it wakes me up. Nate has had a heart attack and he was with another woman, one of our friends, one of my friends.

I want to kill him and I want him to live. I didn't know my mind could hold two such opposing views, but it can. I sit in the little lounge just outside the coronary care, where the television is turned on and where another man sits staring blindly at the box. It's a grainy TV, not a thing of hi-definition beauty and *Murder, She Wrote* is playing. The man and I don't speak. He's staring into the middle distance, his eyes wet. I haven't cried a single tear: shock, I think.

Shock, horror and betrayal. I gulp down my hideous coffee and think that I have to be strong. Strong for Rachel and Joey, strong for myself, and perhaps strong for Nate. All I know is that I love the man on the other side of the perspex doors. And now I hate him too.

'You can come in now,' says the nurse, popping her head

around the door and looking at me. I gulp down the rest of my coffee, throw the cup in the bin and follow her. Cardiac care is utterly frightening, a land of machines with nurses and doctors walking slowly around. In the middle of the beeping and winking and many corded machines, lies my husband.

'We think he's too weak for an angiogram, therefore we are going to do some imaging on his heart and the arteries surrounding it. We need to get a vision of whether he has blockages or not. But we don't want to push him until he's out of danger.'

I nod.

A nurse gave me a number for the ward. 'We don't let people sit in coronary care overnight,' she says, 'it's too difficult for them and us. So if you want, you can sit with him for ten minutes. We will call you if anything changes or you can call the unit directly. We will need some forms filled in as well, so you could do that on the way out, so we have your phone number. The next-of-kin number,' she says. And the way she says it made me think that news of my husband's arrival with one woman and subsequent movement up to the cardiac care unit with another has not bypassed the hospital bush telegraph.

I sit with him and hold his hand again.

Nate, I want to say, why did you do it, why did you risk what we had? But instead I said, 'I love you, Nate, please be strong, please fight this, so that Rachel and Joey can come in and hug you and you can get out of hospital and we can begin again. We don't have to talk about any of this,' I whisper, stroking his forehead and his cheek, 'I just want you well, please understand that, please be well.'

After ten minutes, I am gently extracted from Nate's bedside and brought out into the corridor where a clipboard awaits me to fill in all his and my details.

'You'll ring me if anything happens?'

'Yes, we'll ring you. But this will not be a quick process, so you need sleep,' said an older nurse. 'Go home. We'll phone you after the new shift takes over about half eight, quarter to nine, we'll have a good vision of how he passed the night and that's a good litmus test for his strength. He's young, he has that on his side.'

'Forty-six,' I say.

'We need to take care of him now, you need to let him go into our hands.'

'OK,' I say.

I'm not sure how I leave the hospital or even make it to the car. I drive home feeling both dizzy with tiredness and wide awake at the same time. What am I going to tell the children?

Your father has had a heart attack and he's in hospital, and I wasn't with him because he wasn't home, he was with someone else . . .?

There's no way of saying any of these things, no way at all. I close my eyes. I'll try to figure out the right thing to do. But right now, I just have to survive this. I just have to exist, that's all.

Everything looks different, the roads seem unfamiliar. Maybe it's the fact that I'm driving in the early morning and dawn is thinking about creeping over the horizon. It's a cold morning and a few early-bird workers are on their morning commute. I'm going in the other direction, home. *Home.*

Even the words seem strange. Home implies a place where you are safe and you live with your loved ones. But, my husband is lying in coronary care after having a heart attack when he was with his mistress, who is also my friend, *was* my friend. I practise saying this out loud and it sounds stranger, every time I say it.

What am I going to tell Rachel? With Joey, I can fib a bit, he's still young enough not to see through a lie, so I can say he was out with friends. But Rachel, she's an adult, I don't want to lie to her.

I'm not ready to tell my mother, she'd have a story printed in the local free sheet newspaper, castigating Nate and with pictures of him saying, 'cheater' if she could possibly get away with it. And if she couldn't, she'd be handing out leaflets. Dominic will hug me. And that's when I do cry, thinking of being hugged by someone whom I know loves me. All the pain of thinking that Nate didn't, all the worry that's been bubbling inside me for months now, breaks. I cry for much of the journey home.

And to think I worried about Angie. Or maybe it was Angie too. Maybe Nate has lots of women.

I get home at half six and I make strong tea, which then makes me feel nauseous. I run to the bathroom and throw it all up.

In half an hour, I have to wake Joey, make him breakfast, pretend this is a normal day. Do the same with Rachel. Or do I? Normality has gone out the window. I have a showing this afternoon but I'm not going into work, no way.

Instead of our usual Friday routine, I sit and wait for everyone to get up.

Even though it's too early, I still ring the hospital, get put through to the coronary care ward. And a nurse tells me that he's doing well but that the cardiology team will be on their rounds later. Soon but still later.

'Can I talk to the cardiologist?' I say.

'Possibly this afternoon we'll have some news for you, because they'll have to have a team meeting to decide what to do.'

'OK, but he's stable?'

'Stable, absolutely, passed a good night. We'll call you if there is anything else we need to tell you, Mrs Stanley,' said the nurse. Even her saying my name makes a flush of pain rise inside me. I'm the woman whose husband was brought in with someone else.

'Mum?'

I turn swiftly and Rachel is standing at the door to the

kitchen, still in her pyjamas. She looks me up and down. I always shower and dress after breakfast. Now, I'm wearing my boots and proper clothes, not my slippers and comfortable fleecy dressing gown. 'What are you doing up so early, Mum?'

The note must have fallen off her bed, I think, and she didn't see it.

'I haven't been to bed actually,' I say.

'Why, what's wrong?'

She's beside me in a flash, slender fingers clutching one arm. And suddenly she is not grown-up Rachel who's ready to travel around the world: she's my idealistic daughter, who idolises her father, who thinks everything is normal and simple in life and that things will work out the way she wants them to work out.

'It's your dad,' I say, and years of training kick in. I cannot tell her the truth. 'He's going to be fine, but he had a heart attack, a cardiac episode.' I fumble around a bit trying to find the correct words, words that won't frighten her. 'He's in hospital and he's OK. I was with him last night for a little while, but they sent me home.'

'Why didn't you wake me?'

'I didn't want to worry you, darling,' I said, thinking back to that moment when I was leaving the house and I really wanted to wake her. Just to hug her and hold her. 'You needed to sleep and there was nothing you could do. I didn't want to put you through that. Now he's fine, I've just been on to the hospital, he's stable. And they are going to decide what to do later. He might need some surgery after this, who knows. But your dad is young and strong and fit.'

'Poor Dad,' she says and she starts crying, rubbing at her eyes, making the mascara she hadn't quite taken off properly smudge across them. 'He's very fit, but will he be all right? Did they say that, did they promise?'

'They don't promise things like that, darling, but he's in the right place.'

I'm not sure the message is coming across very well right

now, but I'm doing my best. No matter what has gone on in the night, I am still Marin, mother, mother lioness and I'm going to take care of things.

'It's all right, darling, he's going to be all right.'

'You don't know that,' she says, with unerring accuracy.

'I do,' I said, 'they told me so.'

I wonder how many more lies I'll have to tell. There's no way Rachel can ever find out how her father got into hospital. It would destroy her. And suddenly I want to be beside Nate in the hospital so I can slap him hard across the face. He hasn't just betrayed me, he's betrayed Rachel too.

Rachel goes up to get dressed and I am so angry with Nate, that I want to tell someone.

Finn, I think, I'll ring Finn, because he knew, he must have known, he is so close to Nate. And if he knew and he didn't tell me, he's never coming near my house again, our friendship is over. I know I might be a little unhinged right now, but I dial Finn's number and he answers on about the fourth ring.

'Yes?'

'It's Marin,' I snap. 'I've been at the hospital. Nate's had a heart attack.'

'Oh, Marin, I'm so sorry, I'll come right over.'

'There's no need,' I say. 'Somebody brought him in.'

'Well that's good,' says Finn, a hint of confusion in his voice. 'Somebody . . .? Where did it happen?'

'Bea brought him in, because he was with Bea, you know, our friend. Overnight.'

'Bea?'

Nobody can sound so astonished on purpose. Nobody who hasn't graduated from acting school and got a few Oscar nominations along the way.

'Our Bea? Are you sure, like how do you know he was with her?'

'They thought she was his wife and she travelled with him

288

in the ambulance. They got in at two o'clock in the morning. It was written all over her face, Finn,' I say, coolly, 'just tell me one thing, did you know about this?'

'About Bea and Nate? No, I hadn't a clue. I can't believe it, Marin, honestly –'

'You swear?'

'I swear.'

'Would Steve have known?'

'Steve? Steve isn't interested in other people in that way,' says Finn. 'Love him like a brother, but he's – you know, pretty self-obsessed.'

'Has Nate ever done this before?' I waited for a pause but there was none.

'Marin, I've been Nate's friend for a very long time and I have never seen or heard of him being involved with any other women. I can't believe this, there must be some explanation. Bea would never do this to you, either. She's been trying to date these past few months and I'm pretty sure none of the dates have gone beyond a first one. There has been literally nobody since Jean-Luc died.'

'OK, well, if you can come up with an explanation as to why Bea was with my husband at two o'clock in the morning, and was the one who accompanied him to the hospital in the ambulance and sat by his bed until I got there, and then said sorry and left . . . If you have any other way that explains those facts, please tell me, because I'm home now and I've just avoided telling our daughter that her dad's a cheat and it was very hard, let me tell you.'

I hang up, with a mild pang for Finn but really, I don't care. I just need to be angry with somebody.

It turns out that her somewhat chaotic life means April does trauma and disaster marvellously.

'Marin, you need a hug,' she says when I open the door to her. She was the second person I phoned.

There are two carrier bags on the step behind her, full of food with flowers and a blanket for some reason which escapes me, and the latest magazines. April, dear April, is coming to take care of us. I think I might cry. But I cried enough last night and I have certainly dried out my entire tear duct supply already and it's going to take quite a lot of water and coffee to get them working again.

'Thank you, darling, you're a lifesaver, I couldn't call Ma.'

'Only if you were having a psychotic breakdown,' says April cheerfully. 'And if you call Dad, well, she'd know, she'd want to be here. It would be your fault, either way.'

'That's true,' I say.

I look at April with renewed respect. Normally, she doesn't want to talk about our family and gets upset if she has to discuss Ma at all, because Ma is such a judgemental, angry character. In fact, I was under the impression that April prefers to pretend she doesn't exist. A bit in the same way she pretends to imagine that her prince will come. But this no-men-for-six-months thing is clearly changing her.

'Have you told Rachel anything?' says April quietly.

'No, not going to yet, maybe not ever.'

'It's your call,' says April more decisively than she ever normally says anything. 'But if you ask him to leave, then you'll have to tell her. It's your secret in one way but in another, it's Nate's. He's the one who got caught with Bea. Bea! I am astonished, I have to tell you. Joey and I will have a lovely day here. I've got supplies,' she displays many supermarket cartons of ready-made food, 'so that whenever you come back we'll have food and we can watch nice movies and play games and do whatever.'

'You're wonderful,' I say.

'Oh, Aunt April.' Rachel has suddenly appeared in the room and throws herself into my sister's arms.

What did she hear? I think in horror. But her next words prove that she didn't hear any painful truths.

'Poor Dad, I don't want to cry, I shouldn't cry in front of him, should I?'

'Your dad loves you, he'll be fine. And I'm sure he's going to be all right,' says April.

I look at her thinking, where is my sister and what have you done with her? But then maybe I never needed April before. Maybe being needed is what *she* needs.

I don't have time to think about that now. It's time to go into hospital and see my husband and pretend that he was not brought in with another woman. I kiss Joey goodbye.

'We'll ring you with Dad when we get in, OK? But it's probably better if you don't come in today, just until later and we know how he is and he's out of the intensive care place, which he's going to be out of later today, OK?'

I am lying again. I know nothing. I merely want to make him feel that everything is under control.

'I want to come, Mum,' says Joey tearfully.

'Well, you know younger people bring in lots of germs, so I think probably the best thing is, if you don't come in now. But we can go in again later.'

'He's going to be fine,' says April. 'Your dad's so strong. Doesn't do all that swimming and weightlifting and all those running things for nothing, you know. This will be nothing for him, Joey. I dare say he'll be doing next year's marathon in aid of people who have had heart attacks.'

Joey grins. 'That's Dad,' he says, looking cheered up.

'Now, Rachel, it's perfectly fine to cry when you see Dad,' I say to Rachel, as we park in the hospital car park. 'Hospitals scare all of us.'

I'm saying this because I want her to feel strong. I don't want her to be undone by seeing her father in the hospital bed. I've no idea what I'm going to do. Hit him, hug him, tell him he's not coming back to our house? None of those things.

I can't tell my husband he's being thrown out of our house and our marriage while he's in coronary care. There's probably a law against it. I realise that the trauma seems to have brought out my funny side. Not suitable right now, Marin, I tell myself.

'Are you all right, Mum?' Rachel squeezes my hand. 'You look scared.'

'Yes I'm fine, I'm fine. We're going to get through this. Just got to be calm and let the doctors and nurses do their jobs,' I say, and silently add, and not let on that my husband came in with another woman.

The nurse on the desk outside coronary care tells us Nate had a good night, which I already knew, and says we can both go in and see him. 'He can tell you himself what the doctors have been saying. It's going to be a slow recovery, but he's doing well.'

There's still no let up on the numbers of machines surrounding Nate in the bed. And in the way hospital beds always diminish even the strongest people, he does look smaller, paler against the snowy white sheets.

'Dad,' says Rachel, throwing her arms around him.

'Oh Rach, sweetie,' he says and his face crumbles in a way I've never seen it crumble before. This is Nate, my alpha male husband, and he's crying, actually crying. He cried when both children were born, but I don't think I've ever seen this before, not since.

Then he turns and looks at me.

'Marin,' he says, and he knows I know. And at that moment I have to choose, because there's a choice: I can turn around and walk away, or I can walk over to him and try to fix this for Rachel and Joey and our family. And there's no choice. Strangely, weirdly, there's no choice. I thought I'd go in first and shout at him if he was awake and I knew I couldn't. Now seeing him with Rachel crying into his shoulder, I can't. I lean over and kiss him on the lips.

'Gave us all quite a fright.'

'Oh Marin,' he says and he pulls me closer. 'I'm sorry, I'm so sorry,' he says.

'It's not your fault, Dad,' says Rachel, 'people have heart attacks.'

'Exactly,' I say.

Who knows what kind of stabilising, calming, tranquillising medication he's on? I don't want him saying, I'm sorry I was with Bea last night when I was brought in. One of us is going to have to be strong here, and it's going to be me.

'There's nothing to be sorry for,' I say. 'Tell us what the doctors have said to you?'

'I'm having an angiogram this afternoon and then, depending on what they see, stents inserted in two places.'

'Whatever happens you're going to be fine,' I say, sounding weirdly like my mother, who makes pronouncements.

'I love you, both of you, both my girls,' he says, tearful again. 'Where's Joey?'

'We thought we'd wait until we saw you were OK.'

'Oh I want to see him.'

'I'll ring April, bring him in, just for a moment, we don't want to tire you out.'

'OK.'

And as I look at him there in bed I think, it's going to be OK, we're going to get through this. I'm going to make sure we are going to get through this. I'm not letting my family fall apart.

40
Bea

Luke is delighted when I pick him up that afternoon.

'Sausage did a poop outside,' he tells me happily as I drive him home from school.

'On the grass and everything! Shazz doesn't mind. She says she's cleaned up lots of my and Raffie's poop when we were small. I said yuck!!!!'

I am exhausted and shaking, so shaky, in fact, that I am probably a danger in the car but still, we drive home slowly and as Luke chatters, I think about everything that's happened.

I, Bea, have cheated on my dear friend, Marin, with her husband, and I have destroyed her. What sort of a person am I?

'Mum, are you OK? You look sad,' says Luke suddenly.

I almost haven't the energy to skip into Mummy mode and lie, but I do: it's my instinct. Protect my child. Keep him safe by making him the focus of my life and in the process, make him fatherless because he's never had a chance to have another father figure and also, make myself so lonely I actually sleep with the first man who really holds me in a loving way since Jean-Luc died.

What sort of evil person am I?

'I'm sleepy,' I say, faking a giant yawn.

Finn's Mini is parked outside ours when we get there and instantly I know that Marin has phoned him.

'Finn!!!' yells Luke, delighted to see his favourite uncle.

Will Finn still be a part of our lives now that he knows what I've done? He knows me, surely?

I get out warily.

'Afternoon,' I say.

'Hello, Bea,' he says gently. 'Just thought I'd pop around, see how the two little biscuit monsters were.'

'They're not biscuit monsters,' says Luke happily as the two of them extract the dogs from the car, a tricky task at the best of times. 'They do like biscuits, though.'

I open up and let us inside. Nate's jacket is not lying on the floor because I remembered to bring it in the ambulance. If only I'd let them take him on his own but I couldn't. If something happened, he needed to have someone he knew with him and despite knowing exactly what it would mean, I'd chosen to go with him in the ambulance.

'Bring the girls out the back and see if they poo in our garden too,' I say in a faux cheery voice to Luke.

Once I've let him and the girls into the garden, I boil the kettle and face the window, looking at my son, waiting for judgement. But I've been so busy castigating myself, I've forgotten I am with Finn. He is not a man who judges.

'Talk to me, Bea,' he says. 'Marin thinks you spent the night with Nate, have been spending lots of nights with Nate, because you were with him in the hospital . . .'

I sigh.

'I wish I could tell you she was wrong but I can't,' I say. 'I was with Nate last night but –' this sounds so hollow and lame – 'he'd come in the week before to fix a leak in the kitchen, and I was feeling vulnerable and he –'

'He moved in,' he finishes.

I nod. I still can't look at him.

'Last night he just turned up. Shazz had taken Luke because I was sick with guilt and self-hate all week. I wasn't sleeping, was sick, so she said – she didn't know what had happened – that I needed a rest.' I laugh without humour. 'She had Luke on a sleepover so I could sleep and Nate turned up here unannounced, ready to rock and roll again. I said no, Finn.'

I finally turn away from the window. 'I said no. I told him to leave or I'd call the police and that's when he had the attack.'

Finn looks as if the whole of mankind has let him down. That's two beautiful people whom I love that I've managed to hurt.

'I had to accompany him to the hospital. What if he –'

'Died?'

I nod.

Finn shrugs. 'You did what you thought was right.'

'But it didn't turn out to be right, did it?' I say. Then I ask the question I've wanted to ask, the one which is ludicrous because I know the answer in my heart.

'How's Marin?'

Finn, who danced at my wedding, whom I would call one of my closest friends, looks at me sadly: 'How do you think?' he says.

I start to cry. I feel so hopeless and now I'm losing Finn too. One night lost me Marin and now Finn will join her in the list of people who will cross the road if they see me coming.

But Finn hugs me like the brother I've always felt him to be.

'It's OK, Bea,' he says, holding me tight.

I sob into his shoulder. 'I never meant it to happen,' I sob.

'Of course you didn't,' he says. 'You wouldn't think of it, but men are different, Bea, and Nate –' He pauses. 'I hate what he did,' he says. 'He messed you and Marin up. I can't forgive him for that.'

'I can't forgive me,' I say tearfully.

'Nonsense. You've been alone a long time. You were vulnerable, the stupid moron just picked up on it. You'll always be my friend, Bea.'

'What about Marin and Nate?'

'Marin's my friend too but Nate, well, I'm not sure I want to be his friend anymore. I know you and I know Nate. I know which one carries the can for this one, Bea. And it's not the one who's been alone for ten years bringing up her son, being a proper friend to us all.'

I lean against him, weak with relief. He's not judging me. I might survive this after all, I think, if I still have some people who believe in me.

41

Sid

I have just settled myself perfectly on the couch with the cushions just so to rest my neck on, a cup of tea, my Saturday-morning toast and the various remotes within easy distance. My perfect Saturday morning at home. I'm still in my PJs and fluffy socks because I get cold feet. Giselle is the same, runs in the family, she said, your grandmother was exactly the same. I have only a faint memory of my grandmother because she and my mother didn't get on; the whole happy commune-living style of life didn't go down too well in the leafy suburb my mother came from, but that's OK. If Granny Harrington had wanted to know me, she would have known me. So here I am: feet warm, ready to dive into a new episode of— The doorbell rings. I jerk so quickly that I spill my tea. I really do have a very intense startle reflex. Sometimes people notice it but most of the time they don't. Cursing a little bit I put the tea on the coffee table, wipe myself down, aware that I am now drenched with warm tea and go to the door, muttering that if it's some member of the residence committee with the newsletter about moving the bins a quarter of a centimetre to the right, then there is a very good possibility I will whack them over the head with the pottery vase in the hall. This is a Saturday morning and it's sacrosanct. I peer through my peephole to see who is on the other side. I have to stand on my tippy-toes to do it because those little holes are made for really tall people. At this point all I can see is a bit of a neck and then I see a zipped-up fleece and realise it's Finn.

What's Finn doing here? He's never been in my apartment,

we haven't got that far yet, although I've asked him, and he's going to cook me dinner in his tonight. What's he doing here hours earlier when he's due to pick me up at seven?

I open the door. 'Hello. You're a bit early.'

'Can I come in? Sorry for turning up unannounced but I need someone to talk to.'

In all the time I have known Finn, which, admittedly, is not very long, he's never looked like this, upset, anxious, distressed.

'Sure,' I say, letting him in, thinking, maybe he is slightly mentally unstable and is off his meds and is now going to produce a hatchet from behind his back. I really must stop watching the true-crime stuff. Too many people kill other people with hatchets, who'd have known? I follow him carefully into the sitting room and note that unless he has the hatchet stuffed down his trousers, he's hiding it very well.

'Really sorry to barge in on you like this,' he says, and plonks himself down on the armchair, not even looking around or commenting upon the semi-bare state of the apartment. Marc did take a fair amount of the furniture with him.

'Do you want a cup of tea?' I say, scooping up my cup.

'Tea, that would be lovely,' he says distractedly.

I'm not really sure what to do with this new distressed Finn, so I hide in the kitchen peering around the wall to see what he's doing now. He's sitting back staring into space and I think that this would be the time when a companion animal, preferably a cat, would be very beneficial, because the cat could go and sit on Finn and calm him. Maybe I should get one of those TV cats that you can turn on and look at. I must look into that. I return with tea and sugar, because even though he doesn't take sugar in his coffee, which I know from having multiple coffees with him, he might with tea. He eschews the sugar, pours milk carefully into the tea and looks up at me.

'Biscuits,' I say, 'biscuits.' The one thing I'm fully supplied with at all times is biscuits, because box sets and chocolate and wine or tea and sitting on your own a lot, means biscuits. So far none of this has told on my waist but I feel sure from listening to other people around the office that there will come a point in my life when everything I have ever eaten decides to lodge itself around my belly. Still, hasn't happened yet: onwards with the biscuits. I bring another, more chocolatey pack in and sit at the other end of the couch just in case.

'So what's up?' I say.

'It's Nate, he has had a heart attack.'

'Oh, oh I'm so sorry, Finn,' and suddenly I understand. Nate, Finn and Steve have been friends since college, which is a long time ago. They are very close friends.

'I'm really sorry, how is he, was it a serious attack? How's Marin?'

It's then that Finn looks at me and I see he has got a haunted cast to his face.

'Marin is in bits,' he says, 'Nate is still in cardiac care and there's more to this story.'

'Spit it out,' I say.

'He was with Bea when it happened. I was round with her yesterday and apparently they had a one-night thing. It sounds like Nate tried it on when Bea was vulnerable, and she's devastated. I mean, she is so not that person –'

'If she's been on her own since her son was a baby, she's lonely, Finn,' I said.

'I know she is. So Nate turns up and hugs her –'

'And gets her into bed because, God forbid, if Nate doesn't get what he wants –' I say harshly.

Finn is a little astonished at my tone but says nothing. 'So he goes over there again on Thursday night and when Bea tried to throw him out, he had a heart attack. Bea brought him in the ambulance. The middle of the night.'

To my credit I don't blink or gasp or do any of those things. In fact, I don't know if I'm that surprised. But the feeling sends a shiver up me. I knew I was right about Nate. He went back again and Bea had to threaten to call the police.

'When the hospital phoned Marin, she turned up and Bea was there.'

'Very brave to wait it out,' I say. 'She knew that, somehow, it would come out that she was with Nate, so she stayed to face the music. That's brave.' I move and sit closer to Finn and pat him gently on the hand.

'I'm really sorry,' I say. 'How's Marin, have you been to see her?'

He shakes his head. 'Not yet. I will. She's angry but she hasn't been angry with him, and she can't tell the kids. I wish I could help but I can't. And the thing is,' he looks at me with anguished eyes now, 'I had no idea. I see Nate all the time. We swim, we used to cycle but not anymore, we talk in the sauna – I know this man, he's like my brother. And yet I didn't know that he had this double life, I didn't know he could do this to Marin. He's very flirty, you know. He must have done this before. Jean-Luc was our friend. If he can seduce his widow, then I don't know what sort of person he is.'

I can tell he's getting angry now.

'Sometimes people surprise you, shock you,' I say, calmly. I know all this for a fact.

'Did you suspect?' Finn looks at me quickly.

'I'm not sure I liked Nate that much. I'm good at reading people and I think he left Marin to do all the work. He was very keen on Angie, too, which wasn't nice. He kept talking to her and at worst it was a type of emotional infidelity, ignoring poor Marin slaving away, and, who knows where that can lead to. If I was Marin,' I considered, 'I'd probably go into the hospital and pull out all Nate's leads.'

Finn looks at me and for the first time he laughs.

'You would, wouldn't you.'

'Yep, every single one of them. I mean, that's probably technically murder or attempted murder, depending how fast the doctors and nurses got there, but, you know, I would want to get my point across.'

'You're amazing,' says Finn, and he looks relaxed for the first time since he arrived. 'Seriously, what would you do really if you were Marin, not just go into the hospital and pull out all the plugs?'

I look at him and answer honestly.

'I think all my neuro-pathways would be standing in a corner chain-smoking and having anxiety attacks, and I'd be wondering what I had done wrong.'

He looks at me. 'You wouldn't have done anything wrong.'

I take a breath. He sees me, I think.

'Sorry for barging in on a Saturday morning but I've been thinking about it all day yesterday, couldn't sleep last night, and I just needed to talk to someone about this. Steve is trying to take care of Angie who's taking it really badly.'

'It's upsetting,' I say, 'when people you have known forever and are close to you suddenly do something that's abhorrent to you. It changes how you feel about them, changes how you feel about everyone, about life in general. Pulls the rug from under your feet.' I was speaking from experience now. 'Marin is going to need all the friends she can get. And even though you started off as Nate's friend, you are her friend too, so be there for her and the kids. Be there for Steve, because it's tricky, he'll probably be rethinking Nate and Angie now.'

I make Finn eat a few biscuits.

'What are you going to do next?' I say.

'I don't know – go into the hospital and rage at Nate. I don't blame Bea. I honestly don't. I have never seen a sign of this with her. She's so dedicated to Luke, it's like she won't allow herself to have a life. To mess with that . . . she's had enough pain. I'm so angry with Nate.'

'Good,' I say, 'rage you can work with.'

I hand him the whole packet of biscuits.

'I know this is not good swimmer-cycling-person food, but it will help. You need sugar.'

I was about to stand up, give him the signal that it was OK, that he could go and be with his friends. And suddenly I realise I don't want him to go. I want to comfort him, I want him to stay with me. I want him to comfort me, and it's really hard to get my brain to process this. Because my body has already processed it and worked it out, but my brain hasn't quite caught up yet. But if the body can remember trauma, it can let it go too, slowly. I've been healing for a while and Finn's been a big part of that.

Despite hearing about poor Marin and Bea, and scuzzy Nate, I have this lovely man in my flat. I'm in my pyjamas and he's having the effect on me that he always has on me. The one I can't quite believe I am capable of. The feeling of wanting him to hold me naked and kiss me and I want to kiss him back. I want us to be in bed together. I want to feel him, touch him, let him touch me, kiss him. And I stop thinking, because he's staring at me as if he can see right into my brain.

'Are you OK?' says Finn.

'Fine,' I say. 'I'm thinking of tonight and how much I've been looking forward to it. And now, instead of having to wait for tonight, I don't have to.' And before I know what I'm doing I say, 'I want you to kiss me.'

'Are you sure?' His voice is low. And I know absolutely without being told, without going through my brain, but with purely going through what I sense, that he knows I've been hurt.

And that he's asking my permission.

I nod.

He reaches out with one big hand and strokes my cheek and then his hand is gently around the back of my neck and he's leaning towards me. His fingers are so soft, and his mouth is close to mine, but he's hesitating.

'Just kiss me,' I say.

And he is kissing me and it's like I've never been kissed before, I haven't been kissed for so long. It's wonderful, this beautiful man, holding me, taking care of me and I shift and suddenly we're jammed close together. He gently angles me so that I'm sitting on his lap and my arms are around his neck, my fingers tangling in his hair, his arms wrapped around me.

'Oh Sid,' he says. 'We can't rush this, I don't want to rush this.'

He's kissing near my ear now. His lips soft around my neck, nibbling, and I'm arching my head backwards, as his mouth moves down towards my throat, lazily kissing my collar bone. And his hand is stroking my shoulder which is suddenly the most erogenous spot in the world. His fingers are soft on my body.

'I've been hurt,' I say, 'long ago and I haven't done this for so long, but I want to, I want to do it now with you.'

He moves away, slowly.

'Was it Marc?'

'Marc and I were friends,' I say, 'we ran away together, it's that simple. He was my boyfriend for a time but I wasn't really ready, and we just stayed with each other out of habit. By then it was easier to let everyone think we were together, but we weren't. We were like brother and sister.'

'You ran away? But you love your home,' he says, confused. 'Who hurt you, my darling Sid, what did they do?'

'No.' I put a finger against his lips. 'No. That was then and this is now. I let that define me for so long, not anymore. You've smoothed away the hurt piece.'

And I climb off him and take his hand and he gets up off the couch.

'Come on, we'll go into my bedroom.'

It's sort of girlish, a bit like the bedroom I used to live in at Rivendell.

'Marc never slept in here with me after the first few months, because he had his own bedroom, where he had all his super-hero stuff and his TV for the computer games he used to play. Whenever Vilma came up, she'd sleep on the couch and I'd say that Marc snored so much he had to have his own bedroom, it was the only way. And she believed me, poor darling. I owe it to her to tell her, but not now.'

The room is smaller with Finn inside it. He fills the space.

'Say no at any point,' he tells me. 'Understand?'

'You don't want to do this?' I say, suddenly vulnerable.

'Oh no.' His eyes are dark with desire. 'I want to do this, I think I've wanted to do this since the day we went hiking and you asked me what I had in my rucksack and I just loved you then. You're so funny and clever and beautiful and spiky, like the hedgehog pet you told me about. A little bit bristly but soft. And lovely when one opens up to you.'

'You don't get to give me a nickname now, I'm not going to be hedgehog.'

'Oh no, you are going to be my own beautiful Sid.' And then he bends down and wraps his arms around me and carries me over to my own bed.

I wake up later in the afternoon to this incredible feeling of another naked body warm beside mine and it's glorious. I move, feeling the softness of the sheets, the comfort of the bed, the smoothness of the skin, warmness spooned against me and then one big arm reaches round and tucks me in closer. I feel his face burrowing into the soft place behind my ear and he's whispering. 'Good afternoon, gorgeous.'

'Good afternoon, gorgeous yourself,' I say, 'this is a lovely way to wake up.'

'We could wake up this way all the time,' says Finn. And I can feel the smile in his voice, so I wriggle onto my back and turn to face him. He's supporting his head on one big hand, leaning on his elbow, and I reach up and kiss him and then suddenly I'm lying on top of him and his arms are around me. And I feel so happy.

'Would you like some Saturday very late brunch, madam, or slow, passionate love?' He reaches up and sucks one of my breasts and I arch my back against the exquisite sensation of it.

305

'Brunch can wait.'

'Perfect,' he murmurs, taking his mouth off my nipple for one brief moment. 'That's the answer I was hoping for.'

An hour later, I feel heavy limbed and indolent. But Finn gets out of bed and says, 'I have to cook for you. I'm not a cook by any means but I've become competent at morning stuff like pancakes.'

'Really? I know you're very good at other things,' I say.

And he smiles, 'So are you.'

'I have no practice, well very little practice.'

'We'll have to do something about that. We could draw up a schedule.'

'Do you have a calendar in the kitchen?'

'We'll mark in the dates: every morning and at the weekends, twice, maybe . . .?' he says, 'so we'll get you all practised again.' And then he smiles, strokes my hair and kisses my forehead, takes my face in his hands and says, 'You're perfect, never change anything. I'm going to throw myself in the shower and I'm going to make you something wonderful for breakfast. What do you want?'

'Well, that depends what's in the fridge,' I say. And I don't really care what's in the fridge. Normally people aren't over in my house – except Vilma, and she generally gives out about the contents in my fridge, but I don't care about Finn seeing it, because Finn likes me for me. I don't have to be anything I'm not. With Finn, I feel good enough just the way I am.

Five minutes later he's out of the shower, hair slicked back, wearing his jeans and a T-shirt.

'Right,' he says, and stalks off to the kitchen.

I throw on a T-shirt and go and follow him. I brush my teeth but don't stop to comb my hair: I don't care, this is me. Finn likes me for me. Imagine!

He's in the kitchen making coffee and I walk up behind him, put my arms around his waist and lean into him, my head barely comes up to his shoulder blades.

'You feel good there,' he says but he turns to face me, still with us enmeshed. 'Are you still feeling good, Sid, happy?' He really has the most beautiful eyes and they are looking at me with such understanding and concern.

'Why might I not be happy?' I say, looking up at him.

He keeps staring down at my face and says: 'You're so strong and feisty but underneath it all you're fragile. I don't want to hurt you. Please tell me I haven't hurt you or scared you.'

'Stop,' I say, 'I don't know what miracle this is, I honestly don't know, because for almost fifteen years, apart from a brief time with Marc, I haven't been with anyone.'

'Really?'

'Really,' I say. 'You're on the money – something happened to me and it made me really scared. Scared, guilty and ashamed. I ran away and hid behind funny remarks and black clothes. And then you came into my life and I stopped wanting to run away. I stopped feeling ashamed.'

'Whoever hurt you is the one who should be ashamed,' he said. And there's something in his voice I've never heard before, anger.

'I've been angry,' I say, 'I've been angry for a very long time. But anger doesn't work. Or rage, sometimes the rage comes and gets me. When I'm in the rage place, I think if anyone banged into me in a pub or a club, I'd explode with anger, which would not be good.

'But now –' I smile at him. 'I feel happy. You make me happy.'

'Will you tell me what happened?'

For a moment I don't want to ruin what we have, this glorious happiness. Him standing there, in T-shirt and jeans with his feet bare; me in a T-shirt, more undressed than I've been with another human for years, my hair all bed messed, the scent of him on my skin.

'How about we have coffee and breakfast, go back to bed?'

'One cup,' he says, 'I think that's all I can cope with before I do this again.' And he sits me up on the counter, puts his hands around my face and kisses me deep. 'You can open up to me, Sid. I'm not going anywhere.'

I take a deep breath. 'OK. I'll tell you.'

42

Sid

Fifteen years ago . . .

It's hard to know which one of us is more excited about my new job: Me or my mother.

We're in my bedroom and she is eyeing the sedate clothes I've bought to impress all in Lowther & Quinn, the legal firm I'm interning in. I want to get into family law but the only company I can get any work in is a company offering four-month internships for minuscule pay. Lowther & Quinn specialise in commercial law and I know it will be scut work but it's a foot in the door.

'It's all very . . . grey,' Giselle says doubtfully. My mother thinks grey is an absence of colour and has no place in clothing.

'I need to blend in until I can make my mark and then, mix it up a bit,' I say, closing the wardrobe on my college clothes which were funkier.

On my college work placement, I realised that my version of sedate was not quite sedate enough, so this time, with my first real job since college, I want to nail it. There will be two interns in the company and I am determined to be the one who gets even a quarter of a job.

White shirts, a plain woollen coat that cost half of my savings, two skirts, a silky blouse and a couple of cheap dark grey suits from Marks and Spencer's. Personally, I think it's all hideous but societal mores insist on a certain kind of dressing for junior business people.

The sort of dressing mum and I abhor.

She fingers a light-grey suit jacket and shudders.

'You'll blend into the walls, lovie.'

Mum is wearing her standard uniform of a floral quilted kaftan (patchwork purple today), belted with a crocheted Obi, olive-green cargo pants and heavy socks because her boots for working in the polytunnels are just inside the back door. The restaurateurs who buy her heritage tomatoes and tiny aubergines and edible flowers think she could wear a bin liner and they wouldn't care.

'I'll stand out when they all think I'm fabulous, but not before,' I say. 'I want them to notice me for the right reasons.'

'Why does what you wear matter?'

'It shouldn't,' I mutter, following her out of the room.

Giselle goes gracefully downstairs in our small farmhouse with me in tow. My mother is graceful, with tiny wrists, sleek limbs and stands at five two in her socks. I am precisely the same, only twenty-two to her thirty-eight. With our Matrioska doll caps of shining dark hair and Giselle's remarkably unlined and perpetually smiling face, we do resemble sisters more than mother and daughter, but then she was sixteen when I was born, and she fought fiercely to keep me.

Our kitchen is chaotic but beautifully so. Gertrude, our sheepdog, is on the couch near the stove, smiling, wagging her tail and shedding black and white fur everywhere. Vilma, my little sister, four and three quarters, and gravely kneeling at the kitchen table making a very long necklace out of pasta shapes, doesn't even look up when we come in.

'It's six foot tall,' she announces. 'As tall as Daddy. I want to be as tall as Daddy. He's hidden the chocolate biscuits up in the high cupboard.'

The adorable little face, with those keen dark eyes, is raised to us as though to say that if being tall gives a person an unfair advantage, then Vilma wants it too.

Stefan walks into the kitchen at that precise moment. He has to bend his head to enter the door and, as ever, he beams to see us. He really is very tall, six foot five or thereabouts like all his family, a glorious melting pot of Lithuanians who are all carpenters, like Stefan. Some people bring happiness to the world – the combination of my mother, my stepfather and little Vilma brings utter happiness to mind.

I quash down the anxiety about starting a new job in my grey dressing-up clothes on Monday. I have tonight and to-morrow afternoon left of the weekend to bask in their presence before I head to the city and my rented box room in a shared house where my new life begins.

By day three of working in Lowther & Quinn in the city, I've been in Dublin for a week and I feel I've got a routine.

First, I'm adding to my grey wardrobe: a dotted silk scarf I picked up in a second-hand shop, my Sarah-Janes that look so much better than shoes with a little heel. A flower brooch that Daisy, who also lives in the shared house, made with pale turquoise tulle and silk.

Second, I get up early and have a coffee in a cute café near the office, where I can watch the city walk past and make my list for the day.

Me: country girl at heart is now city slicker and I like it.

I feel like one of the *Sex and the City* girls – myself and Lois, also new in the firm and from my year in college, better ward-robe though, and I discuss which character we are. As it's our second week and we've actually got some money now, we go out to lunch.

'Samantha,' says Lois, admiring her nails for the nth time. Her second manicure ever. Lois is ignoring the fitting-in con-cept and her nails are too. They're Rouge Noir, a sexy midnight burgundy. They look like they're made for ripping things.

'How many guys have you slept with, then?' I ask daringly. Lois is the sort of person who won't hit you if you ask her this. She wears her utter ease with herself with such glorious pride.

'Five and a half,' she replies, after a moment ticking on her fingers.

'A half?' We both giggle.

'He fell asleep,' Lois explains.

'Which half?'

We snort into our sandwiches and it takes a while before we can eat again.

'You next,' she says.

I flush a little, wishing for some of Lois' easy sensuality.

'One,' I say, 'a long term thing. We were together for a whole year. Since then, I obviously have my boyfriend-repellant on.' I'm only half-joking.

'Guys are unsure of you,' Lois says. 'That kooky arty look scares them off. Plus, there's the black nail varnish.'

'True. I had to get rid of it for here.' I gaze at my nails with their badly applied layer of see-through pink. With black, you just slop it on and it always looks right.

'If you want a job, look like the person they'd want to hire,' we parrot, courtesy of one of the Getting A Job seminars we went to.

'It worked, though,' says Lois. 'I'm wearing a blouse instead of a Doors T-shirt and you've cornered the market on white shirts and skirts. Skirts! You're Charlotte.'

'Am not!'

'Yes, you are. You want one lovely man, not a string of lovers. And you look Charlotte-y in those on-the-knee numbers.'

Like Mum, I've always seen myself as a free spirit in the world and I have to fit into the legal world with my conservative clothes. But one day, in a smaller firm and with my own clients, I can be myself.

When we get back to the office there's a buzz in the air. Alex Quinn, one of the company directors, has been on holiday, somewhere hot and expensive, and he's just returned to the office, the reek of Chanel's Eau Sauvage and a hint of After Sun flood the place. I sneak a peek from behind my partition and see a middle-aged guy with white-blond hair, a handsome face, and a tan that looks as if only rich people can buy it.

'Hello, team,' he says loudly.

Even his voice is rich and Michelle, second year there, rolls her eyes and yet stands up and says, 'Hello, Alex, welcome back.'

Like a celebrity visiting a disaster site, he tours the office, a laughing comment here, a pat on the shoulder there, a shake of Lois' hand when he reaches her corner.

I notice him looking her up and down appraisingly, but Lois doesn't smile at him.

Some Samantha, I'll tease her later.

'And you must be Sidonie, our other new intern.'

Suddenly he's standing in front of me, and I feel something sparkle inside me: this man, he's one of the company's partners and he's noticing me, an intern. Maybe he's heard I'm good at what I do!

'Yes,' I say, beaming. 'It's really lovely here, Mr Quinn, everyone has been so nice.'

'Oh, call me Alex,' he says, and he smiles. He's forty, definitely. Which is like miles older, even Stefan isn't forty, Mum isn't quite forty. But this guy, forty seems younger. He's got this vibrant energy and something else, I can't put my finger on it . . . charisma, that's what it is.

He comes around behind the partition and leans against it, one long leg crossing the other.

'So,' he said, 'how do you like it here?' He's got a low deep voice. And I feel very flustered by all this attention. So far I've been treated like a normal young member of staff and there has been a lot of coffee runs, shouted commands to get files, boring document searches, and 'Can somebody work out where my phone charger went?' Stuff like that. The sort of thing you get to do as an intern.

Lois, somehow, doesn't do most of those jobs.

'If you do those jobs, people will think that is all you are capable of,' she's told me, firmly. 'You've got to show them you are here to work, not to be a run around. You didn't go to law school to find that bitch Michelle's phone charger.'

'I know,' I say, but there's a part of me that's always been built in to what I'm supposed to do, helping out. I help people, that's what I do. That's how I got on in school, I worked hard and made Mum proud of me and then Vilma and Stefan. I've always been a good girl.

'Good girls finish last,' Lois said.

'That's just wrong, the world doesn't work like that,' I pointed out.

And now here's Alex Quinn, smiling down at me like I'm the only person in the world. It's a heady feeling. I think he must have heard that I've been working really hard and he's come over to say thank you. And I know I've done the right thing. I'm proving myself an important part of the business and that's what I want to do.

'It's been lovely working here, and I'm really here to learn and I'm so grateful for the opportunity,' I stammer.

'Well, that's good to hear,' he said. 'I'll have to bring you out to lunch to talk to you about this; I like to bring all the interns out to lunch. I think you lovely girls need to get out of the office and see the real world we are dealing with.'

'Oh, well, I do lunch from half twelve to a quarter past one, so I don't know how we could do that. But I'll ask Michelle.' Michelle is in charge of myself and Lois.

'Oh it will be fine with Michelle,' says Alex. 'Anyway, we'll work it out, put it in our diaries. Anyway, nice meeting you.' And he pats me on the shoulder, his hand for a moment touching my hair. And I feel that frisson of excitement at having been noticed by this demigod of a person. Oh wow. I sit there for a minute in silence staring at my computer. And then Lois pokes her head around the partition.

'What is he like? He really loves himself that guy.'

'Shush,' I say, 'he'll hear you.'

'Don't care if he hears me,' she says.

'No, he's lovely, he was welcoming us in.'

'Yeah, right,' says Lois.

She shuffles off and before I can think about it any longer, Michelle appears with a mission for me to deliver some papers to an office up the street.

'Course,' I say, bright, shiny. 'That's what I'm here for.'

'Yup,' says Michelle.

I don't really think she likes me and I don't know why. But as Mum always says, strangers are just friends you haven't met and Michelle and I haven't made friends properly yet, that's going to take time, maybe. But we'll get there, I know.

It's Friday night and normally the partners are gone a bit earlier than us. They have dinners to go to, wives to go to. It's a very male practice, with the exception of people like Michelle and ourselves and the accounts and legal secretaries. There's not much of an after-work culture. I'm sitting at my desk tidying up some loose ends, still determined to be the best employee ever. I'm going home tomorrow morning to Rivendell and I can't wait, because it's just been such an amazing two weeks and I have been telling Mum and Stefan all about it. And I've told Vilma I'll bring her a lovely present. I've got her a really pretty little zippy rucksack with sparkles on it, and I know she's going to love it. I'll have money, wages, it's really exciting. I'm trying to think what I'll get, maybe some wine, although Mum is not much into wine. Stefan really likes beer, but wine seems like the sort of thing you bring home after your successful first two weeks as a woman with an actual job. Oh and chocolates, I might bring chocolates – some of those fancy ones that are handmade and have cream in them. I'm thinking this, as I'm tidying up my desk and pretty much everyone is gone. There's a guy cleaning the offices, pulling along the big red Henry Hoover. He's nice and we nod, but don't talk and I smile in a sort of, 'Hi, how you doing' way, and he smiles in a 'Hi, I'm doing OK' way, but we haven't got as far as actual conversation yet. I know I'm shy, I'm really trying. Nobody ever thinks I'm shy. Everyone assumes that if you are brought up in a place like Rivendell, you must have loads of friends and be marvellous at talking to people.

'Hello, Sidonie, you're working late,' says a charming urbane voice.

I look up and there's Alex.

'Oh, hi, hi,' I say, and I know I sound like some idiot kid with a crush on a movie star or something. But he seems so glamorous, like someone from another world. He's the big boss and he knows my name.

'Lovely name, Sidonie,' he says. 'You must come from an interesting family, I think?'

'Yes,' I say, all bursting enthusiasm and then wish I hadn't sounded like such a moron. I have to try to appear cool. 'I'm just getting ready to go,' I say. 'I thought I was the last one here?'

'No, just you and me, that's all.'

He doesn't appear to count the guy dragging the hoover around. For a second I feel shocked by Alex Quinn. He doesn't count the man cleaning. But maybe the Alex Quinns in the world don't notice someone who does the cleaning, and I don't like that. Still, as Mum always says, 'People are strange, not everyone thinks the way we do.'

'I am just about ready to finish up,' he says, 'but I finished a big case today and it's all gone very well. Litigation is the toughest, you have got to be able to fight,' he says. And I swear I can see his canines as he says it. Beautiful canines too, it has to be said. Lois thinks he's too full of himself and says he's got veneers and probably a sunbed tan.

When she said this, I replied: 'No, no, I've heard from Glenda that he's got a boat, and people with boats are always tanned, aren't they?'

'I was just about to open a bottle of wine to celebrate,' he says now. 'But you can't open a bottle of wine on your own, can you?'

I don't know how to answer this.

Myself and Daisy only open bottles of wine together in the teeny apartment, and even then they are really cheap, screw-top ones.

'I'm sure you can't,' I say and, astonished at my daring: 'you could bring it home and have it with your wife to celebrate?'

'She's got a committee meeting this evening, Lady Captain stuff.'

'Golf?' I question.

'Yes.' He seems amused by the question. 'You don't play golf, do you?'

I shake my head. All I know about golf is that people who play golf have bigger cars and kids who go to private school, because that's how it was in Greystones and I personally don't know anyone who plays golf. I mean, there were lots of people who played pitch and putt, but that's different. I don't think they have lady captains in pitch and putt. But I could be wrong.

'Could you do me a favour, lovely Sidonie?'

'Yes,' I say, sitting up perkily. Work, I can do more work, I am a working machine.

'Come into my office and share a glass with me and then I will have laid this case to rest. I can go off for the weekend feeling it is put to bed.'

'O-kay,' I say, and I don't know if this is the right or wrong answer, because it seems really weird. I mean, why does he want me to come in with him? But, he's the boss and you do what you are told. Same way as when Mr Kinnehan, the vice principal at school, asked people to stay behind and do the litter pick-up in the playing fields, we all stayed behind and did the litter pick-up in the playing fields – except for the people who put the litter there in the first place, who really couldn't care less and were truanting from school.

'Of course, I'll just tidy up here.'

I run into the bathroom first, because I know I pull my hair out of my ponytail when I'm concentrating and I want to look perfectly professional. I sweep the brush through and retie it up: there, the picture of a professional young woman.

Daisy said I looked really nice today when I went out.

'You're finally moving away from the waitress uniform,' she said approvingly.

I felt the little cardigan with the embroidered flowers around the top was really nice. The little flowers sat just above my collarbone, so it's both work-like, lady-like and suitable for a legal office. My skirt is a little bit below the knee because I can't afford to get it turned up, and I'm wearing black fifteen denier tights. A lot of the women in the office wear ten deniers, but I can't really afford them yet because they rip so easily. So, I'm still on the fifteen deniers. Cheap ones, too. With my hair freshly brushed, I grab my bag, turn off my computer and pick up my extra bits and bobs, and my coat in case it's cooler on the way home. I walk in the direction of Alex Quinn's office. The man with the Henry the Hoover is obviously in another part of the offices, because I can hear the drone, but I can't see him. The partners' offices are richly glamorous in a different area to where us newbies and the secretarial staff work. Our part of the office is very boring, but theirs is full of nice wood, big doors, high ceilings and huge windows looking out onto busy streets. They reek of money, entitlement and knowledge. Huge legal books line the wall. And I think that maybe one day I'll have an office like this. I think of all the sorts of law I want to practise and I think, I could get there, I just need to find my way up the ladder, that's all.

There's a large desk, what I believe they call a partner's desk and it's bare of practically everything, except one of those Lucite lamps that look intelligent, as if having one on your desk raises your IQ by about 25 per cent. All the files are neatly locked away. And there's a picture of a very attractive woman of Alex's age, blonde, lovely, with two young children in the background.

'Your family look nice,' I say and I think that's cheeky, I shouldn't have said that. Personal comments shouldn't be made.

'They are,' he says, 'they're wonderful, busy lives, of course. You know, when you are in this business you spend a lot of time in the office.'

'Of course,' I say, making a note to self: have to spend a lot of time in the office. Well, I do spend a lot of time in the office. It's a Friday night and I'm the last one here, except him and the lovely cleaning man.

There's a round antique desk with antique chairs set around it. And then there's an area with a couch and two armchairs and a coffee table in front of it. It's a huge office, absolutely enormous. The tiny little apartment that Daisy and I share could fit in here three times over.

'Sit down.' He gestures in the direction of the couch, and I sit. Knees primly together. Maybe he's going to talk to me about mentoring me, I think.

He opens the bottle easily. My hands take a very full delicate wine glass, full to the brim of red wine.

'Gosh,' I say, 'it's a big glass.'

'Oh, we're celebrating,' he says.

He takes an equally full glass and sits down on the chair opposite me.

'So tell me about yourself, Sidonie, I want to hear everything.'

'OK.' I take a sip of wine. It's lovely, not that I know anything about wine but. Still, I'm sure it is.

'What made you decide to study law?'

This I can talk about.

'I grew up with a lot of people who didn't have a lot of money and I felt that it would be wonderful to know how to help them when they got into trouble.'

'And yet you're here. We don't do much pro bono work,' he says. 'Commercial law might not be your arena.'

'I know, oh I know, I need to know all about the law. I mean, you know, you have an idea in the beginning and then maybe find the right thing for you. But I like how the law makes things right, sorts things out, it's so important, isn't it?'

'You're very young,' he says, paternalistically. 'Have some more wine.' He shoves over a little dish of cashew nuts and I start nibbling. They're lovely but dry, so I have to keep drinking the wine to stop my throat from tickling. And it's ages since I had lunch and that was a very quick three quarters of a cheese sandwich, because I was late.

Before long, I'm somehow drinking a second glass of wine and he's regaling me with stories of his early career and ideas he had for the law and what he was going to do. His father was a lawyer and his father before him.

'It's in the family,' says Alex, one long arm encompassing the beautiful office. His watch is some gold expensive thing and I know I should recognise it. I think that Lois would definitely recognise it, but I haven't a clue what it is. I've always been terrible at expensive stuff.

'You're from Wicklow but you're living in Dublin? With whom?'

'With my friend Daisy; we grew up together in Greystones and we thought it would be good to have an apartment in town. Well, it's really a flat,' I slur, realising I'm definitely on the way to being drunk. 'You know, an apartment is bigger and better and a flat is just like small and a bit messy. We can't get the bath clean. We've tried everything, scrubbing and more scrubbing. So we just have showers. I'm going home this weekend and I can't wait to have a bath.'

He leans back against the couch. I know at this point that I am drunk, because two huge glasses of wine, very little lunch and a few cashew nuts are not really enough for a person of my size. And I've just told my boss I want a bath at the weekend.

'And is it pretty, this little flat?'

'We try and make it pretty. My mum is very into crafts and she sent up lots of hangings for the walls and we have got posters, of course, film posters. Daisy's mum gave us a really beautiful old couch. I mean, it's lots of different colours, so we got some throws on it, white ones to make it nice.'

'And boyfriends?'

He was filling my glass again and I protested and said, 'No, not for me.'

'We have to finish the bottle,' he says.

I can't imagine that any bottle can have that much in it. But I think I can't be rude and say no. So I'll just let him fill it and not drink it.

'Boyfriends, well, not now. Work is too important. I did have a boyfriend.'

'What was his name?'

'Daniel, we grew up together.'

'That's lovely. And you're still seeing him?'

'No, not now.'

'Fancy free,' says Alex. 'You're footloose and fancy free.'

And then he's suddenly closer to me, beside me on the couch. And I know he shouldn't be closer to me. But I don't know what to say. Why is he closer to me? So I move just a little bit, but his hand reaches my knee.

'No, don't go, you're such a lovely girl, this is great. We should talk more often like this; it's important, you know, for me to get to know the staff, to be able to help them make good life choices later, you know. Understand the business, and where you fit within it.'

'Right,' I say trying to concentrate, because I definitely feel dizzy.

'And you have a stepfather, you were saying?'

'Yes, Stefan, he's lovely, he's Lithuanian.'

'Oh how nice, very nice. And a little sister?'

'Yes . . .'

His hand is moving up past my knee. I don't know what to say: get your hand off my knee? He's my boss. He's older. This can't be right?

'I don't think we should be doing this, Alex, Mr Quinn.'

'Nonsense,' he says, 'nonsense. There's nothing wrong with this, just a little drinkie after work, way of winding down after the week. People do it all the time. It's business. There has to be a little fun in life, doesn't there?'

Suddenly he's pushing me back onto the couch and he's actually lying on me. His mouth is pressed up against mine, and his tongue is forcing its way into my mouth. And I'm saying, 'No, no, no, Mr Quinn, stop.'

But he doesn't care and he's holding my ponytail tightly with one hand, holding my head back. It hurts, I feel trapped. He's moved away from my mouth and I'm saying 'No!' and his head's down at my collarbone which is hidden by my little frilled cardigan. And he rips it. Just rips it viciously.

'Oh, that's nice, little lady. You like that, don't you?'

'No, I don't like that,' I beg. 'This is wrong, Mr Quinn. Please stop, please.' I'm crying but it's coming out as whispering because I'm so scared. How is this happening? How did we go from us having a chat in his office to him kissing me, lying on top of me? How?

What did I do wrong? I must have done something for this to happen. Wine, I had wine and I talked and told him about the bath and . . .

'Come on, don't be a tease, you knew what this was about. Stay late, look at me, smile up at me, hello, Mr Quinn. I know your type.'

'No, I don't do that,' and I go to scream and his hand is suddenly clamped over my mouth so I can barely breathe and I feel paralysed with fear, because I know exactly what's going to happen now and the fear does something to my body. Every muscle tenses up and vibrates, the fear radiating out like a pulse, a physical Morse code sign of distress. Ancient knowledge takes over. I feel like a small animal where everything is shutting down to cope with an ongoing threat and my voice has receded along with my understanding because I know what's coming. I know and it's my fault for not seeing, for not understanding. He's so much bigger than me, stronger, and his hand's still pulling my ponytail back, so I'm pulled backwards, arched towards him.

I'm five foot two, he's six foot, and all the urbane clothes mean nothing because under them all he's a bigger animal than I am and he can fight me and win. He's pressing his body weight against me and he's pulling at my cardigan and he's got it open and he scrapes me as he rips it. But even though I'm aware of the rip of skin, I almost can't feel it. My mind is aware but my body has gone somewhere else with the fear.

His hands are pulling up my bra and he's got one of my breasts out. He's biting me.

'No, stop! Don't, please don't do that.'

My voice is so weak now. A hopeless whisper.

'You want it, you know you want it. You've been smiling up at me ever since I came in. Hello, Mr Quinn, hello, Mr Quinn. Yeah, I know girls like you.' And then his other hand is up under my skirt and he's pulling at my tights, ripping them. He tears them away and his hands are in my knickers and now he's touching me –

I can't move at all then: all I can feel is my heart beating to the vibrations of fear in my body and my eyes are closed, but tears are leaking out of the corners. His hands are hurting me, abrading me. Like a pulse in my brain, I think if only someone can come and rescue me.

'Touch me,' he says.

I shake my head and he slaps my face and again, the pain almost doesn't register. I don't know how he manages it but somehow his trousers are open, he's forcing himself inside me and then, I feel pain that makes the earlier handling like nothing.

I keep my eyes closed, let myself fall entirely numb because I can't allow myself to think. If I think, my mind will drop into some place it can never come back from. I'm fully animal now – prey gone silent with fear.

I can only scream silently in my head until I feel his strain. He groans and collapses onto me.

'You're a good girl,' he says.

He's panting and he pulls himself off and away from me. He gets up, adjusts himself. I'm lying there splayed, clothes ripped obscenely and my hands pull my skirt over my body. I drag myself into the corner of the couch and I'm shaking. It's like I'm there and I'm not there. Still the animal knowing the predator is watching, waiting. Still not safe.

'Clean yourself up,' he says, looking at me. 'Maybe next week, a little more wine, be nice.' And he leans down to kiss me and I fall off the couch, moving away.

'No, get away from me.'

'Oh no, you're not going to do something silly now, are you?' he says. There's menace in his voice. How had I ever thought he sounded charming? 'You wanted it. Don't tell anyone otherwise. I'm going, and you need to get out of here before me. Fix yourself up.'

My fingers are shaking as I pull my coat on and gather my belongings together. My clothes feel tattered under the coat, so I do up my coat buttons.

'This is between you and me, right?' he growls.

I leave the room and then I'm out on the street, shaking. I run.

43
Sid

Coming out of remembering is like entering back into a new world and I'm enclosed in Finn's arms and he's holding me so tightly and he's shaking. I'm shaking too.

'I'm going to kill him,' he says. 'I want to kill him, for what he did to you.'

'My mum always thought people were good,' I say. 'And people think rapists are strangers, stranger danger. You know, when you get off the bus and walk strong on the street and things like that. You don't think it happens where you work, you don't expect that. And I've had a lot of time to think about it and a lot of time not to think about it. And I was just there. I was ready for a predator. He saw me, he marked me off.'

'But what did you do?'

'I gathered my stuff and I never went back. I left a note on Lois phone. Said there was a family emergency and I wouldn't be back. Daisy wasn't there in our flat when I got home. She'd gone out for the night with some friends. I got into the shower and I scrubbed everything I could. I had a loofah, I was very proud of that loofah, because they were dear and I scrubbed myself till I was raw, till I bled. In the morning I went to the Family Planning Clinic and I got the Morning After Pill, which made me really sick. They begged me to report it but I said no. I'd studied law. I knew how it worked.'

'How?' he says and he's genuinely confused. Finn thinks fair should work all the time but it doesn't, not with rape cases. The number of known reported rape cases and the number of actual rape cases are always vastly different, all over the world.

The number of convictions is always a tiny number. I knew this fifteen years ago. How could I have known that and not known how to avoid someone like Alex Quinn? But book knowledge and actual inherent, body memory knowledge are two very different things. I'd known nothing, as it turned out, for all my years in college. So clever and yet so dumb all at the same time.

'Can you imagine trying to get him on the stand?' I asked. 'A big shot lawyer and me, just a little girl who'd come to work in his office. They'd rip me to shreds in court. I didn't want to be exploited a second time. Now, I'd do it. Now, I'd tell everyone.

'But I told nobody. Not my flatmate, my family –'

'Why not your family?'

'The shame,' I whispered. Shame was the hardest thing to explain to someone who didn't understand. 'The sense that it was my fault too, that if I'd been smarter, if I'd known more, I could have avoided it. If I'd cried out, if I'd hit him . . . if I hadn't gone into his office. All the ifs you go through. That's shame. That you are culpable.'

Finn is silent but his eyes stay on mine, warm with love.

'I stayed in bed for a week. I cried and I couldn't eat, and this is going to sound really stupid but I cut up that cardigan, I cut it up into pieces and I burnt it in the fire. Wool really smells when it burns. Then I cut my hair off, because it was always pretty. I was pretty. Pretty, naive and stupid. I didn't know what happens because nobody had ever told me.'

Finn runs gentle fingers through my hair.

'Didn't look much different from the way it looks today,' I say. 'I wanted to be invisible, I didn't want anyone to ever look at me and see anything different because, being naive, thinking the best of people, had got me raped and I didn't think I'd ever get over it.'

By now, he's rocking me and I can feel his heart beating fast and furious through his T-shirt.

'I stayed in bed all week. Mum rang and Stefan rang and I said I'd got some terrible bug. The office rang and I pretended to be Daisy and I said that Sidonie was really sick and wouldn't be back. I got a job waitressing, so I could pay the rent, but I couldn't go home. I told Daisy something had happened, but not all of it. I think she guessed, but I told her she was never to tell anyone. I told her my boss had tried it on and it scared me.'

'He raped you, he didn't try it on. He deserves to pay. I want him to pay for what he did.'

'That was fifteen years ago,' I said flatly. 'It's too late and Finn, I can't go through that and I won't. He victimised me once and he won't do it again. It's just my word against his word. And you know, I sat in his room and I drank his wine; it doesn't help me.'

'He was your boss. You were twenty-one, he was what? Forty something. That's, oh Jesus, I want to kill him.'

'No.' I had to make Finn understand this. 'I need you to listen to me,' I say. 'Not avenge me or fix me. I moved away from Daisy, because I couldn't deal with that. And eventually I went back to Rivendell. Started wearing black clothes and never going out. Both Mum and Stefan knew something was wrong but I wouldn't tell them, I wasn't going to tell them. I rang the Rape Crisis Centre, but I told them I wasn't going to report it. I just needed to talk to someone. They were so amazing and they told me it wasn't my fault. But I knew it was my fault, I believed it was my fault. I should have known better. And it took years, years and years and years to let go of that. And I had lots of therapy, healing. Marc was from near me at home and his dad used to beat him up. He wanted to move out and I wanted a man with me so I felt safer. Because I never felt safe from then on. So we moved in together. We let people think that we were together because it was easier, you know. We were broken and we tried to love each other that way, but we were too messed up. Still, we were happy, you know, we had each other.'

Finn kisses me as if I might break.

'I'm so terrified of hurting you now. I wish you'd told me before we . . .'

'If I'd told you before, you would have seen me differently. I needed you to see *me*, to want *me*. I'm sorry I used you.'

He looked at me, his eyes heartbroken, and I smiled.

'No really, I'm making a joke. I know you think I can't make a joke right now. But I've had fifteen years of living with this, Finn. So I can make a joke about it, because I know what is mine, I own it.'

'But that bastard is still running around?'

'I did one thing, one right thing, that I think helped. I told Lois from the law office. She came round after three weeks. I was sitting there and rocking my new goth look, you know, all black: black eyeliner, black eye-shadow, black nails. We were talking and she just knew it was something to do with Quinn. She was adamant I had to do something about it. I said no, I don't have to do anything, I told her.

'Someone needs to know.'

'Well, you can figure out how to tell them,' I said. 'But I'll explain it to you really simply, don't bring me into it. Because if you do, I will deny everything. But they won't listen to you anyway.'

'My father will listen to me,' said Lois.

'Your father who got you the job?'

'Yeah,' says Lois, 'he'll listen to me.'

'OK, good,' I said. 'Don't keep me informed, I don't want to know.'

Lois wasn't exactly touchy feely, but she tried to reach out and touch me, but I wasn't touching, you know. I'm not so good at touching. That's why I hated Nate when I first met him, because he was so handsy.'

'I know, I saw.'

'And I don't know what happened, where he is, what he's doing. But the name Quinn isn't on the company branding anymore. I used to dream about killing him. The rage is very fierce but most of the time, I can deal with it.'

'I love you, you're so brave, so brave. But I do still want to kill him.'

'No,' I say, 'hold me, Finn, just hold me and love me and be you. And let's just talk about this some other time, because for you now this is a huge thing. But for me, I've lived with it for a very long time and I have come to terms with it in my own way. And you unlocked me, like I don't know, Sleeping Beauty, Cinderella, whichever one of them was locked up. Not that I'm a princess who needed to be saved no, but –'

'Nobody needed to save you, you saved yourself,' he says instantly. And he pulls me to him and I can feel him rocking backwards and forwards, as if he's in absolute pain.

'I told you this, so we can have a future, OK?'

'A future.' He looks at me and his eyes are wet.

'Yes, a future. Now either you can deal with me having been raped, and you might not be able to, or you can't, but, either way, what we have just had is amazing.'

'Of course I can . . . I've the most amazingly strong warrior woman ever here. I'm not going anywhere. You've got me for good.'

'OK,' I say. 'That's wonderful.' And I reach forward and I kiss him. Kiss this beautiful man who has given me back something I never thought I'd have again. And I have it because I was finally ready, I managed to let go.

I loved Marc, but we had held each other back. Together, we'd just stayed in our little cosy prison cell. And his leaving had allowed me out. He'd unlocked the door and now I was in the world again and I'd found Finn. I was free.

44

Marin

The person who has helped me most while Nate has been in hospital is April. I never ever thought she could help me through something like this. Help me through anything. My whole life, I've been helping April, being her confidante, cheering her up when she's been dumped, hiding what's going on in her life from Ma's prying ears, rescuing her. Now she's rescuing me. It's quite astonishing.

'What's different, April?' I say, in the morning as we are changing the bed in the spare room, getting it ready for Nate. Ostensibly, the reason he's going to be sleeping in the spare room is because he's had stents delivered via the angiogram and he must not have the groin area banged into. So this is our excuse to keep him safe. In reality, it's because I cannot have him back in my bed. But to everyone, to Rachel and Joey, who are so excited and thrilled he's coming home; to his mother, who has been on the phone three times already; even to Steve, Nate's return is the most wonderful thing ever. Steve has already discussed a party. Unfortunately, he said it to Rachel on the phone, who ran upstairs, her eyes shining, saying 'Mum, wouldn't that be wonderful, you know how much Dad loves parties and we could welcome him home with something fantastic like that, it would be brilliant.'

She's grown up so much in the last few months of working. I'm going to miss her when she goes off on her six-month round-the-world trip with Megan, which is happening in just a few weeks' time. And then I think how young she still is, because I'm still fooling her by not saying, *He was with Bea, the person you consider your auntie, the night he was in hospital.*

'Oh a party is not a good idea,' says April swiftly.

I beam at her.

'No,' April goes on, 'he needs time to rest and recuperate and then maybe a wonderful big party sometime in the summer,' she says. 'Have the family and a few friends over when he comes home, that's all, just for a pot of tea and then off again. Your father will need to rest.'

'Dad would love a big party and I won't be here in the summer,' says Rachel, suddenly forlorn.

'We'll wait till you have come home and you are ready to start college,' says April. 'Your father will love that and he'll be strong by then, because he has to take care and do exercises and things.'

'Yes, you're right,' says Rachel thoughtfully. And April shoots me a side eye that gives me the message that the only exercising Nate will be doing if she has her way will be trying to pull a knife out of his heart; she has said as much. And I laugh. I think I might be going nuts. I was given twenty Xanax by my doctor and I am eking them out, to make sure I don't completely lose the run of myself and giggle at some inopportune moment. Because everyone else is treating Nate getting out of hospital like the return of the king, when to me it's the return of the lying, cheating scumbag. Now that he's getting better, the fear of losing him has subsided and the rage over what he did has reared its head.

'Now, are we all ready to go to the hospital?' says April. She's coming, even though it will be a bit of a squash, even in Nate's big super-duper car. She knows I can't bear to be on my own with him. Not yet, I have to build myself up to it. I know this is the right thing to do, it's the right thing to do for our family. I need to hear him explain what happened and tell me how he came to be with Bea, and we can hardly get into that in the hospital. April bustles us out, managing us all.

Finn has been there for me too. Darling Finn, I believe him

that he had no idea. But he's talking to Bea as well, and I can't hear about her yet. We came close to falling out when he tried to explain it all to me.

'Marin, I've talked to Bea and it was one night when she was at an emotional low. He had the heart attack because he came around again and she threatened to call the police if he didn't go, and that set him off . . .'

'Stop,' I said, 'I don't want to hear it. Not now. Not yet. I don't want to know, Finn, and if that's the message you're bringing from her, well, then, bring it right back.'

'I'm not bringing any message from her,' he says. 'It's just the way it is. And you need to talk to her.'

'I don't need to talk to anyone. I'm just trying to get through every day as it comes. The man I loved has betrayed me. Do you understand that?'

'I understand,' he says. 'And I'm so sorry. But it's not what you think.'

'I know exactly what it is,' I say to Finn, 'don't try and dress it up. I know you are trying to make it better because you're his friend, and Bea's too. But I don't want to hear it.'

And now I'm bringing him home for the first time in weeks.

It's amazing how, after having three stents put in and being told he'll have to be monitored and be on aspirin and all sorts of cholesterol drugs for the rest of his life, Nate still looks sickeningly healthy. Paler, yes, but that's just because he's been trapped inside.

'Oh Dad, you look tired,' says Rachel, holding on to her dad. Then there's Joey's delighted face, as he hangs off his father's other side. And I know I have got to keep doing this for my kids.

Within half an hour, we're home. And despite all plans not to have even the smallest party, everyone, it seems, has turned up to greet us.

There's my mother, who throws herself at Nate, even though

I have never really thought she liked him. Dominic hugs him tightly. Dear Dom hasn't a clue but his heart is in the right place.

Dad is gentle. 'Good man, Nate,' he says, 'good man. Bit of gardening, that's what you need. It's very good for the heart. If you look at all the head gardeners at all the big gardens around the country, you will see that they all live forty-five years from when they're made head gardener. This is the interesting bit,' Dad goes on, 'they are all made head gardener when they are fifty. So, you see, it's a real area of work where people live a long time. Gardening: it's the way forward.'

'Oh Denis, shut up. Nobody wants to hear about head gardeners,' says Ma, rudely.

Something growls inside me.

'I want to hear about head gardeners,' I say, and I turn and give her a gaze that would do Maleficent proud. My mother takes a step backwards.

'All I was saying was –'

'You're always interrupting people,' I say, 'stop.'

From the corner of the room, April giggles. Dominic opens his mouth and stares in total silence. Ma stalks off, indignant.

'Thanks, lovie,' says Dad. And then he whispers, 'She's going to kill me later.'

'No, she's not, because I'm not going to let her,' I say.

'Is everything all right, pet?'

'Yes, Dad,' I say, 'just, you know, the whole near-death thing. Makes you really think of life,' I say. I hate lying to poor darling Dad. But he shouldn't have to put up with my mother, any more than I should have to put up with bloody Nate.

Steve and Angie are here, and they brought some catered sandwiches and nibbles. It's all laid out on the dining-room table. There's no sign of Finn or of Sid or, luckily, Bea. Bea is not welcome here. Not that I've told her that but she's not stupid: she knows.

'Where's Finn?' says Nate.

I look him straight in the eye, probably the first time since he has come into the house.

'He couldn't come,' I say.

'Oh, OK,' says my husband, sounding very much not like my husband.

I'm coming downstairs after having taken a moment upstairs, because the general laughing and hilarity and everything being wonderful is getting to me a bit. And I meet Angie in the hall.

'Can I talk to you for a minute?' she says.

She looks different, although I can't quite put my finger on what it is. Her clothes are still perfect and she looks like she should be on the *just seen at a fashion show* part of a glossy magazine. But it doesn't affect me in the same way. Filling the gaping emotional hole with clothes has done absolutely nothing for me. All it has done has made me ignore what was going on around me.

'Of course,' I say, a clammy feeling in my stomach. What's she going to say? Is she going to say she's been seeing Nate too and she's declaring herself? I'm not able for this.

'Come on out, into the garden, it's a bit cool.' She guides me out by the shoulder. 'I've got wine and two glasses because I'm not driving home and you don't have to do anything. I'll tidy up all the catering stuff and then you can sit down and relax.'

I note that she doesn't say, 'and look after Nate for the rest of the evening' and that cheers me up a bit. Because so far all the conversations have been about how wonderfully I'm going to be looking after my husband and the amazingly low-cholesterol meals I'll be cooking for him and how I'll be helping him get back to full fitness. As if minding my darling Nate is going to be the most important thing in my life.

The garden is a bit of a wreck beyond the pergola. We've got nice back-garden furniture, a dark rattan sort of colour that doesn't change come winter or summer. In the good weather you can stick a few cushions on it and it all looks very nice. We've got a state-of-the-art barbecue, naturally, because Nate loves barbecuing. But Angie has set up a little spot near a wall where I keep my beloved sedums. Nate has no time for these lovely succulent plants, lovely joyous fat little creatures that fall over each other like puppies as they grow, happy and smiling and really needing so little work.

Angie pops the cork out of the wine. I haven't had anything to drink since I came in apart from a strong coffee because I'm not sleeping well, and I need the coffee to keep me awake.

'You will have a glass?' she says. 'I noticed you drinking the coffee earlier. Is it because you want to stay up at night and keep an eye on him?'

I look at her full on. She has an amazingly steady gaze. There's no side to Angie, I realise. I don't know why I thought there was before. I don't know why I thought she talked to the men and ignored the women. That was my own prejudice.

In fact, she has often tried to be there for me. Tried to help at the dinner parties, said things like, 'I wouldn't do it, Steve knows better than to expect me to drum up a party after a hard day at the office.' And I'd always taken it to mean that her work was so much more important than mine, that she couldn't possibly do something like this, because it was beneath her. But now I think she wasn't saying that: she was standing up for me.

'It's about Nate, isn't it?' I say, looking at her.

She nods.

'He, didn't . . .?'

I look at her and I think, *prepare yourself for this body blow.* She hands me half a glass of wine.

'He tried.'

'He tried. Why am I not surprised. At the Christmas party? I knew something was off,' I say. She nods back at me. 'Why are you telling me this now?'

'Because Steve knows about Bea.'

I feel as if someone punched me in the solar plexus. I manage to squash a couple of my little succulents as I collapse down onto the little wall.

335

'I'm sorry, I didn't mean to upset you. I just wanted to be honest. And I wanted to talk to you about Bea. She's very proud, she wouldn't ever say this to you herself. Nate really took advantage of her at a very weak moment, just after something had happened with Luke,' she says.

'What?'

'It's true. I know because Finn and Steve have talked. Now Finn is different to Steve. Steve idolises Nate, he thinks he is wonderful. Mind you, if Steve ever tried to emulate Nate, I'd be gone so fast, he wouldn't know what had hit him. Now about the other women, I don't know much – but Bea was a one-off.'

'A one-off that got him in hospital,' I say, my voice rising. So there had been others.

'She was shocked the first time, but she was at a very weak moment and he totally took advantage of her. But he went back for more and she screamed at him, called the cops. And then he had a heart attack. Which serves him right,' she says.

'I doubt he's learned his lesson.'

'Are you keeping him?' It was like she was talking about a dog who'd just peed on the rug. But you can also train a dog not to pee on the rug. You shouldn't have to train a person who's supposed to love you not to cheat on you. Humans are who they are. They act their better selves if they really want to. Nate just didn't want to.

'How do you know about the other women?' I say.

'I saw him once, with another woman, not Bea.' She looks down. 'I am so sorry, Marin. I didn't know how to tell you. I should have. She was blonde, they were walking out of a hotel in town together which, in itself, means nothing but –'

In the pause, we both think of the 'but'.

'Did Finn know?'

'No. Finn's a straight arrow. I told Steve but Steve never told him.'

'So how do I find out about the other women?' I say.

'You could ask him but I'd say he'll lie. So check the bank statements,' says Angie. 'You need a forensic accountant and a decent lawyer for the divorce.'

'I wasn't going to divorce him,' I say. 'I thought if he was going to leave, he'd have left.'

'Yeah,' Angie gets up and pats my hand, 'I wouldn't bet on it. You deserve so much more, Marin. I don't want you to think I'm experiencing any happiness telling you this, I just wanted you to know. I've always hated the way he treated you and you're a good woman, Marin. And I'd like it if we could be friends. Somehow we haven't really managed that in all these years.'

'I felt intimidated by you,' I say, 'your make-up, your hair, your clothes, you always look so amazing.'

'Clothes are nothing,' laughs Angie, astonished.

'No, no they're not; clothes are fabulous. I love clothes. Clothes are armour and they're the armour I just can't get right.'

'You're so much more than clothes, Marin. I don't see your clothes when I see you, not like with some women. On some women, all I see are the jeans or the shoes or the handbag. With you, I see you. We give clothes too much power. *We* have the power – they just emphasise it if we're in the mood.'

I'm considering this when Angie gets up to go. She's right – clothes have too much power. *We* have it.

'I'll leave you and please, let's do that coffee. Oh, I meant to say, your sister, April, she's changed, hasn't she? I love her. She was telling me that Nate is sleeping in a separate room in case he hurts his groin.' Angie has a slightly wicked look on her face. 'If he was my husband, I'd hurt his groin.'

I laugh and it feels good. I'm so lucky to have all these other women in my life.

45

Bea

Three months later . . .

The introduction to Sean comes by stealth. Not an attack by Shazz from her how-to-find-a-hot-man dating app, which was a small mercy. No, Mum organised this one, although, as she insists, it's just by total accident that he happened to be there when I was.

Once every three weeks her book club meet, having actually read the book, and then they talk for hours, laugh, discuss things and drink too much gin. There are a few fantastic cooks among them, so there are always lots of delicious nibbles, and it's pretty much one of the few events where Mum actually drinks. She's not a big wine drinker but she loves a little glass of sherry or a gin and tonic made by a light hand. Elma, the friend, whose house they are in tonight, has a heavy hand with the sherry. So every three weeks on a Friday I drop her to one of her friend's houses, or help her host the evening. It's the least I can do given how utterly amazing she is to me and Luke.

'I'm not amazing,' she always says, batting me away with one delicate hand. 'I love you both, what else would I do but mind you.'

'Oh Mum,' I say, 'you do so much more than mind us. You love us, you give us so much of your time, this is the least I can do.'

On the book-club evenings, Luke spends the night with Shazz or Christie and her twins. Tonight it's Elma's and I know Mum, with her very weak head for the sherry, will be happy and chatty in the car coming home, the signs of someone quite unaccustomed to three glasses of sherry, chatting and laughing, enjoying being with her friends. It's the best medicine for everything in life: sharing stories, talking of the book they had read, what they were going to read next, whether they liked the last book.

Today, I know it's almost three months since Nate got home from hospital and I can't stop thinking about how much I want to see Marin and cry my eyes out to her. I can't, of course. No matter that Finn has pleaded my case with her, even though I told him not to, Marin has not appeared to tell me how much she hates me. I'd prefer that. It might make up for how much I hate myself right now.

The only joy is the fact that in a month, myself and Luke are flying to the Auvergne for the weekend with Jean-Luc's mother. He's so excited that he tries to speak French at every meal.

I'm seeing a therapist now. The pain of everything from the Family Tree to the disastrous encounter with Nate has made me see that I can't wither away trying to keep everyone happy while I fall apart myself.

Or, as Shazz puts it, 'You've got to forgive yourself, you daft mare.'

It's been a long week at work. Two of the doctors have retired but the practice is busier than ever because two much younger GPs have bought in.

However, today it wasn't too manic and I managed to get a hair cancellation in the afternoon.

'Do you think you should do something about that grey?' Shazz had pointed out to me one day, with her customary bluntness.

'Ah no, I'm letting it go grey because I think, you know, younger guys really fancy older grey women,' I deadpanned.

'Yeah, Mrs Robinson, I'm sure they do,' she says. 'But it's not working on you. Before you know it, you'll have grey pubes.'

'Ah Shazz,' I groan, 'don't go there.'

Christie had laughed. 'She'll be telling you to get it all shaved into a sexy topiary love heart next.'

I groaned again. 'Forget it, girls. I'm au natural all the way and if the guy doesn't like it, he's toast.'

Still, Shazz was right about the grey hairs near my temples. And something the therapist said has stayed with me: 'Luke will see how you live and think that's the way to live. If you never take care of yourself, how can he learn how to take care of himself?' So I take myself to a salon in Blackrock where a lovely colourist put a semi-permanent rinse through my hair to see if I liked it.

'It's really your own mahogany colour,' she says, 'perhaps a little lighter. But as we age, our skin goes paler and so does the skin on our scalp, so it's hard to keep up the same level of darkness, the same depth. You might want to think about getting some paler low-lights in later.'

'OK,' I said, taking it all in, 'it looks amazing.'

'I have a great canvas to work with,' she says, smiling.

Luke, being ten, didn't notice. But Christie said it was gorgeous.

'About time,' she said, as I brought Luke and his overnight bag to hers.

'Are you two having conferences about how bad my hair is getting?' I said dryly, referring to her and Shazz.

'Do I look like I have conferences with people about other people's hair?' said Christie with a laugh.

Her own hair was platinum blonde and cut pretty short in a sexy style. She dyed it herself.

'I like the wash-and-go sort of method with a blast of home dye every month. I've never seen you get your hair dyed – ever. You look amazing, Bea, stunning.'

'Thanks,' I say.

As I drive over to Elma's to pick up Mum that evening, I think how nice it was to make an effort with my hair and it flickers into my head that Jean-Luc, wherever he was, might appreciate that I was no longer letting myself wither away.

There's plenty of parking outside Elma's, because most of the ladies have taken taxis or have been dropped off. Elma herself opens the door.

'Oh, look at you,' she said delightedly. 'Did you get your hair done?' she says.

There are no flies on Elma. Before she retired she was a teacher. And it's obvious in every part of her warm, clever face that she spots absolutely everything.

'Yes, it is. Thank you, Elma,' I say, kissing her on both cheeks, French style.

'Really suits you,' she says. 'Come on in. I know you won't drink because you are driving, but you can have some herbal tea. We are not quite wrapped up yet. I don't know, this book just took ages to talk about.'

I follow her in and find the usual eight ladies sitting around Elma's dining-room table, nibbling cheese, crackers and grapes, all with full glasses. They're clearly long beyond the book stage of the conversation. Interspersed between them are the drivers, two husbands and one man who's going around the table with what is unmistakably a green tea teapot. He looks up as I come in, and at that same moment I catch sight of my mother, who positively beams at me.

'Bea,' she says, 'you're here. You must meet Sean. We're lucky he's gracing our company tonight.'

I look up and there he is: the man from the trendy new restaurant in the city, the guy Christie knew where we'd had a lovely night out with Shazz. I'd seen him then as I was coming back from the ladies' and he, busy running his restaurant, had barely noticed me and I'd felt horribly invisible.

Tonight, it's different. Tonight, he looks at me admiringly.

The entire tableful beams at us en masse, and I'm struck by the impression that if Sean had dragged me upstairs caveman-style, they'd all wave to see us go and say, 'Have fun, lots of love, we'll come up in the morning.'

My mother played a part in this, I think darkly, watching her. Shazz's 'find a man for Bea' campaign has clearly gone viral.

'Sean moved back from Hong Kong to set up the restaurant and it's doing brilliantly, and he's home for good,' says Elma firmly. Just in case Sean had any ideas about what he might want to do with his own life.

He grins. 'Hello, Bea,' he says, with a faint bow, 'would you like some green tea and an apology for the matchmaking?'

I laugh and decide to give in gracefully to a cup of green tea. The eight ladies around the table have not got the combined ages of about five centuries for nothing. At speed, everyone moves and Sean and I are sitting right beside each other, two cups of green tea in front of us. Everyone else has most ostentatiously moved away to talk about other things.

'Does this feel like a set-up to you?' I say, looking down at my cup and not at Sean, who, close up, is definitely several years younger than me. He's late thirties, while I'm like the conveyor belt at Dublin Airport: full of baggage and a bit creaky with a complicated history.

'Sorry,' he says. 'This is a crazy night for us in the restaurant but she begged me to come tonight and meet some of her friends and as I'm so busy and feel guilty, I said yes . . .' His voice trails off a little bit and I laugh.

'Women who want to be grandmothers rule the world, you know, or at least they should,' I say. 'We were both walked into this.'

'Oh I don't know,' he says admiringly. 'Mum has been telling me about you for the past week.'

'Telling you what exactly?' I say, anxiously. And then I stop myself. Elma is a lovely person and she only would have wanted the best for me, like Mum. She won't have said anything negative.

'You OK?' says Sean. I've spaced out on him.

'I'm fine,' I say, 'let's start this again. I just felt a bit thrown because I had an uncomfortable situation with an old boyfriend recently, and I didn't realise I was being set up tonight.'

'You do know that the Chinese characters for crisis also say danger – and opportunity.' He gives me another admiring look and I raise an eyebrow.

'Really?'

'I feel as if I've met you before,' he adds. 'Have we –? I honestly wouldn't forget someone like you.'

'Is that a line that usually works?' I ask.

'Not a line,' he says, shaking his head ruefully. 'I've been too busy to have lines. But for you –' He breaks off and he's doing that admiring thing again. 'I might manage to think up a line or two.'

'We have met before,' I say. 'In your restaurant.'

He looks genuinely sorry. 'I'm really sorry – that's unforgiveable in my trade. You'll have to let me buy you dinner to make up for it.'

'Now that *is* a line –' I begin.

'No,' he interrupts. 'Just a thought. A very, very nice thought.'

In the car going home, Mum looks like the cat who's got the cream.

'You liked Sean,' she says, even her tone blissful. 'He is handsome. Charming and decent. Elma's good stuff and so's her husband.'

'Mum, he's six years younger than me. And when a woman is older it's counted in dog years. People have no trouble with the whole older-man-younger-woman dynamic but they're very cruel when it's reversed.'

'But you don't care what people think,' says Mum, happily.

'No, I don't care what people think, but Sean is thirty-seven. Thirty-seven-year-old young guys want women who can have kids with them. I don't want any more children and I don't know if I could have one even if I started now. I'm happy with Luke.'

'I just want to see you settled.'

I think of Nate and Marin and everything that has gone on. How can any relationship be settled? They were together for so long.

'Mum, I don't think I can date anyone, not after what happened with Marin and Nate.'

'That wasn't your fault.' My mother play slaps my knee which is the only safe bit to touch when I'm driving. 'Stop this,' she says, 'stop punishing yourself. One day, darling Luke is going to go off and have a life and you are going to be sitting there with nothing. Because you gave everything to him. And you can't do that. Whatever you believe in, Bea, you must believe that there can be happiness again. Maybe you won't find someone forever, but you might have ten beautiful years with a new man. Or maybe you'll have a few years before you grind up some glass and put it in his porridge.'

I burst out laughing at the thought that my mother even knows such a thing.

'Don't laugh,' she says, 'we read lots of different types of books in the book club. So what's wrong with going out with Sean? I know you're going to be terribly shocked with me when I say this – go to bed with him, sleep with him. Let Luke see that his mother can have relationships. Don't drag him home by his hair and say, Luke, go and play your Xbox. Do it gently, slowly. Lord knows, you haven't introduced anyone to him up to now, so it's not as if Luke has had a litany of "uncles" coming into his life. So why not go out for a drink with Sean and eventually drag him up to your lair.'

'I did get rid of the mattress.'

'Well, that was a very good idea,' says my mother, in a matter-of-fact tone.

'Mum, you are surprising me tonight, you really can't hold your alcohol.'

We pull into her driveway where the light above the door is on, shining a warm amber, lighting up the pots underneath it. I stop the car and turn off the engine.

'I know, dear. Your father always said that.'

I reach over and give her the biggest hug possible in a small car. 'I've been mean to you – Sean's already asked me out and I said yes.'

'Brat,' she says, laughing. 'I'm so thrilled. You've waited far too long. Sean might show you some fun and it'll get you used to going out at night. And stop beating yourself over the head because of Nate.'

'It's Marin,' I think, 'it's Marin I feel so bad about.'

'Maybe one day you'll be able to talk to her, I don't know. But life moves on, darling, and if anyone knows that, you do.'

She's right. It's true for both me and Luke. It's time to move on.

46

Sid

Finn has been renovating his apartment and he's asked me to move in with him when it's finished. I'm dithering but, secretly, I want to. When I first saw it, I loved it because it's in an old Georgian building and it's so elegant and unusual.

It's so lived in. It's full of stuff and it's not dusty.

'Do you have OCD?' I ask, as I wander around picking up odd things and looking at them and saying: 'What is this?'

'It's an astrolabe,' he says.

'It's very nicely polished, anyway; you must be a very good housekeeper.'

'Someone has to come in and do it,' he says, grinning.

He shows me how to use it.

'I love this sort of stuff,' he says happily, one hand on my waist as he puts it back.

I love the way he touches me as if he can't bear to let me out of reach. In fact, I adore it. 'Must be a nightmare to polish.'

'It is, I have polished it myself, I admit, although it's fiddly. When you live on your own and you get to my age, you've got to be tidy, or else you are just living surrounded by tins of baked beans and growing experiments that Alexander Fleming would be delighted with.'

'Yes, I often wonder why gone-off bread tastes so weird, when I tried to convince myself that it must be good for me,' I say.

I open his breadbin, 'No gone-off bread here, look at you, you are a proper caretaker man.'

'Not only am I a proper caretaker man, I can open tins and

order takeaways and Marin is one day going to teach me how to cook.'

We are both silent for a moment, the music playing in the background, some soft jazzy thing he'd put on that I didn't recognise, but it was beautifully calming and comforting.

'If I show you the rest of the apartment, I'll be showing you the bedroom and then, when the delivery person comes, we'll be in bed.'

'So, you'll just have to go and open the door with no clothes on,' I say, giving him my best winning grin.

'Not a problem.'

Tonight, we wander around the nearly finished apartment and I think that I'm going to tell Finn I'm taking him up on his offer. I want to move in with him. He's the kindest, most gentle man I've ever met. He understands me sexually, gets that a woman who's been violated needs tenderness and love. He's just marvellous at tenderness and love.

Vilma is taking all the credit for our being together, and when Stefan and Mum met Finn for the first time, Stefan grabbed my sister in a bear hug and whispered to her in Lithuanian, which she only understands a little.

When he puts her down, he turns to Finn: 'I want to welcome you and say thank you for bringing our Sidonie home. She was lost for a time.'

'It's an honour. I will take care of her.'

'I don't need –' I begin but Stefan shushes me.

'I know you are a warrior woman, my Sidonie,' he says, 'but sometimes, let us men take care of you? Just sometimes – and this one, he adores you.'

Mum laughs and hugs me.

'He's a keeper,' she whispers. 'And tall. There's something lovely about a tall man.'

I blush. My mother is talking to me about tall men and I think about how when Finn and I are in bed, it doesn't matter that he's taller than me. I blush some more.

If Mum, notices, she says nothing.

The more she knows Finn, the more she adores him and makes him stews, so I complain that he's never going to learn to cook and look after me.

Adrienne particularly approves of him.

'Well done with Mr Stella,' she said the first time she met him. 'Any more like him at home?' she asked.

'He's a one-off,' I said.

'Just my luck.'

Tonight, we finally make it into the bedroom where there are high ceilings.

'Oh,' I say, pretending my phone has just pinged with a news alert. 'Look!'

He obligingly looks down at it and I pull his head lower so I can whisper into his ear.

'You still want a roommate? A small one, lots of black clothes, biker boots, has furry pyjamas?'

His response is to grab me, lift me up and whirl me round.

'Like it? I love that idea,' says Finn, and, still holding me up, he kisses me. This, I think, is my reward for all the pain, this glorious man. I am so lucky.

47
Marin

The day Rachel is leaving for her travels, I'm up early. I have so much to do before she goes, so many plans. I want it all to go off like clockwork and I'm excited.

I dress quickly because I've sold off all my excess clothes, cut up my credit cards and am part of an online group of shopaholics who keep in touch to discuss how we are coping with the 'no shopping for three months' rule. It's getting easier, plus getting dressed in the morning is a doddle.

First up, Finn and Sid want to come over to say goodbye to Rachel, before she goes off on her travels.

'That's brilliant,' I say, 'she's going to love that.'

Sid is a revelation, a complete revelation. I knew there was something nervy about her when I met her first. But since she and Finn have got together it's like watching a beautiful flower blossom. She's still fiery and funny and oh, quirky with knobs on. But she laughs a lot, touches Finn all the time. Mind you, he can't keep his hands off her either.

She had a pretty intense talk with Rachel as well about travelling with Megan. Both girls told us in confidence – because Sid told them to – that she had been raped by someone she knew, a boss.

Somehow, Sid has managed to talk to Rachel about being careful on her travels in a way I couldn't manage to.

'It can be stranger danger but it's much more likely to be someone you know,' Sid has told them.

Louise is grateful at this advice for Megan.

I'm still in the angry stage because of Nate and growl to

Louise that someone needed to teach the girls that 'it's rarely the strangers who hurt us.'

'Great for you that you are going to make it work with Nate,' Louise says cautiously, ignoring the outburst. I told her about Bea because, in the early days, I was so desperate to vent, that I rang her up and blurted it all out.

'Throw his ass out!' she said.

'I'm not going to,' I said quickly and she was silent.

It's been a bit tense between us since then but things might lighten up, I hope.

'So you got those moves,' says Sid, hugging Rachel goodbye.

'I've got those moves.'

'And it's your body, your choice, consent, no crap. And remember, when you're physically weaker, you have to be clever, work with other women, work as a team. Remember: not everyone is good.'

'Don't scare the hell out of her,' says Nate. And I glare at him, not that he notices. Nate thinks everything is back to normal.

He's been out of hospital nearly two months and his recovery is excellent. Although, he's still not cycling or swimming. His regimen is cardiac care, walking and light weights till his next check-up.

He wants to come back into our bed.

'Let's just leave things the way they are,' I said the last time he asked.

He had to make do with that, for the moment.

'I'm going to miss you,' says Joey to his sister.

'I'll be home before you know it,' says Rachel.

'She will, you know. You could probably take over her bedroom,' I say to Joey naughtily, to break the tension.

'Mum!' says Rachel. 'You wouldn't.'

I laugh: 'I promise I won't let him.'

'But we can think about doing interesting things with your bedroom,' I say to Joey.

350

'Yeah,' he says, 'but just you and me and Dad now, we're going to have loads of fun.'

Finn and Sid are arm in arm and about to leave.

'Good luck,' Sid mouths as she hugs me goodbye.

'I don't know, I really think that woman has something psychic going on, because it's like she can see into my head,' I say to Finn.

'She's good at watching people, she picks things up that other people don't. Fabulous, isn't she?' he says, love in his eyes.

'Yes,' I say, 'fabulous.'

Bea has sent money to Rachel. I still haven't been able to see her. But I think I will afterwards, because I understand better now: human vulnerability, how complicated life is. It's harder to get my head round the notion that one person can be our *everything*, while that one person doesn't feel the same way. When that person needs more. Much more, so much more that it tears you apart.

We pile into the car. We are driving in convoy. At the airport we hug and even though I really meant not to cry, I do.

'I'm going to miss you, honey,' I say, 'but this is going to be so good for you. Just be careful. I want you to come back safe, strong, having used your brains to take care of yourselves. It's a big adventure, everyone deserves a big adventure.'

'I know.' My girl is grown.

The two families stand there as the girls go off. We turn to walk back to the car park. And Louise and I fall into walking beside each other.

'It just feels awful having them gone,' says Louise.

'I know,' I say. 'But we always knew they were going to go at some point and this is just the first little going.'

'I suppose,' says Louise tearfully. 'Do you think you guys would come over to us for takeaway dinner tonight, maybe fill the gap, make this all feel not so lonely?'

'No,' I say, 'sorry, just something I've got to do.'

'OK,' says Louise, 'maybe another time.'

'Another time.'

We drive home and on the way drop Joey at his best friend's house.

'I'll be back in two hours,' I say, as I watch him go the front door and ring the doorbell and see him ushered inside.

'It'll take his mind off his big sister,' Nate says. He doesn't know my real plan.

Nate sits down at the kitchen table when we get home. 'Nothing feels quite the same, does it?'

'No,' I say.

All the way home I'd been going over what I was about to say. I've been thinking about it for a month, actually. I decided I'd wait until Rachel was gone. Because that way she'd be away having fun when her father left. It's going to be tricky with Joey and I hate putting him through the pain but having parents living a lie is not going to do him any favours. He'll grow up thinking it's fine to cheat on your wife, the way Dom has grown up thinking it's fine to be a perpetual teenager. At least he's got his own place now and has learned – Sue would be pleased – that there is no laundry fairy.

'So Nate, you and I: the future.'

He looks at me cautiously. 'What do you mean *the future*?'

'Our future,' I say brightly. 'Or rather, our lack of future.'

'Course we have a future, we have everything, we've kids, we've family, we've a mortgage,' he says, his usual bullish self.

'What we have is a very loyal wife, two beautiful kids, one an adult and one a child. And one husband who doesn't take anything seriously. Who thinks we are all at his beck and call. Who takes me for granted, who's clearly been spending our money on someone else.'

His face flushes.

'I've found I'm really talented at forensic accountancy,' I say. 'It's amazing. Sid has a friend who helped me with that.'

He's still brazening it out. 'Sid! You brought Sid into this? She'll tell Finn.'

'Oh Finn knows,' I say.

Nate's face is a picture.

'It transpires that you spent a lot of money on dinners for two, jewellery I've never seen and lingerie. Some of the shops you've gone to, Nate, they're way kinkier than I gave you credit for. But of course, if I'd looked properly a long time ago, I'd have realised you have another credit card. But I didn't, because I trusted you. Trust is a lovely concept, but the person has to be trustworthy in the first place.'

'I am trustworthy.'

'No, you're not,' I say.

'Oh come on, come on,' he says, 'you're just over-wrought because Rachel's gone.'

'It's over, Nate, so I'd advise you to go upstairs and pack your bags and move out.'

'What?' I think it's hitting him now. 'What – what about Joey?'

'I'm going to tell Joey that you are working away for a while and frankly I don't care where you go. But you are going to go. And you are not going to talk to our daughter and tell her what's happening until I'm ready to. Nothing much is going to change with Joey anyway, because I bring him to school and I pick him up from school and I bring him to his football matches, because you don't do that sort of stuff.'

'I do.'

'No, you don't, you do your own thing and then you go off with your girlfriends.'

'I don't have girlfriends.'

'Don't bullshit me.' I think of the blonde Louise saw him with. How did I ever suspect lovely Angie, who has been a tower of strength for me.

'I was worried about you, Marin,' she'd said one day. 'He was all over Bea that night of the party – I was giving him a dressing down and he didn't like that.'

Nate stands up and suddenly he doesn't look so big or strong anymore. He's just a guy whom I trusted and I believed was a good person. Probably the way Sid believed the guy she worked for all those years ago was a good person, until she found out he wasn't.

'Just go, Nate,' I say.

I pour myself a glass of wine and after half an hour I hear him dragging two big suitcases downstairs.

'You're going to regret this,' he says, a little flush on his face now he's angry.

'Have you got your meds?' I say, last act of a kind wife. But he's a big boy, he can look after himself at whichever girlfriend's house he's going to. He's not my problem anymore.

'Yes,' he says.

'All right,' I say, 'don't let the door hit you on the way out. Oh yeah, you can leave your keys.'

'You've no right to ask me for the keys.'

'You want a bet?' I say.

He throws his keys down on the table. Then he's gone.

I sit there for a minute, breathing heavily, and then I ring April.

'You can come round now,' I say, 'he's gone.'

'Oh goody,' says April. 'Maybe we should have a party.'

And we both laugh.

Credits

Cathy Kelly and Orion Fiction would like to thank everyone at Orion who worked on the publication of *Other Women* in the UK.

Editorial
Charlotte Mursell
Harriett Bourton
Sanah Ahmed

Copy editor
Marian Reid

Proof reader
Linda Joyce

Audio
Paul Stark
Amber Bates

Contracts
Anne Goddard
Paul Bulos
Jake Alderson

Publicity
Leanne Oliver

Design
Rachael Lancaster
Joanna Ridley
Nick May
Helen Ewing

Editorial Management
Charlie Panayiotou
Jane Hughes
Alice Davis

Finance
Jasdip Nandra
Afeera Ahmed
Elizabeth Beaumont
Sue Baker

Marketing
Helena Fouracre

Production
Ruth Sharvell

Sales

Jen Wilson
Esther Waters
Victoria Laws
Rachael Hum
Ellie Kyrke-Smith
Frances Doyle
Georgina Cutler

Operations

Jo Jacobs
Sharon Willis
Lisa Pryde
Lucy Brem

Don't miss the next deliciously heartwarming and
refreshingly relatable story by Cathy Kelly about
sisterhood, love and friendship . . .

The Wedding Party

Four sisters.

One secret.

A day they'll never forget . . .

The story follows the four Robicheaux sisters as they return
home for their parents' wedding, at the beautiful Hotel
Sorrento where they all grew up as children.

For the first time in 15 years, the sisters are back together –
and it doesn't take long for long-buried secrets to surface . . .

Available to pre-order now!

The Family Gift

'Honest, funny, clever, it sparkled with witty wry observations on modern life'
Marian Keyes

Freya Abalone has a big, messy, wonderful family. She has an exciting career as a celebrity chef. She has a new home that makes her feel safe.

But behind the happy front, Freya feels pulled in a hundred directions. Life has thrown Freya some lemons – and she's learned how to juggle! But she's keeping a secret from her family, and soon something is going to crashing down . . .

All families have their struggles and strengths. So can Freya pull everyone – and herself – together when they need it most?

The Year that Changed Everything

**Three women. Three birthdays.
One year that will change everything . . .**

Ginger isn't spending her thirtieth the way she would have planned. Tonight might be the first night of the rest of her life - or a total disaster.

Sam is finally pregnant after years of trying. When her waters break on the morning of her fortieth birthday, she panics: forget labour, how is she going to be a mother?

Callie is celebrating her fiftieth at a big party in her Dublin home. Then a knock at the door mid-party changes everything . . .

Help us make the next generation of readers

We – both author and publisher – hope you enjoyed this book. We believe that you can become a reader at any time in your life, but we'd love your help to give the next generation a head start.

Did you know that 9 per cent of children don't have a book of their own in their home, rising to 13 per cent in disadvantaged families*? We'd like to try to change that by asking you to consider the role you could play in helping to build readers of the future.

We'd love you to think of sharing, borrowing, reading, buying or talking about a book with a child in your life and spreading the love of reading. We want to make sure the next generation continue to have access to books, wherever they come from.

And if you would like to consider donating to charities that help fund literacy projects, find out more at **www.literacytrust.org.uk** and **www.booktrust.org.uk**.

THANK YOU

*As reported by the National Literacy Trust